'When I play, opponent who is

'I'm tougher than I corner of Lily's m to be nervous. If rumour is correct, you emotionless vacuum—and that means you're in no danger from someone like little me.'

Nik had a feeling 'little me' was the most dangerous thing he'd encountered in a long while. 'If I'm a "cold, emotionless vacuum", why would you want to climb into my bed?'

'Because you are *insanely* sexy, and all the things that make you so wrong for me would make you perfect for rebound sex.'

He looked into those blue eyes and tried to ignore the surge of sexual hunger that had gripped him from the moment he'd laid eyes on that pale silky hair, tumbling damp round her gleaming wet body.

Never before had doing the right thing felt so wrong.

Nik cursed under his breath and rose to his feet. 'We're leaving.'

'Good decision.' She slid her hand into his, rose on tiptoe and whispered in his ear. 'I'll be gentle with you.'

With her wide smile and laughing eyes it was like being on a date with a beam of sunshine. He felt heat spread through his body, his arousal so brutal he was tempted to haul her behind the nearest lockable door, rip off that dress and acquaint himself with every part of her luscious naked body.

USA TODAY bestselling author **Sarah Morgan** writes hot, happy contemporary romance, and her trademark humour and sensuality have gained her fans across the globe. She has been nominated four years in row for the prestigious RITA® Award from the Romance Writers of America, and has won the award twice.

Sarah lives near London with her family. When she isn't writing she loves spending time outdoors. Visit her website at www.sarahmorgan.com

Other titles by Sarah Morgan available in eBook from www.millsandboon.co.uk:

LOST TO THE DESERT WARRIOR
SOLD TO THE ENEMY
WOMAN IN A SHEIKH'S WORLD
　(The Private Lives of Public Playboys)
A NIGHT OF NO RETURN
　(The Private Lives of Public Playboys)
THE FORBIDDEN FERRARA
ONCE A FERRARA WIFE…
DOUKAKIS'S APPRENTICE
THE TWELVE NIGHTS OF CHRISTMAS
ONE NIGHT…NINE-MONTH SCANDAL
BOUGHT: DESTITUTE YET DEFIANT
POWERFUL GREEK, UNWORLDLY WIFE
CAPELLI'S CAPTIVE VIRGIN
THE PRINCE'S WAITRESS WIFE
THE VASQUEZ MISTRESS

PLAYING BY THE GREEK'S RULES

BY
SARAH MORGAN

All rights reserved including the right of reproduction in whole or in part in any form. This edition is published by arrangement with Harlequin Books S.A.

This is a work of fiction. Names, characters, places, locations and incidents are purely fictional and bear no relationship to any real life individuals, living or dead, or to any actual places, business establishments, locations, events or incidents. Any resemblance is entirely coincidental.

This book is sold subject to the condition that it shall not, by way of trade or otherwise, be lent, resold, hired out or otherwise circulated without the prior consent of the publisher in any form of binding or cover other than that in which it is published and without a similar condition including this condition being imposed on the subsequent purchaser.

® and TM are trademarks owned and used by the trademark owner and/or its licensee. Trademarks marked with ® are registered with the United Kingdom Patent Office and/or the Office for Harmonisation in the Internal Market and in other countries.

Published in Great Britain 2015
by Mills & Boon, an imprint of Harlequin (UK) Limited,
Eton House, 18-24 Paradise Road, Richmond, Surrey, TW9 1SR

© 2015 Sarah Morgan

ISBN: 978-0-263-25049-7

Harlequin (UK) Limited's policy is to use papers that are natural, renewable and recyclable products and made from wood grown in sustainable forests. The logging and manufacturing processes conform to the legal environmental regulations of the country of origin.

Printed and bound in Spain
by CPI, Barcelona

PLAYING BY THE GREEK'S RULES

To the wonderful Joanne Grant,
for her enthusiasm, encouragement
and for always keeping the door open.

CHAPTER ONE

LILY PULLED HER hat down to shade her eyes from the burn of the hot Greek sun and took a large gulp from her water bottle. 'Never again.' She sat down on the parched, sunbaked earth and watched as her friend carefully brushed away dirt and soil from a small, carefully marked section of the trench. 'If I ever, *ever* mention the word "love" to you, I want you to bury me somewhere in this archaeological site and never dig me up again.'

'There is an underground burial chamber. I could dump you in there if you like.'

'Great idea. Stick a sign in the ground. *"Here lies Lily, who wasted years of her life studying the origin, evolution and behaviour of humans and still couldn't understand men".*' She gazed across the ruins of the ancient city of Aptera to the sea beyond. They were high on a plateau. Behind them, the jagged beauty of the White Mountains shimmered in the heat and in front lay the sparkling blue of the Sea of Crete. The beauty of it usually lifted her mood, but not today.

Brittany sat up and wiped her brow with her forearm. 'Stop beating yourself up. The guy is a lying, cheating rat bastard.' Reaching for her backpack, she glanced across the site to the group of men who were deep in conversation. 'Fortunately for all of us he's flying back to London tomorrow to his wife. And all I can say to that is, God help the woman.'

Lily covered her face with her hands. 'Don't say the word "wife". I am a terrible person.'

'Hey!' Brittany's voice was sharp. 'He told you he was single. He *lied*. The responsibility is all his. After tomorrow you won't have to see him again and I won't have to struggle not to kill him.'

'What if she finds out and ends their marriage?'

'Then she might have the chance of a decent life with someone who respects her. Forget him, Lily.'

How could she forget when she couldn't stop going over and over it in her head?

Had there been signs she'd missed?

Had she asked the wrong questions?

Was she so desperate to find someone special that she'd ignored obvious signs?

'I was planning our future. We were going to spend August touring the Greek Islands. That was before he pulled out a family photo from his wallet instead of his credit card. Three little kids wrapped around their dad like bindweed. He should have been taking them on holiday, not me! I can't bear it. How could I have made such an appalling error of judgement? That is a line I *never* cross. Family is sacrosanct to me. If you asked me to pick between family and money, I'd pick family every time.' It crossed her mind that right now she had neither. No money. No family. 'I don't know which is worse—the fact that he clearly didn't know me *at all*, or the fact that when I checked him against my list he was perfect.'

'You have a list?'

Lily felt herself grow pink. 'It's my attempt to be objective. I have a really strong desire for permanent roots. Family.' She thought about the emotional wasteland of her past and felt a sense of failure. Was the future going to look the same way? 'When you want something badly it can distort your decision-making process, so I've put in some layers of protection for myself. I know the basic qualities I need in a man to be happy. I never date anyone who doesn't score highly on my three points.'

Brittany looked intrigued. 'Big wallet, big shoulders and big—'

'No! And you are appalling.' Despite her misery, Lily laughed. 'First, he has to be affectionate. I'm not interested in a man who can't show his feelings. Second, he has to be honest, but short of getting him to take a lie detector test I don't know how to check that one. I thought Professor Ashurst was honest. I'm never calling him David again, by the way.' She allowed herself one glance at the visiting archaeologist who had dazzled her during their short, ill-fated relationship. 'You're right. He's a rat pig.'

'I didn't call him a rat pig. I called him a rat b—'

'I know what you called him. I never use that word.'

'You should. It's surprisingly therapeutic. But we shouldn't be wasting this much time talking about him. Professor Asshat is history, like this stuff we're digging up.'

'I can't believe you called him that.'

'You should be calling him far worse. What's the third thing on your list?'

'I want a man with strong family values. He has to want a family. But not several different families at the same time. Now I know why he gave off all those signals about being a family man. Because he already *was* a family man.' Lily descended into gloom. 'My checklist is seriously flawed.'

'Not necessarily. You need a more reliable test for honesty and you should maybe add "single" to your list, that's all. You need to chill. Stop looking for a relationship and have some fun. Keep it casual.'

'You're talking about sex? That doesn't work for me.' Lily took another sip of water. 'I have to be in love with a guy to sleep with him. The two are welded together for me. How about you?'

'No. Sex is sex. Love is love. One is fun and the other is to be avoided at all costs.'

'I don't think like that. There is something wrong with me.'

'There's nothing wrong with you. It's not a crime to want a relationship. It just means you get your heart broken more than the average person.' Brittany pushed her hat back from her face. 'I can't believe how hot it is. It's not even ten o'clock and already I'm boiling like a lobster.'

'And you know all about lobsters, coming from Maine. It's summer and this is Crete. What did you expect?'

'Right now I'd give anything for a few hours back home. I'm not used to summers that fry your skin from your body. I keep wanting to remove another layer of clothing.'

'You've spent summers at digs all over the Mediterranean.'

'And I moaned at each and every one.' Brittany stretched out her legs and Lily felt a flash of envy.

'You look like Lara Croft in those shorts. You have amazing legs.'

'Too much time hiking in inhospitable lands searching for ancient relics. I want your gorgeous blonde hair.' Brittany's hair, the colour of polished oak, was gathered up from her neck in a ponytail. Despite the hat, her neck was already showing signs of the sun. 'Listen, don't waste another thought or tear on that man. Come out with us tonight. We're going to the official opening of the new wing at the archaeological museum and afterwards we're going to try out that new bar on the waterfront. My spies tell me that Professor Asshat won't be there, so it's going to be a great evening.'

'I can't. The agency rang this morning and offered me an emergency cleaning job.'

'Lily, you have a masters in archaeology. You shouldn't be taking these random jobs.'

'My research grant doesn't pay off my college loans and

I want to be debt free. And anyway, I love cleaning. It relaxes me.'

'You love cleaning? You're like a creature from another planet.'

'There's nothing more rewarding than turning someone's messy house into a shiny home, but I do wish the job wasn't tonight. The opening would have been fun. A great excuse to wash the mud off my knees and dress up, not to mention seeing all those artefacts in one place. Never mind. I'll focus on the money. They're paying me an emergency rate for tonight.'

'Cleaning is an emergency?'

Lily thought about the state of some of the houses she cleaned. 'Sometimes, but in this case it's more that the owner decided to arrive without notice. He spends most of his time in the US.' She dug in her bag for more sunscreen. 'Can you imagine being so rich you can't quite decide which of your many properties you are going to sleep in?'

'What's his name?'

'No idea. The company is very secretive. We have to arrive at a certain time and then his security team will let us in. Four hours later I add a gratifyingly large sum of money to my bank account and that's the end of it.'

'Four hours? It's going to take five of you four hours to clean one house?' Brittany paused with the water halfway to her mouth. 'What is this place? A Minoan palace?'

'A villa. It's big. She said I'd be given a floor plan when I arrive, which I have to return when I leave and I'm not allowed to make copies.'

'A *floor plan*?' Brittany choked on her water. 'Now I'm intrigued. Can I come with you?'

'Sure—' Lily threw her a look '—because scrubbing out someone's shower is so much more exciting than having cocktails on the terrace of the archaeological museum while the sun sets over the Aegean.'

'It's the Sea of Crete.'

'Technically it's still the Aegean, and either way I'm missing a great party to scrub a floor. I feel like Cinderella. So what about you? Are you going to meet someone tonight and do something about your dormant love life?'

'I don't have a love life, I have a sex life, which is not at all dormant fortunately.'

Lily felt a twinge of envy. 'Maybe you're right. I need to lighten up and use men for sex instead of treating every relationship as if it's going to end in confetti. You were an only child, weren't you? Did you ever wish you had brothers or sisters?'

'No, but I grew up on a small island. The whole place felt like a massive extended family. Everyone knew everything, from the age you first walked, to whether you had all A's on your report card.'

'Sounds blissful.' Lily heard the wistful note in her own voice. 'Because I was such a sickly kid and hard work to look after, no one took me for long. My eczema was terrible when I was little and I was always covered in creams and bandages and other yucky stuff. I wasn't exactly your poster baby. No one wanted a kid who got sick. I was about as welcome as a stray puppy with fleas.'

'Crap, Lily, you're making me tear up and I'm not even a sentimental person.'

'Forget it. Tell me about your family instead.' She loved hearing about other people's families, about the complications, the love, the experiences woven into a shared history. To her, family seemed like a multicoloured sweater, with all the different coloured strands of wool knitted into something whole and wonderful that gave warmth and protection from the cold winds of life.

She picked absently at a thread hanging from the hem of her shorts. It felt symbolic of her life. She was a single fibre, loose, bound to nothing.

Brittany took another mouthful of water and adjusted the angle of her hat. 'We're a normal American family, I guess. Whatever that is. My parents were divorced when I was ten.

My mom hated living on an island. Eventually she remarried and moved to Florida. My dad was an engineer and he spent all his time working on oil rigs around the world. I lived with my grandmother on Puffin Island.'

'Even the name is adorable.' Lily tried to imagine growing up on a place called Puffin Island. 'Were you close to your grandmother?'

'Very. She died a few years ago, but she left me her cottage on the beach so I'd always have a home. I take several calls a week from people wanting to buy the place but I'm never going to sell.' Brittany poked her trowel into the ground. 'My grandmother called it Castaway Cottage. When I was little I asked her if a castaway ever lived there and she said it was for people lost in life, not at sea. She believed it had healing properties.'

Lily didn't laugh. 'I might need to spend a month there. I need to heal.'

'You'd be welcome. A friend of mine is staying at the moment. We use it as a refuge. It's the best place on earth and I always feel close to my grandmother when I'm there. You can use it any time, Lil.'

'Maybe I will. I still need to decide what I'm going to do in August.'

'You know what you need? Rebound sex. Sex for the fun of it, without all the emotional crap that goes with relationships.'

'I've never had rebound sex. I'd fall in love.'

'So pick someone you couldn't possibly fall in love with in a million years. Someone with exceptional bedroom skills, but nothing else to commend him. Then you can't possibly be at risk.' She broke off as Spyros, one of the Greek archaeologists from the local university, strolled across to them. 'Go away, Spy, this is girl talk.'

'Why do you think I'm joining you? It's got to be more interesting than the conversation I just left.' He handed Lily a can of chilled Diet Coke. 'He's a waste of space, *theé mou.*' His voice was gentle and she coloured, touched by his kindness.

'I know, I know.' She lifted the weight of her hair from her neck, wishing she'd worn it up. 'I'll get over it.'

Spy dropped to his haunches next to her. 'Want me to help you get over him? I heard something about rebound sex. I'm here for you.'

'No thanks. You're a terrible flirt. I don't trust you.'

'Hey, this is about sex. You don't need to trust me.' He winked at her. 'What you need is a real man. A Greek man who knows how to make you feel like a woman.'

'Yeah, yeah, I know the joke. You're going to hand me your laundry and tell me to wash it. This is why you're not going to be my rebound guy. I am not washing your socks.' But Lily was laughing as she snapped the top of the can. Maybe she didn't have a family, but she had good friends. 'You're forgetting that when I'm not cleaning the villas of the rich or hanging out here contributing nothing to my college fund, I work for the ultimate in Greek manhood.'

'Ah yes.' Spyros smiled. 'Nik Zervakis. Head of the mighty ZervaCo. Man of men. Every woman's fantasy.'

'Not mine. He doesn't tick a single box on my list.'

Spy raised his eyebrows and Brittany shook her head. 'You don't want to know. Go on, Lily, dish the dirt on Zervakis. I want to know everything from his bank balance to how he got that incredible six pack I saw in those sneaky photos of him taken in that actress's swimming pool.'

'I don't know much about him, except that he's super brilliant and expects everyone around him to be super brilliant, too, which makes him pretty intimidating. Fortunately he spends most of his time in San Francisco or New York so he isn't around much. I've been doing this internship for two months and in that time two personal assistants have left. It's a good job he has a big human resources department because I can tell you he gets through *a lot* of human resources in the average working week. And don't even start me on the girlfriends. I need a spreadsheet to keep it straight in my head.'

'What happened to the personal assistants?'

'Both of them resigned because of the pressure. The workload is inhuman and he isn't easy to work for. He has this way of looking at you that makes you wish you could teleport. But he *is* very attractive. He isn't my type so I didn't pay much attention, but the women talk about him all the time.'

'I still don't understand why you're working there.'

'I'm trying different things. My research grant ends this month and I don't know if I want to carry on doing this. I'm exploring other options. Museum work doesn't pay much and anyway, I don't want to live in a big city. I could never teach—' She shrugged, depressed by the options. 'I don't know what to do.'

'You're an expert in ceramics and you've made some beautiful pots.'

'That's a hobby.'

'You're creative and artistic. You should do something with that.'

'It isn't practical to think I can make a living that way and dreaming doesn't pay the bills.' She finished her drink. 'Sometimes I wish I'd read law, not archaeology, except that I don't think I'm cut out for office work. I'm not good with technology. I broke the photocopier last week and the coffee machine hates me, but apparently having ZervaCo on your résumé makes prospective employers sit up. It shows you have staying power. If you can work there and not be intimidated, you're obviously robust. And before you tell me that an educated woman shouldn't allow herself to be intimidated by a guy, try meeting him.'

Spyros rose to his feet. 'Plenty of people would be intimidated by Nik Zervakis. There are some who say his name along with the gods.'

Brittany pushed her water bottle back into her backpack.

'Those would be the people whose salary he pays, or the women he sleeps with.'

Lily took off her hat and fanned herself. 'His security team is briefed to keep them away from him. We are not allowed to put any calls through to him unless the name is on an approved list and that list changes pretty much every week. I have terrible trouble keeping up.'

'So his protection squad is there to protect him from women?' Brittany looked fascinated. 'Unreal.'

'I admire him. They say his emotions have never played a part in anything he does, business or pleasure. He is the opposite of everything I am. No one has ever dumped him or made him feel less of a person and he always knows what to say in any situation.' She glanced once across the heat-baked ruins of the archaeological site towards the man who had lied so glibly. Thinking of all the things she could have said and hadn't plunged her into another fit of gloom. 'I'm going to try and be more like Nik Zervakis.'

Brittany laughed. 'You're kidding, right?'

'No, I'm not kidding. He is like an ice machine. I want to be like that. How about you? Have either of you ever been in love?'

'No!' Spy looked alarmed, but Brittany didn't answer. Instead she stared sightlessly across the plateau to the ocean.

'Brittany?' Lily prompted her. 'Have you been in love?'

'Not sure.' Her friend's voice was husky. 'Maybe.'

'Wow. Ball-breaking Brittany, in love?' Spy raised his eyebrows. 'Did you literally fire an arrow through his heart?' He spread his hands as Lily glared at him. 'What? She's a Bronze Age weapons expert and a terrifyingly good archer. It's a logical suggestion.'

Lily ignored him. 'What makes you think you might have been in love? What were the clues?'

'I married him.'

Spyros doubled up with soundless laughter and Lily stared.

'You—? Okay. Well that's a fairly big clue right there.'

'It was a mistake.' Brittany tugged the trowel out of the ground. 'When I make mistakes I make sure they're *big*. I guess you could call it a whirlwind romance.'

'That sounds more like a hurricane than a whirlwind. How long did it last?'

Brittany stood up and brushed dust off her legs. 'Ten days. Spy, if you don't wipe that smile off your face I'm going to kick you into this trench and cover your corpse with a thick layer of dirt and shards of pottery.'

'You mean ten *years*,' Lily said and Brittany shook her head.

'No. I mean days. We made it through the honeymoon without killing each other.'

Lily felt her mouth drop open and closed it again quickly. 'What happened?'

'I let my emotions get in the way of making sane decisions.' Brittany gave a faint smile. 'I haven't fallen in love since.'

'Because you learned how not to do it. You didn't go and make the same mistake again and again. Give me some tips.'

'I can't. Avoiding emotional entanglement came naturally after I met Zach.'

'Sexy name.'

'Sexy guy.' She shaded her eyes from the sun. 'Sexy rat bastard guy.'

'Another one,' Lily said gloomily. 'But you were young and everyone is allowed to make mistakes when they're young. Not only do I not have that excuse, but I'm a habitual offender. I should be locked up until I'm safe to be rehabilitated. I need to be taken back to the store and reprogrammed.'

'You do not need to be reprogrammed.' Brittany stuffed her trowel into the front of her backpack. 'You're warm, friendly and lovable. That's what guys like about you.'

'That and the fact it takes one glance to know you'd look great naked,' Spy said affably.

Lily turned her back on him. 'Warm, friendly and lovable are great qualities for a puppy, but not so great for a woman. They say a person can change, don't they? Well, I'm going to change.' She scrambled to her feet. 'I am not falling in love again. I'm going to take your advice and have rebound sex.'

'Good plan.' Spy glanced at his watch. 'You get your clothes off, I'll get us a room.'

'Not funny.' Lily glared at him. 'I am going to pick someone I don't know, don't feel anything for and couldn't fall in love with in a million years.'

Brittany looked doubtful. 'Now I'm second-guessing myself. Coming from you it sounds like a recipe for disaster.'

'It's going to be perfect. All I have to do is find a man who doesn't tick a single box on my list and have sex with him. It can't possibly go wrong. I'm going to call it Operation Ice Maiden.'

Nik Zervakis stood with his back to the office, staring at the glittering blue of the sea while his assistant updated him. 'Did he call?'

'Yes, exactly as you predicted. How do you always know these things? I would have lost my nerve days ago with those sums of money involved. You don't even break out in a sweat.'

Nik could have told him the deal wasn't about money, it was about power. 'Did you call the lawyers?'

'They're meeting with the team from Lexos first thing tomorrow. So it's done. Congratulations, boss. The US media have turned the phones red-hot asking for interviews.'

'It's not over until the deal is signed. When that happens I'll put out a statement, but no interviews.' Nik felt some of the tension leave his shoulders. 'Did you make a reservation at The Athena?'

'Yes, but you have the official opening of the new museum wing first.'

Nik swore softly and swung round. 'I'd forgotten. Do you have a briefing document on that?'

His PA paled. 'No, boss. All I know is that the wing has been specially designed to display Minoan antiquities in one place. You were invited to the final meeting of the project team but you were in San Francisco.'

'Am I supposed to give a speech?'

'They're hoping you will agree to say a few words.'

'I can manage a few words, but they'll be unrelated to Minoan antiquities.' Nik loosened his tie. 'Run me through the schedule.'

'Vassilis will have the car here at six-fifteen, which should allow you time to go back to the villa and change. You're picking up Christina on the way and your table is booked for nine p.m.'

'Why not pick her up after I've changed?'

'That would have taken time you don't have.'

Nik couldn't argue with that. The demands of his schedule had seen off three assistants in the last six months. 'There was something else?'

The man shifted uncomfortably. 'Your father called. Several times. He said you weren't picking up your phone and asked me to relay a message.'

Nik flicked open the button at the neck of his shirt. 'Which was?'

'He wants to remind you that his wedding is next weekend. He thinks you've forgotten.'

Nik stilled. *He hadn't forgotten.* 'Anything else?'

'He is looking forward to having you at the celebrations. He wanted me to remind you that of all the riches in this world, family is the most valuable.'

Nik, whose sentiments on that topic were a matter of public record, made no comment.

He wondered why anyone would see a fourth wedding as a cause for celebration. To him, it shrieked of someone who hadn't learned his lesson the first three times. 'I will call him from the car.'

'There was one more thing—' The man backed towards the door like someone who knew he was going to need to make a rapid exit. 'He said to make sure you knew that if you don't come, you'll break his heart.'

It was a statement typical of his father. Emotional. Unguarded.

Reflecting that it was that very degree of sentimentality that had made his father the victim of three costly divorces, Niklaus strolled to his desk. 'Consider the message delivered.'

As the door closed he turned back to the window, staring over the midday sparkle of the sea.

Exasperation mingled with frustration and beneath that surface response lay darker, murkier emotions he had no wish to examine. He wasn't given to introspection and he believed that the past was only useful when it informed the future, so finding himself staring down into a swirling mass of long-ignored memories was an unwelcome experience.

Despite the air conditioning, sweat beaded on his forehead and he strode across his office and pulled a bottle of iced water from the fridge.

Why should it bother him that his father was marrying again?

He was no longer an idealistic nine-year-old, shattered by a mother's betrayal and driven by a deep longing for order and security.

He'd learned to make his own security. Emotionally he was an impenetrable fortress. He would never allow a relationship to explode the world from under his feet. He didn't believe in love and he saw marriage as expensive and pointless.

Unfortunately his father, an otherwise intelligent man, didn't share his views. He'd managed to build a successful business from nothing but the fruits of the land around him, but for some reason he had failed to apply that same intellect to his love life.

Nik reflected that if he approached business the way his father approached relationships, he would be broke.

As far as he could see his father performed no risk analysis, gave no consideration to the financial implications of each of his romantic whims and approached each relationship with the romantic optimism entirely inappropriate for a man on his fourth marriage.

Nik's attempts to encourage at least some degree of circumspection had been dismissed as cynical.

To make the situation all the more galling, the last time they'd met for dinner his father had actually lectured him on his lifestyle as if Nik's lack of divorces suggested a deep character flaw.

Nik closed his eyes briefly and wondered how everything in his business life could run so smoothly while his family was as messy as a dropped pan of spaghetti. The truth was he'd rather endure the twelve labours of Hercules than attend another of his father's weddings.

This time he hadn't met his father's intended bride and he didn't want to. He failed to see what he would bring to the proceedings other than grim disapproval and he didn't want to spoil the day.

Weddings depressed him. All the champagne bubbles in the world couldn't conceal the fact that two people were paying a fortune for the privilege of making a very public mistake.

Lily dumped her bag in the marble hallway and tried to stop her jaw from dropping.

Palatial didn't begin to describe it. Situated on the headland overlooking the sparkling blue of the sea, Villa Harmonia epitomised calm, high-end luxury.

Wondering where the rest of the team were, she wandered out onto the terrace.

Tiny paths wound down through the tumbling gardens to a private cove with a jetty where a platform gave direct swimming access to the sea.

'I've died and gone to heaven.' Disturbed from her trance by the insistent buzz of her phone, she dug it out of her pocket. Her simple uniform was uncomfortably tight, courtesy of all the delicious thyme honey and Greek yoghurt she'd consumed since arriving in Crete. Her phone call turned out to be the owner of the cleaning company, who told her that the rest of the team had been involved in an accident and wouldn't make it.

'Oh no, are they hurt?' On hearing that no one was in hospital but that the car was totalled, Lily realised she was going to be on her own with this job. 'So if it normally takes four of us four hours, how is one person going to manage?'

'Concentrate on the living areas and the master suite. Pay particular attention to the bathroom.'

Resigned to doing the best she could by herself, Lily set to work. Choosing Mozart from her soundtrack, she pushed in her earbuds and sang her way through *The Magic Flute* while she brushed and mopped the spacious living area.

Whoever lived here clearly didn't have children, she thought as she plumped cushions on deep white sofas and polished glass tables. Everything was sophisticated and understated.

Realising that dreaming would get her fired, Lily hummed her way up the curving staircase to the master bedroom and stopped dead.

The tiny, airless apartment she shared with Brittany had a single bed so narrow she'd twice fallen out of it in her sleep. *This* bed, by contrast, was large enough to sleep a family of six comfortably. It was positioned to take advantage of the incredible view across the bay and Lily stood, drooling with envy, imagining how it must feel to sleep in a bed this size. How many times could you roll over before finding yourself on the floor? If it were hers, she'd spread out like a starfish.

Glancing quickly over her shoulder to check there was no sign of the security team, she unclipped her phone from her pocket and took a photo of the bed and the view.

One day, she texted Brittany, I'm going to have sex in a bed like this.

Brittany texted back, I don't care about the bed, just give me the man who owns it.

With a last wistful look at the room, Lily tucked her phone carefully into her bag and strolled into the bathroom. A large tub was positioned next to a wall of glass, offering the owner an uninterrupted view of the ocean. The only way to clean something so large was to climb inside it, so she did that, extra careful not to slip.

When it was gleaming, she turned her attention to the large walk-in shower. There was a sophisticated control panel on the wall and she looked at it doubtfully. Remembering her disastrous experience with the photocopier and the coffee machine, she was reluctant to touch anything, but what choice was there?

Lifting her hand, she pressed a button cautiously and gasped as a powerful jet of freezing water hit her from the opposite wall.

Breathless, she slammed her hand on another button to try and stop the flow but that turned on a different jet and she was blasted with water until her hair and clothes were plastered to her body and she couldn't see. She thumped the wall blindly and was alternately scalded and frozen until finally she managed to turn off the jets. Panting, her hair and clothes plastered to her body, she sank to the floor while she tried to get her breath back, shivering and dripping like a puppy caught in the rain.

'I hate, hate, *hate* technology.' She pushed her hair back from her face, took it in her hands and twisted it into a rope, squeezing to remove as much of the water as she could. Then she stood up, but her uniform was dripping and stuck to her skin. If she walked back through the villa like this, she'd drip water everywhere and she didn't have time to clean the place again.

Peeling off her uniform, she was standing in her underwear wringing out the water when she heard a sound from the bedroom.

Assuming it must be one of the security team, she gave a whimper of horror. 'Hello? If there's anyone out there, don't come in for a moment because I'm just—' She stilled as a woman appeared in the doorway.

She was perfectly groomed, her slender body sheathed in a silk dress the colour of coral, her mouth a sheen of blended lipstick and lip-gloss.

Lily had never felt more outclassed in her life.

'Nik?' The woman spoke over her shoulder, her tone icy. 'Your sex drive is, of course, a thing of legend but for the record it's always a good idea to remove the last girlfriend before installing a new one.'

'What are you talking about?' The male voice came from the bedroom, deep, bored and instantly recognisable.

Still shivering from the impact of the cold water, Lily closed her eyes and wondered if any of the buttons on the control panel operated an ejector seat.

Now she knew who owned the villa.

Moments later he appeared in the doorway and Lily peered through soaked lashes and had her second ever look at Nik Zervakis. Confronted by more good looks and sex appeal than she'd ever seen concentrated in one man before, her tummy tumbled and she felt as if she were plunging downhill on a roller coaster.

He stood, legs braced apart, his handsome face blank of expression as if finding a semi-naked woman in his shower wasn't an event worthy of an emotional response. 'Well?'

That was all he was going to say?

Braced for an explosion of volcanic proportions, Lily gulped. 'I can explain—'

'I wish you would.' The woman's voice turned from ice

to acid and her expensively shod foot tapped rhythmically on the floor. 'This should be worth hearing.'

'I'm the cleaner—'

'Of course you are. Because "cleaners" always end up naked in the client's shower.' Vibrating with anger, she turned the beam of her angry glare onto the man next to her. 'Nik?'

'Yes?'

Her mouth tightened into a thin, dangerous line. 'Who is she?'

'You heard her. She's the cleaner.'

'*Obviously* she's lying.' The woman bristled. 'No doubt she's been here all day, sleeping off the night before.'

His only response to that was a faint narrowing of those spectacular dark eyes.

Recalling someone warning her on her first day with his company that Nik Zervakis was at his most dangerous when he was quiet, Lily felt her anxiety levels rocket but apparently her concerns weren't shared by his date for the evening, who continued to berate him.

'Do you know the worst thing about this? Not that you have a wandering eye, but that your eye wanders to someone as fat as her.'

'*Excuse* me? I'm not fat.' Lily tried vainly to cover herself with the soaking uniform. 'I'll have you know that my BMI is within normal range.'

But the woman wasn't listening. 'Was she the reason you were late picking me up? I *warned* you, Nik, no games, and yet you do this to me. Well, you gambled and you lost because I don't do second chances, especially this early in a relationship and if you can't be bothered to give an explanation then I can't be bothered to ask for one.' Without giving him the chance to respond, his date stalked out of the room and Lily flinched in time with each furious tap of those skyscraper heels.

She stood in awkward silence, her feelings bruised and her spirits drenched in cold water and guilt. 'She's very upset.'

'Yes.'

'Er—is she coming back?'

'I sincerely hope not.'

Lily wanted to say that he was well rid of her, but decided that protecting her job was more important than honesty. 'I'm *really* sorry—'

'Don't be. It wasn't your fault.'

Knowing that wasn't quite true, she squirmed. 'If I hadn't had an accident, I would have had my clothes on when she walked into the room.'

'An accident? I've never considered my shower to be a place of danger but apparently I was wrong about that.' He eyed the volume of water on the floor and her drenched clothing. 'What happened?'

'Your shower is like the flight deck of a jumbo jet, that's what happened!' Freezing and soaked, Lily couldn't stop her teeth chattering. 'There are no instructions.'

'I don't need instructions.' His gaze slid over her with slow, disturbing thoroughness. 'I'm familiar with the workings of my own shower.'

'Well I'm not! I had no idea which buttons to press.'

'So you thought you'd press all of them? If you ever find yourself on the flight deck of a Boeing 747 I suggest you sit on your hands.'

'It's not f-f-funny. I'm soaking wet and I didn't know you were going to come home early.'

'I apologise.' Irony gleamed in those dark eyes. 'I'm not in the habit of notifying people of my movements in advance. Have you finished cleaning or do you want me to show you which buttons to press?'

Lily summoned as much dignity as she could in the circumstances. 'Your shower is clean. Extra clean, because I wiped myself around it personally.' Anxious to make her exit as fast as possible, she kept her eyes fixed on the door and away from that tall, powerful frame. 'Are you sure she isn't coming back?'

'No.'

Lily paused, torn between relief and guilt. 'I've ruined another relationship.'

'Another?' Dark eyebrows lifted. 'It's a common occurrence?'

'You have no idea. Look—if it would help I could call my employer and ask her to vouch for me.' Her voice tailed off as she realised that would mean confessing she'd been caught half naked in the shower.

He gave a faint smile. 'Unless you have a very liberal-minded employer, you might want to rethink that idea.'

'There must be some way I can fix this. I've ruined your date, although for the record I don't think she's a very kind person so she might not be good for you in the long term and with a body that bony she won't be very cuddly for your children.' She caught his eye. 'Are you laughing at me?'

'No, but the ability to cuddle children isn't high on my list of necessary female attributes.' He flung his jacket carelessly over the back of a sofa that was bigger than her bed at home.

She stared in fascination, wondering if he cared at all that his date had walked out. 'As a matter of interest, why didn't you defend yourself?'

'Why would I defend myself?'

'You could have explained yourself and then she would have forgiven you.'

'I never explain myself. And anyway—' he shrugged '—you had already given her an explanation.'

'I don't think she saw me as a credible witness. It might have sounded better coming from you.'

He stood, legs spread, his powerful shoulders blocking the doorway. 'I assume you told her the truth? You're the cleaner?'

'Of course I told her the truth.'

'Then there was nothing I could have added to your story.'

In his position she would have died of humiliation, but he seemed supremely indifferent to the fact he'd been publicly dumped. 'You don't seem upset.'

'Why would I be upset?'

'Because most people are upset when a relationships ends.'

He smiled. 'I'm not one of those.'

Lily felt a flash of envy. 'You're not even a teeny tiny bit sad?'

'I'm not familiar with that unit of measurement but no, I'm not even a "teeny tiny" bit sad. To be sad I'd have to care and I don't care.'

To be sad I'd have to care and I don't care.

Brilliant, Lily thought. *Why* couldn't she have said that to Professor Ashurst when he'd given her that fake sympathy about having hurt her? She needed to memorise it for next time. 'Excuse me a moment.' Leaving a dripping trail behind her, she shot past him, scrabbled in her bag and pulled out a notebook.

'What are you doing?'

'I'm writing down what you said. Whenever I'm dumped I never know the right thing to say, but next time it happens I'm going to say *exactly* those words in exactly that tone instead of producing enough tears to power a water feature at Versailles.' She scribbled, dripping water onto her notebook and smearing the ink.

'Being "dumped" is something that happens to you often?'

'Often enough. I fall in love, I get my heart broken, it's a cycle I'm working on breaking.' She wished she hadn't said anything. Although she was fairly open with people, she drew the line at making public announcements about not being easy to love.

That was her secret.

'How many times have you fallen in love?'

'So far?' She shook the pen with frustration as the ink stalled on the damp page, 'Three times.'

'*Cristo*, that's unbelievable.'

'Thanks for not making me feel better. I bet you've never been unlucky in love, have you?'

'I've never been in love at all.'

Lily digested that. 'You've never met the right person.'

'I don't believe in love.'

'You—' She rocked back on her heels, her attention caught. 'So what do you believe in?'

'Money, influence and power.' He shrugged. 'Tangible, measurable goals.'

'You can measure power and influence? Don't tell me—you stamp your foot and it registers on the Richter scale.'

He loosened his tie. 'You'd be surprised.'

'I'm already surprised. Gosh, you are *so* cool. You are my new role model.' Finally she managed to coax ink from the pen. 'It is never too late to change. From now on I'm all about tangible, measurable goals, too. As a matter of interest, what is your goal in relationships?'

'Orgasm.' He gave a slow smile and she felt herself turn scarlet.

'Right. Well, that serves me right for asking a stupid question. That's definitely a measurable goal. You're obviously able to be cold and ruthlessly detached when it comes to relationships. I'm aiming for that. I've dripped all over your floor. Be careful not to slip.'

He was leaning against the wall, watching her with amusement. 'This is what you look like when you're being cold and ruthlessly detached?'

'I haven't actually started yet, but the moment my radar warns me I might be in danger of falling for the wrong type, *bam*—' she punched the air with her fist '—I'm going to turn on my freezing side. From now on I have armour around my heart. Kevlar.' She gave him a friendly smile. 'You think I'm crazy, right? All this is natural to you. But it isn't to me. This is the first stage of my personality transplant. I'd love to do the whole thing under anaesthetic and wake up all new and perfect, but that isn't possible so I'm trying to embrace the process.'

A vibrating noise caught her attention and she glanced across the room towards his jacket. When he didn't move, she looked at him expectantly. 'That's your phone.'

He was still watching her, his gaze disturbingly intent. 'Yes.'

'You're not going to answer it?' She scrambled to her feet, still clutching the towel. 'It might be her, asking for your forgiveness.'

'I'm sure it is, which is why I don't intend to answer it.'

Lily absorbed that with admiration. 'This is a perfect example of why I need to be like you and not like me. If that had been my phone, I would have answered it and when whoever was on the end apologised for treating me badly, I would have told him it was fine. I would have forgiven them.'

'You're right,' he said. 'You do need help. What's your name?'

She shifted, her wet feet sticking to the floor. 'Lily. Like the flower.'

'You look familiar. Have we met before?'

Lily felt the colour pour into her cheeks. 'I've been working as an intern at your company two days a week for the past couple of months. I'm second assistant to your personal assistant.' *I'm the one who broke the photocopier and the coffee machine.*

Dark eyebrows rose. 'We've met?'

'No. I've only seen you once in person. I don't count the time I was hiding in the bathroom.'

'You hid in the bathroom?'

'You were on a firing spree. I didn't want to be noticed.'

'So you work for me two days a week, and on the other three days you're working as a cleaner?'

'No, I only do that job in the evenings. The other three days I'm doing fieldwork up at Aptera for the summer. But that's almost finished. I've reached a crossroads in my life and I've no idea which direction to take.'

'Fieldwork?' That sparked his interest. 'You're an archaeologist?'

'Yes, I'm part of a project funded by the university but that part doesn't pay off my massive college loans so I have other jobs.'

'How much do you know about Minoan antiquities?'

Lily blinked. 'Probably more than is healthy for a woman of twenty-four.'

'Good. Get back into the bathroom and dry yourself off while I find you a dress. Tonight I have to open the new wing of the museum. You're coming with me.'

'Me? Don't you have a date?'

'I had a date,' he said smoothly. 'As you're partially responsible for the fact she's no longer here, you're coming in her place.'

'But—' She licked her lips. 'I'm supposed to be cleaning your villa.'

His gaze slid from her face to the wash of water covering the bathroom floor. 'I'd say you've done a pretty thorough job. By the time we get home, the flood will have spread down the stairs and across the living areas, so it will clean itself.'

Lily gave a gurgle of laughter. She wondered if any of his employees realised he had a sense of humour. 'You're not going to fire me?'

'You should have more confidence in yourself. If you have knowledge of Minoan artefacts then I still have a use for you and I never fire people who are useful.' He reached for the towel and tugged it off, leaving her clad only in her soaking wet underwear.

'What are you doing?' She gave a squeak of embarrassment and snatched at the towel but he held it out of reach.

'Stop wriggling. I can't be the first man to see you half naked.'

'Usually I'm in a relationship when a man sees me naked.

And being stared at is very unnerving, especially when you've been called fat by someone who looks like a toast rack—' Lily broke off as he turned and strolled away from her. She didn't know whether to be relieved or affronted. 'If you want to know my size you could ask me!'

He reached for his phone and dialled. While he waited for the person on the other end to answer, he scanned her body and gave her a slow, knowing smile. 'I don't need to ask, *theé mou*,' he said softly. 'I already know your size.'

CHAPTER TWO

NIK LOUNGED IN his seat while the car negotiated heavy evening traffic. Beside him Lily was wriggling like a fish dropped onto the deck of a boat.

'Mr Zervakis? This dress is far more revealing than anything I would normally wear. And I've had a horrible thought.' Her voice was breathy and distracting and Nik turned his head to look at her, trying to remind himself that girls with sweet smiles who were self-confessed members of Loveaholics Anonymous were definitely off his list.

'Call me Nik.'

'I can't call you Nik. It would feel wrong while I'm working in your company. You pay my salary.'

'I pay you? I thought you said you were an intern.'

'I am. You pay your interns far more than most companies, but that's a different conversation. I'm still having that horrible thought by the way.'

Nik dragged his eyes from her mouth and tried to wipe his brain of X-rated thoughts. 'What horrible thought is that?'

'The one where your girlfriend finds out you took me as your date tonight.'

'She will find out.'

'And that doesn't bother you?'

'Why would it?'

'Isn't it obvious? Because she didn't believe I was the cleaner. She thought you and I—well...' she turned scarlet

'...if she finds out we were together tonight then it will look as if she was right and we were lying, even though if people used their brains they could work out that if she's your type then I couldn't possibly be.'

Nik tried to decipher that tumbled speech. 'You're concerned she will think we're having sex? Why is that a horrible thought? You find me unattractive?'

'That's a ridiculous question.' Lily's eyes flew to his and then away again. 'Sorry, but that's like asking a woman if she likes chocolate.'

'There are women who don't like chocolate.'

'They're lying. They might not eat it, but that doesn't mean they don't like it.'

'So I'm chocolate?' Nik tried to remember the last time he'd been this entertained by anyone.

'If you're asking if I think you're very tempting and definitely bad for me, the answer is yes. But apart from the fact we're totally unsuited, I wouldn't be able to relax enough to have sex with you.'

Nik, who had never had trouble helping a woman relax, rose to the challenge. 'I'm happy to—'

'No.' She gave him a stern look. 'I know you're competitive, but forget it. I saw that photo of you in the swimming pool. No way could I ever be naked in front of a man with a body like yours. I'd have to suck everything in and make sure you only saw my good side. The stress would kill any passion.'

'I've already seen you in your underwear.'

'Don't remind me.'

Nik caught his driver's amused gaze in the mirror and gave him a steady stare. Vassilis had been with him for over a decade and had a tendency to voice his opinions on Nik's love life. It was obvious he thoroughly approved of Lily.

'It's true that if you turn up as my guest tonight there will be people who assume we are having sex.' Nik returned his attention to the conversation. 'I can't claim to be intimately acquainted with the guest list, but I'm assuming a few of the people there will be your colleagues. Does that bother you?'

'No. It will send a message that I'm not broken-hearted, which is good for my pride. In fact the timing is perfect. Just this morning I embarked on a new project. Operation Ice Maiden. You're probably wondering what that is.'

Nik opened his mouth to comment but she carried on without pausing.

'I am going to have sex with no emotion. That's right.' She nodded at him. 'You heard me correctly. Rebound sex. I am going to climb into bed with some guy and I'm not going to feel a thing.'

Hearing a sound from the front of the car, Nik pressed a button and closed the screen between him and Vassilis, giving them privacy.

'Do you have anyone in mind for—er—Operation Ice Maiden?'

'Not yet, but if they happen to think it's you that's fine. You'd look good on my romantic résumé.'

Nik leaned his head back against the seat and started to laugh. 'You, Lily, are priceless.'

'That doesn't sound like a compliment.' She adjusted the neckline of her dress and her breasts almost escaped in the process. 'You're basically saying I'm not worth anything.'

Dragging his gaze from her body, Nik decided this was the most entertaining evening he'd had in a long time.

'There are photographers.' As they pulled up outside the museum Lily slunk lower in her seat and Nik closed his hand around her wrist and hauled her upright again.

'You look stunning. If you don't want them all surmising that we climbed out of bed to come here then you need to stop looking guilty.'

'I saw several TV cameras.'

'The opening of a new wing of the museum is news.'

'The neckline of this dress might also be news.' She

tugged at it. 'My breasts are too big for this plunging style. Can I borrow your jacket?'

'Your breasts deserve a dress like that and no, you may not borrow my jacket.' His voice was a deep, masculine purr and she felt the sizzle of sexual attraction right through her body.

'Are you flirting with me?' He was completely different from the safe, friendly men who formed part of her social circle. There was a brutal strength to him, a confidence and assurance that suggested he'd never met a man he hadn't been able to beat in a fight, whether in the bar or the boardroom.

Her question appeared to amuse him. 'You're my date. Flirting is mandatory.'

'It unsettles me and I'm already unsettled at the thought of tonight.'

'Because you're with me?'

No way was she confessing how being with him really made her feel. 'No, because the opening of this new museum wing is a really momentous occasion.'

'You and I have a very different idea of what constitutes a momentous occasion, Lily.' There was laughter in his eyes. 'Never before has my ego been so effectively crushed.'

'Your ego is armour plated, like your feelings.'

'It's true that my feelings of self-worth are not dependent on the opinion of others.'

'Because you think you're right and everyone else is wrong. I wish I were more like you. What if the reporters ask who I am? What do I say? I'm a fake.'

'You're the archaeologist. I'm the fake. And you say whatever you want to say. Or say nothing. Your decision. You're the one in charge of your mouth.'

'You have no idea how much I wish that was true.'

'Tell me why you're excited about tonight.'

'You mean apart from the fact I get to dress up? The new wing houses the biggest collection of Minoan antiquities anywhere in Greece. It has a high percentage of provenanced material, which means archaeologists will be able to restudy material from old excavations. It's exciting. And I love the dress by the way, even though I'll never have any reason to wear it again.'

'Chipped pots excite you?'

She winced. 'Don't say that on camera. The collection will play an active role in research and in university teaching as well as offering a unique insight for the general public.'

As the car pulled up outside the museum one of Nik's security team opened the door and Lily emerged to what felt like a million camera flashes.

'Unreal,' she muttered. 'Now I know why celebrities wear sunglasses.'

'Mr Zervakis—' Photographers and reporters gathered as close as they could. 'Do you have a statement about the new wing?'

Nik paused and spoke directly to the camera, relaxed and at ease as he repeated Lily's words without a single error.

She stared at him. 'You must have an incredible short-term memory.'

A reporter stepped forward. 'Who's your guest tonight, Nik?'

Nik turned towards her and she realised he was leaving it up to her to decide whether to give them a name or not.

'I'm a friend,' she muttered and Nik smiled, took her hand and led her up the steps to the welcome committee at the top.

The first person she spotted was David Ashurst and she stopped in dismay. In answer to Nik's questioning look, she shook her head quickly, misery and panic creating a sick cocktail inside her. 'I'm fine. I saw someone I didn't expect to see, that's all. I didn't think he'd have the nerve to show up.'

'That's him?' His gaze travelled from her face to the man looking awkward at the top of the steps. 'He is the reason you're hoping for a personality transplant?'

'His name is Professor Ashurst. He has a *wife*,' she muttered in an undertone. 'Can you believe that? I actually cried over that loser. Do I have time to get my notebook out of my bag? I can't remember what I wrote down.'

'I'll tell you what to say.' He leaned closer and whispered something in her ear that made her gasp.

'I can't say that.'

'No? Then how's this for an alternative?' Sliding his arm round her waist, he pressed his hand to the base of her spine and flattened her against him. She looked up at him, hypnotised by those spectacular dark eyes and the raw sexuality in his gaze. Before she could ask what he was doing he lowered his head and kissed her.

Pleasure screamed through her, sensation scorching her skin and stoking a pool of heat low in her belly. She'd been kissed before, but never like this. Nik used his mouth with slow, sensual expertise and she felt a rush of exquisite excitement burn through her body. Her nerve endings tingled, her tummy flipped like a gymnast in a competition, and Lily was possessed by a deep, dark craving that was entirely new to her. Oblivious to their audience, she pushed against his hard, powerful frame and felt his arms tighten around her in a gesture that was unmistakably possessive. It was a taste rather than a feast, but it left her starving for more so that when he slowly lifted his head she swayed towards him dizzily, trying to balance herself.

'Wh-why did you do that?'

He dragged his thumb slowly across her lower lip and released her. 'Because you didn't know what to say and sometimes actions speak louder than words.'

'You're an amazing kisser.' Lily blinked as a flashbulb went off in her face. 'Now there's *no* chance your girlfriend will believe I'm the cleaner.'

'No chance.' His gaze lingered on her mouth. 'And she isn't my girlfriend.'

Her head spun and her legs felt shaky. She was aware of the women staring at her enviously and David gaping at her, shell-shocked.

As she floated up the last few steps to the top she smiled at him, feeling strong for the first time in days. 'Hi, Professor Ass—Ashurst.' She told herself it was the heat that was making her dizzy and disorientated, not the kiss. 'Have a safe flight home tomorrow. I'm sure your family has missed you.'

There was no opportunity for him to respond because the curator of the museum stepped forward to welcome them, shaking Nik's hand and virtually prostrating himself in gratitude.

'Mr Zervakis—your generosity—this wing is the most exciting moment of my career—' the normally articulate man was stammering. 'I know your schedule is demanding but we'd be honoured if you'd meet the team and then take a quick tour.'

Lily kept a discreet distance but Nik took her hand and clamped her next to his side, a gesture that earned her a quizzical look from Brittany, who was looking sleek and pretty in a short blue dress that showed off her long legs. She was standing next to Spy, whose eyes were glued to Lily's cleavage, confirming all her worst fears about the suitability of the dress.

The whole situation felt surreal.

One moment she'd been half naked and shivering on the bathroom floor, the next she'd been whisked into an elegant bedroom by a team of four people who had proceeded to style her hair, do her make-up and generally make her fit to be seen on the arm of Nik Zervakis.

Three dresses had magically appeared and Nik had strolled into the room in mid phone call, gestured to one of them and then left without even pausing in his conversation.

It had been on the tip of Lily's tongue to select a different dress on principle. Then she'd reasoned that not only had he provided the dress, thus allowing her to turn up at the museum opening in the first place, but that he'd picked the dress she would have chosen herself.

All the same, she felt self-conscious as her friends and

colleagues working on the project at Aptera stood together while she was treated like a VIP.

As the curator led them towards the first display Lily forgot to be self-conscious and examined the pot.

'This is early Minoan.'

Nik stared at it with a neutral expression. 'You know that because it's more cracked than the others?'

'No. Because their ceramics were characterised by linear patterns. Look—' She took his arm and drew him closer to the glass. 'Spirals, crosses, triangles, curved lines—' She talked to him about each one and he listened carefully before strolling further along the glass display cabinet.

'This one has a bird.'

'Naturalistic designs were characteristic of the Middle Minoan period. The sequencing of ceramic styles has helped archaeologists define the three phases of Minoan culture.'

He stared down in her eyes. 'Fascinating.'

Her heart bumped hard against her chest and as the curator moved away to answer questions from the press she stepped closer to him. 'You're not really fascinated, are you?'

'I am.' His eyes dropped to her mouth with blatant interest. 'But I think it might be because you're the one saying it. I love the way you get excited about things that put other people to sleep, and your mouth looks cute when you say "Minoan". It makes you pout.'

She tried not to laugh. 'You're impossible. To you it's an old pot, but it can have tremendous significance. Ceramics help archaeologists establish settlement and trading patterns. We can reconstruct human activity based on the distribution of pottery. It gives us an idea of population size and social complexity. Why are you donating so much money to the museum if it isn't an interest of yours?'

'Because I'm interested in preserving Greek culture. I donate the money. It's up to them to decide how to use it. I don't micromanage and gifts don't come with strings.'

'Why didn't you insist that it was called "The Zervakis

Wing" or something? Most benefactors want their name in the title.'

'It's about preserving history, not about advertising my name.' His eyes gleamed. 'And ZervaCo is a modern, forward-thinking company at the cutting edge of technology development. I don't want the name associated with a museum.'

'You're joking.'

'Yes, I'm joking.' His smile faded as Spy and Brittany joined them.

'They're good friends of mine,' Lily said quickly, 'so you can switch off the full-wattage intimidation.'

'If you're sure.' He introduced himself to both of them and chatted easily with Spy while Brittany pulled Lily to one side.

'I don't even know where to start with my questions.'

'Probably just as well because I wouldn't know where to start with my answers.'

'I'm guessing he's the owner of Villa You-Have-to-be-Kidding-Me.'

'He is.'

'I'm not going to ask,' Brittany muttered and then grinned. 'Oh hell, yes I am. I'm asking. What happened? He found you in the cellar fighting off the ugly sisters and decided to bring you to the ball?'

'Close. He found me on the floor of his bathroom where I'd been attacked and left for dead by his power shower. After I broke up his relationship, he needed a replacement and I was the only person around.'

Brittany started to laugh. 'You were left for dead by his power shower?'

'You said you wouldn't ask.'

'These things only ever happen to you, Lily.'

'I am aware of that. I am really not good with technology.'

'Maybe not, but you know how to pick your rebound guy. He is spectacular. And you look stunning.' Brittany's curious gaze slid over her from head to foot. 'It's a step up from dusty shorts and hiking boots.'

Lily frowned. 'He isn't my rebound guy.'

'Why not? He is smoking hot. And there's something about him.' Her friend narrowed her eyes as she scanned Nik's broad shoulders and powerful frame. 'A suggestion of the uncivilised under the civilised, if you know what I mean.' Brittany put her hand on her arm and her voice was suddenly serious. 'Be careful.'

'Why would I need to be careful? I'm never setting foot in his shower again, if that's what you mean.'

'It isn't what I mean. That man is not tame.'

'He's surprisingly amusing company.'

'That makes him even more dangerous. He's a tiger, not a pussycat and he hasn't taken his eyes off you for five seconds. I don't want to see you hurt again.'

'I have never been in less danger of being hurt. He isn't my type.'

Brittany looked at her. 'Nik Zervakis is the man equivalent of Blood Type O. He is everyone's type.'

'Not mine.'

'He kissed you,' Brittany said dryly, 'so I'm guessing he might have a different opinion on that.'

'He kissed me because I didn't know what to say to David. I was in an awkward position and he helped me out. He did that for me.'

'Lily, a guy like him does things for himself. Don't make a mistake about that. He does what he wants, with whoever he wants to do it, at a time that suits him.'

'I know. Don't worry about me.' Smiling at Brittany, she moved back to Nik. 'Looks like the party is breaking up. Thanks for a fun evening. I'll post you the dress back and any time you need your shower cleaned let me know. I owe you.'

He stared down at her for a long moment, ignoring everyone around them. 'Have dinner with me. I have a reservation at The Athena at nine.'

She'd heard of The Athena. Who hadn't? It was one of the most celebrated restaurants in the whole of Greece. Eating there was a once-in-a-lifetime experience for most people and a never-in-this-lifetime experience for her.

Those incredible dark eyes held hers and Brittany's voice flitted into her head.

He's a tiger, not a pussycat.

From the way he was looking at her mouth, she wondered if he intended her to be the guest or the meal.

'That's a joke, right?' She gave a half-smile and looked away briefly, awkward, out of her depth. When she looked back at him she was still the only one smiling.

'I never joke about food.'

Something curled low in her stomach. 'Nik…' she spoke softly '…this has been amazing. Really out of this world and something to tell my kids one day, but you're a gazillionaire and I'm a—a—'

'Sexy woman who looks great in that dress.'

There was something about him that made her feel as if she were floating two feet above the ground.

'I was going to say I'm a dusty archaeologist who can't even figure out how to use your power shower.'

'I'll teach you. Have dinner with me, Lily.' His soft command made her wonder if anyone had ever said no to him.

Thrown by the look in his eyes and the almost unbearable sexual tension, she was tempted. Then she remembered her rule about never dating anyone who didn't fit her basic criteria. 'I can't. But I'll never forget this evening. Thank you.' Because she was afraid she'd change her mind, she turned and walked quickly towards the exit.

What a crazy day it had been.

Part of her was longing to look back, to see if he was watching her.

Of course he wouldn't be watching her. Look at how quickly he'd replaced Christina. Within two minutes of her refusal, Nik Zervakis would be inviting someone else to dinner.

David stood in the doorway, blocking her exit. 'What are you doing with him?'

'None of your business.'

His jaw tightened. 'Did you kiss him to make me jealous or to help you get over me?'

'I kissed him because he's a hot guy, and I was over you the moment I found out you were married.' Realising it was true, Lily felt a rush of relief but that relief was tempered by the knowledge that her system for evaluating prospective life partners was seriously flawed.

'I know you love me.'

'You're wrong. And if you really knew me, you'd know I'm incapable of loving a man who is married to another woman.' Her voice and hands were shaking. 'You have a wife. A family.'

'I'll work something out.'

'Did you really just say that to me?' Lily stared at him, appalled. 'A family is *not* disposable. You don't come and go as it suits you, nor do you "work something out". You stick by them through thick and thin.' Disgusted and disillusioned, she tried to step past him but he caught her arm.

'You don't understand. Things are tough right now.'

'I don't care.' She dug her fingers into clammy palms. Knowing that her response was deeply personal, she looked away. 'A real man doesn't walk away when things get tough.'

'You're forgetting how good it was between us.'

'And you're forgetting the promises you made.' She dragged her arm out of his grip. 'Go back to your wife.'

He glanced over her shoulder towards Nik. 'I never thought you were the sort to be turned on by money, but obviously I was wrong. I hope you know what you're doing because all that man will ever give you is one night. A man like him is only interested in sex.'

'What did you say?' Lily stared at him and then turned her

head to look at Nik. The sick feeling in her stomach eased and her spirits lifted. 'You're right. Thank you so much.'

'For making you realise he's wrong for you?'

'For making me realise he's perfect. Now stop looking down the front of my dress and go home to your wife and kids.' With that, she stalked past him and spotted the reporter who had asked her identity on the way in. 'Lily,' she said clearly. 'Lily Rose. That's my name. And yes, Rose is my second name.'

Then she turned and stalked back into the museum, straight up to Nik, who was deep in conversation with two important-looking men in suits.

All talk ceased as Lily walked up to him, her heels making the same rhythmic tapping sound that Christina's had earlier in the evening. She decided heels were her new favourite thing for illustrating mood. 'What time is that restaurant reservation?'

He didn't miss a beat. 'Nine o'clock.'

'Then we should leave, because we don't want to be late.' She stood on tiptoe and planted a kiss firmly on his mouth. 'And just so that you know, whatever you're planning on doing with the dress, I'm keeping the shoes.'

CHAPTER THREE

THE ATHENA WAS situated on the edge of town, on a hill overlooking Souda Bay with the White Mountains dominating the horizon behind them.

Still on a high after her confrontation with David, Lily sailed into the restaurant feeling like royalty. 'You have no idea how good it felt to tell David to go home to his wife. I felt like punching the air. You see what a few hours in your company has done for me? I'm already transformed. Your icy control and lack of emotional engagement is contagious.'

Nik guided her to his favourite table, tucked away behind a discreet screen of vines. 'You certainly showed the guy what he was missing.'

Lily frowned. 'I didn't want to show him what he was missing. I wanted him to learn a lesson and never lie or cheat again. I wanted him to think of his poor wife. Marriage should be for ever. No cheating. Mess around as much as you like before if that's what you want, but once you've made that commitment, that's it. Don't you agree?'

'Definitely. Which is why I've never made that commitment,' he said dryly. 'I'm still at the "messing around" stage and I expect to stay firmly trapped in that stage for the rest of my life.'

'You don't want a family? We're very different. It's brilliant.' She smiled at him and his eyes narrowed.

'Why is that brilliant?'

'Because you're completely and utterly wrong for me. We don't want the same things.'

'I'm relieved to hear it.' He leaned back in his chair. 'I hardly dare ask what you want.'

She hesitated. 'Someone like you will think I'm a ridiculous romantic.'

'Tell me.'

She dragged her gaze from his and looked over the tumbling bougainvillea to the sea beyond. *Was she a ridiculous romantic?*

Was she setting herself unachievable goals?

Seduced by the warmth of his gaze and the beauty of the spectacular sunset, she told the truth. 'I want the whole fairy tale.'

'Which fairy tale? The one where the stepmother poisons the apple or the one where the prince has to deal with a heroine with narcolepsy?'

She laughed. 'The happy-ending part. I want to fall in love, settle down and have lots of babies.' Enjoying herself, she looked him in the eye. 'Am I freaking you out yet?'

'That depends. Are you expecting to do any of that with me?'

'No! Of course not.'

'Then you're not freaking me out.'

'I start every relationship in the genuine belief it might go somewhere.'

'I presume you mean somewhere other than bed?'

'I do. I have never been interested in sex for the sake of sex.'

Nik looked amused. 'That's the only sort of sex I'm interested in.'

She sat back in her chair and looked at him. 'I've never had sex with a man I wasn't in love with. I fall in love, then I have sex. I think sex cements my emotional connection to someone.' She sneaked another look at him. 'You don't have that problem, do you?'

'I'm not looking for an emotional connection, if that's what you're asking.'

'I want to be more like you. I decided this morning I'm going to have cold, emotionless rebound sex. I'm switching everything off. It's going to be wham, bam, thank you, man.'

The corners of his mouth flickered. 'Do you have anyone in mind for this project?'

She sensed this wasn't the moment to confess he was right at the top of her list. 'I'm going to pick a guy I couldn't possibly fall in love with. Then I'll be safe. It will be like—' she struggled to find the right description '—emotional contraception. I'll be taking precautions. Wearing a giant condom over my feelings. Protecting myself. I bet you do that all the time.'

'If you're asking if I've ever pulled a giant condom over my feelings, the answer is no.'

'You're laughing at me, but if you'd been hurt as many times as I have you wouldn't be laughing. So if emotions don't play a part in your relationships, what exactly is sex to you?'

'Recreation.' He took a menu from the waiter and she felt a rush of mortification. As soon as he walked away, she gave a groan.

'How long had he been standing there?'

'Long enough to know you're planning on having cold, unemotional rebound sex and that you're thinking of wearing a giant condom over your feelings. I think that was the point he decided it was time to take our order.'

She covered her face with her hands. 'We need to leave. I'm sure the food here is delicious, but we need to eat somewhere different or I need to take my plate under the table.'

'You're doing it again. Letting emotions govern your actions.'

'But he *heard* me. Aren't you embarrassed?'

'Why would I be embarrassed?'

'Aren't you worried about what he might think of you?'

'Why would I care what he thinks? I don't know him. His role is to serve our food and make sure we enjoy ourselves sufficiently to want to come back. His opinion on anything else is irrelevant. Carry on with what you were saying. It was fascinating. Dining with you is like learning about an alien species. You were telling me you're going to pick a guy you can't fall in love with and use him for sex.'

'And you were telling me sex is recreation—like football?'

'No, because football is a group activity. I'm possessive, so for me it's strictly one on one.'

Her heart gave a little flip. 'That sounds like a type of commitment.'

'I'm one hundred per cent committed for the time a woman is in my bed. She is the sole focus of my attention.'

Her stomach uncurled with a slow, dangerous heat. 'But that might only be for a night?'

He simply smiled and she leaned back with a shocked laugh.

'You are so *bad*. And honest. I love that.'

'As long as you don't love *me*, we don't have a problem.'

'I could never love you. You are so wrong for me.'

'I think we should drink to that.' He raised a hand and moments later champagne appeared on the table.

'I can't believe you live like this. A driver, bottles of champagne—' She lifted the glass, watching the bubbles. 'Your villa is bigger than quite a few Greek islands and there is only one of you.'

'I like space and light and property is always a good investment.' He handed the menu back to the waiter. 'Is there any food you don't eat?'

'I eat everything.' She paused while he spoke to the waiter in Greek. 'Are you seriously ordering for me?'

'The menu is in Greek and you were talking about sex so I was aiming to keep the interaction as brief as possible in order to prevent you from feeling the need to dine under the table.'

'In that case I'll forgive you.' She waited until the waiter had walked away with their order. 'So if property is an investment that means you'd *sell* your home?'

'I have four homes.'

Her jaw dropped. 'Four? Why does one person need four homes? One for every season or something?'

'I have offices in New York, San Francisco and London and I don't like staying in hotels.'

'So you buy a house. That is the rich man's way of solving a problem. Which one do you think of as home?' Seeing the puzzled look on his face, she elaborated. 'Where do your family live? Do you have family? Are your parents alive?'

'They are.'

'Happily married?'

'Miserably divorced. In my father's case three times so far, but he's always in competition with himself so I'm expecting a fourth as soon as the wedding is out of the way.'

'And your mother?' She saw a faint shift in his expression.

'My mother is American. She lives in Boston with her third husband who is a divorce lawyer.'

'So do you think of yourself as Greek American or American Greek?'

He gave a careless lift of his broad shoulders. 'Whichever serves my purpose at the time.'

'Wow. So you have this big, crazy family.' Lily felt a flash of envy. 'That must be wonderful.'

'Why?'

'You don't think it's wonderful? I guess we never appreciate something when we have it.' She said it lightly but felt his dark gaze fix on her across the table.

'Are you going to cry?'

'No, of course not.'

'Good. Because tears are the one form of emotional expression I don't tolerate.'

She stole an olive from the bowl on the table. 'What if someone is upset?'

'Then they need to walk away from me until they've sorted themselves out, or be prepared for me to walk away. I never allow myself to be manipulated and ninety-nine per cent of tears are manipulation.'

'What about the one per cent which are an expression of genuine emotion?'

'I've never encountered that rare beast, so I'm willing to play the odds.'

'If that's your experience, you must have met some awful women in your time. I don't believe you'd be that unsympathetic.'

'Believe it.' He leaned back as the waiter delivered a selection of dishes. 'These are Cretan specialities. Try them.' He spooned beans in a rich tomato sauce onto her plate and added local goat's cheese.

She nibbled the beans and moaned with pleasure. 'These are delicious. I still can't believe you ordered for me. Do you want to feed me, too? Because I could lie back and let you drop grapes into my mouth if that would be fun. Or you could cover my naked body with whipped cream. Is that the sort of stuff you do in bed?'

There was a dangerous glitter in his eyes. 'You don't want to know the sort of "stuff" I do in bed, Lily. You're far too innocent.'

She remembered what Brittany had said about him not being tame. 'I'm not innocent. I have big eyes and that gives people a false impression of me.'

'You remind me of a kitten that's been abandoned by the side of the road.'

'You've got me totally wrong. I'd say I'm more of a panther.' She clawed the air and growled. 'A little bit predatory. A little bit dangerous.'

He gave her a long steady look and she blushed and lowered her hand.

'All right, maybe not a *panther* exactly but not a kitten either.' She thought about what lay in her past. 'I'll have you know I'm pretty tough. Tell me more about your family. So you have a father and a few stepmothers. How about siblings?'

'I have one half-sister who is two.'

Lily softened. 'I love that age. They're so busy and into everything. Is she adorable?'

'I've no idea. I've never met her.'

'You've—' She stared at him, shocked. 'You mean it's been a while since you've seen her.'

'No. I mean I've never seen her.' He lifted his champagne. 'Her mother extracted all the money she could from my father and then left. She lives in Athens and visits when she wants something.'

'Oh, my God, that's *terrible*.' Lily's eyes filled. 'Your poor, poor father.'

He put his glass down slowly. 'Are you crying for my father?'

'No.' Her throat was thickened. 'Maybe. Yes, a little bit.'

'A man you've never met and know nothing about.'

'Maybe I'm the one per cent who cares.' She sniffed and he shook his head in exasperation.

'This is your tough, ruthless streak? How can you be sad for someone you don't know?'

'Because I sympathise with his situation. He doesn't see his little girl and that must be so hard. Family is the most important thing in the world and it is often the least appreciated thing.'

'If you let a single tear fall onto your cheek,' he said softly, 'I'm walking out of here.'

'I don't believe you. You wouldn't be that heartless. I think it's all a big act you put on to stop women slobbering all over you.'

'Do you want to test it?' His tone was cool. 'Because I suggest you wait until the end of the meal. The lamb *kleftiko* is the best anywhere in Greece and they make a house special with honey and pistachio nuts that you wouldn't want to miss.'

'But if you're the one walking out, then I can stay here and eat your portion.' She helped herself to another spoonful of food from the dish closest to her. 'I don't know why you're so freaked out by tears. It's not as if I was expecting you to hug me. I've taught myself to self-soothe.'

'Self-soothe?' Some of the tension left him. 'You hug yourself?'

'It's important to be independent.' She'd been self-sufficient from an early age, but the ability to do everything for herself hadn't removed the deep longing to share her life with someone. 'Why did your dad and his last wife divorce?'

'Because they married,' he said smoothly, 'and divorce is an inevitable consequence of marriage.'

She wondered why he had such a grim view of marriage. 'Not all marriages.'

'All but those infected with extreme inertia.'

'So you're saying that even people who stay married would divorce if they could be bothered to make the effort.'

'I think there are any number of reasons for a couple to stay together, but love isn't one of them. In my father's case, wife number three married him for his money and the novelty wore off.'

'Does "wife number three" have a name?'

'Callie.' His hard tone told her everything she needed to know about his relationship with his last stepmother.

'You don't like her?'

'Are you enjoying your meal?'

She blinked, thrown by the change of subject. 'It's delicious, but—'

'Good. If you're hoping to sample dessert, you need to talk about something other than my family.'

'You control everything, even the conversation.' She wondered why he didn't want to talk about his family. 'Is this where you bring all the women you date?'

'It depends on the woman.'

'How about that woman you were with earlier—Christina? She definitely wouldn't have eaten any of this. She had carb-phobia written all over her.'

Those powerful shoulders relaxed slightly. 'She would have ordered green salad, grilled fish and eaten half of it.'

'So why didn't you order green salad and grilled fish for me?'

'Because you look like someone who enjoys food.'

Lily gave him a look. 'I'm starting to understand why women cry around you. You basically called me fat. For your information, most women would storm out if you said that to them.'

'So why didn't you storm out?'

'Because eating here is a once-in-a-lifetime experience and I don't want to miss it. And I don't think you meant it that way and I like to give people the benefit of the doubt. Tell me what happens next on a date. You bring a woman to a place like this and then you take her back to your villa for sex in that massive bed?'

'I never talk about my relationships.'

'You don't talk about your family and you don't talk about your relationships.' Lily helped herself to rich, plump slices of tomato salad. 'What do you want to talk about?'

'You. Tell me about your work.'

'I work in your company. You know more about what goes on than I do, but one thing I will say is that with all these technology skills at your disposal you need to invent an app that syncs all the details of the women who call you. You have a busy sex life and it's easy to get it mixed up, especially as they're all pretty much the same type.' She put her fork down. 'Is that the secret to staying emotionally detached? You date women who are clones, no individual characteristics to tell them apart.'

'I do not date clones, and I don't want to talk about my work, I want to talk about your work. Your archaeological work.' His eyes gleamed. 'And try to include the word "Minoan" at least eight times in each sentence.'

She ignored that. 'I'm a ceramics expert. I did a masters in archaeology and since then I've been working on an internationally funded project replicating Minoan cooking fabrics. Among other things we've been looking at the technological shift Minoan potters made when they replaced hand-building methods with the wheel. We can trace patterns of production, but also the context of ceramic consumption. The word ceramic comes from the Greek, *keramikos,* but you probably already know that.'

He reached for his wine glass. 'I can't believe you were cleaning my shower.'

'Cleaning your shower pays well and I have college debts.'

'If you didn't have college debts, what would you be doing?'

She hesitated, unwilling to share her dream with a stranger, especially one who couldn't possibly understand having to make choices driven by debt. 'I have no idea. I can't afford to think like that. I have to be practical.'

'Why Crete?'

'Crete had all the resources necessary to produce pottery. Clay, temper, water and fuel. Microscopic ceramic fabric analysis indicate those resources have been used for at least eight thousand years. The most practical way of understanding ancient technology is to replicate it and use it and that's what we've been doing.'

'So you've been trying to cook like a Minoan?'

'Yes. We're using tools and materials that would have been available during the Cretan Bronze Age.'

'That's what you're digging for?'

'Brittany and the team have different objectives, but while they're digging I'm able to access clay. I spend some of my time on site and some of my time at the museum with a small team, but that's all coming to an end now. Tell me what you do.'

'You work in my company. You should know what I do.'

'I don't know *specifically* what you do. I know you're a technology wizard. I guess that's why you have a shower that looks like something from NASA. I bet you're good with computers. Technology isn't really my thing, but you probably already know that.'

'If technology isn't your thing, why are you working in my company?'

'I'm not dealing with the technology side. I'm dealing with people. I did a short spell in Human Resources—you keep them busy by the way—and now I'm working with your personal assistants. I still haven't decided what I want to do with my life so I'm trying different things. It's only two days a week and I wanted to see how I enjoyed corporate life.'

'And how are you enjoying "corporate life"?'

'It's different.' She dodged the question and he gave her a long, speculative look.

'Tell me why you became involved with that guy who looked old enough to be your father.'

Her stomach lurched. *Because she was an idiot.* 'I never talk about my relationships.'

'On short acquaintance I'd say the problem is stopping you talking, not getting you talking. Tell me.' Something about that compelling dark gaze made it impossible not to confide.

'I think I was attracted to his status and gravitas. I was flattered when he paid me attention. A psychologist would probably say it has something to do with not having a father around when I was growing up. Anyway, he pursued me pretty heavily and it got serious fast. And then I found out he was married.' She lowered her voice and pulled a face. 'I hate myself for that, but most of all I hate him for lying to me.' Knowing his views on marriage, she wondered if he'd think she was ridiculously principled but his eyes were hard.

'You cried over this guy?'

'I think perhaps I was crying because history repeated

itself. My relationships always follow the same pattern. I meet someone I'm attracted to, he's caring, attentive and a really good listener—I fall in love, have sex with him, start planning a future and then suddenly that's it. We break up.'

'And this experience hasn't put you off love?'

Perhaps it should have done.

No one had ever stayed in her life.

From an early age she'd wondered what it was about her that made it so easy for people to walk away.

The dishes were cleared away and a sticky, indulgent dessert placed in the centre of the table.

She tried to pull herself together. 'If you have one bad meal you don't stop eating, do you? And by the way this is the best meal I've ever had in my whole life.' She stuck her spoon in the pastry and honey oozed over the plate. She decided this was the perfect time to check a few facts before finally committing herself. 'Tell me what happens in your relationships. We'll talk hypothetically as you don't like revealing specifics. Let's say you meet a woman and you find her attractive. What happens next?'

'I take her on a date.'

'What sort of date?' Lily licked the spoon. 'Dinner? Theatre? Movie? Walk on the beach?'

'Any of those.'

'Let's say it's dinner. What would you talk about?'

'Anything.'

'Anything as long as it isn't to do with your family or relationships.'

He smiled. 'Exactly.'

'So you talk, you drink expensive wine, you admire the romantic view—then what? You take her home or you take her to bed?'

'Yes.' He paused as their waiter delivered a bottle of clear liquid and two glasses and Lily shook her head.

'Is that raki? Brittany loves it, but it gives me a headache.'

'We call it *tsikoudia*. It is a grape liqueur—an important part of Cretan hospitality.'

'I know. It's been around since Minoan times. Archaeologists have found the petrified remains of grapes and grape pips inside *pithoi*, the old clay storage jars, so it's assumed they knew plenty about distillation. Doesn't change the fact it gives me a headache.'

'Then you didn't drink it with enough water.' He handed her a small glass. 'The locals think it promotes a long and healthy life.'

Lily took a sip and felt her throat catch fire as she swallowed. 'So now finish telling me about your typical date. You don't fall in love, because you don't believe in love. So when you take a woman to bed, there are no feelings involved at all?'

'There are plenty of feelings involved.' The look he gave her made her heart pump faster.

'I mean emotions. You have emotionless sex. You don't say *I love you*. You don't feel anything here—' Lily put her hand on her heart. 'No feelings. So it's all about physical satisfaction. This is basically a naked workout, yes? It's like a bench press for two.'

'Sex may not be emotional, but it's intimate,' he said softly. 'It requires the ultimate degree of trust.'

'You can do that and still not be emotionally involved?'

'When I'm with a woman I care about her enjoyment, her pleasure, her happiness and her comfort. I don't love her.'

'You don't love women?'

'I do love women.' The corners of his mouth flickered. 'I just don't want to love one specific woman.'

Lily stared at him in fascination.

There was no way, *no way*, she would ever fall in love with a man like Nik. She didn't even need to check her list to know he didn't tick a single one of the boxes.

He was perfect.

'There's something I want to say to you and I hope you're

not going to be shocked.' She put her glass down and took a deep breath. 'I want to have rebound sex. No emotions involved. Sex without falling in love. Not something I've ever done before, so this is all new to me.'

He watched her from under lowered lids, his expression unreadable. There was a dangerous stillness about him. 'And you're telling me this because—?'

'Because you seem to be the expert.' Her heart started to pound. 'I want you to take me to bed.'

CHAPTER FOUR

NIK SCANNED HER in silence. The irony was that his original plan had been to do exactly that. Take her to bed. She was fun, sexy and original but the longer he spent in her company the more he realised how different her life goals were from his own. By her own admittance, Lily wasn't the sort to emotionally disengage in a relationship. In the interests of self-protection, logic took precedence over his libido.

'It's time I took you home.'

Far from squashing her, the news appeared to cheer her. 'That's what I was hoping you'd say. I promise you won't regret it. What I lack in experience I make up for in enthusiasm.'

She was as bright as she was pretty and he knew her 'misunderstanding' was deliberate.

'*Theé mou*, you should *not* be saying things like that to a man. It could be taken the wrong way.'

She sliced into a tomato. 'You're taking it the way I intended you to take it.'

Nik glanced at the bottle of champagne and tried to work out how much she'd had. 'I'm not taking you to my home, I'm taking you to *your* home.'

'You don't want to do that. My bed is smaller than a cat basket and you're big. I have a feeling we're going to get very hot and sweaty, and I don't have air conditioning.'

Nik's libido was fighting against the restraining bonds of logic. 'I will give you a lift home and then I'm leaving.'

'Leaving?' Disappointment mingled with uncertainty. 'You don't find me attractive?'

'You're sexy as hell,' he drawled, 'but you're not my type.'

'That doesn't make any sense. You don't like sexy?'

'I like sexy. I don't like women who want to fall in love, settle down and have lots of babies.'

'I thought we'd already established I didn't want to do any of that with you. You don't score a single point on my checklist, which is *exactly* why I want to do this. I know I'd be safe. And so would you!'

He decided he didn't even want to know about her checklist. 'How much champagne have you had?'

'I'm not drunk, if that's what you're suggesting. Ask me anything. Make me walk in a straight line. I'll touch my nose with my eyes closed, or I'll touch *your* nose with my eyes closed if you prefer. Or other parts of you—' She gave a wicked grin and leaned forward. 'One night. That's all it would be. You will not regret it.'

Nik deployed the full force of his will power and kept his eyes away from the softness of her breasts. 'You're right. I won't, because it's not going to happen.'

'I do yoga. I'm very bendy.'

Nik gave a soft curse. 'Stop talking.'

'I can put my legs behind my head.'

'*Cristo*, you should *definitely* stop talking.' His libido was urging logic to surrender.

'What's the problem? One night of fun. Tomorrow we both go our own ways and if I see you in the office I'll pretend I don't know you. Call your lawyer. I'll sign a contract promising not to fall in love with you. A pre-non-nuptial agreement. All I want is for you to take me home, strip me naked, throw me onto that enormous bed of yours and have sex with me in every conceivable position. After that I will walk out of your door and you'll never see me again. Deal?'

He tried to respond but it seemed her confusing mix of innocence and sexuality had short-circuited his brain. 'Lily—' he spoke through his teeth '—trust me, you do *not* want me to take you home, strip you naked and throw you onto my bed.'

'Why not? It's just sex.'

'You've spent several hours telling me you don't do "just sex".'

'But I'm going to this time. I want to be able to separate sex from love. The next time a man comes my way who might be the one, I won't let sex confuse things. I'll be like Kevlar. Nothing is getting through me. Nothing.'

'You are marshmallow, not Kevlar.'

'That was the old me. The new me is Kevlar. I don't understand why you won't do this, unless—' She studied him for a long moment and then leaned forward, a curious look in her eyes. 'Are you *scared*?'

'I'm sober,' he said softly, 'and when I play, I like it to be with an opponent who is similarly matched.'

'I'm tougher than I look.' A dimple appeared in the corner of her mouth. 'Drink another glass of champagne and then call Vassilis.'

'How do you know my driver's name?'

'I listen. And he has a kind face. There really is no need to be nervous. If rumour is correct, you're a cold, emotionless vacuum and that means you're in no danger from someone like little me.'

He had a feeling 'little me' was the most dangerous thing he'd encountered in a long while. 'If I'm a "cold, emotionless vacuum", why would you want to climb into my bed?'

'Because you are *insanely* sexy and all the things that make you so wrong for me would make you perfect for rebound sex.'

He looked into those blue eyes and tried to ignore the surge of sexual hunger that had gripped him from the moment he'd laid eyes on that pale silky hair tumbling damp round her gleaming wet body.

Never before had doing the right thing felt so wrong.

Nik cursed under his breath and rose to his feet. 'We're leaving.'

'Good decision.' She slid her hand into his, rose on tiptoe and whispered in his ear. 'I'll be gentle with you.'

With her wide smile and laughing eyes, it was like being on a date with a beam of sunshine. He felt heat spread through his body, his arousal so brutal he was tempted to haul her behind the nearest lockable door, rip off that dress and acquaint himself with every part of her luscious, naked body.

Vassilis was waiting outside with the car and Nik bundled her inside and sat as far from her as possible.

All his life, he'd avoided women like her. Women who believed in romance and 'the one'. For him, the myth of love had been smashed in childhood along with Santa and the Tooth Fairy. He had no use for it in his life.

'Where do you live?' He growled the words but she simply smiled.

'You don't need to know, because we're going back to your place. Your bed is almost big enough to be seen from outer space.'

Nik ran his hand over his jaw. 'Lily—'

Her phone signalled a text and she dug around in her bag. 'I need to answer this. It will be Brittany, checking I'm all right. She and Spy are probably worried because they saw me go off with you.'

'Maybe you should pay attention to your friends.'

'Hold that thought—'

Having rebound sex. She mouthed the words as she typed. Speak to you tomorrow.

Nik was tempted to seize the phone and text her friends to come and pick her up. 'Brittany was the girl in the blue dress?'

'She's the female version of you, but without the money.

She doesn't engage emotionally. I found out today that she was married for ten days when she was eighteen. Can you believe that? Ten days. I don't know the details, but apparently it cured her of ever wanting a repeat performance.' She pressed send and slid the phone back into her bag. 'I grew up in foster homes so I don't have any family. I think that's probably why my friends are so important to me. I never really had a sense of belonging anywhere. That's a very lonely feeling as a child.'

He felt something stir inside him, as if she'd poked a stick into a muddy, stagnant pool that had lain dormant and undiscovered for decades. Deeply uncomfortable, he shifted in his seat. 'Why are you telling me this?'

'I thought as we're going to have sex, you might want to know something about me.'

'I don't.'

'That's not very polite.'

'I'm not striving for "polite". This is who I am. It's not too late for my driver to drop you home. Give him the address.'

She leaned forward and pressed the button so that the screen closed between him and the driver. 'Sorry, Vassilis, but I don't want to corrupt you.' She slid across the seat, closed her eyes and lifted her face to his. 'Kiss me. Whatever it is you do, do it now.'

Nik had always considered himself to be a disciplined man but he was rapidly rethinking that assessment. With her, there was no discipline. He looked down at those long, thick eyelashes and the pink curve of her mouth and tried to remember when he'd last been tempted to have sex in the back of his car.

'No.' He managed to inject the word with forceful conviction but instead of retreating, she advanced.

'In that case I'll kiss you. I don't mind taking the initiative.' Her slim fingers slid to the inside of his thigh. He was so aroused he couldn't even remember why he was fighting this, and instead of pushing her away he gripped her hand hard and turned his head towards her.

His gaze swept her flushed cheeks and the lush curve of her mouth. With a rough curse he lowered his head, driving her lips apart with his tongue and taking that mouth in a kiss that was as rough as it was sexually explicit. His intention was to scare her off, so there was no holding back, no diluting of his passion. He kissed her hard, expecting to feel her pull back but instead she pressed closer. She tasted of sugar and sweet temptation, her mouth soft and eager against his as she all but wriggled onto his lap.

The heavy weight of her breasts brushed against his arm and he gave a groan and slid his hand into her hair, anchoring her head for the hard demands of his kiss. She licked into his mouth, snuggling closer like a kitten, those full soft curves pressing against him. It was a kiss without boundaries, an explosion of raw desire that built until the rear of the car shimmered with stifling heat and sexual awareness.

He slid his hand under her dress, over the smooth skin of her thigh to the soft shadows between her legs. It was her thickened moan of pleasure that woke him up.

Cristo, they were in the car, in moving traffic.

Releasing her as if she were a hot coal, he pushed her away. 'I thought you were supposed to be smart.'

Her breathing was shallow and rapid. 'I'm very, very smart. And you're an amazing kisser. Are you as good at everything else?'

His pulse was throbbing and he was so painfully aroused he didn't dare move. 'If you really want to come home with me then you're not as smart as you look.'

'What makes you think that?'

'Because a woman like you should steer clear of men like me. I don't have a love life, I have a sex life. I'll use you. If you're in my bed it will be all about pleasure and nothing else. I don't care about your feelings. I'm not kind. I'm not gentle. I need you to know that.'

There was a long, loaded silence and then her gaze slid to his mouth. 'Okay, I get it. No fluffy kittens in this relationship. Message received and understood. Can this car go any faster because I don't think I've ever been this turned on in my life before.'

She wasn't the only one. His self-control was stretched to breaking point. Why was he fighting it? She was an adult. She wasn't drunk and she knew what she was doing. Logic didn't just surrender to libido, it was obliterated. All the same, something made him open one more exit door. 'Be very sure, Lily.'

'I'm sure. I've never been so sure of anything in my life. Unless you want to be arrested for performing an indecent act in a public place you'd better tell Vassilis to break a few speed limits.'

Lily walked into the villa she'd cleaned earlier, feeling ridiculously nervous. In the romantic setting of the restaurant this had seemed like a good idea. Now she wasn't quite so sure. 'So why did you hire a contract cleaning company?'

'I didn't.' He threw his jacket over the back of a chair with careless disregard for its future appearance. 'I have staff who look after this place. Presumably they arranged it. I didn't give them much notice of my return. I don't care how they do their job as long as it gets done.'

She paced across the living room and stared across the floodlit shimmer of the infinity pool. 'It's pretty at night.' It was romantic, but she knew this had nothing to do with romance. Her other relationships had been with men she knew and cared about. This scenario was new to her. 'Do you have something to drink?'

'You're thirsty?'

Nervous. 'A little.'

He gave her a long look, strolled out of the room and returned moments later carrying a glass of water.

'I want you sober,' he said softly. 'In fact I insist on it.'

Realising they were actually going to do this, she suddenly found she was shaking so much the water sloshed out of the glass and onto the floor. 'Oops. I'm messing up the floor I cleaned earlier.'

He was standing close to her and her gaze drifted to the bronzed skin at the base of his throat and the blue-shadowed jaw. Everything about him was unapologetically masculine. He wasn't just dangerously attractive, he was lethal and suddenly she wondered what on earth she was doing. Maybe she should have taken up Spy's offer of rebound sex, except that Spy didn't induce one tenth of this crazy response in her. A thrilling sense of anticipation mingled with wicked excitement and she knew she'd regret it for ever if she walked away. She knew she took relationships too seriously. If she was going to try a different approach then there was surely no better man to do it with than Nik.

'Scared?' His voice was deep, dark velvet and she gave a smile.

'A little. But only because I don't normally do this and you're not my usual type. It's like passing your driving test and then getting behind the wheel of a Ferrari. I'm worried I'll crash you into a lamppost.' She put the glass down carefully on the glass table and ran her damp hands over her thighs. 'Okay, let's do this. Ignore the fact I'm shaking, go right ahead and do your bad, bad thing, whatever that is.'

He said nothing. Just looked at her, that dark gaze uncomfortably penetrating.

She waited, heart pounding, virtually squirming on the spot. 'I'm not good with delayed gratification. I'm more of an instant person. I like to—'

'Hush.' Finally he spoke and then he reached out and drew her against him, the look in his eyes driving words and thoughts from her head. She felt the warmth of his hand against the base of her spine, the slow, sensitive stroke of his fingers low on her back and then he lifted his hands and cupped her face, forcing her to look at him. 'Lily Rose—'

She swallowed. 'Nik—'

'Don't be nervous.' He murmured the words against her lips. 'There's no reason to be nervous.'

'I'm not nervous,' she lied. 'But I'm not really sure what happens next.'

'I'll decide what happens next.'

Her heart bumped uncomfortably against her ribs. 'So—what do you want me to do?'

His mouth hovered close to hers and his fingers grazed her jaw. 'I want you to stop talking.'

'I'm going to stop talking right now this second.' Her stomach felt as if a thousand butterflies were trying to escape. She hadn't expected him to be so gentle, but those exploring fingers were slow, almost languorous as they stroked her face and slid over her neck and into her hair.

She stood, disorientated by intoxicating pleasure as he trailed his mouth along her jaw, tormenting her with dark, dangerous kisses. Heat uncurled low in her pelvis and spread through her body, sapping the strength from her knees, and she slid her hands over those sleek, powerful shoulders, feeling the hard swell of muscle beneath her palms. His mouth moved lower and she tilted her head back as he kissed her neck and then the base of her throat. She felt the slow slide of his tongue against supersensitive skin, the warmth of his breath and then his hand slid back into her hair and he brought his mouth back to hers. He kissed her with an erotic expertise that made her head spin and her legs grow heavy. With each slow stroke of his tongue, he sent her senses spinning out of control. It was like being drugged. She tried to find her balance, her centre, but just when she felt close to grasping a few threads of control, he used his mouth to drive every coherent thought from her head. Shaky, she lifted her hand to his face, felt the roughness of his jaw against her palm and the lean, spare perfection of his bone structure.

She slid her fingers into his hair and felt his hand slide down her spine and draw her firmly against him.

She felt him, brutally hard through the silky fabric of her dress, and she gave a moan, low in her throat as he trapped her there with the strength of his arms, the power in those muscles reminding her that this wasn't a safe flirtation, or a game.

His kisses grew rougher, more intimate, more demanding and she tugged at his shirt, her fingers swift and sure on the buttons, her movements more frantic with each bit of male muscle she exposed.

His chest was powerful, his abs lean and hard and she felt a moment of breathless unease because she'd never had sex with a man built like him.

He was self-assured and experienced and as she pushed the shirt from his shoulders she tried to take a step backwards.

'I'd like to keep my clothes on, if that's all right with you.'

'It's not all right.' But there was a smile in his voice as he slid his hand from her hips to her waist, pulling her back against him. His fingers brushed against the underside of her breast and she moaned.

'You look as if you spend every spare second of your life working out.'

'I don't.'

'You get this way through lots of athletic sex?'

His mouth hovered close to hers. 'You promised to stop talking.'

'That was before I saw you half naked. I'm intimidated. That photo didn't lie. Now I know what you look like under your clothes I think I might be having body-image problems.'

He smiled, and she felt his hands at the back of her dress and the slow slither of silk as her dress slid to the floor.

Standing in front of him in nothing but her underwear and high heels, she felt ridiculously exposed. It didn't matter that he'd already seen her that way. This was different.

He eased back from her, his eyes slumberous and dangerously dark. 'Let's go upstairs.'

Her knees were shaking so much she wasn't sure she could walk but the next moment he scooped her into his arms and she gave a gasp of shock and dug her hands in his shoulder.

'Don't you dare drop me. I bruise easily.' She had a close-up view of his face and stared hungrily at the hard masculine lines, the blue-black shadow of his jaw and the slim, sensual line of his mouth. 'If I'd known you were planning on carrying me I would have said no to dessert.'

'Dessert was the best part.' They reached the top of the stairs and he carried her into his bedroom and lowered her to the floor next to the bed.

She didn't see him move, and yet a light came on next to the bed sending a soft beam over the silk covers. Glancing around her, Lily realised that if she lay on that bed her body would be illuminated by the wash of light.

'Can we switch the lights off?'

His eyes hooded, he lowered his hands to his belt. 'No.' As he removed the last of his clothes she let her eyes skid downwards and felt heat pour into her cheeks.

It was only a brief glance, but it was enough to imprint the image of his body in her brain.

'Do you model underwear in your spare time? Because seriously—' Her cheeks flooded with colour. 'Okay so I think this whole thing would be easier in the dark—then I won't be so intimidated by your supersonic abs.'

'Hush.' He smoothed her hair back from her face. 'Do you trust me?' His voice was rough and she felt a flutter of nerves low in her belly.

'I—yes. I think so. Why? Am I being stupid?'

'No. Close your eyes.'

She hesitated and then closed them. She heard the sound of a drawer opening and then felt something soft and silky being tied round her eyes.

'What are you doing?' She lifted her hand but he closed

his fingers round her wrist and drew her hands back to her sides.

'Relax.' His voice was a soft purr. 'I'm taking away one of your senses. The one that's making you nervous. There's no need to panic. You still have four remaining. I want you to use those.'

'I can't see.'

'Exactly. You wanted to do this in the dark. Now you're in the dark.'

'I meant that you should put the lights out! It was so you couldn't see me, not so that I couldn't see you.'

'Shh.' His lips nibbled at hers, his tongue stroking over her mouth in a slow, sensual seduction.

She was quivering, her senses straining with delicious anticipation as she tried to work out where he was and where he'd touch her next.

She felt his lips on her shoulder and felt his fingers slide the thin straps of her bra over her arms. Wetness pooled between her thighs and she pressed them together, so aroused she could hardly breathe.

He took his time, explored her neck, her shoulder, the underside of her breast until she wasn't sure her legs would hold her and he must have known that because he tipped her back onto the bed, supporting her as she lost her balance.

She could see nothing through the silk mask but she felt the weight of him on top of her, the roughness of his thigh against hers and the slide of silk against her heated flesh as he stripped her naked.

She was quivering, her senses sharpened by her lack of vision. She felt the warmth of his mouth close over the tip of her breast, the skilled flick of his tongue sending arrows of pleasure shooting through her over-sensitised body.

She gave a moan and clutched at his shoulders. 'Do we need a safe word or something?' She felt him pause.

'Why would you need a safe word?'

'I thought—'

'I'm not going to do anything that makes you uncomfortable.'

'What do I say if I want you to stop?'

His mouth brushed lightly across her jaw. 'You say "stop".'

'That's it?'

'That's it.' There was a smile in his voice. 'If I do one single thing that makes you uncomfortable, tell me.'

'Is embarrassed the same as uncomfortable?'

He gave a soft laugh and she felt the stroke of his palm on her thigh and then he parted her legs and his mouth drifted from her belly to her inner thigh.

He paused, his breath warm against that secret place. 'Relax, *erota mou*.'

She lifted her hands to remove the blindfold but he caught her wrists in one hand and held them pinned, while he used the other to part her and expose her secrets.

Unbearably aroused, melting with a confusing mix of desire and mortification, she tried to close her legs but he licked at her intimately, opening her with his tongue, exploring her vulnerable flesh with erotic skill and purpose until all she wanted was for him to finish what he'd started.

'Nik—' She writhed, sobbed, struggled against him and he released her hands and anchored her hips, holding her trapped as he explored her with his tongue.

She'd forgotten all about removing the blindfold.

The only thing in her head was easing the maddening ache that was fast becoming unbearable.

She dug her fingers in the sheets, moaning as he slid his fingers deep inside her, manipulating her body and her senses until she tipped into excitement overload. She felt herself start to throb round those seeking fingers, but instead of giving her what she wanted he gently withdrew his hand and eased away from her.

'Please! Oh, please—' she sobbed in protest, wondering what he was doing.

Was he leaving her?

Was he stopping?

With a whimper of protest, she writhed and reached for him and then she heard a faint sound and understood the reason for the brief interlude.

Condom, she thought, and then the ability to think coherently vanished because he covered her with the hard heat of his body. She felt the blunt thrust of his erection at her moist entrance and tensed in anticipation, but instead of entering her he cupped her face in his hand and gently slid off the blindfold.

'Look at me.' His soft command penetrated her brain and she opened her eyes and stared at him dizzily just as he slid his hand under her bottom and entered her in a series of slow, deliciously skilful thrusts. He was incredibly gentle, taking his time, murmuring soft words in Greek and then English as he moved deep into the heart of her. Then he paused, kissed her mouth gently, holding her gaze with his.

'Are you all right? Do you want to use the safe word?' His voice was gently teasing but the glitter in his eyes and the tension in his jaw told her he was nowhere near as relaxed as he pretended to be.

In the grip of such intolerable excitement she was incapable of responding, Lily simply shook her head and then moaned as he withdrew slightly and surged into her again, every movement of his body escalating the wickedly agonising pleasure.

She slid her hands over the silken width of his shoulders, down his back, her fingers clamping over the thrusting power of his body as he rocked against her. His hand was splayed on her bottom, his gaze locked on hers as he drove into her with ruthlessly controlled strength and a raw, primitive rhythm. She wrapped her legs around him as he brought pleasure raining down on both of them. She cried out his name and he took her mouth, kissing her deeply, intimately, as the first ripple of orgasm took hold of her body. They didn't stop kissing, mouths locked, eyes locked as her body contracted around his and dragged him over the edge of control. She'd never experienced anything like it, the whole experience a shattering revelation about her capacity for sensuality.

It was several minutes before she was capable of speaking and longer than that before she could persuade her body to move.

As she tried to roll away from him, his arms locked around her. 'Where do you think you're going?'

'I'm sticking to the rules. I thought this was a one-night thing.'

'It is.' He hauled her back against him. 'And the night isn't over yet.'

CHAPTER FIVE

NIK SPENT TEN minutes under a cold shower, trying to wake himself up after a night that had consisted of the worst sleep of his life and the best sex. He couldn't remember the last time he hadn't wanted to leave the bed in the morning.

A ton of work waited for him in the office, but for the first time ever he was contemplating working from home so that he could spend a few more hours with Lily. After her initial shyness she'd proved to be adventurous and insatiable, qualities that had kept both of them awake until the rising sun had sent the first flickers of light across the darkened bedroom.

Eventually she'd fallen into an exhausted sleep, her body tangled around his as dawn had bathed the bedroom in a golden glow.

It had proved impossible to extract himself without waking her so Nik, whose least favourite bedroom activity was hugging, had remained there, his senses bathed in the soft floral scent of her skin and hair, trapped by those long limbs wrapped trustingly around him.

And he had no one to blame but himself.

She'd offered to leave and he'd stopped her.

He frowned, surprised by his own actions. He had no need for displays of affection or any of the other meaningless rituals that seemed to inhabit other people's relationships. To him, sex was a physical need, no different from hunger and thirst. Once satisfied he moved on. He had no desire for anything deeper. He didn't believe anything deeper existed.

When he was younger, women had tried to persuade him differently. There had been a substantial number who had believed they had what it took to penetrate whatever steely coating made his heart so inaccessible. When they'd had no more success than their predecessors they'd withdrawn, bruised and broken, but not before they'd delivered their own personal diagnosis on his sorry condition.

He'd heard it all. That he didn't have a heart, that he was selfish, single minded, driven, too focused on his work. He accepted those accusations without argument, but knew that none explained his perpetually single status. Quite simply, he didn't believe in love. He'd learned at an early age that love could be withdrawn as easily as it was given, that promises could be made and broken in the same breath, that a wedding ring was no more than a piece of jewellery, and wedding vows no more binding than one plant twisted loosely around another.

He had no need for the friendship and affection that punctuated other people's lives.

He'd taught himself to live without it, so to find himself wrapped in the tight embrace of a woman who smiled even when she was asleep was as alien to him as it was unsettling.

For a while, he'd slept, too, and then woken to find her locked against him. Telling himself that she was the one holding him and not the other way round, he'd managed to extract himself without waking her and escaped to the bathroom where he contemplated his options.

He needed to find a tactful way of ejecting her.

He showered, shaved and returned to the bedroom. Expecting to find her still asleep, he was thrown to find her dressed. She'd stolen one of his white shirts and it fell to mid-thigh, the sleeves flapping over her small hands as she talked on the phone.

'Of course he'll be there.' Her voice was as soothing as

warm honey. 'I'm sure it's a simple misunderstanding…well, no I agree with you, but he's very busy…'

She lay on her stomach on the bed, her hair hanging in a blonde curtain over one shoulder, the sheets tangled around her bare thighs.

Nik took one look at her and decided that there was no reason to rush her out of the villa.

They'd have breakfast on the terrace. Maybe enjoy a swim.

Then he'd find a position they hadn't yet tried before sending her home in his car.

Absorbed in her conversation, she hadn't noticed him and he strolled round in front of her and slowly released the towel from his waist.

He saw her eyes go wide. Then she gave him a smile that hovered somewhere between cheeky and innocent and he found himself resenting the person on the end of the phone who was taking up so much of her time.

He dressed, aware that she was watching him the whole time, her conversation reduced to soothing, sympathetic noises.

It was the sort of exchange he'd never had in his life. The sort that involved listening while someone poured out their woes. When Nik had a problem he solved it or accepted it and moved on. He'd never understood the female urge to dissect and confide.

'I know,' she murmured. 'There's nothing more upsetting than a rift in the family, but you need to talk. Clear the air. Be open about your feelings.'

She was so warm and sympathetic it was obvious to Nik that the conversation was going to be a long one. Someone had rung in the belief that talking to Lily would make them feel better and he couldn't see a way that this exchange would ever end as she poured a verbal Band-Aid over whatever wound she was being asked to heal. Who would want to hang up when they were getting the phone equivalent of a massive hug?

Outraged on her behalf, Nik sliced his finger across his throat to indicate that she should cut the connection.

When she didn't, he was contemplating snatching the phone and telling whoever it was to get a grip, sort out their own problems and stop encroaching on Lily's good nature when she gestured to the phone with her free hand.

'It's for you,' she mouthed. 'Your father.'

His *father*?

The person she'd been soothing and placating for the past twenty minutes was his *father*?

Nik froze. Only now did he notice that the phone in her hand was his. 'You answered my phone?'

'I wouldn't have done normally, but I saw it was your dad and I knew you'd want to talk to him. I didn't want you to miss his call because you were in the shower.' Clearly believing she'd done him an enormous favour, she wished his father a cheery, caring goodbye and held out the phone to him. The front of his shirt gapped, revealing those tempting dips and curves he'd explored in minute detail the night before. The scrape of his jaw had left faint red marks over her creamy skin and the fact that he instantly wanted to drop the phone in the nearest body of water and take her straight back to bed simply added to his irritation.

'That's my shirt.'

'You have so many, I didn't think you'd miss one.'

Reflecting on the fact she was as chirpy in the morning as she was the rest of the day, Nik dragged his gaze from her smiling mouth, took the phone from her and switched to Greek. 'You didn't need to call again. I got your last four messages.'

'Then why didn't you call me back?'

'I've been busy.'

'Too busy to talk to your own father? I have rung you every day this week, Niklaus. Every single day.'

Aware that Lily was listening Nik paced to the window, turned his back on her and stared out over the sea. 'Is the wedding still on?'

'Of course it is on! Why wouldn't it be? I love Diandra and she loves me. You would love her, too, if you took the time to meet her and what better time than the day in which we exchange our vows?' There was a silence. 'Nik, come home. It has been too long.'

Nik knew exactly how long it had been to the day.

'I've been busy.'

'Too busy to visit your own family? This is the place of your birth and you never come home. You have a villa here that you converted and you don't even visit. I know you didn't like Callie and it's true that for a long time I was very angry with you for not making more of an effort when she showed you so much love, but that is behind us now.'

Reflecting on exactly what form that 'love' had taken, Nik tightened his hand on the phone and wondered if he'd been wrong not to tell his father the unpalatable truth about his third wife. He'd made the decision that since she'd ended the relationship anyway there was nothing to be gained from revealing the truth, but now he found himself in the rare position of questioning his own judgement.

'Will Callie be at the wedding?'

'No.' His father was quiet. 'I wanted her to bring little Chloe, but she hasn't responded to my calls. I don't mind admitting it's a very upsetting situation all round for everyone.'

Not everyone, Nik thought. He was sure Callie wasn't remotely upset. Why would she be? She'd extracted enough money from his father to ensure she could live comfortably without ever lifting a finger again. 'You would really want her at your wedding?'

'Callie, no. But Chloe? Yes, of course. If I had my way she would be living here with me. I still haven't given up hope that might happen one day. Chloe is my child, Nik. My daughter. I want her to grow up knowing her father. I don't want her thinking I abandoned her or chose not to have her in my life.'

Nik kept his eyes forward and the past firmly suppressed. 'These things happen. They're part of life and relationships.'

His father sighed. 'I'm sorry you believe that. Family is the most important thing in the world. I want that for you.'

'I set my own life goals, and that isn't on the list,' Nik drawled softly. Contemplating the complexity of human relationships, he was doubly glad he'd successfully avoided them himself. Like every other area of his life, he had his feelings firmly under control. 'Would Diandra really want Chloe to be living with you?'

'Of course! She'd be delighted. She wants it as much as I do. And she'd really like to meet you, too. She's keen for us to be a proper family.'

A proper family.

A long-buried memory emerged from deep inside his brain, squeezing itself through the many layers of self-protection he'd used to suppress it.

It had been so long the images were no longer clear, a fact for which he was grimly grateful. Even now, several decades later, he could still remember how it had felt to have those images replaying in his head night after night.

A man, a woman and a young boy, living an idyllic existence under blue skies and the dazzle of the sun. Growing up, he'd learned a thousand lessons about living. How to cook with leaves from the vine, how to distil the grape skins and seeds to form the potent *tsikoudia* they drank with friends. He'd lived his cocooned existence until one day his world had crumbled and he'd learned the most important lesson of all.

That a family was the least stable structure invented by man.

It could be destroyed in a moment.

'Come home, Niklaus,' his father said quietly. 'It has been too long. I want us to put the past behind us. Callie is no longer here.'

Nik didn't tell him that the reason he avoided the island had nothing to do with Callie.

Whenever he returned there it stirred up the same memory of his mother leaving in the middle of the night while he watched in confusion from the elegant curve of the stairs.

Where are you going, Mama? Are you taking us with you? Can we come, too?

'Niklaus?' His father was still talking. 'Will you come?'

Nik dragged his hand over the back of his neck. 'Yes, if that's what you want.'

'How can you doubt it?' There was joy in his father's voice. 'The wedding is Tuesday but many of our friends are arriving at the weekend so that we can celebrate in style. Come on Saturday then you can join in the pre-wedding celebrations.'

'Saturday?' His father expected him to stay for four days? 'I'll have to see if I can clear my diary.'

'Of course you can. What's the point of being in charge of the company if you can't decide your own schedule? Now tell me about Lily. I like her very much. How long have the two of you been together?'

Ten memorable hours. 'How do you know her name?'

'We've been talking, Niklaus! Which is more than you and I ever do. She sounds nice. Why don't you bring her to the wedding?'

'We don't have that sort of relationship.' He felt a flicker of irritation. Was that why she'd spent so much time on the phone talking to his father? Had she decided that sympathy might earn her an invite to the biggest wedding of the year in Greece?

Exchanging a final few words with his father, he hung up. 'Don't ever,' he said with silky emphasis as he turned to face her, 'answer my phone again.' But he was talking to an empty room because Lily was nowhere to be seen.

Taken aback, Nik glanced towards the bathroom and then noticed the note scrawled on a piece of paper by his pillow.

Thanks for the best rebound sex ever. Lily.

The best rebound sex?

She'd left?

Nik picked up the note and scrunched it in his palm. He'd been so absorbed in the conversation with his father he hadn't heard her leaving.

The dress from the night before lay neatly folded on the chair but there was no sign of the shoes or his shirt. He had no need to formulate a plan to eject her from his life because she'd removed herself.

She'd gone.

And she hadn't even bothered saying goodbye.

'No need to ask if you had a good night, it's written all over your face.' Brittany slid her feet into her hiking boots and reached for her bag. 'Nice shirt. Is that silk?' She reached out and touched the fabric and gave a murmur of appreciation. 'The man has style, I'll give him that.'

'Thanks for your text. It was sweet of you to check on me. How was your evening?'

'Nowhere near as exciting as yours apparently. While you were playing Cinderella in the wolf's lair, I was cataloguing pottery shards and bone fragments. My life is so exciting I can hardly bear it.'

'You love it. And I think you're mixing your fairy tales.' Aware that her hair was a wild mass of curls after the relentless exploration of Nik's hands, Lily scooped it into a ponytail. She told herself that eventually she'd stop thinking about him. 'Did you find anything else after I left yesterday?'

'Fragments of plaster, conical cups—' Brittany frowned. 'We found a bronze leg that probably belongs to that figurine that was discovered last week. Are you listening to me?'

Lily was deep in an action replay of the moment Nik had removed the mask from her eyes. 'That's exciting! I'm going to join you later.'

'We're removing part of the stone mound and exploring the North Eastern wall.' Brittany eyed her. 'You might want to rethink white silk. So am I going to hear the details?'

'About what?'

'Oh, please—'

'It was fun. All right, incredible.' Lily felt her cheeks burn and Brittany gave a faint smile.

'That good? Now I'm jealous. I haven't had incredible sex since—well, let's just say it's been a while. So are you seeing him again?'

'Of course not. The definition of rebound sex is that it's just one night. No commitment.' She parroted the rules and tried not to wish it could have lasted a little more than one night. The truth was even in that one night Nik had made her feel special. 'Do we have food in our fridge? I'm starving.'

'He helped you expend all those calories and then didn't feed you before you left? That's not very gentlemanly.'

'He didn't see me leave. He had to take a call.' And judging from the reluctance he'd shown when she'd handed him the phone, if it had been left to him he wouldn't have answered it.

Why not?

Why wouldn't a man want to talk to his father?

It had been immediately obvious that whatever issues Nik might have in expressing his emotions openly weren't shared by his father, who had been almost embarrassingly eager to share his pain.

She'd squirmed with discomfort as Kostas Zervakis had told her how long it was since his son had come home. Even on such a short acquaintance she knew that family was one of the subjects Nik didn't touch. She'd felt awkward listening, as if she were eavesdropping on a private conversation, but at the same time his father had seemed so upset she hadn't had the heart to cut him off.

The conversation had left her feeling ever so slightly sick, an emotion she knew was ridiculous given that she hadn't ever met Kostas and barely knew his son. Why should it bother her that there were clearly problems in their relationship?

Her natural instinct had been to intervene but she'd recognised instantly the danger in that. Nik wasn't a man who appreciated the interference of others in anything, least of all his personal life.

The black look he'd given her had been as much responsible for her rapid exit as her own lack of familiarity with the morning-after etiquette following rebound sex.

She'd taken advantage of his temporary absorption in the phone call to make a hasty escape, but not before she'd heard enough to make her wish for a happy ending. Whatever damage lay in their past, she wanted them to fix their problems.

She always wanted people to fix their problems.

Lily blinked rapidly, realising that Brittany was talking. 'Sorry?'

'So he doesn't know you left?'

'He knows by now.'

'He won't be pleased that you didn't say goodbye.'

'He'll be delighted. He doesn't want emotional engagement. No awkward conversations. He will be relieved to be spared a potentially awkward conversation. We move in different circles so I probably won't ever see him again.' And that shouldn't bother her, should it? Although a one-night stand was new to her, she was the expert at transitory relationships. Her entire life had been a series of transitory relationships. No one had ever stuck in her life. She felt like an abandoned railway station where trains passed through but never stopped.

Brittany glanced out of the window at the street below and raised her eyebrows. 'I think you're going to see him again a whole lot sooner than you think.'

'What makes you say that?'

'Because he's just pulled up outside our apartment.'

Lily's heart felt as if it were trying to escape from her chest. 'Are you sure?'

'Well there's a Ferrari parked outside that costs more than I'm going to earn in a lifetime, so, unless there is someone else living in this building that has attracted his attention, he clearly has things he wants to say to you.'

'Oh *no*.' Lily shrank against the door of the bedroom. 'Can you see his face? Does he look angry?'

'What reason would he have to be angry?' Brittany glanced out of the window again and then back at Lily. 'Is this about the shirt? He can afford to lose one shirt, surely?'

'I don't think he's here because of the shirt,' Lily said weakly. 'I think he's here because of something I did this morning. I'm going to hide on the balcony and you're going to tell him you haven't seen me.'

Brittany looked at her curiously. 'What did you do?'

Lily flinched as she heard a loud hammering on the door. 'Remember—you haven't seen me.' She fled into the bedroom they shared and closed the door.

What was he doing here?

She'd seen the flash of anger in his eyes when he'd realised it was *his* phone she'd answered, but surely he wouldn't care enough to follow her home?

She heard his voice in the doorway and heard Brittany say, 'Sure, come right on in, Nik—is it all right if I call you Nik?—she's in the bedroom, hiding.' The door opened a moment later and Brittany stood there, arms folded, her eyes alive with laughter.

Lily impaled her with a look of helpless fury. 'You're a traitor.'

'I'm a friend and I am doing you a favour,' Brittany murmured. 'The man is seriously *hot*.' Having delivered that assessment, she stepped to one side with a bright smile. 'Go ahead. The space is a little tight, but I guess you folks don't mind that.'

'No! Brittany, don't—er—hi…' Lily gave a weak smile

as Nik strolled into the room. His powerful frame virtually filled the cramped space and she wished she'd picked a different room as a refuge. Being in a bedroom reminded her too much of the night before. 'If you're mad about the shirt, then give me two minutes to change. I shouldn't have taken it, but I didn't want to do the walk of shame through the middle of Chania wearing an evening dress that doesn't belong to me.'

'I don't care about the shirt.' His hair was glossy dark, his eyes dark in a face so handsome it would have made a Greek god weep with envy. 'Do you seriously think I'm here because of the shirt?'

'No. I assume you're mad because I answered your phone, but I saw that it was your father and thought you wouldn't want to miss his call. If I had a dad I'd be ringing him every day.'

His face revealed not a flicker of emotion. 'We don't have that sort of relationship.'

'Well I know that *now,* but I didn't know when I answered the phone and once he started talking he was so upset I didn't want to hang up. He needed to talk to someone and I was in the right place at the right time.'

'You think so?' His voice was silky soft. 'Because I would have said you were in the wrong place at the wrong time.'

'Depends how you look at it. Did you manage to clear the air?' She risked a glance at the hard lines of his face and winced. 'I'm guessing the answer to that is no. If I made it worse by handing you the phone, I'm sorry.'

He raised an eyebrow. 'Are you?'

She opened her mouth and closed it again. 'No, not really. Family is the most important thing in the world. I don't understand how anyone could not want to try and heal a rift. But I could see you were very angry that I'd answered the call and of course your relationship with your father is none of my business.' But she wanted to make it her business so badly she virtually had to sit on her hands to stop herself from interfering.

'For someone who realises it's none of her business, you seem to be showing an extraordinary depth of interest.'

'I feel strongly about protecting the family unit. It's my hot button.'

His searing glance reminded her he was intimately familiar with all her hot buttons. 'Why did you walk out this morning?'

The blatant reminder of the night before brought the colour rushing to her cheeks.

'I thought the first rule of rebound sex was that you rebound right out of the door the next morning. I have no experience of morning-after conversation and frankly the thought of facing you over breakfast after all the things we did last night didn't totally thrill me. And can you honestly tell me you weren't standing in that shower working out how you were going to eject me?' The expression on his face told her she was right and she nodded. 'Exactly. I thought I'd spare us both a major awkward moment and leave. I grabbed a shirt and was halfway out of the door when your father rang.'

'It didn't occur to you to ignore the phone?'

'I thought it might be important. And it was! He was *so* upset. He told me he'd already left a ton of messages.' Concern overwhelmed her efforts not to become involved. 'Why haven't you been home for the past few years?'

'A night in my bed doesn't qualify you to ask those questions.' The look in his eyes made her confidence falter.

'I get the message. Nothing personal. Now back off. Last night you were charming and fun and flirty. This morning you're scary and intimidating.'

He inhaled deeply. 'I apologise,' he breathed. 'It was not my intention to come across as scary or intimidating, but you should *not* have answered the phone.'

'What's done is done. And I was glad to be a listening ear for someone in pain.'

'My father is not in pain.'

'Yes, he is. He misses you. This rift between you is causing him agony. He wants you to go to his wedding. It's breaking his heart that you won't go.'

'Lily—'

'You're going to tell me it's none of my business and you're right, it isn't, but I don't have a family at all. I don't even have the broken pieces of a family, and you have no idea how much I wish I did. So you'll have to forgive me if I have a tendency to try and glue back together everyone else's chipped fragments. It's the archaeologist in me.'

'Lily—'

'Just because you don't believe in love, doesn't mean you have to inflict that view on others and judge them for their decisions. Your father is happy and you're spoiling it. He loves you and he wants you there. Whatever you are feeling, you should bury it and go and celebrate. You should raise a glass and dance at his wedding. You should show him you love him no matter what, and if this marriage goes wrong then you'll be there to support him.' She stopped, breathless, and waited to be frozen by the icy wind of his disapproval but he surprised her yet again by nodding.

'I agree.'

'You do?'

'Yes. I've been trying to tell you that but you wouldn't stop talking.' He spoke through clenched teeth. 'I am convinced that I should go to the wedding, which is why I'm here.'

'What does the wedding have to do with me?'

'I want you to come with me.'

Lily gaped at him. 'Me? Why?'

He ran his hand over the back of his neck. 'I am willing to be present if that is truly what my father wants, but I don't have enough faith in my acting skills to believe I will be able to convince anyone that I'm pleased to be there. No matter how much he tells me Diandra is "the one", I cannot see how this match will have a happy ending. You, however, seem to see happy endings where none exist. I'm hoping that by taking you, people will be blinded in the dazzling beam of your sunny optimism and won't notice the dark thundercloud hovering close by threatening to rain on the proceedings.'

The analogy made her smile. 'You're the dark thundercloud in that scenario?'

His eyes gleamed. 'You need to ask?'

'You really believe this marriage is doomed? How can you say that when you haven't even met Diandra?'

'When it comes to women, my father has poor judgement. He follows his heart and his heart has no sense of direction. Frankly I can't believe he has chosen to get married again after three failed attempts. I think it's insane.'

'I think it's lovely.'

'Which is why you're coming as my guest.' He reached out and lifted a small blue plate from her shelf, tipping off the earrings that were stored there. 'This is stylish. Where did you buy it?'

'I didn't buy it, I made it. And I haven't agreed to come with you yet.'

'You *made* this?'

'It's a hobby of mine. There is a kiln at work and sometimes I use it. The father of one of the curators at the museum is a potter and he's helped me. It's interesting comparing old and new techniques.'

He turned it in his hands, examining it closely. 'You could sell this.'

'I don't want to sell it. I use it to store my earrings.'

'Have you ever considered having an exhibition?'

'Er—no.' She gave an astonished laugh. 'I've made about eight pieces I didn't throw away. They're all exhibited around the apartment. We use one as a soap dish.'

'You've never wanted to do this for a living?'

'What I want to do and what I can afford to do aren't the same thing. It isn't financially viable.' She didn't even allow her mind to go there. 'And where would our soap live? Let's talk about the wedding. A wedding is a big deal. It's intimate and special, an occasion to be shared with friends and loved ones. You don't even know me.' The moment the words left her mouth she realised how ridiculous that statement was given the night they'd spent. 'I mean obviously there are *some* things about me you know very well, but other things like my favourite flower and my favourite colour, you don't know.'

Still holding her plate, he studied her with an unsettling intensity. 'I know all I need to know, which is that you like weddings almost as much as I hate them. Did you study art?'

'Minoan art. This is a sideline. And if I go with you, people will speculate. How would you explain our relationship to your father? Would you want us to pretend to be in a relationship? Are we supposed to have known one another for ages or something?'

'No.' His frown suggested that option hadn't occurred to him. 'There is no need to tell anything other than the truth, which is that I'm inviting you to the wedding as a friend.'

'Friend with benefits?'

He put the plate back down on the shelf and replaced the earrings carefully. 'That part is strictly between us.'

'And if your father asks how we met?'

'Tell him the truth. He'd be amused, I assure you.'

'So you don't want to pretend we're madly in love or anything? I don't have to pose as your girlfriend?'

'No. You'd be going as yourself, Lily.' A muscle flickered in his lean jaw. 'God knows, the wedding will be stressful enough without us playing roles that feel unnatural.'

It was his obvious distaste for lies and games that made up her mind. After David, a man whose instinct was to tell the truth was appealing. 'When would we leave?'

'Next Saturday. The wedding is on Tuesday but there will be four days of celebrations.' It was obvious from his expression he'd rather be dragged naked through an active volcano than join in those celebrations and a horrible thought crept into her mind.

'You're not going because you're planning to break off the wedding, are you?'

'No.' His gaze didn't shift from hers. 'But I won't tell you it didn't cross my mind.'

'I'm glad you rose above your natural impulse to wreck someone else's happiness. And if you really think it would help to have me there, then I'll come, if only to make sure you don't have second thoughts and decide to sabotage your father's big day.' Lily sank down onto the edge of her bed, thinking. 'I'll need to ask for time off.'

'Is that a problem? I could make a few calls.'

'No way!' Imagining how the curator at the museum would respond to personal intervention from Nik Zervakis, Lily recoiled in alarm. 'I'm quite capable of handling it myself. I don't need to bring in the heavy artillery, I'll simply ask the question. I'm owed holiday and my post ends in a couple of weeks anyway. Where exactly are we going? Where is "home" for you?'

'My father owns an island off the north coast of Crete. You will like it. The western part of the island has Minoan remains and there is a Venetian castle on one of the hilltops. It is separated from Crete by a lagoon and the beaches are some of the best anywhere in Greece. When you're not reminding me to smile, I'm sure you'll enjoy exploring.'

'And he *owns* this island? So tourists can't visit.'

'That's right. It belongs to my family.'

Lily looked at him doubtfully. 'How many guests will there be?'

'Does it matter?'

'I wondered, that's all.' She wanted to ask where they'd be sleeping but decided that if his father could afford a private island then presumably there wasn't a shortage of beds. 'I need to go shopping.'

'Given that you are doing me a favour, I insist you allow me to take care of that side of things.'

'No. Apart from last night, which wasn't real, I buy my own clothes. But thanks.'

'Last night didn't feel real?' He gave her a long, penetrating look and she felt heat rush into her cheeks as she remembered all the very real things he'd done to her and she'd done to him.

'I mean it wasn't really my life. More like a dreamy moment you know is never going to happen again.' Realising it was long past time she kept her mouth shut, she gave a weak smile. 'I'll buy or borrow clothes, don't worry. I'm good at putting together a wardrobe. Colours are my thing. The secret is to accessorise. I won't embarrass you even if we're surrounded by people dressed head to toe in Prada.'

'That possibility didn't enter my head. My concern was purely about the pressure on your budget.'

'I'm creative. It's not a problem.' She remembered she was wearing his shirt. 'I'll return this, obviously.'

A smile flickered at the corners of his mouth. 'It looks better on you than it does on me. Keep it.'

His gaze collided with hers and suddenly it was hard to breathe. Sexual tension simmered in the air and she was acutely aware of the oppressive heat in the small room that had no air conditioning. Blistering, blinding awareness clouded her vision until the only thing in her world was him. She wanted so badly to touch him. She wanted to lean into that muscled power, rip off those clothes and beg him to do all the things he'd done to her the night before. Shaken, she assumed she was alone in feeling that way and then saw something flare in his eyes and knew she wasn't. He was sexually aroused and thinking all the things she was thinking.

'Nik—'

'Saturday.' His tone was thickened, his eyes a dark, dangerous black. 'I will pick you up at eight a.m.'

She watched him leave, wondering what the rules of engagement were when one night wasn't enough.

CHAPTER SIX

NIK PUT HIS foot down and pushed the Ferrari to its limits on the empty road that led to the north-western tip of Crete.

He spent the majority of his time at the ZervaCo offices in San Francisco. When he returned to Crete it was to his villa on the beach near Chania, not to the island that had been his home growing up.

For reasons he tried not to think about, he'd avoided the place for the past few years and the closer he got to their destination, the blacker his mood.

Lily, by contrast, was visibly excited. She'd been waiting on the street when he'd arrived, her bag by her feet and she'd proceeded to question him non-stop. 'So will this be like *My Big Fat Greek Wedding*? I loved that movie. Will there be dancing? Brittany and I have been learning the *kalamatianós* at the *taverna* near our apartment so I should be able to join in as long as no one minds losing their toes.' She hummed a Greek tune to herself and he sent her an exasperated look.

'Are you ever *not* cheerful?'

The humming stopped and she glanced at him. 'You want me to be miserable? Did I misunderstand the brief, because I thought I was supposed to be the sunshine to your thundercloud. I didn't realise I had to be a thundercloud, too.'

Despite his mood, he found himself smiling. 'Are you capable of being a thundercloud?'

'I'm human. I have my low moments, same as anyone.'

'Tell me your last low moment.'

'No, because then I might cry and you'd dump me by the side of the road and leave me to be pecked to death by buzzards.' She gave him a cheery smile. 'This is the point where you reassure me that you wouldn't leave me by the side of the road, and that there are no buzzards in Crete.'

'There are buzzards. Crete has a varied habitat. We have vultures, Golden Eagle, kestrel—' he slowed down as he approached a narrow section of the road '—but I have no intention of leaving you by the side of the road.'

'I'd like to think that decision is driven by your inherent good nature and kindness towards your fellow man, but I'm pretty sure it's because you don't want to have to go to this wedding alone.'

'You're right. My actions are almost always driven by self-interest.'

'I don't understand you at all. I love weddings.'

'Even when you don't know the people involved?'

'I support the principle. I think it's lovely that your father is getting married again.'

Nik struggled to subdue a rush of emotion. 'It is not lovely that he is getting married again. It's ill advised.'

'That's your opinion. But it isn't what *you* think that matters, is it? It's what *he* thinks.' She spoke with gentle emphasis. 'And he thinks it's a good idea. For the record, I think it says a lot about a person that he is prepared to get married again.'

'It does.' As they hit a straight section of road, he pushed the car to its limits and the engine gave a throaty roar. 'It says he's a man with an inability to learn from his mistakes.'

'I don't see it that way.' Her hair whipped around her face and she anchored it with her hand and lifted her face to the sun. 'I think it shows optimism and I love that.'

Hearing the breathy, happy note in her voice he shook his head. 'Lily, how have you survived in this world without being eaten alive by unscrupulous people determined to take advantage of you?'

'I've been hurt on many occasions.'

'That doesn't surprise me.'

'It's part of life. I'm not going to let it shatter my belief in human nature. I'm an optimist. And what would it mean to give up? That would be like saying that love isn't out there, that it doesn't exist, and how depressing would *that* be?'

Nik, who lived his life firmly of the conviction that love didn't exist, didn't find it remotely depressing. To him, it was simply fact. 'Clearly you are the perfect wedding guest. You could set up a business, weddingguests.com. Optimists-R-us. You could be the guaranteed smile at every wedding.'

'Your cynicism is deeply depressing.'

'Your optimism is deeply concerning.'

'I prefer to think of it as inspiring. I don't want to be one of those people who think that a challenging past has to mean a challenging future.'

'You had a challenging past?' He remembered that she'd mentioned being brought up in foster care and hoped she wasn't about to give him the whole story.

She didn't. Instead she shrugged and kept her eyes straight ahead. 'It was a bit like a bad version of *Goldilocks and the Three Bears*. I was never "just right" for anyone, but that was my bad luck. I didn't meet the right family. Doesn't mean I don't believe there are loads of great families out there.'

'Doesn't what happened to you cause you to question the validity of any of these emotions you feel? The fact that the last guy lied to you *and* his wife doesn't put you off relationships?'

'It was one guy. I know enough about statistics to know you can't draw a reliable conclusion from a sample of one.' She frowned. 'If I'm honest, I'm working from a bigger sample than that because he's the third relationship I've had, but I still don't think you can make a judgement on the opposite sex based on the behaviour of a few.'

Nik, who had done exactly that, stayed silent and of course she noticed because she was nothing if not observant.

'Put it this way—if I'm bitten by a shark am I going to avoid swimming in the sea? I could, but then I'd be depriving myself of one of my favourite activities so instead I choose to carry on swimming and be a little more alert. Life isn't always about taking the safe option. Risk has to be balanced against the joy of living. I call it being receptive.'

'I call it being ridiculously naïve.'

She looked affronted. 'You're cross and irritable because you're not looking forward to this, but there is no reason to take it out on me. I'm here as a volunteer, remember?'

'You're right. I apologise.'

'Accepted. But for your father's sake you need to work on your body language. If you think you're a thundercloud you're deluding yourself because right now you're more of a tropical cyclone. You have to stop being judgemental and embrace what's happening.'

Nik took the sharp right-hand turn that led down to the beach and the private ferry. 'I am finding it hard to embrace something I know to be a mistake. It's like watching someone driving their car full speed towards a brick wall and not trying to do something to stop it.'

'You don't know it's a mistake,' she said calmly. 'And even if it is, he's an adult and should be allowed to make his own decisions. Now smile.'

He pulled in, killed the engine and turned to look at her.

Those unusual violet eyes reminded him of the spring flowers that grew high in the mountains. 'I will not be so hypocritical as to pretend I am pleased, but I promise not to spoil the moment.'

'If you don't smile then you *will* spoil the moment! Poor Diandra might take one look at your face and decide she doesn't want to marry into your family and then your father would be heartbroken. I can't believe I'm saying this, but be hypocritical if that's what it takes to make you smile.'

'Poor Diandra will not be poor for long so I think it unlikely she'll let anything stand in the way of her wedding, even my intimidating presence.'

Her eyes widened. 'Is that what this is about? You think she's after his money?'

'I have no idea but I'd be a fool not to consider it.' Nik saw no reason to be anything but honest. 'He is mega wealthy. She was his cook.'

'What does her occupation have to do with it? Love is about people, not professions. And I find it very offensive that you'd even think that. You can't judge a person based on their income. I know plenty of wealthy people who are slimeballs. In fact if we're going with stereotypes here, I'd say that generally speaking in order to amass great wealth you have to be prepared to be pretty ruthless. There are plenty of wealthy people who aren't that nice.'

Nik, who had never aspired to be 'nice', was careful not to let his expression change. 'Are you calling me a slimeball?'

'I'm simply pointing out that income isn't an indicator of a person's worth.'

'You mean because you don't know the level of expenditure?'

'No! Why is everything about money with you? I'm talking about *emotional* worth. Your father told me about Diandra. He was ill with flu last winter after Callie left. He was so ill at one point he couldn't drag himself from the bed. I sympathised because it happened to me once and I hope I never get flu again. Anyway, Diandra cared for him the whole time. She was the one who called the doctor. She made all his meals. That was kind, don't you think?'

'Or opportunistic.'

'If you carry on thinking like that you are going to die lonely. He met her when she cooked him her special moussaka to try and tempt him to eat. I *love* that he doesn't care what she does.'

'He should care. She stands to gain an enormous amount financially from this wedding.'

'That's horrible.'

'It is truly horrible. Finally we find something we agree on.'

'I wasn't agreeing with you! It's your attitude that's horrible, not this wedding. You're not only a judgemental cynic, you're also a raging snob.'

Nik breathed deeply. 'I am not a raging snob, but I am realistic.'

'No, what you are is damaged. Not everything has a price, Nik, and there are things in life that are far more important than money. Your father is trying to make a family and I think that's admirable.' She fumbled with the seat belt. 'Get me out of this car before I'm contaminated by you. Your thundercloud is about to rain all over my sunny patch of life.'

Your father is trying to make a family.

Nik thought about everything that had gone before.

He'd buried the pain and hurt deep and it was something he had never talked about with anyone, especially not his father, who had his own pain to deal with. What would happen when this relationship collapsed?

'If my father entered relationships with some degree of caution and objective contemplation then I would be less concerned, but he makes the same mistake you make. He confuses physical intimacy with love.' He saw the colour streak across her cheeks.

'I'm not confused. Have I spun fairy tales about the night we spent together? Have I fallen in love with you? No. I know exactly what it was and what we did. You're in a little compartment in my brain labelled "Once in a Lifetime Experiences" along with skydiving and a helicopter flight over the New York skyline. It was amazing by the way.'

'The helicopter flight was amazing?'

'No, I haven't done that yet. I was talking about the night with you, although there were moments that felt as nerve-racking as skydiving.' Her mouth tilted into a self-conscious smile. 'Of course it's also a little embarrassing looking at you in daylight after all those things we did in the dark, but I'm trying not to think about it. Now stop being annoying. In fact, stop talking for a while. That way I'm less likely to kill you before we arrive.'

Nik refrained from pointing out she'd been the only one in the dark. He'd had perfect vision and he'd used it to his own shameless advantage. There wasn't a single corner of her body he hadn't explored and the memory of every delicious curve was welded in his brain.

He tried to work out what it was about her that was so appealing. Innocence wasn't a quality he generally admired in a person so he had to assume the power of the attraction stemmed from the sheer novelty of being with someone who had managed to retain such an untarnished view of the world.

'Are you embarrassed about the night we spent together?'

'I would be if I thought about it, so I'm not thinking about it. I'm living in the moment.' Having offered that simple solution to the problem, she reached into the back of the car for her hat. 'You could take the same approach to the wedding. You're not here to fix it or protect anyone. You're here as a guest and your only responsibility is to smile and look happy. Is this it? Are we here? Because I don't see an island. Maybe your father might have changed the venue when he saw the black cloud of your presence approaching over the horizon.'

Nik dragged his gaze from her mouth to the jetty. 'This is it. From here, we go by boat.'

Lily stood in the prow of the boat feeling the cool brush of the wind on her face and tasting the salty air. The boat skimmed and bounced over the sparkling ocean towards the large island in the distance, sending a light spray over her face and tangling her hair.

Nik stood behind the wheel, legs braced, eyes hidden behind a pair of dark glasses. Despite the unsmiling set of his mouth, he looked more approachable and less the hard-headed businessman.

'This is so much fun. I think I might love it more than your Ferrari.'

He gave a smile that turned him from insanely good-looking to devastating, and she felt the intensity of the attraction like a physical punch.

It was true he didn't seem to display any of the family values that were so important to her, but that didn't do anything to diminish the sexual attraction.

As far as she could tell, he couldn't be more perfect for a short-term relationship.

For the whole trip in the car she'd been aware of him. As he'd shifted gear his hand had brushed against her bare thigh and she'd discovered that being with him was an exciting, exhilarating experience that was like nothing she'd experienced before.

There had been a brief moment when they'd pulled into the car park that she'd thought he might be about to kiss her. He'd looked at her mouth the way a panther looked at its prey before it devoured it, but just when she'd been about to close her eyes and take a fast ride to bliss, he'd sprung from the car, leaving her to wonder if she'd imagined it.

She'd followed him to the jetty, watching in fascination as the group of people gathered there sprang to attention. If she needed any more evidence of the power he wielded, she had only to observe the way people responded to him. He behaved with an authority that was instinctive, his air of command unmistakable even in this apparently casual setting.

It was a good job he didn't possess any of the qualities she was looking for, she thought, otherwise she'd be in trouble.

Her gaze lingered on his bronzed throat, visible at the open neck of his shirt. He handled the boat with the same confident assurance he displayed in everything and she was sure that no electrical device had ever dared to misbehave under his expert touch.

Trying not to think about just how expert his touch had been, she anchored her hair and shouted above the wind. 'The beaches are beautiful. People aren't allowed to bathe here?'

'You can bathe here. You're my guest.' As they approached the island, he slowed the speed of the boat and skilfully steered against the dock.

Two men instantly jumped forward to help and Nik sprang from the boat and held out his hand to her.

'I need to get my bag.'

'They will bring our luggage up to the villa later.'

'I have a gift for your father and it's only one bag,' she muttered. 'I can carry a single bag.'

'You bought a gift?'

'Of course. It's a wedding. I couldn't come without a small gift.' She stepped out of the bobbing boat and allowed herself to hold his hand for a few seconds longer than was necessary for balance. She felt warmth and strength flow through her fingers and had to battle the temptation to press herself against him. 'So how many bedrooms does your father have? Are you sure there is room for me to stay?'

The question seemed to amuse him. 'There will be room, *theé mou*, don't worry. As well as the main villa, there are several other properties scattered around the island. We will be staying in one of those.'

As they walked up a sandy path she breathed in the wonderful scents of sea juniper and wild thyme. 'One of the things I love most about Crete is the thyme honey. Brittany and I eat it for breakfast.'

'My father keeps bees so he will be very happy to hear you say that.'

The path forked at the top and he turned right and took the path that led down to another beach. There, nestling in the small horseshoe bay of golden sand with the water almost lapping at the whitewashed walls, was a beautiful contemporary villa.

Lily stopped. '*That's* your father's house?' The position

was idyllic, the villa stunning, but it looked more like a honeymoon hideaway than somewhere to accommodate a large number of high-profile international guests.

'No. This is Camomile Villa. The main house is fifteen minutes' walk in the other direction, towards the small Venetian fort. I thought we'd unpack and breathe for an hour or so before we face the guests.'

Witnessing his tension, she felt a rush of compassion. 'Nik—' She put her hand on his cheek and turned his face to hers. 'This is a wedding, not the sacking of Troy. You do not need to find your strength or breathe. Your role is to smile and enjoy yourself.'

His gaze locked on hers and she wished she hadn't touched him. His blue-shadowed jaw was rough beneath her fingers and suddenly she was remembering that night in minute detail.

Seriously unsettled, she started to pull her hand away but he caught her wrist in his fingers and held it there.

'You are a very unusual woman.' His voice was husky and she gave a faint smile, ignoring the wild flutter of nerves low in her stomach.

'I am not even going to ask what you mean by that. I'm simply going to take it as a compliment.'

'Of course you are.' There was a strange gleam in his eyes. 'You see positive in everything, don't you?'

'Not always.' She could have told him that she saw very little positive in being alone in the world, having no family, but given his obvious state of tension she decided to keep that confidence to herself. 'So how do you know we're staying in Camomile Villa? Cute name, by the way. Maybe your father has given it to one of the other guests. Shouldn't you go and check?'

'Camomile belongs to me.'

Lily digested that. 'So actually you own five properties, not four.'

'I don't count this place.'

'Really? Because if I owned this I'd be spending every spare minute here.' She walked up the path, past silvery green olive trees, nets lying on the ground ready for harvesting later in the year. A small lizard lay basking in the hot sun and she smiled as it sensed company and darted for safety into the dry, dusty earth.

The path leading down to the villa cut through a garden of tumbling colour. Bougainvillaea in bright pinks and purples blended and merged against the dazzling white of the walls and the perfect blue of the sky.

Nik opened the door and Lily followed him inside.

White beamed ceilings and natural stone floors gave the interior a cool, uncluttered feel and the elegant white interior was lifted by splashes of Mediterranean blue.

'If you don't want this place, I might live here.' Lily looked at the shaded terrace with its beautiful infinity pool. 'Why does anyone need a pool when the sea is five steps from the front door?'

'Some people don't like swimming in the sea.'

'I'm not one of those people. I adore the sea. Nik, this place is—' she felt a lump in her throat '—it's really special.'

He opened the doors to the terrace and gave her a wary look. 'Are you going to cry?'

'It's perfect.' She blinked. 'And I'm fine. Happy. And excited. I love Crete, but I never get the chance to enjoy it like a tourist. I'm always working.' And never in her life had she experienced this level of luxury.

She and Brittany were always moaning about the mosquitoes and lack of air conditioning in their tiny apartment. At night they slept with the windows open to make the most of the breeze from the sea, but in the summer months it was almost unbearable indoors.

'You are the most unusual woman I've ever met. You enjoy small things.'

'This is not a small thing. And you're the unusual one.' She picked up her bag. 'You take this life for granted.'

'That is not true. I know how fortunate I am.'

'I don't think you do, but I'm going to be pointing it out to you every minute for the next few days so hopefully by the time we leave you will.' She glanced around her and then looked at him expectantly. 'My bedroom?'

For a wild, unnerving moment she hoped he was going to tell her there was just one bedroom, but he gestured to a door that led from the large spacious living area.

'The guest suite is through there. Make yourself comfortable.'

Guest suite.

So he didn't intend them to share a room. For Nik, it really had been one night.

Telling herself it was probably for the best, she followed his directions and walked through an open door into a bright, airy bedroom. The bed was draped in layers of cream and white, deep piles of cushions and pillows inviting the occupant to lounge and relax. The walls were hung with bold, contemporary art, slashes of deep blue on large canvases that added a stylish touch to the room. In one corner stood a tall, elegant vase in graduated blues, the colour shifting under the dazzling sunlight.

Lily recognised it instantly. 'That's one of Skylar's pots.'

He looked at her curiously. 'You know the artist?'

'Skylar Tempest. She and Brittany were roommates at college. They're best friends, as close as sisters. I would know her work anywhere. Her style, her use of colour and composition is unique, but I know that pot specifically because I talked to her about it. Brittany introduced us because Skylar wanted to talk to me about ceramics. She's incorporated a few Minoan designs into some of her work, modernised, of course.' She knelt down and slid her hand over the smooth surface of the glass. 'This is from her *Mediterranean Sky* collection. She had a small exhibition in New York, not only glass and pots but jewellery and a couple of paintings. She's insanely talented.'

'You were at that exhibition?'

'Sadly no. I don't move in those circles. Nor do I pretend to claim any credit for any of her incredible creations, but I did talk to her about shapes and style. Of course the Minoans used terracotta clay. It was Sky's idea to reproduce the shape in glass. Look at this—' She trailed her finger lightly over the surface. 'The Minoans usually decorated their pots with dark on light motifs, often of sea creatures, and she's taken her inspiration from that. It's genius. I can't believe you own it. Where did you find it?'

'I was at the exhibition.'

'In New York? How did you even know about her?'

'I saw her work in a small artisan jewellers in Greenwich Village and I bought one of her necklaces for—' He broke off and Lily looked at him expectantly.

'For? For one of your women? We're not in a relationship, Nik. You don't have to censor your conversation. And even if we were in a relationship you still wouldn't need to censor it.'

'In my experience, most women do not appreciate hearing about their predecessors.'

'Yes, well the more I hear about the women you've known in your life, the more I'm not surprised. Now tell me about how you discovered Skylar.'

'I asked to see more of her work and was told she was having an exhibition. I managed to get myself invited.'

Lily rocked back on her heels. 'She never mentioned that she met you.'

'We never met. I didn't introduce myself. I went on the first night and she was surrounded by well-wishers, so I simply bought a few pieces and left. That was two years ago.'

'So she doesn't know she sold pieces to Nik Zervakis?'

'A member of my team handled the actual transaction.'

Lily scrambled to her feet. 'Because you don't touch real money? She would be so excited if she knew her work was here in your villa. Can I tell her?'

He looked amused. 'If you think it would interest her, then yes.'

'Interest her? Of course it would interest her.' Lily pulled her phone out of her bag and took a photo. 'I must admit that pot looks perfect there. It needs a large room with lots of light. Did you know she has another exhibition coming up?' She slipped her phone back into her bag. 'December in London. An upmarket gallery in Knightsbridge is showing her work. She's really excited. Her new collection is called *Ocean Blue*. It's still sea themed. Brittany showed me some photos.'

'Will you be going?'

'To an exhibition in Knightsbridge? Sure. I thought I'd fly in on my private jet, spend a night in the Royal Suite at The Savoy and then get my driver to take me to the exhibition.' She laughed and then saw something flicker in his eyes. 'Er—that's exactly what you're going to be doing, isn't it?'

'My plans aren't confirmed.'

'But you do have a private jet.'

'ZervaCo owns a Gulfstream and a couple of Lear jets.' He said it as if it was normal and she shook her head, trying not to be intimidated.

For her, wealth was people and family, not money, but still—

'Seriously, Nik. What am I doing here? To you a Gulfstream is a mode of transport, to me it's a warm Atlantic current. I used to own a rusty mountain bike until the wheel fell off. I'm the one who works in a dusty museum, digs in the dirt in the summer and cleans other people's houses to give myself enough money to live. And living doesn't include jetting across Europe to a friend's exhibition. I have no idea where I'll even be in December. I'm job hunting.'

'Wherever you are, I'll fly you there. And for your information, I wouldn't be staying in the Royal Suite.'

'Because you already own an apartment that most royals would kill for.' His lack of response told her she was right and she rolled her eyes. 'Nik, we had an illuminating conversation earlier during which you confessed that you think your new stepmother is only interested in your father's money. Money is obviously a very big deal to you, so I'm hardly likely to take you up on your offer of a ride in your private jet, am I?'

'That is different. I'm grateful that you agreed to come here with me,' he said softly, 'and taking you to Skylar's exhibition would be my way of saying thank you.'

'I don't need a thank you. And to be honest I'm here because of the conversation I had with your father. My decision didn't have anything to do with you. We had one night, that's all. I mean, the sex was great, but I had no trouble walking out of your door that morning. There were no feelings involved.' She shook her head to add emphasis. 'Kevlar, that's me.'

He gave her a long, steady look. 'I have never met anyone who less resembles that substance.'

'Up until a week ago I would have agreed with you, but now I'm a changed person. Seriously, I'm enjoying being with you. You're smoking hot and surprisingly entertaining despite your warped view of relationships, but I am no more in love with you than I am with your supersonic shower. And you don't owe me anything for bringing me here—in fact I owe you.' She glanced across the room to the terrace outside. 'This is the nearest I've come to a vacation in a long time. It's not exactly a hardship being here. I am going to lie in the sun like that lizard out there.'

'You haven't met my family yet.' He paused, his gaze fixed on hers. 'Think about it. If you change your mind about coming to Skylar's London exhibition, let me know. The invitation stands. I won't withdraw it.'

It was a different world.

What would it be like, she wondered, not to have to think about your budget? Not to have to make choices between forfeiting one thing to buy another?

This close she could see the flecks of gold in those dark eyes, the blue-black shadow of his jaw and the almost unbelievably perfect lines of his bone structure. If a scale had been invented to measure sex appeal, she was pretty sure he would have shattered it. She couldn't look at his mouth without remembering all the ways he'd used it on her body and remembering made her want it again. She wanted to reach out and slide her fingers into that silky dark hair and press her mouth to his. And this time she wanted to do it without the blindfold.

Aware that her mind was straying into forbidden territory she took a step back, reminding herself that money came a poor second to family and this man seemed to be virtually estranged from his father.

'I won't change my mind.'

Dragging her gaze from his, she dropped her bag on the floor and unzipped it. 'I need to hang up my dresses or they'll be creased. I don't want to make a bad impression.'

'There are staff over in the main villa who will help you unpack. I can call them.'

'Are you kidding?' Amused by yet more evidence of the differences between their respective lifestyles, she pulled out her clothes. 'This will take me five minutes at most. And I'd be embarrassed to ask anyone else to hang up a tee shirt that cost the same amount as a cup of coffee. So what happens next?'

'We are joining my father and Diandra for lunch.'

'Sounds good to me.'

The expression on his face told her he didn't share her sentiments. 'I need to make some calls. Make yourself at home. The fridge is stocked, there are books in the living room. Feel free to use the pool. If there is anything you need, let me know. I'll be using the office on the other side of the living room.'

What else could she possibly need?

Lily glanced round the villa, which was by far the most luxurious and exclusive place she'd ever stayed.

She had a feeling the only thing she was going to need was a reality check.

He hadn't been back here since that summer five years before. It had been an attempt to put the past behind him, but ironically it had succeeded only in making things worse.

The memory of his last visit sat in his head like a muddy stain.

Nik strolled out onto the terrace, hoping the view would relieve his tension, but being here took him right back to his childhood and that was a place he made a point of avoiding.

With a soft curse, he walked back into the room he'd had converted into an office and switched on his laptop.

For the next hour he took an endless stream of calls and then finally, when he couldn't postpone the moment any longer, he took a quick shower and changed for lunch.

Another day, another wedding.

Mouth grim, he pocketed his phone and strolled through the villa to find Lily.

She was sitting in the shade on the terrace, a glass of iced lemonade by her hand and a book in her lap, staring out across the bright turquoise blue of the bay.

She hadn't noticed him and he stood for a moment, watching her. The tension left him to be replaced by tension of a different source. That one night he'd spent with her hadn't been anywhere near long enough.

He wanted to rip off that pretty blue sundress and take her straight back to bed but he knew that, no matter what she said, she wasn't the sort of woman to be able to keep her emotions out of the bedroom so he gave her a cool smile as he strolled onto the terrace.

'Are you ready?'

'Yes.' She slid her feet into a pair of silver ballet flats and put her book on the table. 'Is there anything I should know? Who will be there?'

'My father and Diandra. They wanted this lunch to be family only.'

'In other words your father doesn't want your first meeting for a long while to be in public.' She reached for her glass and finished her drink. 'Don't worry about me while we're here. I'm sure I can find a few friendly faces to talk to while you're mingling.'

He looked down at the curve of her cheeks and the dimple in the corner of her mouth and decided she was the one with the friendly face. If he had to pick a single word to describe her, it would be approachable. She was warm, friendly and he was sure there would be no shortage of guests eager to talk to her. The thought should have reduced his stress because it gave him one less responsibility, but it didn't.

Despite her claims to being made of Kevlar, he wasn't convinced she'd managed to manufacture even a thin layer of protection for herself.

He offered to drive her to avoid the heat but she chose to walk and on the way up to the main house she grilled him about his background. Did his father still work? What exactly was his business? Did he have any other family apart from Nik?

His suspicion that she was more comfortable with this gathering than him was confirmed as soon as he walked onto the terrace.

He saw the table by the pool laid for four and felt Lily sneak her hand into his.

'He wants you to get to know Diandra. He's trying to build bridges,' she said softly, her fingers squeezing his. 'Don't glare.'

Before he could respond, his father walked out onto the terrace.

'Niklaus—' His voice shook and Nik saw the shimmer of tears in his father's eyes.

Lily extracted her hand from his. 'Hug him.' She made it sound simple and Nik wondered whether bringing someone as idealistic as Lily to a reunion as complicated as this one had been entirely sensible, but she and his father obviously thought alike because he walked towards them, arms outstretched.

'It's been too long since you were home. Far too long, but the past is behind us. All is forgiven. I have such news to tell you, Niklaus.'

Forgiven?

His feet nailed to the floor by the past and the weight of the secrets his father didn't know, Nik didn't move and then he felt Lily's small hand in his back pushing, harder this time, and he then stepped forward and was embraced by his father so tightly it knocked the air from his lungs.

He felt a heaviness in his chest that had nothing to do with the intensity of his father's grip. Emotions rushed towards him and he was beginning to wish he'd never agreed to this reunion when Lily stepped forward, breaking the tension of the moment with her warmest, brightest smile and an extended hand that gave his father no choice but to release Nik.

'I'm Lily Rose. We spoke on the phone. You have a very beautiful home, Mr Zervakis. It's kind of you to invite me to share your special day.' Blushing charmingly, she then attempted to speak a few words of Greek, a gesture that both distracted his father and guaranteed a lifetime of devotion.

Nik watched as his dazzled father melted like butter left in the hot sun.

He kissed her hand and switched to heavily accented English. 'You are welcome in my home, Lily. I'm so happy you are able to join us for what is turning out to be the most special week of my life. This is Diandra.'

For the first time Nik noticed the woman hovering in the background.

He'd assumed she was one of his father's staff, but now she stepped forward and quietly introduced herself.

Nik noticed that she didn't quite meet his eye, instead she focused all her attention on Lily as if she were the lifebelt floating on the surface of a deep pool of water.

Diandra clearly had sophisticated radar for detecting sympathy in people, Nik thought, wondering what 'news' his father had for them.

Experience led him to assume it was unlikely to be good.

'I've brought you a small gift. I made it myself.' Lily delved into her bag and handed over a prettily wrapped parcel.

It was a ceramic plate, similar to the one he'd admired in her apartment, decorated with the same pattern of swirling blues and greens.

Nik could see she had real talent and so, apparently, did his father.

'You made this? But this isn't your business?'

'No. I'm an archaeologist. But I did my dissertation on Minoan ceramics so it's an interest of mine.'

'You must tell me all about it. And all about yourself. Lily Rose is a beautiful name.' His father led her towards the table that had been laid next to the pool. Silver gleamed in the sunlight and bowls of olives gleamed glossy dark in beautiful blue bowls. Kostas put Lily's plate in the centre of the table. 'Your mother liked flowers?'

'I don't know. I didn't know my mother.' She shot Nik an apologetic look. 'That's too much information for a first meeting. Let's talk about something else.'

But Kostas Zervakis wasn't so easily deflected. 'You didn't know your mother? She passed away when you were young, *koukla mou*?'

Appalled by that demonstration of insensitivity, Nik shot him an exasperated look and was about to steer the conversation away from such a deeply personal topic when Lily answered.

'I don't know what happened to her. She left me in a basket in Kew Gardens in London when I was a few hours old.'

Whatever he'd expected to hear, it hadn't been that and Nik, who made a point of never asking about a woman's past, found himself wanting to know more. 'A basket?' Her eyes lifted to his and for a moment the presence of other people was forgotten.

'Yes. I was found by one of the staff and taken to hospital. They called me Lily Rose because I was found among the flowers. They never traced my mother. They assumed she was a teenager who panicked.' She spoke in a matter-of-fact tone but Nik knew she wasn't matter-of-fact about the way she felt.

This was why she had shown so much wistful interest in the detail of his family. At the time he hadn't been able to understand why it would make an interesting topic of conversation, but now he understood that, to her, it was not a frustration or a complication. It was an aspiration.

This was why she dreamed of happy endings, both for herself and other people.

He felt something stir inside him, an emotion that was entirely new to him.

He'd believed himself immune to even the most elaborately constructed sob story, but Lily's revelation had somehow managed to slide under those steely layers of protection he'd constructed for himself. For some reason, her simply stated story touched him deeply.

Unsettled, he dragged his eyes from her soft mouth and promised himself that no matter how much he wanted her, he wasn't going to touch her again. It wouldn't be fair, when their expectations of life were so different. He had no concerns about his own ability to keep a relationship superficial. He did, however, have deep concerns about her ability to do the same and he didn't want to hurt her.

His father, predictably, was visibly moved by the revelation about her childhood.

'No family?' His voice was roughened by emotion. 'So who raised you, *koukla mou*?'

'I was brought up in a series of foster homes.' She poked absently at her food. 'And now I think we should talk about something else because this is *definitely* too much detail for a first meeting, especially when we're here to celebrate a wedding.' Superficially she was as cheerful as ever but Nik knew she was upset.

He was about to make another attempt to change the topic when his father reached out and took Lily's hand.

'One day you will have a family of your own. A big family.'

Nik ground his teeth. 'I don't think Lily wants to talk about that right now.'

'I don't mind.' Lily sent him a quick smile and then turned back to his father. 'I hope so. I think family makes you feel anchored and I've never had that.'

'Anchors keep a boat secured in one place,' Nik said softly, 'which can be limiting.'

Her gaze met his and he knew she was deciding if his observation was random or a warning.

He wasn't sure himself. All he knew was that he didn't want her thinking this was anything other then temporary. He could see she'd had a tough life. He didn't want to be the one to shatter that optimism and remove the smile from her face.

His father gave a disapproving frown. 'Ignore him. When it comes to relationships my son behaves like a child in a sweetshop. He gorges his appetites without learning the benefits of selectivity. He enjoys success in everything he touches except, sadly, his private life.'

'I'm very selective.' Nik reached for his wine. 'And given that my private life is exactly the way I want it to be, I consider it an unqualified success.'

He banked down the frustration, wondering how his father, thrice divorced, could consider himself an example to follow.

His father looked at him steadily. 'All the money in the

world will not bring a man the same feeling of contentment as a wife and children, don't you agree, Lily?'

'As someone with massive college loans, I wouldn't dismiss the importance of money,' Lily said honestly, 'but I agree that family is the most important thing.'

Feeling as if he'd woken up on the set of a Hollywood rom-com in which he'd been cast in the role of 'bad guy', Nik refrained from asking his father which of his wives had ever given him anything other than stomach ulcers and astronomical bills. Surely even he couldn't reframe his romantic past as anything other than a disaster.

'One day you will have a family, Lily.' Kostas Zervakis surveyed her with misty eyes and Nik observed this emotional interchange with something between disbelief and despair.

His father had known Lily for less than five minutes and already he was ready to leave her everything in his will. It was no wonder he'd made himself a target for every woman with a sob story.

Callie had spotted that vulnerability and dug her claws deep. No doubt Diandra was working on the same soft spot.

A dark, deeply buried memory stirred in the depths of his brain. His father, sitting alone in the bedroom among the wreckage of his wife's hasty packing, the image of wretched despair as she drove away without looking back.

Never, before or since, had Nik felt as powerless as he had that day. Even though he'd been a young child, he'd known he was witnessing pain beyond words.

The second time it had happened, he'd been a teenager and he remembered wondering why his father would have risked putting himself through such emotional agony a second time.

And then there had been Callie...

He'd known from the first moment that the relationship was doomed and had blamed himself later for not trying to save his father from that particular mistake.

And now here he was again, trapped in the unenviable position of having to make a choice between watching his father walk into another relationship disaster, or potentially damaging their relationship by trying to intervene.

Lily was right that his father was a grown man, able to make his own decisions. So why did he still have this urge to push his father out of the path of the oncoming train?

Emotions boiling inside him, he glanced across the table to his future stepmother, wondering if it was a coincidence that she'd picked the chair as far from his as possible.

She was either shy or she was harbouring a guilty conscience.

He'd promised he wouldn't interfere, but he was fast rethinking that decision.

He sat in silence, observing rather than participating, while staff discreetly served food and topped up glasses.

His father engaged Lily in conversation, encouraging her to talk about her life and her love of archaeology and Greece.

Forced to sit through a detailed chronology of Lily's life history, Nik learned that she'd had three boyfriends, worked numerous low-paid jobs to pay for college tuition, was allergic to cats, suffered from severe eczema as a child and had never lived in the same place for more than twelve months.

The more he discovered about her life, the more he realised how hard it had been. She'd made a joke about Cinderella, but Lily made Cinderella look like a slacker.

Learning far more than he'd ever wanted to know, he turned to his father. 'What is the "news" you have for me?'

'You will find out soon enough. First, I am enjoying having the company of my son. It's been too long. I have resorted to the Internet to find news of what is happening with you. You have been spending a great deal of time in San Francisco.'

Happy to talk about anything that shifted the focus from Lily, Nik relaxed slightly and talked broadly about some of the technology developments his company was spearheading and touched lightly on the deal he was about to close, but the diversion proved to be brief.

Kostas spooned olives onto Lily's plate. 'You must persuade Nik to take you to the far side of the island to see the Minoan remains. You will need to go early in the day, before it is too hot. At this time of year everything is very dry. If you love flowers, then you will love Crete in the spring. In April and May the island is covered in poppies, daisies, camomile, iris.' He beamed at her. 'You must come back here then and visit.'

'I'd like that.' Lily tucked into her food. 'These olives are delicious.'

'They come from our own olive groves and the lemonade in your fridge came from lemons grown on our own trees. Diandra made it. She is a genius in the kitchen. You wait until you taste her lamb.' Kostas leaned across and took Diandra's hand. 'I took one mouthful and fell in love.'

Losing his appetite, Nik gave her a direct look. 'Tell me about yourself, Diandra. Where were you brought up?' He caught Lily's urgent glance and ignored it, instead listening to Diandra's stammered response.

From that he learned that she was one of six children and had never been married.

'She never met the right person, and that is lucky for me,' his father said indulgently.

Nik opened his mouth to speak, but Lily got there first.

'You're so lucky having been born in Greece,' she said quickly. 'I've travelled extensively in the islands but living here must be wonderful. I've spent three summers on Crete and one on Corfu. Where else do you think I should visit?'

Giving her a grateful look, Diandra made several suggestions, but Nik refused to be deflected from his path.

'Who did you work for before my father?'

'Ignore him,' Lily said lightly. 'He makes every conversation feel like a job interview. The first time I met him I wanted to hand over my résumé. This lamb is *delicious* by the way. You're so clever. It's even better than the lamb Nik and I ate last week and that was a top restaurant.' She went on to describe what they'd eaten in minute detail and Diandra offered a few observations of her own about the best way to cook lamb.

Deprived of the opportunity to question his future stepmother further, Nik was wondering once again what 'news' his father was preparing to announce, when he heard the sound of a child crying inside the house.

Diandra shot to her feet and exchanged a brief look with his father before scurrying from the table.

Nik narrowed his eyes. 'Who,' he said slowly, 'is that?'

'That's the news I was telling you about.' His father turned his head and watched as Diandra returned to the table carrying a toddler whose tangled blonde curls and sleepy expression announced that she'd recently awoken from a nap. 'Callie has given me full custody of Chloe as a wedding present. Niklaus, meet your half-sister.'

CHAPTER SEVEN

Lily sat on the sunlounger in the shade, listening to the rhythmic splash from the infinity pool. Nik had been swimming for the past half an hour, with no break in the relentless laps back and forth across the pool.

Whatever had possessed her to agree to come for this wedding?

It had been like falling straight into the middle of a bad soap opera.

Diandra had been so intimidated by Nik she'd barely opened her mouth and he, it seemed, had taken that as a sign that she had nothing worth saying. Lunch had been a tense affair and the moment his father had produced his little half-sister Nik had gone from being coolly civil to remote and intimidating. Lily had worked so hard to compensate for his frozen silence she'd virtually performed cartwheels on the terrace.

And she couldn't comprehend his reaction.

He was too old to care about sharing the affections of his father, and too independently wealthy to care about the impact on his inheritance. The toddler was adorable, a cherub with golden curls and a ready smile, and his father and Diandra had been so obviously thrilled by the new addition to the family Lily couldn't understand the problem.

On the walk back from lunch she'd tentatively broached

the subject but Nik had cut her off and made straight for his office where he'd proceeded to work without interruption.

Trying to cure her headache, Lily had drunk plenty of water and then read her book in the shade but she'd been unable to concentrate on the words.

She knew it was none of her business, but still she couldn't keep her mouth shut and when Nik finally vaulted from the pool in an athletic movement that displayed every muscle in his powerful frame, she slid off her sunlounger and blocked his path.

'You were horrible to Diandra at lunch and if you want to heal the rift with your father, that isn't the way. She is *not* a gold-digger.'

His face was an uncompromising mask. 'And you know this on less than a few minutes' acquaintance?'

'I'm a good judge of character.'

'This from a woman who didn't know a man was married?'

She felt herself flush. 'I was wrong about him, but I'm not wrong about Diandra, and you have to stop giving her the evil eye.'

Droplets of water clung to his bronzed shoulders. 'I was not giving her the evil eye.'

'Nik, you virtually grilled her at the table. I was waiting for you to throw her on the barbecue along with the lamb. You were terrifying.'

'*Theé mou,* that is *not* true. She behaved like a woman with a guilty conscience.'

'She behaved like a woman who was terrified of you! How can you be so *blind*?' And then she realised in a flash of comprehension that she was the one who was blind. He wasn't being small-minded, or prejudiced. That wasn't what was happening. She saw now that he was afraid for his father. His actions all stemmed from a desire to protect him. In his own way he was displaying the exact loyalty she valued so highly. Like a gazelle approaching a sleeping lion, she tiptoed carefully. 'I think your perspective may be a little skewed because of what happened with your father's other relationships. Do you want to talk about it?'

'Unlike you, I don't have the desire to verbalise every thought that enters my head.'

Lily stiffened. 'That was a little harsh given that I'm trying to help, but I'm going to forgive you because I can see you're very upset. And I think I know why.'

'Don't forgive me. If you're angry, say so.'

'You told me not to verbalise every thought that enters my head.'

Nik wiped his face with the towel and sent her a look that would have frozen molten lava. 'I don't need help.'

Lily tried a different approach. 'I can see that this situation has the potential for all sorts of complications, not least that Diandra has been given another woman's child to raise as her own just a few days before the wedding, but she seemed thrilled. Your father is clearly delighted. They're happy, Nik.'

'For how long?' His mouth tightened. 'How long until it all falls apart and his heart is broken again? What if this time he doesn't heal?' His words confirmed her suspicions and she felt a rush of compassion.

'This isn't about Diandra, it's about you. You love your father deeply and you're trying to protect him.' It was ironic, she thought, that Nik Zervakis, who was supposedly so cold and aloof, turned out to have stronger family values than David Ashurst, who on the surface had seemed like perfect partner material. It was something that her checklist would never have shown up. 'I love that you care so much about him, but has it occurred to you that you might be trying to save him from the best thing that has ever happened in his life?'

'Why will this time be different from the others?'

'Because he loves her and she loves him. Of course having a toddler thrown into the mix will make for a challenging start to the relationship, but—' She frowned as she examined that fact in greater depth. 'Why did Callie choose to do this now? A child is a person, not a wedding present. You think she was hoping to derail your father's relationship with Diandra?'

'The thought had occurred to me but no, that isn't what she is trying to do.' He hesitated. 'Callie is marrying again and she doesn't want the child.'

He delivered that news in a flat monotone devoid of emotion, but this time Lily was too caught up in her own emotions to think about his.

Callie didn't want the child?

She felt as if she'd been punched in the gut. All the air had been sucked from her lungs and suddenly she couldn't breathe.

'Right.' Her voice was croaky. 'So she gives her up as if she's a dress that's gone out of fashion? I'm not surprised you didn't like her. She doesn't sound like a very likeable person.' Horrified by the intensity of her response and aware he was watching her closely, she moved past him. 'If you're sure you don't want to talk then I think I'm going to have a rest before dinner. The heat makes me sleepy.'

He frowned. 'Lily—'

'Dinner is at eight? I'll be ready by then.' She steered her shaky legs towards her bedroom and closed the door behind her.

What was the matter with her?

This wasn't her family.

It wasn't her life.

Why did she have to take everything so *personally*?

Why was she worrying about how little Chloe would feel when she was old enough to ask about her mother when it wasn't really any of her business? Why did she care about all the potential threats she could see to his family unit?

The door behind her opened and she stiffened but kept her back to him. 'I'm about to lie down.'

'I upset you,' he said quietly, 'and that was not my intention. You were generous enough to come here with me, the least I can do is respond to your questions in a civil tone. I apologise.'

'I'm not upset because you didn't want to talk. I understand you don't find it helpful.'

'Then what's wrong?' When she didn't reply he cursed softly. 'Talk to me, Lily.'

'No. I'm having lots of feelings of my own and you hate talking about feelings. And no doubt you'll find some way to interpret what I'm feeling in a bad way, because that seems to be your special gift. You twist everything beautiful into something dark and ugly. You really should leave now. I need to self-soothe.'

She expected to hear the pounding of feet and the sound of a door closing behind him, but instead felt the warm strength of his hands curve over her shoulders.

'I do not twist things.'

'Yes, you do. But that's your problem. I can't deal with it right now.'

'I don't want you to self-soothe.' The words sounded as if they were dragged from him. 'I want you to tell me what's wrong. My father asked you a lot of personal questions over lunch.'

'I don't mind that.'

'Then what? Is this about Chloe?'

She took a juddering breath. 'It's a little upsetting when adults don't consider how a child might feel. It's lovely that she has a loving father, but one day that little girl is going to wonder why her mother gave her away. She's going to ask herself whether she cried too much or did something wrong. Not that I expect you to understand.'

There was a long pulsing silence and his grip on her arms tightened. 'I do understand.' His voice was low. 'I was nine when my mother left and I asked myself all those questions and more.'

She stood still, absorbing both the enormity and the implications of that revelation. 'I didn't know.'

'I don't talk about it.'

But he'd talked about it now, with her. Warmth spread through her. 'Did seeing Chloe stir it all up for you?'

'This whole place stirs it up,' he said wearily. 'Let's hope Chloe doesn't ask herself those same questions when she's older.'

'I was a baby and I still ask myself those questions.' And she had questions for him, so many questions, but she knew they wouldn't be welcome.

'I appreciate you listening to me, but I know you don't really want to talk about this so you should probably leave now.'

'Seeing as I am indirectly responsible for the fact you're upset by bringing you here in the first place, I have no intention of leaving.'

'You should.' Her voice was thickened. 'It's the situation, not you. You've never even met your half-sister so you can't be expected to love her and your father is obviously pleased, but a toddler is a lot of work and he's about to be married. What if he decides he doesn't want Chloe either?'

'He won't decide that.' His hands firm, he turned her to face him. 'He has wanted her from the first day, but Callie did everything she could to keep the child from him. I have no idea what my father will say when Chloe is old enough to ask, but he is a sensitive man—much more sensitive than I am as you have discovered—and he will say the right thing, I'm sure.' His hands stroked her bare arms and she gave a little shiver.

She could see the droplets of water clinging to dark hair that shadowed his bare chest.

Unable to help herself, she lifted her hand to his chest and then caught herself and pulled back.

'Sorry—' She took a step backwards but he muttered something under his breath in Greek and hauled her back against him. Her brain blurred as she was flattened against the heat and power of his body, his arm holding her trapped. He used his other hand to tilt her face to his and she drowned in the heated burn of his eyes in the few seconds before he bent his head and kissed her. And then there was nothing but the hunger of his mouth and the erotic slide of his tongue and it felt every bit as good as it had the first time. So good that she forgot everything except the pounding of her pulse and the desperate squirming heat low in her pelvis.

Pressed against his hard, powerful chest she forgot about feeling miserable and unsettled.

She forgot all the reasons this wasn't a good idea.

She forgot everything except the breathtaking excitement he generated with his mouth and hands. His kiss was unmistakably sexual, his tongue tangling with hers, his gaze locked on hers as he silently challenged her.

'Yes, yes.' With a soft murmur of acquiescence, she wrapped her arms round his neck, feeling the damp ends of his hair brush her wrists.

The droplets of water on his chest dampened her thin sundress until it felt as if there were nothing between them.

She felt him pull her hard against him, felt his hand slide down her back and cup her bottom so that she was pressed against the heavy thrust of his erection.

'I promised myself I wasn't going to do this but I want you.' He spoke in a thickened tone, and she gave a sob of relief.

'I want you, too. You have no idea how much. Right through lunch I wanted to rip your clothes off and remove that severe look from your face.'

He lifted his mouth from hers, his breathing uneven, the smouldering glitter of his eyes telling her everything she needed to know about his feelings. 'Do I look severe now?'

'No. You look incredible. This has been the longest week of my life.' She backed towards the bed, pulling him with her. If he changed his mind she was sure she'd explode. 'Don't have second thoughts. I know this is about sex and nothing else. I don't love you, but I'd love a repeat of all those things you did to me the other night.'

With sure hands, he dispensed with her sundress. 'All of them?'

'Yes.' She wanted him so badly it was almost indecent and when he lowered his head and trailed his mouth along her neck she almost sobbed aloud. 'Please. Right now. I want your whole repertoire. Don't hold anything back.'

'You're shy, it's still daylight,' he growled, 'and I don't have a blindfold.'

'I'm not shy. Shy has left the party. I don't care, I don't care.' Her hands moved over his chest and lower to his damp swimming shorts. She struggled to remove them over the thrusting force of his erection but finally her frantic fumbling proved successful and she covered him with the flat of her hand.

He groaned low in his throat and tipped her onto the bed, covering her body with his, telling her how much he wanted her, how hard she made him, until the excitement climbed to a point where she was a seething, writhing mass of desire. She tore at his shirt with desperate hands and he swore under his breath and wrenched it over his head, his fingers tangling with hers.

'Easy, slow down, there's no rush.'

'Yes, there is.' She rolled him onto his back and pressed her mouth to the hard planes of his chest and lower until she heard him groan. She tried to straddle him but he flipped her onto her back and caught her shifting hips in his hands, anchoring her there.

Despite the simmering tension, there was laughter in his eyes. 'It would be a criminal waste to rush this, *theé mou*.'

'No, it wouldn't.' She slid her hands over the silken muscles of his back. 'It might kill me if you don't.'

It was hard to know which of them was most aroused. She saw it in the glitter of his eyes and heard it in his uneven breathing. Felt it in the slight shake of his fingers as he unhooked her bra and peeled it away from her, releasing her breasts, taking his time. Everything he did was slow, unhurried, designed to torture her and she wondered how he could exercise so much control, such brutal discipline, because if it had been up to her the whole thing would have been over by now. He kept her still with his weight, with soft words, with skilled kisses and the sensual slide of his hand that dictated both position and pace.

She felt the cool air from the ceiling fan brush the heated surface of her skin and then moaned aloud as he drew her into the dark heat of his mouth. Sensation was sweet and wild and she arched into him, only to find herself anchored firmly by the rough strength of his thigh. He worked his way down her body with slow exploratory kisses and she shivered as she felt the brush of his lips and the flick of his tongue. Lower, more intimate, his mouth wandered to the shadows between her thighs and she felt the slippery heat of his tongue opening her, tasting her until she could feel the pleasure thundering down on her. She was feverish, desperate, everything in her body centred on this one moment.

'Nik—I need—'

'I know what you need.' A brief pause and then he eased over her and into her, each driving thrust taking him deeper until she didn't know where she ended and he began and then he paused, his hand in her hair and his mouth against hers, eyes half closed as he studied her face. She was dimly aware that he was saying something, soft intimate words that blurred in her head and melted over her skin. She felt the delicious weight of him, the masculine invasion, the solidity of muscle, the scrape of his jaw against hers as he kissed her, murmured her name and told her all the things he wanted to do to her. And she moaned because she wanted him to do them, right now. He was controlling her but she didn't care because he knew things about her she didn't know herself.

How to touch her, where to touch her. All she wanted was more of this breath-stealing pleasure and then he started to move, slowly at first, and then building the rhythm with sure, skilled thrusts until she was aware of nothing but him, of hard muscle and slick skin, of the frenzy of sensation until it exploded and she clung to him, sobbing his name as her body tightened on his, her muscles rippling around the thrusting length of him drawing out his own response.

She heard him groan her name, felt him slide his hand into her hair and take her mouth again so that they kissed their way through the whole thing, sharing every throb, ripple and flutter in the most intimate way possible.

The force of it left her shaken and stunned and she lay, breathless, trying to bring herself slowly back to earth. And then he shifted his weight and gathered her close, murmuring something in Greek as he stroked her hair back from her face and kissed her mouth gently.

They lay for a moment and then he scooped her up and carried her into the shower where, under the soft patter of steamy water, he proceeded to expand her sexual education with infinite skill until her body no longer felt like her own and her legs felt like rubber.

'Nik?' She lay damp and sated on the tangled sheets, deliciously sleepy and barely able to keep her eyes open. 'Is that why you don't like coming back here? Because it reminds you of your childhood?'

He stared down at her with those fathomless black eyes, his expression inscrutable. 'Get some sleep.' His voice was even. 'I'll wake you in time to change for dinner.'

'Where are you going?'

'I have work to do.'

In other words she'd strayed into forbidden territory. Somewhere in the back of her mind there was another question she wanted to ask him, but her brain was already drifting into blissful unconsciousness and she slid into a luxurious sleep.

* * *

Nik returned to the terrace and made calls in the shade, one eye on the open doors of Lily's bedroom.

So much for his resolve not to touch her again.

And what had possessed him to tell her about his mother? It was something he rarely thought about himself, let alone spoke of to other people.

It was being back here that had stirred up memories long buried.

He ignored the part of him that said it was the prospect of another wedding that stirred up the memories, not the place.

To distract himself he worked until the blaze of the sun dimmed and he heard movement from the bedroom.

He ended the call he'd made and a few minutes later she wandered onto the terrace, sleepy eyed and deliciously disorientated. 'Have you been out here the whole time?'

'Yes.'

'You're not tired?'

'No.'

'Because you're stressed out about your father.' She sat down next to him and poured herself a glass of water. 'For what it's worth, I like Diandra.'

He studied the soft curve of her mouth and the kindness in her eyes. 'Is there anyone you don't like?'

'Yes!' She sipped her water. 'I have a deep aversion to Professor Ashurst, and if we're drawing up a list then I should confess I didn't totally fall in love with your girlfriend from the other night, but that might be because she called me fat. And I definitely didn't like you a few hours ago, but you redeemed yourself in the bedroom so I'm willing to overlook the offensive things you said on the journey.' A dimple appeared in the corner of her mouth and Nik felt the instant, powerful response of his body and wondered how he was going to make it through an evening of small talk with people that didn't interest him.

She, on the other hand, interested him extremely.

'We should get ready for the party. The guests will be arriving soon and my father wants us up there early to greet them.'

'Us? You, surely, not me.'

'He wants you, too. He likes you very much.'

'I like him, too, but I don't think I should be greeting his guests. I'm not family. We're not even together.' Her gaze slid to his and away again and he knew she was thinking about what they'd shared earlier.

He was, too. In fact he'd thought of little else but sex with Lily since she'd drenched herself in his shower a week earlier.

Sex had always been important to him, but since meeting her it had become an obsession.

'It would mean a lot to him if you were there.'

'Well, if you're sure that's what he wants. This all feels a bit surreal.'

'Which part feels surreal?'

'All of it. The whole rich-lifestyle thing. Living with you could turn a girl's head. You can snap your fingers and have anything you want.'

Relieved by the lightening of the atmosphere, he smiled. 'I will snap my fingers for you any time you like. Tell me what you want.'

She smiled. 'You can get me anything?'

'Anything.'

'So if I had a craving for lobster mousse, you'd find me one?'

'I would.' He reached for his phone and she covered his hand with hers, laughing.

'I wasn't serious! I don't want lobster mousse.' Her fingers were light on his hand. There was nothing suggestive about her touch. Nothing that warranted his extreme physical reaction.

'Then what?' His voice was husky. 'If you don't want lobster mousse, what can I get you?'

Her eyes met his and colour streaked across her cheeks.

'Nothing. I have everything I need.' She removed her hand quickly and said something, but her words were drowned out by the clacking of a helicopter.

Nik rose reluctantly to his feet. 'We need to move. The guests are arriving.'

'By helicopter?' Her eyes were round, as if it was only now dawning on her that this wasn't an ordinary wedding party. 'Is this party going to be glamorous?'

'Very. Lunch was an informal family affair, but tonight is for my father to show off his new wife.'

'How many guests?'

'A very select party. No more than two hundred, but they're arriving from all over Europe and the US.'

'Two *hundred*? That's a select party?' Her smile faltered. 'I'm a gatecrasher.'

'You are not a gatecrasher. You're my guest.'

She pushed her hair back from her face. 'I'm starting to panic that what I brought with me isn't dressy enough.'

'You look lovely in everything you wear, but I do have something if you'd like to take a look at it.'

'Something you bought for someone else?'

'No. For you.'

'I told you I didn't want anything.'

'I didn't listen.'

'So you bought me something anyway. In case I embarrassed you?'

'No. In case you had a panic that what you'd brought wasn't dressy enough.'

'I should probably be angry that you're calling me predictable, but as we don't have time to be angry I'm going to overlook it. Can I see?' She stood up at the same time he did and her body brushed against his.

'Lily...' He breathed her name, steadied her with his hands and she gave a low moan.

'No.' Her eyes were clouded. 'Seriously, Nik, if we do it again I'll fall asleep and never wake up. The Prince is supposed to wake Sleeping Beauty, not put her to sleep with endless sex.'

He lifted his hand to her flushed cheek and gently stroked her hair back from her face. It took all his will power not to power her back against the wall. 'We could skip the party. Better still, we could grab a couple of bottles of champagne and have our own party here by the pool.'

'No way! Not only would that upset your father and Diandra, but I wouldn't get to ogle all those famous people. Brittany will grill me later so I need to have details. Am I allowed to take photographs?'

'Of course.' With a huge effort of will he let his hand drop. 'You'd better try the dress.'

The dress was exquisite. A long sheath of shimmering turquoise silk with delicate beads hand-sewn around the neckline. It fitted her perfectly.

She picked up her phone, took a quick selfie and sent it to Brittany with a text saying Rebound sex is my new favourite thing.

People were wrong when they thought rebound sex didn't involve any emotion, she mused. Yes, the sex was spectacular, but even though she wasn't in love that didn't mean two people couldn't care about each other. She cared about making this wedding as easy as possible for Nik, and he'd cared enough not to leave her alone when she was upset.

Somewhere deep inside a small part of her wondered if perhaps that wasn't how she was supposed to be feeling, but she dismissed it, picked up her purse and walked through to the living room.

'I could be a little freaked out by how well you're able to guess my size.'

He turned, sleek and handsome in a dinner suit.

Despite the undisputable elegance and sophistication, formal dress did nothing to disguise the lethal power of the man beneath.

Testosterone in a tux, she thought as he reached into his pocket and handed her something.

'What's this?' She took the slim, elegant box and opened it cautiously. There, nestled in deep blue velvet, was a necklace of silver and sapphire she immediately recognised. 'It's one of Skylar's. I admired the picture.'

'And now you can admire the real thing. I thought it would look better on your neck than in a catalogue.' He took it from her and fastened it round her neck while she pressed her fingers to her throat self-consciously.

'When did you buy this?'

'I had it flown in after you admired her pot.'

'You had it *flown in*? From New York? There wasn't time.'

'This piece was in a gallery in London.'

'Unbelievable. So extravagant.'

'Then why are you smiling?'

'Because I like pretty things and Skylar makes the prettiest things.' Smiling, she pulled her phone out of her purse again. 'I need to capture the moment so when I'm sitting in my pyjamas in a cramped apartment in rainy London I can relive this moment. It's a loan, obviously, because I could never accept a gift this generous.' She took a couple of photos and then made him pose with her. 'I promise not to sell these to the newspapers. Can I send it to Sky? I can say *Look what I'm wearing.*'

A smile touched the corners of his mouth. 'It's your photo. You can do anything you like with it.'

'Skylar will be over the moon. I'm going to make sure everyone sees this necklace tonight. Now, tell me how you're feeling.' She'd asked herself over and over again if his earlier confession was something she should mention or not. But how could she ignore it when it was clearly the source of his stress?

His expression shifted from amused to guarded. 'How I'm feeling?'

'This is a party to celebrate your father's impending wedding, which you didn't want to attend. Is it hard to be here thinking about your mother and watching your father marry again? It must make marriage seem like a disposable object.'

'I appreciate your concern, but I'm fine.'

'Nik, I know you're not fine, but if you'd rather not talk about it—'

'I'd rather not talk about it.'

She kept her thoughts on that to herself. 'Then let's go.' She slipped her hand into his. 'I guess everyone will be trying to work out whether you're pleased or not, so for Diandra's sake make sure you smile.'

'Thank you for your counsel.'

'Ouch, that was quite a put-down. I presume that was your way of telling me to stop talking.'

'If I want to stop you talking, I have more effective methods than a verbal put-down.'

She caught his eye. 'If you feel like testing out one of those methods, go right ahead.'

'Don't tempt me.'

She was shocked by how badly she wanted to tempt him. She considered dragging him back inside, but a car was waiting outside the villa for them. 'I didn't realise there were cars on the island. How do they get across here?'

'There is a ferry, but my father usually takes a helicopter to the mainland if he is travelling.'

'We could have walked tonight.'

'There is no way you'd be able to walk that far in those shoes, let alone dance.'

'Who says I'll be dancing?'

His gaze slid to hers. 'I do.'

'You seem very sure of that.'

'I am, because you'll be dancing with me.'

She felt a shiver of excitement, excitement that grew as they drew up outside the imposing main entrance. The villa was situated on the far side of the island, out of sight of the mainland. 'This is a mansion, not a villa. Normal people don't live like this.'

'You think I'm not a normal person?'

'I *know* you're not.' She took his arm as they walked past a large fountain to the floodlit entrance of the villa. 'Normal people don't own five homes and a private jet.'

'The jet is owned by the company.'

'And you own the company.' It was hard not to feel overwhelmed as she walked through the door into the palatial entrance of his father's home. Towering ceilings gave a feeling of space and light and through open doors she caught a glimpse of rooms tastefully furnished with antiques and fine art. 'Tell me again what your father does?'

Nik smiled. 'He ran a very successful company, which he sold for a large sum of money.'

'But not to you.'

'Our interests are different.'

There was no opportunity for him to elaborate because Diandra was hovering and Lily noticed the nervous look she gave Nik.

To break the ice, she enthused over the other woman's dress and hair and then asked after Chloe.

'She's sleeping. My niece is watching her while we greet everyone, then I'm going to check on her. It's been a very unsettling time.' Diandra kept her voice low. 'I wanted to postpone the wedding but Kostas won't hear of it.'

'You're right, I won't.' Kostas took Diandra's hand. 'Nothing is going to stop me marrying you. You worry too much. She will soon settle and in the meantime we have an army of staff to attend to her happiness.'

'She doesn't need an army,' Diandra murmured. 'She needs the security of a few people she knows and trusts.'

'We'll discuss this later.' Kostas drew her closer. 'Our guests are arriving. Lily, you look beautiful. You will stand with us and greet everyone.'

'Oh, but I—'

'I insist.'

Lily quickly discovered that Nik's father was as skilled at getting his own way as his son.

Unable to extract herself, she stood and greeted the guests, feeling as if she were on a movie set as a wave of shimmering, glittering guests flowed past her.

'This isn't my life,' she whispered to Nik but he simply smiled and exchanged a few words with each guest, somehow managing to make everyone feel as if they'd had his full attention.

She discovered that even among this group of influential people everyone wanted a piece of him, especially the women.

It gave her a brief but illuminating insight into his life and she saw how it must be for him, surrounded by people whose motives in wanting to know him were as mixed up and murky as the bottom of the ocean.

She was beginning to understand both his reserve and his cynicism.

The evening was like something out of a dream, except that none of her dreams had ever featured an evening as glittering and extravagant as this.

What would it be like, she wondered, if this really *were* her life?

She pushed that thought aside quickly, preferring not to linger in fantasyland. Wanting a family was one thing, this was something else altogether.

Candles flickered, silverware gleamed and the air was filled with the heady scent of expensive perfume and fresh flowers. The food, a celebration of all things Greek, was served on the terrace so that the guests could enjoy the magnificent sight of the sun setting over the Aegean.

By the time Nik finally swung her onto the dance floor Lily was dizzy with it.

'I talked to a few people while you were in conversation

with those men in suits. I didn't mention the fact I'm a penniless archaeologist.'

'Are you enjoying yourself?'

'What do you think?'

'I think you look stunning in that dress.' He eased her closer. 'I also think you are better at mindless small talk than I am.'

'Are you calling me mindless?' She rested her hand lightly on his chest. 'Did you know that the very good-looking man over there with the lovely wife owns upmarket hotels all over the world? He's Sicilian.'

He glanced over her shoulder. 'Cristiano Ferrara? You think he's good-looking?'

'Yes. And his wife is beautiful. They seem like a happy family.'

He smiled. 'Her name is Laurel.'

'Do you know everyone? She was very down-to-earth. She admired my necklace and he pulled me to one side to ask me for the details. He's going to surprise her for her birthday.'

'If Skylar sells a piece of jewellery to a Ferrara I can assure you she's made. They move in the highest circles.'

'Laurel wants an invitation to her exhibition in London. I have plugged Skylar's jewellery to at least ten *very* wealthy people. I hope you're not angry.'

He curved her against him in a possessive gesture. 'You are welcome to be as shameless as you wish. In fact I'm willing to make a few specific suggestions about how you could direct that shameless behaviour.'

A few heads turned in their direction.

'Thank you for telling this room full of strangers that I'm a sex maniac. Are you sure you don't want to dance with someone else?'

His eyes were half shut, his gaze focused entirely on her. 'Why would I want to dance with anyone else?'

'Because there are a lot of women in this room and they're

looking at you hopefully. Me, they look as if they'd like to kill. They're wondering why you're with me.'

'None of the men are wondering that,' he drawled. 'Trust me on that.'

'Can I tell you something?'

'That depends. Is it going to be a deeply emotional confession that is going to send me running from the room?'

'You can't run anywhere because your father is about to make a speech and—oh—' she frowned '—Diandra looks stressed.' Taking his hand, she tugged him across the crowded dance floor towards Diandra, who appeared to be arguing with Kostas.

'Wait five minutes,' Kostas urged in a low tone. 'You cannot abandon our guests.'

'But she needs me,' Diandra said firmly and Lily intervened.

'Is this about Chloe?'

'She's woken up. I can't bear to think of her upset with people she doesn't know. It's already hard enough on her to have been left here by her mother.'

'Nik and I will go to her,' Lily said immediately and saw Nik frown.

'I don't think—'

'We'll be fine. Make your speech and then come and find us.' Without letting go of Nik's hand, Lily made for the stairs. 'I assume you know where the nursery is or should we use GPS?'

'I really don't think—'

'Cut the excuses, Zervakis. Your little sister needs you.'

'She doesn't know me. I don't see how my sudden appearance in her life can do anything but make things a thousand times worse.'

'Children are sometimes reassured by a strong presence. But stop glaring.' She paused at the top of the stairs. 'Which way?'

He sighed and led the way up another flight of stairs to a suite of rooms and pushed open the door.

A young girl stood there jiggling a red-faced crying toddler. Relief spread across her features when she saw reinforcements.

'She's been like this for twenty minutes. I can't stop her crying.'

Nik took one look at the abject misery on his half-sister's face and took her from the girl, but, instead of her being comforted by the reassuring strength in those arms, Chloe's howls intensified.

Sending Lily a look that said 'I told you so', he immediately handed her over.

'Perhaps you can do a better job than I can.'

She was about to point out that he was a stranger and that Chloe's response was no reflection on him when the toddler flopped onto her shoulder, exhausted.

'You poor thing,' Lily soothed. 'Did you wake and not know where you were? Was it noisy downstairs?' She continued to talk, murmuring soothing nothings and stroking the child's back until the child's eyelids drifted closed. She felt blonde curls tickle her chin. 'There, that's better, you must be exhausted. Are you thirsty? Would you like a drink?' She glanced across the room and saw Nik watching her, his expression inscrutable. 'Say something.'

'What do you want me to say?'

'Something. Anything. You look as if someone has released a tiger from a cage and you're expected to bag it single-handed.'

There was a tension in his shoulders that hadn't been there a few moments earlier and suddenly she wondered if his response to the child was mixed up with his feelings for Callie.

It was obvious he'd disliked his father's third wife, but surely he wouldn't allow those feelings to extend to the child?

And then she realised he wasn't looking at Chloe, he was looking at her.

He lifted his hand and loosened his tie with a few flicks of those long, bronzed fingers. 'You love children.'

'Well I don't love *all* children, obviously, but at this age they're pretty easy to love.' She waited for him to walk across the room and take his sister from her, but he didn't move. Instead he leaned against the doorway, watching her, and then finally eased himself upright.

'You seem to have this under control.' His voice was level. 'I'll see you downstairs when you're ready.'

'No! Nik, wait—' She shifted Chloe onto her other hip and walked across to him, intending to hand over the wriggling toddler so that he could form a bond with her, but he took a step back, his face a frozen mask.

'I'll send Diandra up as soon as she's finished with the speeches.' With that he turned and strode out of the room leaving her holding the baby.

CHAPTER EIGHT

NIK MADE HIS way through the guests, out onto the terrace and down past the cascading water feature that ended in a beautiful pool. Children cried for a million reasons, he knew that, but that didn't stop him wondering if deep down Chloe knew her mother had abandoned her. The fact that he'd been unable to offer comfort had done nothing for his elevated stress levels, but the real source of his tension had been the look on Lily's face.

He could see now he'd made a huge mistake bringing her here. *Cristos*, who was he kidding? The mistake had been taking her back to his place from the restaurant that night, instead of dropping her safely at her apartment and telling her to lock the door behind her.

She was completely, totally wrong for him and he was completely, totally wrong for her.

Cursing under his breath, he yanked off his tie and ran his hand over his jaw.

'Nik?'

Her voice came from behind him and he turned to find her standing there, her sapphire eyes gleaming bright in the romantic light of the pool area. The turquoise dress hugged the lush lines of her body and her blonde hair, twisted into Grecian braids, glowed like a halo. The jewel he'd given her sat at the base of her throat and suddenly all he wanted to do was rip it off and replace it with his mouth. There wasn't a man in the room who hadn't taken a second glance at her and he was willing to bet she hadn't noticed. He'd always considered jealousy to be a pointless and ugly emotion but tonight he'd experienced it in spades. He should have given her a dress of shapeless black, although he had a feeling that would have made no difference to the way he felt. It was a shock to discover that will power alone wasn't enough to hold back the brutal arousal.

'I thought you were with Chloe. Is she asleep?'

'Diandra came to take over. And you shouldn't have walked away from her.' She was stiff. Furious, displaying none of the softness and gentleness he'd witnessed in the nursery.

The wind had picked up and he frowned as he saw her shiver and run her hands over her arms. 'Are you cold? Crete often experiences high winds.'

'I'm not cold. I'm being heated from the inside out because I'm boiling mad, Nik. I don't think it's exactly fair of you to take your feelings for her mother out on a child, that's all.'

Nik took a deep breath, wondering how honest to be. 'That is not what is happening here.'

'No? Well there has to be some reason why you looked at Chloe as if she was a dangerous animal.'

'This is not about Chloe.'

'What then?'

There was a long, throbbing pause. 'It's about you.'

'Me?' She stared at him blankly and he cursed under his breath.

'You are the sort of woman who cannot pass a baby without wanting to pick it up. You see sunshine in a thunderstorm, happy endings everywhere you look and you believe family is the answer to every problem in the world.'

She stared at him with a total lack of comprehension. 'I do like babies, that's true, and I don't see any reason to apologise for the fact I'd like a family one day. I don't see sunshine in every thunderstorm, but I do try and see the positive rather than the negative because that's how I prefer to live my life. I put up an umbrella instead of standing there and getting wet. Sometimes life can be crap, I know that but I've learned not to focus on the crap and I won't apologise for that. But I don't see what that has to do with the situation. None of that explains why you behaved the way you did in that room. You looked as if you'd been hit round the head with a plank of wood and then you walked out. And you say it was about me, but how can it possibly—?'

Her expression changed, the shards of anger in her eyes changing to wariness. 'Oh. I get it. You're worried that because I want a family one day, that because I like babies, it makes me a dangerous person to have sex with, is that right?' She spoke slowly, feeling it out, watching his face the whole time and she must have seen something there that confirmed her suspicions because she made a derisive sound and turned away.

'Lily—'

'No! Don't make excuses or find a tactful way to express how you feel. It's sprayed over you like graffiti.' She hitched up her dress and started to walk away from him and he gritted his teeth because he could see she was truly upset.

'Wait. You can't walk back in those shoes—'

'Of course I can. What do you think I usually do when I'm out? I'd never been in a limo in my life before I met you. I walk everywhere because it's cheaper.' She hurled the words over her shoulder and he strode after her, wondering how to intervene and prevent a broken ankle without stoking her wrath.

'We should talk about this—'

'There is nothing to talk about.' She didn't slacken her pace. 'I cuddled your baby sister and you're afraid that somehow changed our relationship. You're worried that this isn't about sex any more, and that I've suddenly fallen in love with you. Your arrogance is shocking.'

He kept pace with her, ready to catch her if she twisted her ankle in those shoes. 'It is not arrogance. But that incident upstairs reinforced how different we are.'

'Yes, we're different. That's why I picked you for my rebound guy. It's true I want children one day, but believe me you're the last man on earth I'd want to share that with. I don't want a guy who describes a crying child as an "incident".'

'That is not—*Cristos,* will you *stop* for a moment?' He caught her arm and she shrugged him off, turning to face him.

'Believe me, Nik, I have never been *less* likely to fall in love with you than I am right at this moment. A little girl was distressed and all you could think about was how to extract yourself from a relationship you're not even having! That doesn't make you a great catch in my eyes so you're perfectly safe. I understand now why you have emotionless relationships. You're brilliant at the mechanics of sex, but that's it. I'd get as much emotional comfort from a laptop. Seriously, you should stick to your technology, or your investments or whatever it is you do—' She tugged her arm from his grip and carried on walking down the path, her distress evident in each furious tap of her heels.

He stared after her, stunned into silence by her unexpected attack and shaken by his own feelings. In emotional terms, he kept women at a distance. He'd never aspired to a deeper attachment and when his relationships ended he invariably felt nothing. He had no interest in marriage and didn't care about long-term commitment.

But he really, really cared that Lily was upset.

The feeling was uncomfortable, like having a stone in his shoe.

He followed at a safe distance, relieved when she reached the terrace and ripped off her shoes. She dumped them unceremoniously on a sunlounger and carried on walking. The braids of her Grecian goddess hairstyle had been loosened by the wind, and her hair slithered in tumbled curls over her bare shoulders.

A man with a sense of self-preservation would have left her to cool down.

Nik carried on walking. He walked right into the bedroom, narrowly avoiding a black eye as she swung the door closed behind her.

He caught it on the flat of his hand, strode through and slammed it shut behind him.

She turned, her eyes a furious blaze of blue. 'Get out, Nik.'

He shrugged off his jacket and slung it over the nearest chair. 'No.'

'You should, because the way I feel right now I might punch you. No, wait a minute, I know exactly how to make you back out of that door.' She tilted her head and her mouth curved into a smile that didn't reach her eyes. 'You should leave, Nik, because I'm—oh, seconds away from falling in love with your irresistible self.' Her sarcasm made him smile and that smile was like throwing petrol on flame. 'Are you laughing at me?'

'No, I'm smiling because you're cute when you're angry.'

'I'm not cute. I'm fearsome and terrifying.'

What was fearsome and terrifying was how much he wanted her but he kept that thought to himself as he strolled towards her. 'Can we start this conversation again?'

'There is nothing more to say. Stop right there, Nik. Don't take another step.'

He kept walking. 'I should not have left you with Chloe. I behaved like an idiot, I admit it,' he breathed, 'but I'm not used to having a relationship with a woman like you.'

'And you're afraid I don't understand the rules? Trust me, I not only understand them but I applaud them. I wouldn't *want* to fall in love with someone like you. You make Neanderthal man look progressive and I've studied Neanderthal man. And stop looking at me like that because there is no way I can have sex with you when I'm this angry. It's not happening, Nik. Forget it.'

He stopped toe to toe with her, slid his hand into her hair and tilted her face to his. 'You've never had angry sex?'

'Of course not! Until you, I've only ever had "in love" sex. Angry sex sounds horrible. Sex should be loving and gentle. Who on earth would want to—?' Her words died as he silenced her with his mouth.

He cupped her face, feeling the softness of her skin beneath his fingers and the frantic beat of her pulse. He took her mouth with a hunger bordering on aggression and felt her melt against him. Her arms sneaked round his neck and he explored the sweet heat of her mouth, so aroused he was ready to rip off her dress and play out any one of the explicit scenarios running through his brain.

He had no idea what it was about her that attracted him so much, but right now he wouldn't have cared if she was holding an armful of babies and singing the wedding march, he still would have wanted to get her naked.

Without lifting his mouth from hers, he hauled her dress up to her waist and slid his fingers inside the lace of her panties. He heard her moan, felt her slippery hot and ready for him, and then her hands were on his zip, fumbling as she tried desperately to free him. As her cool fingers closed around him his mind blanked. He powered her back against the wall, slid his hands under her thighs and lifted her easily, wrapping her legs around his hips.

'Nik—' She sobbed his name against his mouth, dug her nails into his shoulders and he anchored her writhing hips with his hands and thrust deep. Gripped by tight, velvet softness, he felt his vision blur. Control was so far from his reach he abandoned hope of ever meeting up again and simply surrendered to the out-of-control desire that seemed to happen whenever he was near this woman.

He withdrew and thrust again, bringing thick waves of pleasure cascading down on both of them. From that moment on there was nothing but the wildness of it. He felt her nails digging into his shoulders and the frantic shifting of her hips. He tried to slow things down, to still those sensuous movements, but they were both out of control and he felt the first powerful ripples of her body clenching his shaft.

'*Cristo*—' He gave a deep, throaty groan and tried to hold back but there was no holding back and he surrendered to a raw explosive climax that wiped his mind of everything except this woman.

It was only when he lowered her unsteadily to the floor that he realised he was still dressed.

He couldn't remember when he'd last had sex fully clothed.

Usually he had more finesse, but finesse hadn't been invited to this party.

He felt her sway slightly and curved a protective arm around her, supporting her against him. His cheek was on her hair and he could feel the rise and fall of her chest as she struggled for air.

Finally she locked her hand in the front of his shirt and lifted her head. Her mouth was softly swollen and pink from his kisses, her eyes dazed. 'That was angry sex?'

Nik was too stunned to answer and she gave a faint smile and gingerly let go of the front of his shirt, as if testing her ability to stand unsupported.

'Angry sex is good. I don't feel angry any more. You've taught me a whole new way of solving a row.' She swayed like Bambi and he caught her before she could slide to the floor.

'*Theé mou*, you are *not* going to use sex to solve a row.' The thought of her doing with anyone else what she'd done with him sent his stress levels soaring.

'You did. It worked. I'm not saying I like you, but all my adrenaline was channelled in a different direction so I'm feeling a lot calmer. My karma is calmer.'

Nik was far from calm. 'Lily—'

'I know this whole thing is difficult for you,' she said, 'and you don't need to make the situation more difficult by worrying about me falling in love with you. That is never going to happen. And next time your little sister is upset, don't hand her to someone else. I know you don't like tears, but I think you could make an exception for a distressed two-year-old. Man up.'

Nik, who had never before in his life had his manhood questioned, struggled for a response. 'She needed comfort and I have zero experience with babies.' He spoke through his teeth. 'My approach to all problems is to delegate tasks to whichever person has the superior qualifications—in this instance it was you. She liked you. She was calmer with you. With me, she cried.'

She gave him a look that was blisteringly unsympathetic. 'Every expert started as a beginner. Get over yourself. Next time, pick her up and learn how to comfort her. Who knows, one day you might even be able to extend those skills to grown-ups. If you didn't find it so hard to communicate you might not have gone so long without seeing your father. He adores you, Nik, and he's so proud of you. I know you didn't like Callie, but couldn't you have swallowed your dislike of her for the occasional visit? Would that really have been so hard?'

Nik froze. 'You know nothing about the situation.' Unaccustomed to explaining his actions to anyone, he took a deep breath. 'I did *not* stay away from my father because of my feelings about Callie.'

'What then?'

He was silent for a long moment because it was a topic he had never discussed with anyone. 'I stayed away from him because of her feelings for me.'

'That's what I'm saying! Because the two of you didn't get along, he suffered.'

'Not because I didn't like her. Because she liked me—a little too much.' He spoke with raw emphasis and saw the moment her expression changed and understanding dawned. 'That's right. My stepmother took her desire to be "close" to me to disturbing extremes.'

Lily's expression moved through a spectrum encompassing confusion, disbelief and finally horror. 'Oh, *no*, your poor father—does he know?'

'I sincerely hope not. I stayed away to avoid there ever being any chance he would witness something that might cause him distress. Despite my personal views on Callie I did not wish to see his marriage ended and I certainly didn't want to be considered the cause of it, because that would have created a rift that never would have healed.'

'So you stayed away to prevent a rift between you, but it caused a rift anyway and he doesn't even know the reason. Do you think you should have told him?'

'I asked myself that question over and over again, but I decided not to.' He hesitated. 'She was unfaithful several times during their short marriage and my father knew. There was nothing to be gained by revealing the truth and I didn't want to add to my father's pain.'

'Of course you didn't.' Lily's eyes filled. 'And all this time I was thinking it was because of your stubborn pride, because you didn't like the woman and were determined to punish him. I was *so wrong*. I'm sorry. Please forgive me.'

More unsettled by the tears than he was by her anger, Nik backed away. 'Don't cry. And there is nothing to forgive you for.'

'I misjudged you. I leaped to conclusions and I try never to do that.'

'It doesn't matter.'

'It does to me. You said that she had affairs—' Her eyes widened. 'Do you think that Chloe might not be—?'

He tensed because it was a possibility that had crossed his mind. 'I don't know, but it makes no difference now. My father's lawyers are taking steps to make sure it's a legal adoption.'

'But if she isn't and your father ever finds out—'

'It would make no difference to the way he feels about Chloe. Despite everything, I actually do believe she is my father's child. For a start she has certain physical characteristics that are particular to my family, and then there is the fact that Callie did everything in her power to keep her from him.'

'You really think she used her child as currency?'

'Yes.' Nik didn't hesitate and he saw the distress in her eyes.

'I think I dislike her almost as much as you do.'

'I doubt that.'

'I'm starting to see why you were worried about your father marrying again. Is Callie the reason you don't believe love exists?'

'No.' His voice didn't sound like his own. 'I formed that conclusion long before Callie.'

He waited for her to question him further but instead she leaned forward and hugged him tightly.

Unaccustomed to any physical contact that wasn't sexual, he tensed. 'What's that for?'

'Because you were put in a hideous, *horrible* position with Callie and the only choice you had was to stay away from your father. I think you're a very honourable person.'

He breathed deeply. 'Lily—'

'And because you were let down by a woman at a very vulnerable age. But I know you don't want to talk about that so I won't mention it again. And now why don't we go to bed and have apology sex? That's one we haven't tried before, but I'm willing to give it my all.'

Hours later they lay on top of the bed, wrapped around each other while the night breeze cooled their heated flesh.

Lily thought he was asleep, but then he stirred and tightened his grip.

'Thank you for helping with Chloe. You were very good with her.'

'One day I'd love to have children of my own, but it isn't something I usually admit to out loud. When people ask about your aspirations, they want to hear about your career. Wanting a family isn't a valid life choice. And I'm happy and interested in my job, but I don't want it to be all there is in my life.'

'Why did you choose archaeology?'

'I suppose I'm fascinated by the way people lived in the past. It tells us a lot about where we come from. Maybe it's because I don't know where I come from that it always interested me.'

There was a long silence. 'You know nothing about your mother?'

'Very little. I like to think she loved me, but she wasn't able to care for me. We assume she was a teenager. What I always wonder is why no one helped her. She obviously didn't feel she could even tell anyone she was pregnant. I think about that more than anything and I feel horrible that there wasn't anyone special in her life she could trust. She must have been so lonely and frightened.'

'Have you tried to trace her?'

'The police tried to trace her at the time but they had no success. They thought she was probably from somewhere outside London.' It was something she hadn't discussed with anyone before and she wondered why she was doing so now, with him. Maybe because he, too, had been abandoned by his mother, even though the circumstances were different. Or maybe because his honesty made him surprisingly easy to talk to. He didn't sugar coat his views on life, nor did he lie. After the brutal shock of discovering how wrong she'd been about David Ashurst, it was a relief to be with someone who was exactly who he seemed to be. And although she'd accused Nik of arrogance, part of her could understand how watching her with Chloe might have unsettled him. That moment had highlighted their basic differences and the truth was that his extreme reaction to her 'baby moment' had been driven more by his reluctance to mislead her, than arrogance.

It was obvious that his issues with love and marriage had been cemented early in life.

What psychological damage had his mother caused when she'd walked out leaving her young son watching from the hallway?

What message had that sent to him? That relationships didn't last? If a mother could leave her child, what did that say to a young boy about the enduring quality of love?

He'd been let down by the one person he should have been able to depend on, his childhood rocked by insecurity and lack of trust. Everything that had followed had cemented his belief that relationships were a transitory thing with no substance.

'We're not so different, you and I, Nik Zervakis.' She spoke softly. 'We're each a product of our pasts, except that it sent us in different directions. You ceased to believe true love existed, whereas I was determined to find it. It's why we're both bad at relationships.'

'I'm not bad at relationships.'

'You don't have relationships, Nik. You have sex.'

'Sex is a type of relationship.'

'Not really. It's superficial.'

'Why are we talking about me? Tell me why you think you're bad at relationships.'

'Because I care too much. I try too hard.'

'You want the fairy tale.'

'Not really. When you describe it that way it makes it sound silly and unachievable and I don't think what I want is unrealistic.'

'What do you want?'

There was a faint splash from beyond the open doors as a tiny bird skimmed across the pool.

'I want to be special to someone.' She spoke softly, saying the words aloud for the first time in her life. 'Not just special. I'm going to tell you something, and if you laugh you will be sorry—'

'I promise not to laugh.'

'I want to be someone's favourite person.'

There was a long silence and then his arms tightened. 'I'm sure you're special to a lot of people.'

'Not really.' She felt the hot sting of tears and was relieved it was dark. 'My life has been like a car park. People come and go. No one stays around for long. I have friends. Good friends, but it's not the same as being someone's favourite person. I want to be someone's dream come true. I want to be the person they call when they're happy or sad. The one they want to wake up next to and grow old with.' She wondered why she was telling him this, when his ambitions were diametrically opposed to hers. 'You think I'm crazy.'

'That isn't what I think.' His voice was husky and she turned her head to look at him but his features were indistinct in the darkness.

'Thank you for listening.' She felt sleep descend and suppressed a yawn. 'I know you don't think love exists, but I hope that one day you find a favourite person.'

'In bed, you are definitely my favourite person. Does that count?' He pulled the sheet up over her body, but didn't release her. 'Now get some sleep.'

The next couple of days passed in a whirl of social events. Helicopters and boats came and went, although tucked away on the far side of the idyllic island Lily was barely aware of the existence of other people. For her, it was all about Nik.

There had been a subtle shift in their relationship, although she had a feeling that the shift was all on her side. Now, instead of believing him to be cold and aloof, she saw that he was guarded. Instead of controlling, she saw him as someone determined to be in charge of his own destiny.

In between socialising, she lounged by the pool and spent time on the small private beach next to Camomile Villa.

She loved swimming in the sea and more than once Nik had to extract her with minutes to spare before she was expected to accompany him to another lunch or dinner.

He was absent a lot of the time and she was aware that he'd been spending that time with his father and, judging from the more harmonious atmosphere, that time had been well spent.

After that first awkward lunch, he'd stopped firing questions at Diandra and if he wasn't completely warm in his interactions with her, he was at least civil.

To avoid the madness of the wedding preparations, Nik was determined to show Lily the island.

The day before the wedding he pulled her from bed just before sunrise.

'What time do you call this?' Sleepy and fuzzy-headed after a night that had consisted of more sex than sleep, she grumbled her way to the bathroom and whimpered a protest when he thrust her under cold water. 'You're a sadist.'

'You are going to thank me. Wear sturdy shoes.'

'The Prince never said that to Cinderella and I am never going to thank you for anything.' But she dragged on her shorts and a pair of running shoes, smothering a yawn as she followed him out of the villa. She stopped when she saw the vintage Vespa by the gates. 'I hate to be the one to tell you this but something weird happened to your limo overnight.'

'When I was a teenager this was my favourite way of getting round the island.' He swung his leg over the bike with fluid predatory grace and she laughed.

'You are too tall for this thing.' But her heart gave a little bump as she slid behind him and wrapped her arms round hard male muscle. 'Shouldn't I have a helmet or a seat belt or something?'

'Hold onto me.'

They wound their way along dusty roads, past rocky coves

and beautiful beaches and up to the crumbling ruins of the Venetian fort where they abandoned the scooter and walked the rest of the way. He took her hand and they scrambled to the top as dawn was breaking.

The view was breathtaking, and she sat next to him, her thigh brushing his as they watched the sun slowly wake and stretch out fingers of dazzling light across the surface of the sea.

'I could live here,' she said simply. 'There's something about the light, the warmth, the people—London seems so grey in comparison. I can't believe you grew up here. You're so lucky. Not that you know that of course—you take it all for granted.'

'Not all.'

He'd brought a flask of strong Greek coffee and some of the sweet pastries she adored and she nibbled the corner and licked her fingers.

'I don't believe you made those.'

'Diandra made both the coffee and the pastries.'

'Diandra.' She grinned and nudged him with her shoulder. 'Confess. You're starting to like her.'

'She is an excellent cook.'

'And a good person. You're starting to like her.'

'I admit that what I took for a guilty conscience appears to be shyness.'

'You like her.'

His eyes gleamed. 'Maybe. A little.'

'There, you said it and it didn't kill you. I'll make a romantic of you yet.' She finished the pastry, contemplated another and decided she wouldn't get into the dress she'd brought to wear at the wedding. 'That was the perfect start to the day.'

'Worth waking up for?' His voice was husky and she turned her head, met his sleepy, sexy gaze and felt her tummy tumble.

'Yes. Of course, it would be easier to wake up if you'd let me sleep at night.'

He lowered his forehead to hers. 'Do you want to sleep, *erota mou*?' He curved his hand behind her head and kissed her with lingering purpose. 'I could take you back to bed right now if that is what you want.'

Her heart was pounding. She had to keep telling herself that this was about sex and nothing else. 'What's the alternative?'

'There are Minoan remains west of here if you want to extend the trip.'

'There are Minoan remains all over Crete,' she said weakly, telling herself that she could spend the rest of her life digging around in Minoan remains, but after this trip was over she'd never again get the chance to spend time with Nik Zervakis. 'Bed sounds good to me.'

CHAPTER NINE

THE CREAM OF Europe's great and good turned up to witness the wedding of Kostas Zervakis and Diandra.

'It's busier than Paris in fashion week,' Lily observed as they gathered for the actual wedding.

Nik was looking supremely handsome in a dark suit and whatever reservations he had about witnessing yet another marriage of his parent he managed to hide behind layers of sophisticated charm.

'You're doing well,' Lily murmured, reaching down to rescue the small posy of flowers that Chloe had managed to drop twice already. 'I'm proud of you. No frowning. All you have to do is keep it up for another few hours and you're done.'

He curved his arm round her waist. 'What's my reward for not frowning?'

'Angry sex.'

There was laughter in his eyes. 'Angry sex?'

'Yes. I like that sort. It's good to see you out of control.'

'I'm never out of control.'

'You were totally out of control, Mr Zervakis, and you hate that.' She hooked her finger into the front of his shirt and saw his eyes darken. 'You are used to being in control of everything. The people around you, your work environment, your emotions—angry sex is the only time I've ever seen you lose it. It felt good knowing I was the one responsible for breaking down that iron self-control of yours. Now, stop talking and focus. This is Diandra's moment.'

The wedding went perfectly, Chloe managed to hold onto the posy and after witnessing the ceremony Lily was left in no doubt that the love between Kostas and Diandra was genuine.

'She's his favourite person,' she whispered in a choked voice and Nik turned to her, wry humour in his eyes.

'Of course she is. She cooks for him, takes care of his child and generally makes his life run smoothly.'

'That isn't what makes this special. He could pay someone to do that.'

'He *is* paying her.'

'Don't start.' She refused to let him spoil the moment. 'Have you seen the way he looks at her? He doesn't see anyone else, Nik. The rest of us could all disappear.'

'That's the best idea I've heard in a long time. Let's do it.'

'No. I don't go to many weddings and this one is perfect.' Teasing him, she leaned closer. 'One day that is going to be you.'

He gave her a warning look. 'Lily—'

'I know, I know.' She shrugged. 'It's a wedding. Everyone dreams at weddings. Today, I want everyone to be happy.'

'Good. Let's sneak away and make each other happy.' His eyes dropped to her mouth. 'Wait here. There's one thing I have to do before we leave.' Leaving Lily standing in the shade, he walked across to his new stepmother and took her hands in his.

Lily watched, a lump in her throat, as he drew her to one side.

She couldn't hear what was said but she saw Diandra visibly relax as they talked and laughed together. And then they were joined by Kostas, who evidently didn't want to be parted from his new bride.

The whole event left Lily with a warm feeling and a genuine belief that this family really might live happily. Oh, there would be challenges of course, but a strong family weathered those together and she was sure that, no matter what had gone before, Kostas and Diandra were a strong family.

Just one dark cloud hovered on the horizon, shadowing her happiness. Now that the wedding was over, they'd both be returning to the reality of their lives.

And Nik Zervakis had no place in the reality of her life.

Still, they had one more night and she wasn't going to spoil today by worrying about tomorrow. She was lost in a private and very erotic fantasy about what the night might bring when Kostas drew her to one side.

'I have an enormous favour to ask of you.'

'Of course.' Her mind elsewhere, Lily wondered if it was time to be a bit more bold and inventive in the bedroom. Nik brought a seemingly never-ending source of energy, creativity and sexual expertise to every encounter and she wondered if it was time she took the initiative. Planning ways to give him a night he'd never forget, she remembered Kostas was talking and forced herself to concentrate.

'Would you take Chloe for us tonight? I am thrilled she is with us, but I want this one night with Diandra. Chloe likes you. You have a way with children.'

Lily's plans for an erotic night that Nik would remember for ever evaporated.

How could she refuse when her relationship with Nik was a transitory thing and this one was for ever?

'Of course.' She hid her disappointment beneath a smile, and decided that the news that they were sharing Camomile Villa with a toddler was probably best broken when it was too late for Nik to do anything about it, so instead of enlisting his help to transport Chloe's gear across to the villa, she did it herself, sending a message via Diandra to tell him she was tired and to meet her back there when he was ready.

She'd settled a sleepy Chloe into her bed at the villa when she heard his footsteps on the terrace.

'You should have waited for me.' Nik stopped in the doorway as she put her finger to her lips.

'Shh—she's sleeping.'

'*Who* is sleeping?'

'Chloe.' She pointed to where Chloe lay, splayed like a starfish in the middle of the bed. 'It's their wedding night, Nik. They don't want to have to think about getting up to a toddler. And in case you're thinking you don't want to get up to a toddler either, you don't have to. I'll do it.'

He removed his tie and disposed of his jacket. 'She is going to sleep in the bed?'

'Yes. I thought we could babysit her together.' She eyed him, unsure how he'd react. 'I know this is going to ruin our last night. Are you angry?'

'No.' He undid the buttons on his shirt and sighed. 'It was the right thing to do. I should have thought of it.'

'She might keep us awake all night.'

His eyes gleamed with faint mockery. 'We've had plenty of practice.' He looked at the child on the bed. 'Tell me what you want me to do. This should be my responsibility, not yours. And I want to do the right thing. It's important to me that she feels secure and loved.'

Her insides melted. 'You don't have to "do" anything. And if you'd rather go to bed, that's fine.'

'I have a better idea. We have a drink on the terrace. Open the doors. That way we'll hear her if she wakes up and she won't be able to escape without us seeing.'

'She's a child, not a wild animal.' But his determination to give his half-sister the security she deserved touched her, and Lily stood on tiptoe and kissed him on the cheek. 'And a drink is a good idea. I didn't drink anything at the wedding because I was so nervous that something might go wrong.'

'I know the feeling.' He slid his hand behind her head and tilted her face to his. 'Thank you for coming with me. I have no doubt at all that the wedding was a happier experience for everyone involved because you were there.' His gaze dropped to her mouth and lingered there and her heart started to pound.

All day, she'd been aware of him. Of the leashed power concealed beneath the perfect cut of his suit, of the raw sexuality framed by spectacular good looks.

A cry from the bedroom shattered the moment and she eased away regretfully. 'Could you pick her up while I fetch her a drink? Diandra says she usually has a drink of warm milk before she goes to sleep and I'm sure today was unsettling for her.'

'It was unsettling for all of us,' he drawled and she smiled.

'Do you want warm milk, too? Because I could fix that.'

'I was thinking more of chilled champagne.' He glanced towards the bedroom and gave a resigned sigh. 'I will go to her, but don't blame me when I make it a thousand times worse.'

Perhaps because he was so blisteringly self-assured in every other aspect of his life, she found his lack of confidence strangely endearing. 'You won't make it worse.'

She walked quickly through to the kitchen and warmed milk, tension spreading across her shoulders as she heard Chloe's cries. Knowing that all that howling would simply ensure that Nik didn't offer to help a second time, she moved as quickly as she could. As she left the kitchen, the cries ceased and she paused in the doorway of the bedroom, transfixed by the sight of Nik holding his little sister against his shoulder, one strong, bronzed hand against her back as he supported her on his arm. As she watched, she saw the little girl lift her hand and rub the roughness of his jaw.

He caught that hand in his fingers, speaking to her in Greek, his voice deep and soothing.

Lily had no idea what he was saying, but whatever it was seemed to be working because Chloe's eyes drifted shut and her head thudded onto his broad shoulder as she fell asleep, her blonde curls a livid contrast to the dark shadow of his strong jaw.

Nik stood still, as if he wasn't sure what to do now, and then caught sight of Lily in the doorway. He gave her a rueful smile at his own expense and she smiled.

'Try putting her back down on the bed.'

As careful as if he'd been handling delicate Venetian glass, Nik lowered the child to the bed but instantly she whimpered and tightened her grip around his neck like a barnacle refusing to be chipped away from a rock.

He kept his hand securely on her back and cast Lily a questioning look. 'Now what?'

'Er—sit down in the chair with her in your lap and give her some milk,' Lily suggested, and he strolled onto the terrace, sat on one of the comfortable sunloungers and let the toddler snuggle against him.

'When I said I wanted to spend the evening on the terrace with a woman this wasn't exactly what I had in mind.'

'Two women.' Laughing, she sat down next to him and offered Chloe the milk. 'Here you go, sweetheart. Cow juice.'

Nik raised his eyebrows. 'Cow juice?'

'One of my friends used to call it that because whenever she said "milk" her child used to go demented.' Seeing that the child was sleepy, Lily tried to keep her hold on the cup but small fingers grabbed it, sloshing a fair proportion of the contents over Nik's trousers.

To give him his due, he didn't shift. Simply looked at her with an expression that told her she was going to pay later.

'Thanks to you I now have "cow juice" on my suit.'

'Sorry.' She was trying not to laugh because she didn't want to rouse the sleepy, milk-guzzling toddler. 'I'll have it cleaned.'

'Let me.' He covered Chloe's small fingers with his large hand, holding the cup while she drank.

Lily swallowed. 'You see? You have a natural talent.'

His gaze flickered to hers. 'Take that look off your face. This is a one-time crisis-management situation, never to be repeated.'

'Right. Because she isn't the most adorable thing you've ever seen.'

Nik glanced down at the blonde curls rioting against the crisp white of his shirt. 'I have a fair amount of experience with women and I can tell you that this one is going to be high maintenance.'

'What gave you that idea? The fact that she wouldn't stay in her bed or the fact that she spilled her drink over you?'

'For my father's sake I hope that isn't a foreshadowing of her teenage years.' Gently, he removed the empty cup from Chloe's limp fingers and handed it back to Lily. 'She's fast asleep. Now it's my turn. Champagne. Ice. You.' His gaze met hers and she saw humour and promise under layers of potent sex appeal.

Her stomach dropped and she reached and took Chloe from him. 'I'll tuck her in.'

He rose to his feet, dwarfing her. 'I'll get the champagne.'

Wondering if the intense sexual charge ever diminished when you were with a man like him, Lily tiptoed through to the bedroom and tucked Chloe carefully into the middle of the enormous bed.

This time the child didn't stir.

Lily brushed her hand lightly over those blonde curls and stared down at her for a long moment, a lump in her throat. When she grew up was she going to wonder about her mother? Did Callie intend to be in her life or had she moved on to the next thing?

Closing the doors of the bedroom, Lily took the cup back to the kitchen. By the time she returned Nik was standing on the terrace wearing casual trousers and a shirt.

'You changed.'

'It didn't feel right to be drinking champagne in wet trousers.' He handed her a glass. 'She's asleep?'

'For now. I don't think she'll wake up. She's exhausted.' She sipped the champagne. 'It was a lovely wedding. For what it's worth, I like Diandra a lot.'

'So do I.'

She lowered the glass. 'Do you believe she loves him?'

'I'm not qualified to judge emotions, but they seem happy together. And I'm impressed by how willingly she has welcomed Chloe.'

She slipped off her shoes and sat on the sunlounger. 'I think Chloe will have a loving and stable home.'

He sat down next to her, his thigh brushing against hers. 'You didn't have that.'

She stared at the floodlit pool. 'No. I was a really sickly child. Trust me, you don't want the details, but as a result of that I moved from foster home to foster home because I was a lot of trouble to take care of. When you face the possibility of having to spend half the night in a hospital with a sick kid when you already have others at home, you take the easier option. I was never the easy option.'

He covered her hand with his. 'Was adoption never considered?'

'Older children aren't easy to place. Especially not sickly older children. Every time I arrived somewhere new I used to hope this might be permanent, but it never was. Anyway, enough of that. I've already told you far more than you ever wanted to know about me. You hate talking about family and personal things.'

'With you I do things I don't do with other people. Like attend weddings.' He turned her face to his and kissed her. 'You had a very unstable, unpredictable childhood and yet still you believe that something else is possible.'

'Because you haven't experienced something personally, doesn't mean it doesn't exist. I've never been to the moon but I know it's there.'

'So despite your disastrous relationships you still believe there is an elusive happy ending waiting for you somewhere.'

'Being happy doesn't have to be about relationships. I'm happy now. I've had a great time.' She gave a faint smile. 'Have I scared you?'

He didn't answer. Instead he lowered his head to hers again and she melted under the heat of his kiss, wishing she could freeze time and make this moment last for ever.

When she finally pulled away, she felt shaky. 'I've never met anyone like you before.'

'Cold and ruthlessly detached? Wasn't that what you said to me on that first night?'

'I was wrong.'

'You weren't wrong.'

'You reserve that side of you for the people you don't know very well and people who are trying to take advantage. I wish I were more like you. You're very analytical. There's another side of you that you don't often show to the world, but don't worry—it's our secret.'

His expression shifted from amused to guarded. 'Lily—'

'Don't panic. I still don't love you or anything. But I don't think you're quite the cold-hearted machine I did a week ago.'

I still don't love you.

She'd said the words so many times during their short relationship and they'd always been a joke. It was a code that acted as a reminder that this relationship was all about fun and sex and nothing deeper. Until now. She realised with a lurch of horror that it was no longer true.

She wasn't sure at what point her feelings had changed, but she knew they had and the irony of it was painful.

She'd conducted all her relationships with the same careful, studied approach to compatibility. David Ashurst had seemed perfect on the surface but had proved to be disturbingly imperfect on closer inspection whereas Nik, who had failed to score a single point on her checklist at first glance, had turned out to be perfect in every way when she'd got to know him better.

He'd proved himself to be both honest and unwaveringly loyal to his family.

It was that honesty that had made him hesitate before

finally agreeing to take her home that night and that honesty was part of the reason she loved him.

She wanted to stay here with him for ever, breathing in the sea breeze and the scent of wild thyme, living this life of barefoot bliss.

But he didn't want that and he never would.

The following morning, Nik left Lily to pack while he returned Chloe to his father and Diandra, who were enjoying breakfast on the sunny terrace overlooking the sea.

Diandra took Chloe indoors for a change of clothes and Nik joined his father.

'I was wrong,' he said softly. 'I like Diandra. I like her a great deal.'

'And she likes you. I'm glad you came to the wedding. It's been wonderful having you here. I hope you visit again soon.' His father paused. 'We both love Lily. She's a ray of sunshine.'

Nik usually had no interest in the long-term aspirations of the women he dated, but in this case he couldn't stop thinking about what she'd told him.

I want to be someone's favourite person.

She said she didn't want a fairy tale, but in his opinion expecting a relationship to last for a lifetime was the biggest fairy tale of all. His mouth tightened as he contemplated the brutal wake-up call that awaited her. He doubted there was a man out there who was capable of fulfilling Lily's shiny dream and the thought of the severe bruising that awaited her made him want to string safety nets between the trees to cushion her fall.

'She is ridiculously idealistic.'

'You think so?' His father poured honey onto a bowl of fresh yoghurt. 'I disagree. I think she is remarkably clear-sighted about many things. She's a smart young woman.'

Nik frowned. 'She is smart, but when it comes to relationships she has poor judgement just like—' He broke off and his father glanced at him with a smile.

'Just like me. Wasn't that what you were going to say?' He poured Nik a cup of coffee and pushed it towards him. 'You think I haven't learned my lesson, but every relationship I've had has taught me something. The one thing it hasn't taught me is to give up on love. Which is good, because this twisty, turning, sometimes stony path led me to Diandra. Without those other relationships, I wouldn't be here now.' He sat back, relaxed and visibly happy while Nik stared at him.

'You're seriously trying to convince me that if you could put the clock back, you wouldn't change things? Try and undo the mistakes?'

'I wouldn't change anything. And I don't see them as mistakes. Life is full of ups and downs. All the decisions I made were right at the time and each one of them led to other things, some good, some bad.'

Nik looked at him in disbelief. 'When my mother left you were a broken man. I was scared you wouldn't recover. How can you say you don't regret it?'

'Because for a while we were happy, and even when it fell apart I had you.' His father sipped his coffee. 'I wish I'd understood at the time how badly you were scarred by it all and I certainly wish I could undo some of the damage it did to you.'

'So if you had your time again, you'd still marry her?'

'Without hesitation.'

'And Maria and Callie?'

'The same. There are no guarantees with love, that's true, but it's the one thing in life worth striving to find.'

'I don't see it that way.'

His father gave him a long look. 'When you were building your business from the ground and you hit a stumbling block, did you give up?'

'No, but—'

'When you lost a deal, did you think to yourself that there was no point in going after the next one?'

Nik sighed. 'It is *not* the same. In my business I never make decisions based on emotions.'

'And that,' his father said softly, 'is your problem, Niklaus.'

CHAPTER TEN

THE JOURNEY BACK to Crete was torture. As the boat sped across the waves, Lily looked over her shoulder at Camomile Villa, knowing she'd never see it again.

Nik was unusually quiet.

She wondered if he'd had enough of being with her.

No doubt he was ready to move on to someone else. Another woman with whom he could share a satisfying physical relationship, never dipping deeper. The thought of him with another woman made her feel ill and Lily gripped the side of the boat, a gesture that earned her a concerned frown.

'Are you sea sick?'

She was about to deny that, but realised to do so would mean providing an alternative explanation for her inertia so she gave a little nod and instantly he slowed the boat.

That demonstration of thoughtfulness simply made everything worse.

It had been so much easier to stay detached when she'd thought he was the selfish, ruthless money-making machine everyone else believed him to be.

Now she knew differently.

The drive between the little jetty and his villa should have been blissful. The sun beamed down on them and the scent of lavender and thyme filled the air, but as they grew closer to their destination she grew more and more miserable.

She was lost in her own deep pit of gloom, and it was only

when he stopped at the large iron gates that sealed his villa off from the rest of the world that she realised his mistake.

She stirred. 'You forgot to drop me home.'

'I didn't forget.' He turned to look at her. 'I'll take you home if that's what you want, or you can spend the night here with me.'

Her heart started to pound. 'I thought—' She'd assumed he'd drop her home and that would be the end of it. 'I'd like to stay.'

The look in his eyes made everything inside her tighten in delicious anticipation.

He muttered something under his breath in Greek and then turned his head and focused on the driving, a task that seemed to cost him in terms of effort.

She knew he was aroused and her mood lifted and flew. He might not love her, but he wanted her. That was enough for now.

It wasn't one night.

They'd already had so much more than that.

He shifted gears and then reached across and took her hand and she looked down, at those long, strong fingers holding tightly to hers.

Her body felt hot and heavy and she stole a glance at his taut profile and knew he was as aroused as she was. In the short time they'd been together she'd learned to recognise the signs. The darkening of his eyes, the tightening of his mouth and the brief sideways glance loaded with sexual promise.

He wore a casual shirt that exposed the bronzed skin at the base of his throat and she had an almost overwhelming temptation to lean across and trace that part of him with her tongue. To tease when he wasn't in a position to retaliate.

'Don't you dare.' He spoke through his teeth. 'I'll crash the car.'

'How did you know what I was thinking?'

'Because I was thinking the same thing.'

It amazed her that they could be so in tune with each other, when they were so fundamentally different in every way.

'You need a villa with a shorter drive.'

He gave a laugh that was entirely at his own expense, and then cursed as his phone rang as he pulled up in front of the villa.

'Answer it.' She said it lightly, somehow managing to keep the swell of disappointment hidden inside.

'I'll get rid of them.' He spoke with his usual arrogant assurance before hitting a button on his phone and taking the call.

He switched between Greek and English and Lily was lost in a dream world, imagining the night that lay ahead, when she heard him talking about taking the private jet to New York.

He was flying to New York?

The phone call woke her up from her dream.

What was she doing?

Why was she hanging around like stale fish when this relationship was only ever going to be something transitory?

Was part of her really hoping that she might be the one that changed his mind?

The happiness drained out of her like air from an inflatable mattress.

She never should have come back here. She should have asked him to drop her at her flat and made her exit with dignity.

Taking advantage of the fact he was still on the phone, she grabbed her small bag and slid out of the car.

'Thanks for the lift, Nik,' she whispered. 'See you soon.'

Except she knew she wouldn't.

She wouldn't see him ever again.

He turned his head and frowned. 'Wait—'

'Carry on with your call—I'll grab a cab,' she said hastily, and then proceeded to walk as fast as she could back up his drive in the baking heat.

Why did his drive have to be so *long*?

She told herself it was for the best. It wasn't his fault that her feelings had changed, and his hadn't. Their deal had been rebound sex without emotion. She was the one who'd brought emotion into it. And she'd take those emotions home with her, as she always did, and heal them herself.

Her eyes stung. She told herself it was because the sun was bright and scrabbled in her bag for sunglasses as a car came towards her down the drive. She recognised the sleek lines of the car that had driven her and Nik to the museum opening that night. It slowed down and Vassilis rolled down the window.

He took one look at her face and the suitcase and his mouth tightened. 'It's too hot to walk in this heat, *kyria*. Get in the car. I'll take you home.'

Too choked to argue, Lily slid into the back of the car. The air conditioning cooled her heated skin and she tried not to think about the last time she'd been in this car.

She was about to give Vassilis the address of her apartment, when her phone beeped.

It was a text from Brittany.

Fell on site, broke my stupid wrist and knocked myself out. In hospital. Can you bring clothes?

Horrified, Lily leaned forward. 'Vassilis, could you take me straight to the hospital please? It's urgent.'

Without asking questions, he turned the car and drove fast in the direction of the hospital, glancing at her in his mirror.

'Can I do anything?'

She gave him a watery smile and shook her head. At least worrying about Brittany gave her something else to think about. 'You're already doing it, thank you.'

'Where do you want me to drop you?'

'Emergency Department.'

'Does the boss know you're here?'

'No. And he doesn't need to.' She was glad she'd kept the sunglasses on. 'It was a bit of fun, Vassilis, that's all.' Impulsively she leaned forward and kissed him on the cheek. 'Thank you for the lift. You're a sweetheart.'

Scarlet, he handed her a card. 'My number. Call me when you're ready for a lift home.'

Lily located Brittany in a ward attached to the emergency department. She was sitting, pale and disconsolate, in a room where she was the only occupant. Her face was bruised and her wrist was in plaster and she had a smear of mud on her cheek.

Putting aside her own misery, Lily gave a murmur of sympathy. 'Can I hug you?'

'No, because I'm dangerous. I'm in a filthy mood. It's my right hand, Lil! The hand I dig with, type with, write with, feed myself with, punch with— Ugh. I'm so *mad* with myself. And I'm mad with Spy.'

'Why? What did he do?'

'He made me laugh! I was laughing so hard I wasn't looking where I was putting my feet. I tripped and fell down the damn hole, put my hand out to save myself and smashed my head on a pot we'd dug up earlier. It would be funny if it wasn't so tragic.'

'Why isn't Spy here with you?'

'He was. I sent him away.' Brittany slumped. 'I'm not good company and I couldn't exactly send him to pack my underwear.'

'What's going to happen? Are they keeping you in?'

'Yes, because I banged my head and they're worried my brain might be damaged.' Brittany looked so frustrated Lily almost felt like smiling.

'Your brain seems fine to me, but I'm glad they're treating you with care.'

'I want to go home!'

'To our cramped, airless apartment? Brittany, it will be horribly uncomfortable.'

'I don't mean home to the apartment. I mean home to Puffin Island. There is no point in being here now I can't dig. If I've got to sit and brood somewhere, I'd rather do it at Castaway Cottage.'

'I thought you said a friend was using the cottage.'

'Emily is there, but there's room for two. In fact it will be three, because—' She broke off and shook her head dismissively, as if realising she'd said something she shouldn't. 'Long story. My friends and I lurch from one crisis to another and it looks as if it's my turn. Can you do me a favour, Lil?'

'Anything.'

'Can you book me a flight to Boston? I'll sort out the transfer from there, but if you could get me back home, that would be great. The doctor said I can fly tomorrow if I feel well enough. My credit card is back in the apartment.' She lay back and closed her eyes, her cheeks pale against the polished oak of her hair.

'Have they given you something for the pain?'

'Yes, but it didn't do much. I don't suppose you have a bottle of tequila on your person? That would do it. Crap, I am so selfish—I haven't even asked about you.' She opened her eyes. 'You look terrible. What happened? How was the wedding?'

'It was great.' She made a huge effort to be cheerful. 'I had a wonderful time.'

Brittany's eyes narrowed. 'How wonderful?'

'Blissful. Mind-blowing.' She told herself that all the damage was internal. No one was going to guess that she was stumbling round with a haemorrhaging wound inside her.

'I want details. Lots of them.' Brittany's eyes widened as she saw the necklace at Lily's throat. 'Wow. That's—'

'It's one of Skylar's, from her *Mediterranean Sky* collection.'

'I know. I'm drooling with envy. He *bought* you that?'

'Yes.' She touched her fingers to the smooth stone, knowing she'd always remember the night he'd given it to her.

'He had one of her pots in his villa—do you remember the large blue one? She called it *Modern Minoan* I think. I recognised it and when he found out I knew Skylar, he thought I might like this.'

'So just like that he bought it for you? How the other half lives. That necklace you're wearing cost—'

'Don't tell me,' Lily said quickly, 'or I'll feel I have to give it back.' She'd intended to, but it was all she had to remind her of her time with him.

'Don't you dare give it back. You're supporting Sky. Her business is really taking off. It's thrilling for her. In my opinion she needs to ditch the guy she's dating because he can't handle her success, but apart from that she has a glittering future. That is one serious gift you're wearing, Lily. So when are you seeing him again?'

'I'm not. This was rebound sex, remember?' She said it in a light-hearted tone but Brittany's smile turned to a scowl.

'He hurt you, didn't he? I'm going to kill him. Right after I put a deep gouge in his Ferrari, I'm going to dig out his damn heart.'

Lily gave up the exhausting pretence that everything was fine. 'It's my fault. Everything I did was my choice. It's not his fault I fell in love. I still don't understand how it happened because he is *so* wrong for me.' She sank onto the edge of the bed. 'I thought he didn't fit any of the criteria on my list, and then after a while I realised he did. That's the worst thing about it. I've realised there are no rules I can follow.'

'You're in love with him? Lily—' Brittany groaned '—a man like that doesn't *do* love.'

'Actually you're wrong. He loves his father deeply. He doesn't show it in a touchy-feely way, but the bond between them is very strong. It's romantic love he doesn't believe in. He doesn't trust the emotion.' And she understood why. He'd been deeply hurt and that hurt had bedded itself deep inside him and influenced the way he lived his life. His security had been wrenched away from him at an age when it should have been the one thing he could depend on, so he'd chosen a different sort of security—one he could control. He'd made sure he could never be hurt again.

She ached for him.

And she ached for herself.

Brittany took her hand. 'Forget him. He's a rat bastard.'

'No.' Lily sprang to his defence. 'He isn't. He's honest about what he wants. He would never mislead someone the way David did.'

'Not good enough. He should have seen what sort of person you were on that very first night and driven you home.'

'He did see, and he tried to.' Lily swallowed painfully. 'He spelled out exactly what he was offering but I didn't listen. I made my choice.'

'Do you regret it, Lil?'

'No! It was the most perfect time of my life. I can't stop wishing the ending was different, but—' She took a deep breath and pressed her hand to her heart. 'I'm going to stop doing that fairy-tale thing and be a bit more realistic about life. I'm going to "wise up" as you'd say, and try and be a bit more like Nik. Protect myself, as he does. That way when someone like David comes into my life, I'll be less likely to make a mistake.'

'What about your checklist?'

'I'm throwing it out. In the end it didn't prove very reliable.' And deep down she knew there was no chance of her making a mistake again. No chance of her falling in love again.

'Does he know how you feel?'

'I hope not. That would be truly embarrassing. Now let's forget that. You're the important one.' Summoning the last threads of her will power, Lily stood up and picked up her bag. 'I'm going to go back to our apartment, pack you a case of clothes and book you on the first flight out of here.'

'Come with me. You'd love Puffin Island. Sea, sand and sailing. It's a gorgeous place. There's nothing keeping you here, Lily. Your project is finished and you can't spend August travelling Greece on your own.'

Right now she couldn't imagine travelling anywhere.

She wanted to lie down in a dark room until she stopped hurting.

Brittany reached out and took her hand. 'Castaway Cottage is the most special place on earth. We may not have Greek weather, but right now living here is like being in a range cooker so you might be grateful for that. When I'm home, I sleep with the windows open and I can hear the birds and the crash of the sea. I wake up and look out of the window and the sea is smooth and flat as a mirror. You have to come. My grandmother thought the cottage had healing properties, remember? And it looks as if you need to heal.'

Was healing possible? 'Thanks. I'll think about it.' She gave her friend a gentle hug. 'Don't laugh at any jokes while I'm gone.'

She took a cab home and tried not to think about Nik.

Sweltering in their tiny, airless bedroom, she hunted for a top or a dress that could easily be pulled over a plaster cast.

It was ridiculous to feel this low. Right from the start, there had only been one ending.

She'd be fine as long as she kept busy.

But would he?

The next woman he dated wouldn't know about his past, because he didn't share it.

They wouldn't understand him.

They wouldn't be able to find a way through the steely layers of protection he put between himself and the world and they'd retreat, leaving him alone.

And he didn't deserve to be alone.

He deserved to be loved.

Through the window of her apartment she could see couples walking hand in hand along the street on their way to the nearest beach. Families with small children, the nice gay couple who owned Brittany's favourite bar. Everyone was in pairs. It was like living in Noah's ark, she thought gloomily, two by two.

She resisted the urge to lie down on the narrow bed and sob until her head ached. Brittany needed her. She didn't have time for self-indulgent misery, especially when this whole thing was her own fault.

She found a shirt that buttoned down the front and was folding it carefully when she heard a commotion in the street outside.

Lily felt a flicker of panic. The cab couldn't be here already, surely?

She was about to lean out of the window and ask him to wait when someone pounded on the door.

'Lily?' Nik's voice thundered through the woodwork. 'Open the door.'

The ground shifted beneath her feet and for a moment she thought there had been a minor earthquake. Then she realised it was her knees that were trembling, not the floor.

What was he doing here?

Dragging herself to the door, she opened it cautiously. 'Stop banging. These apartments aren't very well built. A cupboard fell off the wall last week.' She took in his rumpled appearance and the tension in his handsome face and felt a stab of concern. 'Is something the matter? You look terrible. Was your phone call bad news?'

'Are you ill?' He spoke in a roughened tone and she looked at him in astonishment.

'What makes you think I'm ill?'

'Vassilis told me he took you to the emergency department. You *were* very pale on the boat. You should have told me you were feeling so unwell.'

He thought she'd gone to the hospital for herself? 'Brittany is the one in hospital. She had a fall. I'm on my way there now with some stuff. I really need to finish packing. The cab will be here soon.' Knowing she couldn't keep this up for much longer, she turned away but he caught her arm in a tight grip.

'Why did you walk away from me? I thought we agreed you were going to stay another night.'

'I didn't walk. I bounded. That's what happens after rebound sex. You bound.' She kept it light and heard him curse softly under his breath.

'You didn't need to leave.'

'Yes, I did.' Aware that her neighbours were probably enjoying the show, she reached past him and closed the door. 'I shouldn't have agreed to stay in the first place. I wasn't playing by the rules. And as it happened Brittany needed me, so your phone call was perfect timing.'

'It was terrible timing.'

Discovering that being in the same room as him was even harder than not being in the same room as him, Lily walked back to the bedroom and finished packing. 'So you're flying back to New York? That sounds exciting.'

'Business demands I fly back to the US, but I have things to settle here first.'

She wondered if she was one of the things he had to settle.

He was trying to find a tactful way of reminding her their relationship hadn't been serious.

The ache inside grew worse. She tried to think of something to say that would make it easy for him. 'I have to get to the hospital. Brittany fell on site and fractured her wrist. She's waiting for me to bring her clothes and things and then I have to arrange a flight for her back to Maine because she can't stay here. She has invited me to spend August with her. I'm going to say yes.'

'Is that what you want?'

Of course it wasn't what she wanted. 'It will be fantastic.' Her control was close to snapping. 'Did you want something, Nik? Because I have to ring a cab, take some clothes to Brittany at the hospital and then battle with the stupid Wi-Fi to book a ticket and it's a nightmare. I did some research before the Internet crashed and at best it's a nineteen-hour journey with two changes. She's going to have to fly to Athens, then to Munich where she can get a direct flight to Boston. I still have to research how she gets from Boston to Puffin Island, but I can guarantee that by the time she arrives home she'll be half dead. I'm going to fly with her because she can't do it on her own, but I hadn't exactly budgeted for a ticket to the US so I'm having to do a bit of financial juggling.'

'What if I want to change the rules?'

'Sorry?'

'You said you weren't playing by the rules.' His gaze was steady on her face. 'What if I want to change the rules?'

'The way I feel right now, I'd have to say no.'

'How do you feel?'

She was absolutely sure that was one question he didn't want answered. 'My cab is going to be here in a minute and I have to book flights—'

'I'll give you a lift to the hospital and arrange for her to use the Gulfstream. We can fly direct to Boston and she can lie down all the way if she wants to,' he said. 'And I know a commercial pilot who flies between the islands, so that problem is also solved. Now tell me how you feel.'

'Wait a minute.' Lily looked at him, dazed. 'You're offering to transport Brittany home on a private jet? You can't do that. When I told you I was going to have to do some financial juggling I wasn't fishing for a donation.'

'I know. It sounds as if Brittany's in trouble and I'm always happy to help a friend in trouble.'

It confirmed everything she already knew about him but instead of cheering her up, it made her feel worse. 'But she's my friend, not yours.'

He drew in a breath. 'I'm hoping your friends will soon be my friends. And on that topic, *please* can we focus on us for a moment?'

Her heart gave an uneven bump and she looked at him warily. 'Us?'

'If you won't talk about your feelings then I'll talk about mine. Before we left the island this morning, I had a long conversation with my father.'

Lily softened. 'I'm pleased.'

'I'd always believed his three marriages were mistakes, something he regretted, and it wasn't until today that I realised he regretted nothing. Far from seeing them as mistakes, he sees them as a normal part of life, which delivers a mix of good and bad to everyone. Yes, there was pain and hurt, but he never once faltered in his belief that love existed. I confess that came as a surprise to me. I'd assumed if he could have put the clock back and done things differently, he would have done.'

Lily gave a murmur of sympathy. 'Perhaps it was worse for you being on the outside. You only had half the story.'

'When my mother left I saw what it did to him, how vulnerable he was, and it terrified me.' His honesty touched her but she resisted the temptation to fling her arms round him and hug him until he begged for mercy.

'You don't have to tell me this. I know you hate talking about it.'

'I want to. It's important that you understand.'

'I do understand. Your mother walked away from you. That was the one relationship you should have been able to depend on. It's not surprising you didn't believe in love. Why would you? You had no evidence that it existed.'

'Neither did you,' he breathed, 'and yet you never ceased to believe in it.'

She gave a half-smile. 'Maybe I'm stupid.'

'No. You are the brightest, funniest, sexiest woman I've met in my whole life and there is no way, *no way*,' he said in a raw tone, 'I am letting you walk out of my life.'

'Nik—'

'You asked me why I was here. I'm here because I want to renegotiate the terms of our relationship.'

She almost smiled at that. Only Nik could make it sound

like a business deal. 'Is this because you know I have feelings for you and you feel sorry for me? Because, honestly, I'm going to be fine. I'll get over you, Nik. At some point I'll get out there again.' She hoped she sounded more convincing than she felt.

'I don't want you to get over me. And I don't want to think of you "out there", a pushover for anyone who decides to take advantage of you.'

'I can take care of myself. I've learned a lot from you. I'm Kevlar.'

'You are marshmallow-coated sunshine,' he drawled, 'and you need someone with a less shiny view on life to watch out for you. I don't want this to be a rebound relationship, Lily. I want more.'

Suddenly she found it difficult to breathe. 'What exactly are we talking about here? How much more?'

'All of it.' He stroked her hair back from her face with gentle hands. 'You've made me believe in something I never thought existed.'

'Fairy tales?'

'Love,' he said softly. 'You've made me believe in love.'

'Nik—'

'I love you.' He paused and drew breath. 'And unless my reading of this situation is completely wrong, I believe you love me back. Which is probably more than I deserve, but I'm selfish enough not to care about that. When it comes to you, I'll take whatever I can get.'

'Oh.' She felt a constriction in her chest. Her eyes filled and she covered her mouth with her hand. 'I'm going to cry, and you hate that. I'm really sorry. You'd better run.'

'I hate it when you cry, that's true. I don't ever want to see you cry. But I'm not running. Why would I run when the one thing in life that is special to me is right here?'

A lump wedged itself in her throat. She was so afraid of misinterpreting what he said, she was afraid to speak. 'You love me. So y-you're saying you'd like to see me again? Date?'

'No, that's not what I'm saying.' Usually so articulate, this time he stumbled over the words. 'I'm saying that you're my favourite person, Lily. And I apologise for proposing to you in a cramped airless room with no air conditioning but, as you know, I'm very goal orientated and as my goal is to persuade you to marry me then the first step is to ask you.' He reached into his pocket and pulled out a box. 'Skylar doesn't make engagement rings but I hope you'll like this.'

'You want to marry me?' Feeling as if she were running to catch up, she stared at the box. 'I'm your favourite person?'

'Yes. And when you find your favourite person it's important to hold onto them and not let them go.'

'You love me? You're sure?' She blinked as he opened the box and removed a diamond ring. 'Nik, that's *huge*.'

'I thought it would slow you down and make it harder for you to escape from me.' He slid it onto her finger and she stared at it, dazzled as the diamond caught the sun's rays.

'I'm starting to believe in fairy tales after all. I love you, too.' It was her turn to stumble. 'I knew I was in love with you, but I wasn't going to tell you. It didn't seem fair on you. You were clear about the rules right from the beginning and I broke them. That was my fault.'

With a groan, he pulled her against him. 'I knew how you felt. I was going to force you to talk to me, but then I had to take that phone call and you vanished.'

'I didn't want to make it awkward for you by hanging around,' she muttered and he said something in Greek and eased her away from him.

'What about you?' His expression was serious. 'This isn't a first for you. You've fallen in love before.'

'That's the weird thing—' she lifted her hand to take another look at her ring, just to make sure she hadn't imagined it '—I thought I had, but then I spent time with you and told you all those things and I realised that with you it was different. I think I was in love with the idea of love. I thought I knew exactly what qualities I wanted in a person. But you can't use a checklist to fall in love. With you, I wasn't trying and it happened anyway. I need to change. I need to find a new way to protect myself.'

'I don't want you to change. I want you to stay exactly the way you are. And I can be that layer of protection that you don't seem to be able to cultivate for yourself.'

'You're volunteering to be my armour?'

'If that means spending the rest of my life plastered against you that sounds good to me.' His mouth was on hers, his hands in her hair and it occurred to her that this level of happiness was something she'd dreamed about.

'I was going to spend August on Puffin Island with Brittany.'

'Spend it with me. I have to go to New York next week, but we can fly Brittany to Maine first. I have friends in Bar Harbor. That's close to Puffin Island. While I'm at my meeting in New York you could visit Skylar. Then we can fly to San Francisco and take some time to plan our life together. I can't promise you a fairy tale, but I can promise the best version of reality I can give you.'

'You want me to go with you to San Francisco? What job would I do there?'

'Well, they have museums, but I was thinking about that.' He brushed away salty tears from her cheeks. 'How would you feel about spending more time on your ceramics?'

'I can't afford it.'

'You can now, because what's mine is yours.'

'I couldn't do that. I don't ever want our relationship to be about money.' She flushed awkwardly. 'It's important I keep custody of my rusty bike so I'm going to need you to sign one of those pre-nuptial agreement things so I'm protected in case you try and snatch everything I own.'

He was smiling. 'Pre-nuptial agreements are for people whose relationships aren't going to last and ours will last, *theé mou.*' Those words and the sincerity in his voice finally convinced her that he meant it, but even that wasn't enough to convince her this was really happening.

'But seriously, what do I bring to this relationship?'

'You bring optimism and a sunny outlook on life that no amount of money can buy. You're an inspiration, Lily. You're willing to trust, despite having been hurt. You have never known a stable family, and yet that hasn't stopped you believing that such a thing is possible for you. You live the life you believe in and I want to live that life with you.'

'So I bring a smile and you bring a private jet? I'm not sure that's an equitable deal. Not that I know much about deals. That's your area of expertise.'

'It is, and I can tell you I'm definitely the winner in this particular deal.' He kissed her again. 'The money is going to mean I can spoil you, and I intend to do that so you'd better get used to it. I thought being an artist would fit nicely round having babies. We'll split our time between the US and Greece. Several times a year we'll come back here and stay in Camomile Villa so we can see Diandra and Chloe and you can have your fill of Minoan remains.'

'Wait. You're moving too quickly for me. You have to understand I'm still getting used to the idea that I've gone from owning a bicycle, to having part ownership of a private jet.'

'And five homes.'

'I have real-estate whiplash. But at least I know how to clean them!' But it was something else he'd said that had really caught her attention. 'A moment ago—did you mention babies?'

'Have I misunderstood what you want? Am I sounding too traditional? Right now my Greek DNA is winning out,' he groaned, 'but what I'm trying to say is you can do anything you like. Make any choices you like, as long as I'm one of them.'

'You'd want babies?' She flung her arms round him. 'You haven't misunderstood. Having babies is my dream.'

His mouth was on hers. 'How do you feel about starting

right away? I used to consider myself progressive, but all I can think about is how cute you're going to look when you're pregnant so I have a feeling I may have regressed to Neanderthal man. Does that bother you?'

'I've already told you I studied *homo neanderthalensis*,' Lily said happily. 'I'm an expert.'

'You have no idea how relieved I am to hear that.' Ignoring the heat, the size of the room and the width of the bed, he pulled her into his arms and Lily discovered it was possible to kiss and cry at the same time.

'We've had fun sex, athletic sex and angry sex—what sort of sex is this? Baby sex?'

'Love sex,' he said against her mouth. 'This is love sex. And it's going to be better than anything that's gone before.'

* * * * *

If you loved this story, and want to read more about Brittany, don't miss Sarah Morgan's
SOME KIND OF WONDERFUL,
available soon from HQN!

'Don't apologise.' Asim breathed deep, filling the void in his lungs. 'I don't like it when you're...meek.'

The words surprised him as much as her. He felt the shock of the admission reverberate through him even as he saw it ripple across her face.

He didn't approve of the way she argued with him, refusing to be silenced after he'd made a decision. It happened daily when she tried to wheedle access to records or palace staff or ancient pavilions that had been locked up as unsafe generations ago. Yet seeing her hesitant and downcast was like watching a bright light dim.

For long seconds their eyes locked. Long enough for him to notice that in the syrupy late-afternoon light her eyes flashed with shards of gold.

Slowly her mouth eased into a crooked smile.

'In that case, Asim...' Jacqui paused over his name as if savouring it '...I promise not to be meek with you again.'

She scooped up her towel and wrapped it around herself, hurrying towards her room. But her chin was up and her shoulders back and, despite his body's howl of protest at her departure, Asim found himself smiling.

DESERT VOWS

*Two powerful desert princes…
and the only women who can tame them*

Sultan Asim of Jazeer and Sheikh Tariq of Al-Sarath are both bound by honour, duty and tradition. They've always known they must marry, but it will be for the good of their kingdoms—*not* for love. Yet now two very different women threaten the vows Asim and Tariq have always sworn to uphold.

As desire burns hotter than the desert sand can these powerful men withstand the heat of temptation?

Find out in:

THE SULTAN'S HAREM BRIDE
February 2015

THE SHEIKH'S PRINCESS BRIDE
April 2015

THE SULTAN'S HAREM BRIDE

BY
ANNIE WEST

All rights reserved including the right of reproduction in whole
or in part in any form. This edition is published by arrangement with
Harlequin Books S.A.

This is a work of fiction. Names, characters, places, locations and
incidents are purely fictional and bear no relationship to any real
life individuals, living or dead, or to any actual places, business
establishments, locations, events or incidents. Any resemblance is
entirely coincidental.

This book is sold subject to the condition that it shall not, by way of
trade or otherwise, be lent, resold, hired out or otherwise circulated
without the prior consent of the publisher in any form of binding or
cover other than that in which it is published and without a similar
condition including this condition being imposed on the subsequent
purchaser.

® and ™ are trademarks owned and used by the trademark owner
and/or its licensee. Trademarks marked with ® are registered with the
United Kingdom Patent Office and/or the Office for Harmonisation in
the Internal Market and in other countries.

Published in Great Britain 2015
by Mills & Boon, an imprint of Harlequin (UK) Limited,
Eton House, 18-24 Paradise Road, Richmond, Surrey, TW9 1SR

© 2015 Annie West

ISBN: 978-0-263-25049-7

Harlequin (UK) Limited's policy is to use papers that are natural,
renewable and recyclable products and made from wood grown in
sustainable forests. The logging and manufacturing processes conform
to the legal environmental regulations of the country of origin.

Printed and bound in Spain
by CPI, Barcelona

Growing up near the beach, **Annie West** spent lots of time observing tall, burnished lifeguards—early research! Now she spends her days fantasising about gorgeous men and their love-lives. Annie has been a reader all her life. She also loves travel, long walks, good company and great food.

You can contact her at annie@annie-west.com or PO Box 1041, Warners Bay, NSW 2282, Australia.

**Other titles by Annie West available
in eBook from www.millsandboon.co.uk:**

DAMASO CLAIMS HIS HEIR
AN ENTICING DEBT TO PAY
  (At His Service)
IMPRISONED BY A VOW
CAPTIVE IN THE SPOTLIGHT
DEFYING HER DESERT DUTY
UNDONE BY HIS TOUCH
  (Dark-Hearted Tycoons)
GIRL IN THE BEDOUIN TENT
  (Sinful Desert Nights)
PRINCE OF SCANDAL
PASSION, PURITY AND THE PRINCE
  (The Weight of the Crown)
SCANDAL: HIS MAJESTY'S LOVE-CHILD
  (Dark-Hearted Desert Men)
FORGOTTEN MISTRESS, SECRET LOVE-CHILD
  (Regally Wed)
THE SAVAKIS MISTRESS
  (Tall, Dark and Dangerously Sexy)
BLACKMAILED BRIDE, INNOCENT WIFE
  (Innocent Wives)
THE DESERT KING'S PREGNANT BRIDE
  (Unexpected Babies)

To my dear friend Karen
with love and thanks, not just for now, but always.

CHAPTER ONE

'Give it up, Jack. This is a wild goose chase.' Imran's voice came over the hubbub of vehicles, people and livestock thronging the pre-election cavalcade.

'No!' Jacqui shook her head. 'You'll see. It will be worth it.'

It *had* to be worth it. They had a chance to interview one of the world's most hard to meet opposition leaders, an inspirational reformer the authorities would do anything to silence. It was an opportunity not to be missed.

Yet uneasiness stirred. This jammed street was strangely familiar, as if she'd been here before. The pungent aromas of dust, sweat, spices and dung teased her nostrils. A disturbing sense of *déjà vu* made her pause.

Jacqui swung round, looking for Imran's familiar face.

Anxiety speared her. Her nape prickled. 'Imran?'

'Right here, Jack.' She spun round and there he was, large as life, his camera over one shoulder, his laughing eyes narrowed against the sun.

Relief thudded in her chest. For a moment Jacqui had feared… Feared what? Her train of thought dissolved.

'This is a long shot, despite the tip-off,' she said. 'If you'd rather go to the hotel, I'll try to locate him then call you.'

Imran's expression didn't change.

Had she spoken aloud or just thought about it? Confused, she lifted a hand to her hot forehead. Everything felt unreal, strangely distant. Even the faces of the people around them seemed blurred.

All except Imran.

Jacqui blinked and tried to focus. The job. The lead. This would be their best story yet. Their news editor wouldn't believe it if they came in with this exclusive.

It was an opportunity to reveal the truth about this oppressive regime. Then world powers could no longer plead ignorance and turn a blind eye to the violence.

'Come on, Jack. Don't dawdle.' Imran strode ahead, forging easily through the packed street.

Jacqui tried to follow but her feet seemed stuck to the ground, her limbs weighted. With a supreme effort, she struggled forward a pace. Just one. Around her the crowd slowed too, like a film moving frame by frame.

All except Imran, striding through the barely moving people. Each step took him further away.

Jacqui opened her mouth to call his name, urge him to stop. The *déjà vu* was back, stronger this time. Her flesh crawled in horrified premonition. Her throat constricted, silencing her strained vocal cords.

Helplessly she watched him meld into the crowd.

Then it came. The nameless thing she'd been expecting without knowing. A soundless judder of vibration on the air. A quake that made the ground beneath her feet shudder and heave.

Then the cataclysmic roar. A deafening well of sound, spiralling round her. So loud her ears rang and kept on ringing.

Finally her stasis broke. She ran, lungs pumping, breath tearing in her throat. Still she couldn't call out.

She slammed to a stop. Imran's camera lay on the ground, its shattered lens glinting in dusty sunlight. He held it fast, fingers clamped round it.

Jacqui knelt, her brain trying to make sense of the picture before her. The ungainly jumble of limbs, the shapes impossible to comprehend. An unholy cocktail of dust and bright-red liquid spread all round her, soaking the ground, filling her nostrils.

She put out a hand to touch what had once been the man she knew better than anyone. A man fit, whole...

Finally she found her voice. It rose, filling the air, an anguished, wordless scream.

Asim stalked the empty corridor and out into a moonlit courtyard. Annoyance lengthened his stride and made the blood steam in his veins.

What had possessed his ambassador to suggest that woman as a possible bride? Or hint to the old Emir that he should bring his niece? This should have been a simple state visit to finalise an energy venture between their countries. Instead the Emir's visit to Jazeer was a potential diplomatic disaster.

Asim strode past the scented garden and into another passage. The sprawling old palace provided plenty of space to be alone with his impatience.

Not as good as the freedom of a four-wheel drive on the desert dunes but that luxury was denied him. Asim had to remain here to play host to the Emir and his unwanted niece in the morning. He'd need to soothe the Emir's pride but make it clear his choice of bride lay elsewhere.

He grimaced. If beauty were all he required, she might have been a contender. She was one of the most flagrantly gorgeous women he'd met.

That was saying something. In his youth, Asim had acquired a well-deserved reputation as a connoisseur of beautiful women. Blonde, brunette, redhead, slim, curvaceous, tall or petite. He'd enjoyed them all.

Did they believe he'd be so seduced by her charms he'd ignore her character? She'd been demure tonight. But Asim knew that in the exclusive holiday hideaways of the mega-wealthy she had an unrivalled reputation for pleasure, for multiple lovers and chemical stimulants.

Only a fool could think he'd turn a blind eye to that!

The woman Asim married would become wife to the Sultan of Jazeer. She would be intelligent, beautiful and capable; a devoted mother. She would be a woman of dignity and self-control, of impeccable standards. Not the subject of salacious gossip.

His wife would be everything his mother hadn't been.

Oh, she had been beautiful. And loving, in her own way.

An icy finger tracked down Asim's spine.

Fate preserve him from *love*!

That curse had destroyed his parents and now his sister. He had no intention of suffering a similar destiny.

He drew a slow breath. He'd hoped to keep his decision to acquire a wife quiet. Now speculation would be rife and he'd be bombarded with hopeful candidates.

A sharp cry brought Asim up short. He lifted his head, searching for its source.

It came again, an unearthly shriek on the still night air, raising the hairs on the back of his neck. It wasn't a peacock, or a wild dog beyond the city outskirts.

Asim strode down an arched passageway to an even older building, long disused. The cry sounded again as he emerged into a space wilder and less formal than the other gardens.

He knew this place. As a boy he'd listened to the old stories of tragedy and avidly watched for proof that the garden was, indeed, haunted.

Now, at thirty-five, Asim didn't consider the possibility of meeting a ghost. He was more concerned with the flesh and blood source of that scream.

It came again. High, anguished, wordless. Its tenor of distress catapulted him forward. As he neared the pavilion on the far side of the garden a glow caught his eye and adrenalin pumped hard in his blood.

Asim sprinted towards the light. Fire in the centuries-old building would be disastrous.

Yet there was no scent of smoke, no crackle of burning. Perhaps the flames hadn't taken hold.

He slammed through a wide entrance, past dark, empty rooms to a doorway spilling light.

He jerked to a stop, heart pounding. The peace of the scene before him, after the turmoil he'd expected, flummoxed him for a moment and he strove to take it in.

An old-fashioned hanging lamp sent shafts of multi-hued light across the wall murals and inlaid floor. The place was bare of furniture but for a small table, a carved chest and a bed.

It was the bed that caught his attention. He stared, disbelieving, at the woman who lay naked upon it.

Asim sucked in an astonished breath, his fingers curling around the door jamb.

Lamplight painted her bare flesh in delicate rainbow hues. Gold across her long, slim legs, lithe and restless. Rose at her hips, over her smooth, pale belly and the V of reddish-brown pubic hair. Lavender across the perfect swell of firm, high breasts that shook and trembled with her agitated breathing. Pale azure over her neat jaw, slender throat and contorting mouth.

Surprise, curiosity and a surge of raw masculine hunger warred within him at the enticing picture she presented.

With her arms raised high above her head on a satin cushion, she looked like some delectable feast laid out for his enjoyment—an invitation to touch and taste.

Sexual arousal slammed into him, congealing thought.

Asim swallowed as his groin tightened and his blood rushed faster. His gaze drifted from the swell of her dainty breasts to her shifting thighs.

Heaving an unsteady breath, he grappled back to sanity and strode forward.

Spikes of damp, tawny hair splayed over the pillow as she tossed her head. Her throat worked and a soft mew emerged from her lips. It had to be a sound of distress, yet some primitive part of him wondered if that was how she'd sound in the throes of passion.

Heat rose from her. Asim felt it as he stood beside her.

Deliberately he clasped his hands behind his back, conquering the base instinct that made him want to reach out.

He should comfort her. But the compulsion to touch sprang as much from the need to know if her creamy skin was as soft as it looked.

Asim scrubbed an unsteady palm over his face, forcing down impulses that could only be dishonourable.

Who was this woman?

What was she doing in the most ancient part of his palace, alone and naked?

Despite the gravity of his royal position some women had gone to inordinate lengths to offer themselves to him.

Was she one of them? Was this her idea of a tantalising new twist on the age-old mating ritual?

His body's reaction showed she'd succeeded in piquing his interest.

In his wilder youth he might have been tempted by such a tactic. But it was a wife he sought now, not a one-night stand.

Inevitably his gaze was drawn back to her body. She was slim almost to the point of thinness. A model? She was tall enough. Yet she was completely unadorned—not even a ring or gold chain.

He didn't know a woman who didn't wear some jewellery, even if just stud earrings.

She was so…bare.

Yet there was no mistaking the powerful tide of desire sweeping him. The dragging weight in his lower body. His heartbeat's thrum of anticipation. His rapid breathing.

Asim stretched out his arm. He opened his hand a metre above her and imagined he felt the scrape of one pebbled nipple tease his palm. A jolt of electricity rushed from his fingers, up his arm and straight to his groin. He fisted his hand against the urge to reach down and cup her *there*.

Abruptly she moved, scrabbling at the sides of the bed. Her head twisted. She drew an enormous breath that hollowed her belly and thrust her tip-tilted breasts towards him as a muffled sob broke from her lips.

Asim reared back, shame and disbelief scalding him. He'd been acting the voyeur!

'It's time to wake up,' he said, his voice assuming a familiar tone of firm command.

Asim's mouth twisted. If only he'd had such command over his own cruder impulses.

He opened his mouth to repeat the order when she gasped, writhed and screamed at the top of her lungs.

'It's time to wake…time to wake.' The words circled Jacqui's brain like a half-forgotten mantra. The ground shook again, heaving her up and down, a boneless rag doll. She didn't run. Where could she escape to? Why should she? She'd led Imran into danger and now he was dead. How could she even think about surviving herself?

Heat suffused her like an embrace, at odds with the chill in her bones. Still she clung to Imran's hand, wishing she could rewind time. For nothing, she knew, could bring him back from this.

But that voice was insistent, ordering her to pay attention, ordering her to…wake.

The deafening sound stopped abruptly. It took Jacqui a while to realise it was the sound of her own screams. Her throat was raw and her chest heaved. Fear clawed, though the worst panic began to subside.

She'd done this before. She knew what it meant. She'd had one of her dreams. Even as she told herself *this* was reality, this quiet, peaceful place, her brain buzzed anxiously.

'That's better.' It was the voice again. Low, soothing, so deep it shivered right to the core of her. 'You're awake now, aren't you?'

For a moment longer she could swear she grasped Imran's still-warm hand. Then the sensation faded.

He was gone. Grief scooped a hollow in her belly.

Tears flooded her eyes and spilled down her cheeks. Stupid, helpless tears that came too easily now. She rubbed her hand across her face, smearing wetness, trying to scrub it away. A choking ball of emotion lodged in her throat and she swallowed clumsily, heedless of the pain.

Something shifted. The heat on her shoulders abated. Belatedly she realised it was the imprint of long fingers, the touch of hard palms.

The shreds of nightmare faded as realisation hit. Jacqui's eyes snapped open on a pulse of shock.

She wasn't alone.

Ebony eyes, deep set beneath slashing straight brows, met hers. They were so intent, so piercing, she saw nothing else as she gasped in astonishment.

A frown puckered his broad forehead and tiny lines clustered at the corners of his eyes, giving him the look of a man who spent time outdoors in the sun.

Jacqui blinked, unable to do more than digest the fact she was awake *with a total stranger.*

A stranger who transfixed her with his gleaming, dark gaze.

Yet even as she thought it a memory stirred, a hint of recognition. He seemed…familiar.

'You're all right now?' The concern in his voice was echoed in his scrutiny and the line of his compressed lips.

Or was that annoyance?

Muddled and disorientated from the nightmare, she nevertheless felt no fear, sensed no threat. Surely it had been his voice, that warm, deep rumble that had dragged her out of horror and back to reality? Hazily, she registered relief she wasn't alone in the dark.

Jacqui struggled to breathe deeply, gratefully dragging air into her lungs, anything to dispel the sharp, rusty tang of Imran's blood from her nostrils.

The man stood so close she inhaled the scent of his skin, like the deep notes of an expensive cologne, only real, not manufactured. It reminded her of exotic spice and hot, desert breezes.

His breath was warm on her brow and parted lips as she sucked in more air. Long lashes veiled his eyes as his gaze dropped to her mouth. Instantly heat shimmered across her skin and her bloodstream traced fire through her body as if someone had set a match to dry kindling. Her skin flushed and her bare breasts tightened.

Her reaction was so sudden, so shockingly unfamiliar, she simply stared back, stunned, her mind grappling to take in what it meant.

'Yes, thanks. I'm—' Awareness crashed upon her in a flurry of alarm. 'Naked!' she gasped, jack-knifing to sit up.

Dimly she was grateful he stepped back but her focus was on locating the cover she must have flung off. She *hoped* she'd flung it off. That it hadn't been dragged off her by a stranger.

Horror skated skeletal fingers down her spine as Jacqui grabbed for the lavishly embroidered throw that had slipped from the bed. She didn't *feel* like she'd been groped. She couldn't remember anything but the solid, calming warmth of broad hands on her shoulders. But how could she be sure?

Seconds later, with the cover wrapped tight around her overheated body, she swung to face him.

Never turn your back on danger.

The stranger was tall, imposingly tall, which was saying something given her lanky height. Few men made her feel petite. The effect of powerful height was emphasised by the breadth of straight shoulders that filled the doorway. Jacqui's first impression was of hard, lean masculinity. Her second, that he hid something.

His expression was closed, almost stern, yet his gaze belied the sombre attitude. Those eyes looked heavy-lidded and secretive. They remained fixed on her face, thankfully not dropping to where she fumbled, tucking a stray edge of fabric under her arm.

She'd never experienced such an instantaneous physical reaction to any man. That unsettled her almost as much as finding him here, leaning over her.

Jacqui hitched the material higher and set her jaw, trying to control the apprehension tightening her flesh. Even the innocent brush of fabric against her skin seemed evocative, reminding her of her nakedness.

In all her years of travel she'd got packing down to a fine art. It was a sign of her distraction that for the first time ever she'd forgotten to pack her ancient sleep shirt. It hadn't mattered two hours ago, but then she hadn't expected to wake and discover a hero from an *Arabian Nights* fantasy towering over her. Or was he a villain?

'Who are you?' Her voice emerged faint and husky. She hated the tremor in it. She cleared her throat. 'What are you doing here?'

He didn't move yet she had the impression he stood taller, more imposing, if that were possible.

'I believe that's my line.' He paused, brows raised, as if waiting for her to answer.

But Jacqui had learned never to show weakness or doubt. She had a perfect right to be here and she refused to cower as if she'd done something wrong. He was the one who'd invaded her privacy!

Before she could tell him so, he spoke again.

'Who are you and what are you doing in my harem?'

CHAPTER TWO

HIS HAREM?

Jacqui's mouth sagged.

No wonder he'd looked familiar. Yet, in the photos she'd seen of Sultan Asim of Jazeer, his head had been covered.

Jacqui took in the thick, black hair that complemented the burnished bronze of his skin and threatened to flop over his brow. The media had dubbed him one of the world's most eligible bachelors. He had wealth, power and charisma. If the public ever saw him like this, bare-headed and slightly tousled in a way that amplified the potent sexuality of his strong, autocratic features, women would mob him wherever he went.

Though according to Imran plenty of women had already thrown themselves at His Royal Highness.

Imran.

Jacqui pressed a hand to her swooping stomach.

'You should sit.' It wasn't a suggestion but an order, cracking through the tension in the room.

Jacqui pushed back her shoulders and opened her mouth to tell him she was fine.

'The dream was disturbing. You shouldn't exert yourself yet.'

'You know about that?'

'Why do you think I'm here?' His lofty expression made a joke of her fear he might be a sexual predator. What would a man like Sultan Asim want with a woman as plain as Jacqui Fletcher?

Awkwardly, the long coverlet almost tripping her, she subsided on the bed. Silly, how weak her knees felt. But the dream had been so real.

'Are you all right?' He'd moved from the door but kept his distance. Clearly he had no desire to get close.

Grimly Jacqui acknowledged she wasn't in the same league as the sort of women rich, sexy potentates entertained. Nature had skimped on her curves, for a start. Was that why she accepted so easily that his interest wasn't personal?

'I'll be fine soon,' she lied. Experience told her it would take far longer to shake the miasma of that dream. She tugged the covering close.

'Do you get them often?'

Her head snapped up. What did he see as he scrutinised her so closely? Terror? Grief? Guilt?

Instinct urged her to protect her privacy. 'Occasionally.'

'You should see someone about them.'

'You seem awfully interested in my sleeping habits.'

Was that a flush of colour across his cheekbones or a trick of the multi-coloured light?

Jacqui tensed and rubbed her forehead; a headache was beginning. Nerves and stress made her snap at the man who had the power to make or break this venture.

How could she? Everything rode on the Sultan's goodwill.

She wished she could blame her stupidity on being disorientated after the nightmare. Yet Jacqui had an awful suspicion her reaction to the Sultan himself was to blame. He was just… too big, too masculine, too close, though he stood metres away. It was as if the spacious room had shrunk and couldn't accommodate the two of them.

'I'm sorry,' she murmured huskily. 'I apologise.'

'No need. I understand.' His voice was a deep burr that worked its way under her skin and turned her insides to mush. 'The circumstances are…unusual. I should apologise for breaching your privacy. Finding a stranger so close on waking must be disconcerting.'

No mention of her nudity, or his hands on her body.

Yet she had trouble thinking of anything else.

She should be relieved he clearly didn't want to be in her bedroom. What she'd thought was a gleam of sexual interest in those hooded eyes was nothing of the kind.

Yet for some reason tension still eddied between them.

'Now we've got the apologies out of the way...' he paused, as if waiting to be sure they had '...you can answer my question.'

'Your question?' Jacqui felt like a parrot, repeating the word, but her foggy brain was a mess of impressions. Imran. The barely familiar room. The shock of meeting the Sultan. The curious ripple of reaction deep inside when those dark eyes rested on her.

He folded his arms and Jacqui was momentarily distracted as the movement moulded his long robe to a body that was even larger and more powerful than she'd imagined.

'Exactly who are you?'

Amber. Her eyes were a luminous shade of amber. A warm, enticing shade that made him think of sunrise over the desert, or the peachy reflection of late-afternoon light in the pool at his favourite oasis.

Asim had been stunned by that glowing brightness when she'd looked up at him. Those wide-spaced, slightly slanted eyes gave her an intriguing feline look.

He found himself staring.

Better staring at her eyes than her naked flesh, his conscience taunted. He was the lion of Jazeer, ruler, law-giver and leader. He did not ogle defenceless women.

Yet the image of her lithe, streamlined body had lodged in some unrepentant part of his brain and he couldn't shift it.

She hunched her bare shoulders and he realised he was scowling.

'I'm Jacqui Fletcher.' She sat straighter, meeting his eyes

directly, as few in his kingdom did. His pulse pounded as their gazes meshed. That was unprecedented.

Asim waited but she appeared to be pausing for his response. Was he supposed to know her? Something about the name rang a bell but he was sure they'd never met.

She understood his language, had responded in it, though she'd switched to English once she'd become aware of her nudity. Presumably shock had made her revert to her mother tongue.

'How do you come to be here?' His security staff had questions to answer. This section of the palace was well beyond the public audience rooms.

'I was invited.' Her head tipped up, though her gaze slid from his. Instantly he sensed she withheld something.

'Indeed?'

She flushed and Asim watched, fascinated, as colour washed her cheekbones and throat. With her tousled, tawny hair around her shoulders, flushed skin and flimsy covering, she looked alluring yet strangely innocent.

Damn! He needed to focus.

'I don't recall issuing any invitation.'

Again that lift of the chin, baring her slender throat. Did she realise how sexually provocative she looked with all that cream and rose flesh on display and her cover slipping low over her pert breasts?

'It was from the Lady Rania.'

'My grandmother?' What was the old schemer up to now, inviting strange women into the palace? Not just into the palace but deep into the long abandoned heart of it that hadn't been modernised in a century.

Asim sensed intrigue. He had an instinct for it, given the poisonous environment in which he'd grown up.

'Strange she didn't mention this invitation to me.'

A shrug drew his attention back to those bare shoulders, milk-white above the embroidered silk. A dart of heat jabbed low but Asim ignored it. He had more important issues to deal with than sexual awareness.

'Really? I wouldn't know.'

He told himself the husky, nervous voice proved she hid something. But his wayward body was too busy responding to the eroticism of that rough velvet tone.

Asim stood straighter, infuriated by his inability to focus. His day had turned to disaster because of one unwanted female. His night was rapidly going the same way. He fast lost patience.

'Why are you here, Ms Jacqui Fletcher?' A thread of memory tugged in his brain. He knew that name. 'You should be in a guest apartment near my grandmother.'

Something was going on behind his back and he didn't like it. He should have known when the old lady had been so uncharacteristically quiet this last week. His beloved grandmother was many things—opinionated, capable and clever—but never meek. He'd begun to worry she was unwell, that age and grief had finally caught up with her. He should have known better.

'I'm here to research a book. I'm a writer.'

Asim frowned. 'A writer?'

In a blast of realisation, it came to him. He knew where he'd heard of her. He froze, every nerve and sinew stiffening. Incredulity widened his eyes.

'Not Jacqui, but *Jacqueline* Fletcher. Am I right?' He watched her gulp and knew he wasn't mistaken. 'And not a writer, a journalist. Isn't that so?'

Anger spurted in his veins. What was the old woman thinking, bringing a journalist into their midst? Bad enough at any time but *now?* Sheer lunacy! They had too much to lose.

And this wasn't just any journalist. Anger turned to whitehot fury. She'd been there the day Imran died.

Asim drew in a searing breath, forcing back grief. His cousin had been on assignment with this woman. They'd headed out together for an interview. But only one had returned.

* * *

Jacqui clutched the fabric tighter at her chest. The silk kept slipping through her damp palms.

She'd planned to be fully dressed if she met the Sultan. She bit her lip, suppressing an insane urge to giggle. There was nothing remotely funny about this.

Sultan Asim had the power to scupper her project before it got off the ground. How could she convince him of her case, dressed in a bedspread and dazed from her nightmare? He'd never take her seriously.

Instinctively she rose, locking wobbly knees as she pushed the hair from her eyes.

'My by-line is always Jacqui Fletcher.'

'But you were identified as Jacqueline in the official reports.' Accusation rang in his tone and she flinched.

Jacqui knew the reports that he meant. Police reports, diplomatic reports, hospital and media updates. It was amazing the paperwork caused when two foreign news reporters got caught up in a supposed terrorist blast, even if it was in a distant African nation. She swallowed. It felt like broken glass lined her throat, scraping her raw.

'That's my given name but I never use it.'

'No.' His face turned to granite. 'I understand you prefer to be called Jack.'

Imran. Her fragile composure cracked. Imran must have mentioned that to his cousin.

'It's a nickname my colleagues use. Used.' She drew a shaky breath that didn't fill her lungs.

'You were my cousin's partner.' It was a statement, not a question, yet Jacqui had the impression he probed. Did he think them lovers? His gaze scoured so intently she felt it abrade her skin.

Remorse filled her. Here she was in Imran's childhood home, meeting his family, while he…

'We were colleagues, and friends.' He'd been the nearest

she'd had to a best friend. Her throat closed on a searing ball of emotion.

No wonder she'd thought this man familiar. He and Imran shared that superior nose and striking good looks. But, where Imran's eyes had danced with mischief, Jacqui couldn't imagine the Sultan laughing. His brand of handsome was harder than his cousin's. Those features looked like they'd been sculpted into proud, spare elegance by the desert winds.

'I'm sorry for your loss.' Her voice was hoarse. She'd written to Imran's family after he'd died but today was the first time she'd met any of them.

'Thank you.' He inclined his head in a gesture that was at once courtly yet distancing.

As if he didn't want her sympathy. He disapproved of her.

The knot of guilt in her stomach twisted tighter. She couldn't blame him. It was her fault Imran had died. If she hadn't dragged him to what had clearly been a set-up, he'd still be alive.

And she'd still be a journalist.

Brittle ice crackled in her veins and she hugged the bedding tighter. She desperately needed to be alone. But the man before her looked as immoveable as this massive ancient citadel.

Obviously her state of undress didn't faze him. She wished she could say the same. She was used to men, spent most of her time with them, but always fully clothed as one of the guys. Now she felt hyper-aware of her femininity and her nakedness.

'My grandmother invited you *here* to research a book?' Disbelief dripped from every syllable and his sable eyebrows shot up.

'She did.' Jacqui scrabbled for poise. How she wished she wore her charcoal trouser suit, or even the wrinkled cargo pants and long sleeved T-shirt she'd travelled in. Something familiar that would boost her confidence in the face of his imperious disbelief.

Once she'd have taken it in her stride, a challenge to be overcome to reach the next professional goal. But that certainty had been blown apart the day the bomb had exploded. She felt battered and unsure of herself. It wasn't just the trauma of the dream and waking to his disturbing presence. These past months had taken a terrible toll, not only on her career, but her confidence.

She wasn't the woman she'd been.

The realisation stiffened her spine. Hadn't she determined to drag herself out of the dark void of despair and fear? Hadn't she promised she'd make a success of this?

After all, it was all she had left.

She *had* to succeed.

'The Lady Rania was very supportive, and *hospitable*,' she added with deliberate emphasis, ignoring the whisper of her conscience that he had a right to resent her presence. 'She personally invited me to stay here—' her gesture took in the muted beauty of the ancient room '—in the heart of the old palace.' Jacqui forced a smile, as if she couldn't read the Sultan's disbelief. 'I'm most grateful to her.'

His expression grew more brooding.

'Clearly you can't remain.'

Jacqui's smile died. 'But I—'

He gestured in a slashing motion that signified no argument would be brooked. 'This is no place for a guest.'

Jacqui put her palm to her chest where her heart crashed into her ribs. For a moment she thought he'd meant to evict her from the royal residence. That would have been disastrous, the end of all her hopes and plans.

Relief eased the rapid beat of her heart.

'I'm perfectly comfortable, truly.' After some of the places she'd bunked down, this was luxurious, despite the lack of modern facilities.

Again his brows rose. Yet it was true. Besides, the tranquillity here soothed after the bustle of the capital. Even now, months after the explosion, Jacqui was edgy and uncomfortable with crowds or sudden noise.

'Nevertheless, it's not appropriate.' He looked as if he'd

swallowed something sour. It hit her that he might be talking about more than the lack of amenities. Did he think she was going to filch the silver? His stare was disapproving.

Strange how that hurt, though she should have expected it. He clearly blamed her for what had happened to Imran.

But the Sultan's grandmother had been so supportive and kind, first via correspondence and then today in person, that Jacqui had believed she'd be accepted here. She'd let herself believe that in completing the project she and Imran had discussed she could somehow atone for what had happened. Was that even possible?

'I'll have someone move you to another room.' He inclined his head and turned away.

Jacqui's old spirit surfaced. Being dismissed had always rankled.

'That's very thoughtful of you, Your Highness.' She grimaced. It was too late for royal protocol—the man had already seen her naked and screaming her lungs out—yet surely it couldn't hurt. 'Truly, there's no need. I'm just so grateful to the Lady Rania for allowing me such access.'

He stopped in his tracks, his neck and shoulders stiffening. Was he so unused to anyone speaking up once he'd dismissed them?

Imran hadn't talked of his cousin much, apart from occasional references to his focus on duty and royal responsibilities. The man had none of Imran's laughing charm. She guessed he was too self-important to bother charming anyone.

Slowly he turned. His face was impassive, but those night-dark eyes glittered sharply. Jacqui sucked in a breath and fumbled for a better hold on her covering as her fingers momentarily slackened.

Silently she cursed her misfortune in being caught at anything but her professional best. But regret couldn't distract her from the way her body sizzled under his scrutiny. As if he was seeing her naked again.

As if she *wanted* him to!

Abruptly she looked away, stunned. What was happening to her? She didn't react like this to any man. She closed her eyes momentarily, wishing she could wake and find this was all just an extension of her nightmare.

'As you say, Lady Rania is very generous.' He paused as if to let that sink in. 'And I'm sure you'll find a guest suite more than adequate.'

'But...' Jacqui bit the inside of her cheek in rising frustration. Words were her trade. Why couldn't she summon the right ones now she needed them? Had she lost that too, along with her nerve and her best friend?

'Your Highness, it's the private part of the palace I want to research. Not the public function-rooms.' She dredged up what she hoped was a winning smile and forced herself to meet his eyes. 'I'm writing about the women of the palace and their lives here.'

Obviously she'd lost her touch. Far from being persuaded, Sultan Asim's face turned stony. His lips thinned, his nostrils flared and his hand slid to a jewel-encrusted scabbard she hadn't noticed at his side.

Instinctively Jacqui stepped back as the man in the flowing robes transformed from autocrat to warrior in the blink of an eye. He looked dangerous and magnificent. As if he was on a raid into enemy territory.

Except he looked at *her* as if she was the enemy.

Her nape prickled and her breathing shallowed. Instinct told her to run. Her heart hammered.

Surely that curved knife was for show? Sultan Asim was renowned for diplomacy and leadership, not violence. Nevertheless she crept a little further away.

'You intend to write about the women of the palace? And my grandmother *agreed*?' His voice was a bass rumble that made her skin ripple.

Jacqui planted her feet, refusing to back up again. 'She not only agreed, she was enthusiastic.'

What was his problem? He hadn't looked this menacing even when they'd spoken of Imran. This was about something else.

'I find that difficult to believe.' He shook his head, folding his arms across his wide chest. The light of battle disappeared from his eyes, replaced by condescension as he looked down that sexy, arrogant nose of his.

'I assure you, Your Highness, I'm not in the habit of lying.' Anger took her across the room till she stood only an arm's length away. He might be lord of all he surveyed but that didn't give him the right to call her a liar.

She breathed deep then regretted it as she inhaled the hot, enticing scent of his skin. It infuriated her that she noticed it. She fixed her gaze on his face and ignored the predatory glint she saw there. This time, instead of frightening her, it spurred her on.

'When I told your grandmother I wanted to write about the traditions of the harem, she was enthusiastic. That way of life has disappeared and I want to document it.'

'You want to write about women from the *past*?'

'That's what I said.' Jacqui frowned. 'The women of the palace and their lives here. Or perhaps you think women's stories aren't important?' The challenge slid out before she could stop it. She was on a roll, too keyed up to pull back, though she knew she should.

Maybe because living dangerously was far more appealing than the dark nothingness she'd inhabited these past months.

Tonight, for the first time in ages, she felt blood pump in her veins. She felt *alive*.

'History is about more than wars and politics and who runs the country. What happens on a domestic level is important too.'

'Yet you made your name chasing stories about wars and politics and who run countries across the globe.'

Jacqui blinked, rocked by the fact he knew about her career. And by the reminder of all she'd lost.

'I'm interested in a lot of things. My background in news journalism doesn't mean I can't branch into something different.'

At least she hoped it didn't. Nerves made her stomach clench and her palms dampen.

She didn't know yet if she had what it took to make this dream a reality. But it was the only dream left to her. She'd cling to it with both hands. She owed it to her friend and to herself.

The Sultan surveyed her silently, as if she were a curiosity. Because no one ever stood up to him? She was pretty sure royal protocol didn't allow for contradicting the sovereign.

Jacqui drew a shaky breath and prayed she hadn't blown her one chance. She *couldn't* fail before she'd even started.

'Your grandmother is one of the few people who remember such a life here. She's a valuable resource and it would be criminal not to record what she remembers. This is part of Jazeer's culture and history.'

'You're very passionate about this.'

'There's nothing wrong with being passionate about what you do.'

Unless it leads you and your friends into danger.

Unless it destroys lives.

Memory was a sucker-punch to the belly. Her shoulders hunched, the pain almost doubling her over. Here she was, arguing trifles when Imran would never again feel the sun on his face or see his family. Because *she* had led him into danger. Maybe it was only just that she'd lost her career, her old life, as a result. Maybe she deserved to.

A firm hand closed around her upper arm, holding her steady.

'Slow breaths.'

Jacqui closed her eyes and nodded, focusing on breathing out through the pain.

The heat of his big frame radiated against her, counteracting the chill deep in her bones. The reassurance of his grip seeped strength into limbs that had turned limp.

'Here,' he said. 'You'll feel better if you sit.'

Jacqui opened her eyes as he led her to the bed. She almost sighed out loud with relief as she sank onto it. Immediately he withdrew his hand.

'Thank you,' she whispered. 'You're very kind.'

'You shouldn't exert yourself. You were distressed earlier and that took a toll.'

Dully, she nodded. 'I'm...' She shook her head.

What could she say? *I'm a mess right now* might be the truth but she had just enough pride left not to blurt that out. Though after the last half-hour baring herself to this man physically and emotionally she didn't have much dignity left.

'What's so funny?'

Jacqui lifted her face to find him a mere step away, a frown marking that broad, handsome brow.

She bit down a half-hysterical laugh.

'Just myself.'

If she didn't laugh she'd curl up in a ball and sob. She'd probably blown her chance to work on this wonderful project. It had shone like a beacon, dragging her out of the inertia of despair and fear.

'Can you dress yourself?'

Jacqui blinked. Was he offering to do it for her? Her overtired brain boggled.

'Of course.'

'Good. Be dressed and ready to move in ten minutes.' Having given the order, he spun on his heel and strode out of the room, only pausing to be sure the door snicked shut behind him.

CHAPTER THREE

ASIM PACED THE COURTYARD, resolutely dragging his mind from imagining Jacqueline Fletcher discarding her less than adequate covering.

She was an enigma. Passionate and argumentative, not knowing when to give up. Fiery yet vulnerable. That made him want to ignore the danger she represented.

His desire to protect her was equalled by a burning desire of another kind and that was unnerving.

Yet he wanted to blame her for being alive when Imran wasn't.

He spun on his heel.

What was his grandmother thinking, inviting a *journalist* here? Having a professional snoop under the same roof—no matter how large a roof—invited trouble. Any further invasion of his sister Samira's privacy could tip her into a complete breakdown. The doctors hadn't said it outright but it was what they feared.

His stomach knotted. Samira had endured so much because he'd failed to protect her. The knowledge ate at him like acid.

Reluctantly he'd supported her plan to study overseas, only to learn she'd embarked on a passionate affair with a Hollywood actor who was the epitome of shallow self-absorption. But Samira had had stars in her eyes, had talked of marriage and hadn't seen him for what he was.

She'd only found out when he'd been discovered in bed

with his co-star by the woman's wrathful husband. Acrimonious divorce proceedings had ensued, eagerly reported by the press. Scandal grew with stories of multiple infidelities, drug use and even the corruption of minors.

Samira was an innocent party in the morass of stomach-turning revelations about her boyfriend and his co-star. But the press didn't let up. Once the darling of the paparazzi with her stunning looks, aristocratic heritage and high-profile romance, now she was their prey.

She'd sought refuge here. Only he and his grandmother and a few select staff knew that, as well as being heartbroken, Samira had to recuperate physically too. *That* story would never make it into the press.

He'd never known fear such as he'd experienced when he'd thought he might lose her. He'd felt so ineffectual. But this, now, was a situation he could control.

Asim grimaced, raking his fingers through his hair. He'd do whatever it took to keep his little sister safe. He wouldn't fail her again.

Had Jacqueline Fletcher told the truth about writing a book? Or was it a ploy to get a scoop on Samira?

Suspicion ran deep in Asim. How could it not after he'd witnessed the web of lies that had been his parents' marriage? How could he trust the woman who'd been caught up in Imran's death?

Yet he couldn't get a handle on her. He knew she was a respected news reporter. She was Australian, though she'd spent years in Africa, Asia and the Middle East. He knew she'd been with Imran when he died.

Everything else was speculation.

Speculation and an unhealthy dollop of attraction.

Asim shook his head, fed up with his circling thoughts. It was time.

He knocked but didn't enter. Better to be sure she was decently covered. The door swung inwards.

'You!' Those stunning eyes widened and it struck him again how fragile she looked. Was that real or some trick?

Asim stepped inside and she shifted back.

'Sorry,' she murmured. 'You surprised me. I expected one of the servants.'

Is that why she was dressed in drab trousers and a navy top that leached the colour from her face? She wore no make-up and had pulled her hair back in a ponytail.

And still arousal beat low in his belly.

He frowned. Just because he'd seen this woman naked didn't mean he was going to have her in his bed, no matter what his body wanted. He had more sense than to hook up with a journalist. After what had happened to Samira, how could he? Besides, his women were always poised, polished and beautifully dressed, at least to begin with.

Jacqueline Fletcher was…no; not ordinary. Not with those eyes or that mouth. But nor was she sophisticated.

'It's after one a.m. Why wake someone when I can lead the way?' Besides, he intended to keep a personal eye on her.

He scanned the neatly made bed then picked up the single suitcase and laptop bag. She travelled light. His sister had arrived with more than half a dozen cases, probably full of shoes. 'Is this all?'

'Yes, but I'll take the laptop.' She reached out but at a look from him her arm fell.

Why so eager to take the computer? Because she had something there she didn't want him to see or simply a journalist's instinct to protect the tool of her trade? Suspicion stirred anew.

'I can just about manage them both.' He nodded to the door. 'After you.'

She moved with a grace that belied tiredness or nerves. Baggy trousers hid her slender curves but his mind filled the blanks.

Asim turned off the lamp and followed. In the dim corridor it took a moment for his eyes to adjust but he sensed when he reached her. His nostrils twitched as the sweet tang of her perfume reached him. Something fruity and light that made him think of summer.

'I'll lead. Just watch your step. The old tiles are uneven.'

Silently she fell into step.

His mouth quirked. Who'd have thought this woman could be so biddable?

On the other hand, there'd been something curiously refreshing about the way she'd continued to argue her case after he'd stated his decision. Maybe Imran had been right and he was too used to getting his own way now he'd been Sultan so long.

His cousin had liked her, he recalled with a pang that crushed his smile.

'Where are we going?' Her long legs stretched to match his stride. Automatically he eased his pace.

'To a guest apartment where you won't be disturbed.' More to the point, she wouldn't have a chance to disturb anyone else.

'I'm very grateful for you taking the time to see me settled.' She was like a prim little girl reciting polite words she'd been taught.

If only she knew. Asim took her personally to her new accommodation because he didn't trust her. As soon as he had her installed he'd call security to ensure she didn't indulge in any night-time prowling. He refused to compromise Samira's safety.

'Is it in a modern part of the palace?'

'Yes, completed in the last ten years.' When he'd become ruler his one indulgence had been to build a suite of modern rooms for his own use and that of his private guests. The apartments his parents had used were too full of memories he'd rather forget.

'That will be...nice.'

Asim shot her a glance. 'They're very comfortable.'

'I'm sure they are.' She didn't sound enthused.

'But? There's a "but" in there.'

'Of course not.' He waited. Finally she added, 'It's just that I barely had time to explore the old rooms and they were so beautiful. That wall painting, for instance, with the climbing roses and the birds. It was magnificent.'

Curiosity stirred. 'You would like to stay in a place like that? Beautiful but cut off from the world?' It wasn't what he expected.

Moonlight lit her features as they passed through another courtyard. She looked serious, as if considering. 'It has a certain appeal. I'd enjoy it…for a while. But I'm a modern woman. Seclusion would lose its charm and I'd end up feeling trapped with nothing to do.'

'The women who lived there kept busy.'

She turned. 'Pleasing the Sultan? Being available to meet his every need?'

Despite himself Asim's lips twitched. She sounded almost prudish as she skated over the issue of sex.

'You've been reading too much fiction. It wasn't just the lord's wife or lover who lived there, but all his female relatives.'

He gestured for her to precede him into a corridor illuminated by glowing wall lights. Modern marble flooring replaced worn tiles underfoot.

'According to family tradition, that's why my ancestors were so warlike and successful in battle. It gave them an outlet for their frustrations since their female relatives tried to rule the roost at home.'

She slowed and he stopped, turning. Pale before, her face was animated now, delicate colour highlighting regular features. Even her lips looked plumper, rosier.

'There are two sides to every truth. I bet your male ancestors wouldn't have given up the freedom to ride across their kingdom, pick fights with their neighbours and grow rich from trade and war even if it meant living a life of domestic bliss. And as for the right to take the most beautiful girl in the kingdom as their own—'

Asim raised his hand. 'I see you've done your homework.' He shrugged. 'What can I say? Men will be men.' In his family, particularly so. Marauders, warriors and rulers, they had a reputation for fierceness as well as for honour and their impeccable taste in women.

He looked down into wide, seductive eyes and for an instant knew sharp regret that those old days had gone. A hundred years ago he'd have been within his rights to clap an intrusive journalist in irons rather than risk her reporting private family matters.

But he wouldn't have kept Jacqueline Fletcher in a dungeon. He'd have had her in one of those rooms adorned with murals of paradise. The bonds around her wrists would have been silk...

Suddenly she stepped back, her expression wary, as if she read his mind.

Asim blinked and refocused, stunned at his thoughts.

'Not far now,' he murmured, leading the way again.

What had come over him? He'd seen his share of naked women. Some would say more than his share. In his youth sex had been one of his favourite things. It still was, but these past months he'd exercised abstinence, distracted by Samira's problems and the need to finalise the agreement that had been signed tonight.

Maybe that was the problem. Once he'd have celebrated such a significant coup in the arms of a delectable woman. Instead he found himself guarding an unwanted intruder. An intruder with none of the glamorous allure he was used to, yet who provoked lurid thoughts of her naked and responsive in his bed.

He opened the tall entrance door to the Sultan's apartments.

He'd keep Jacqueline Fletcher from his sister. If she decided to wander she'd have to get past him first then his guards. Besides, he couldn't have left her far from anyone after that nightmare. Its trauma had been obvious.

Asim remembered Samira's frantic nightmares years ago when their parents' love-hate relationship had see-sawed violently. After screaming rows and smashing china, was it any wonder his kid sister had had bad dreams? She'd been weak and frightened afterwards.

No, he was doing the right thing, securing this woman close.

'This way.' He walked through the atrium and into a colonnade that ran beside his favourite courtyard.

'This is stunning.' She stopped to stare. 'Absolutely breathtaking.'

Asim followed her gaze. Trees offered shade during the day and the end of the courtyard was taken up by a long swimming pool, illuminated by underwater lights that showed off its aquamarine tiles. Concealed lighting above emphasised the decoratively carved arches of the colonnade, lending a traditional air.

'I'm glad you approve. I had a hand in the design.'

He ushered her through a door into a private sitting room.

'Oh my. It's…'

Asim strode ahead into the bedroom and put her case down. 'Too modern?'

He turned to find her standing in the middle of the room, eyes alight and a hint of a curve on her lips.

His pulse quickened. What effect would a full-blown smile have? He killed the thought, feeling as if it was a betrayal of his cousin.

She shook her head, turning to take in the airy space and the filmy curtains at the windows and pulled back from the bed. 'Absolutely not. It's sumptuous and gorgeous yet comfortable.' Abruptly she fixed him with that disturbingly direct look. 'It doesn't feel like a guest suite.'

Asim shrugged. 'That's what it's designed for.' He didn't add that only his intimates stayed here, one or two close friends and a handful of lovers.

Instantly he imagined her writhing naked on this bed…and she wasn't alone.

Abruptly he gestured to the bathroom, disturbed at the way his mind strayed around her. 'You'll find all you need. If not, call housekeeping. There's a phone beside the bed.' He spun away. 'I'll wish you a good night.'

'Wait!' Her voice came from close on his heels. He turned and there she was, within touching distance.

Clearly he *was* getting too used to being treated with royal distinction. Her nearness surprised him. Outside his family no one but a lover got this close without permission.

A buzz of anticipation filled him. Is that what he wanted from this woman? It was a lunatic idea yet his body's response told its own story.

'You've got my laptop.' She reached but stopped short of grabbing it from under his arm.

For a moment Asim considered refusing to return it. He could search it for anything she'd written about Samira.

Only for a moment. Such an act was beneath him.

Besides, anything she'd written could be rewritten and was probably already saved elsewhere.

With a slight bow he extended the case. 'What would a journalist be without a computer?'

She opened her mouth as if to contradict him then snapped it shut. 'Thank you. And thank you for your hospitality. The rooms are marvellous. I feel very privileged to be able to stay in the palace while I research.'

Asim shook his head, watching dismay tighten her features. 'Enjoy the accommodation but don't thank me so soon, Ms Fletcher. You'll be leaving tomorrow.'

He left before her inevitable protest. Yet he was surprised she didn't scurry after him.

He carried the image of her hurt eyes until he finally slept. Then he dreamed of a slim, pale-skinned woman laid out on his bed, awaiting his pleasure. Her hair was the tawny colour of the Jazeeri lion for which the country was famous and her voice husky as she pleaded for him to do all the things his burning body desired.

Asim paced his grandmother's sitting room. He'd slept badly and dealing with the Emir and his precious niece this morning had sapped his patience. He'd walked a razor-sharp line between hospitality and discretion and hadn't relaxed until he'd finally farewelled his guests. The assembled crowd's gaze had been like a dagger between his shoulders every time he'd even looked at the woman. She, devil take her, had cast him sultry looks and leaned close whenever they spoke.

He sighed and propped one arm on the window embrasure. It was a relief to have the woman out of his palace.

Now he just had one more female to eject.

If only his grandmother wasn't so obstinate about keeping her.

'It won't work. It's naïve to think she can remain if we want to protect Samira.' This time he'd keep her safe, keep control of the situation.

'Of course it will work. I'll see to it. They'll be in separate parts of the palace complex and Ms Fletcher will be busy with her research. She strikes me as a woman of considerable focus.'

Asim looked at the little dumpling of a woman from whom, he suspected, he'd inherited his determination. He wished she'd been here in the palace during his boyhood. She'd have been a welcome addition to their unstable household with her brisk common sense and kind heart. But his mother hadn't taken to her so despite centuries of custom his grandmother had retired to a summer palace in the foothills.

Yet for once Asim felt in sympathy with his departed mother. The Lady Rania, once fixed on an idea, was hard to budge.

He pinched the bridge of his nose, summoning patience.

'It's a recipe for disaster, putting a journalist under the same roof as a beautiful princess who's on the run from the press.'

'Ms Fletcher isn't that sort of journalist. She's not interested in kiss and tell affairs. She's here for a *real* story. I told you about the book she wants to write.'

Yes, he'd heard about the book. The table near his grandmother just happened to be littered with articles Jacqueline Fletcher had published about women's lives in Africa and East Asia. Clearly the woman was a workaholic. Given her demanding news job, he wondered how she'd found time.

'You really think there's a difference between a "news" journalist and the paparazzi?' He couldn't believe her naivety. 'Let either one sniff a story and they'll be onto it in a flash. Right now, Samira is news.'

'Samira is always going to be news.' His grandmother folded her arms. 'With her wealth and looks it can't be avoided. It's a matter of managing that.'

'You think having that woman here will help her manage the fallout?' He couldn't believe what he heard.

His grandmother fixed him with a shrewd stare. 'I think the two matters are quite separate. I see no reason for you to be concerned. I've already had a security assessment done on Ms Fletcher.'

'You have?' So his grandmother hadn't been as blindly trusting as he'd thought.

She nodded. 'Her life's an open book, and most of the pages are about work.' She paused. 'This project is important to her. She wants very strongly to make it a success. She won't jeopardise that by biting the hand that feeds her.'

Asim choked back a comment about taking the money and running. The press would pay handsomely for candid snaps of his sister right now, and even more for an insider's story on her state of mind, true or not.

'But *why* write this book? She's used to the quick adrenalin fix and high profile of current affairs. Why walk away from that at just twenty-eight? She's on the way to big things.' He'd done more checking of his own last night. 'It's too convenient.'

'You're too concerned with conspiracy theories, Asim. She and I have corresponded for some time. Even before Imran…' The old lady sucked in a shuddering breath. Her fingers knotted in her lap. 'He'd suggested she contact me and I believe she views it as her duty to your cousin to see it through.'

'Duty?' Asim bit out. 'It's a little late for that now he's dead.'

His grandmother shook her head. 'You can't blame her for what happened. You read the reports. You know she was as much a victim as Imran.'

Reluctantly he nodded. Logic told him the old lady was right. But Jacqueline Fletcher's presence here still felt wrong.

Not to Lady Rania. 'How can I turn my back on her when it was the last thing Imran asked of me?'

Asim watched his grandmother battle tears and his gut clenched. In seconds the clever, feisty woman he loved was gone, replaced by a fragile, grieving old lady whose distress tore at him. He felt as if someone was slowly disembowelling him with a rusty spoon. She'd always seemed indomitable but his cousin's untimely death had aged her as not even the loss of her son and daughter-in-law had.

Imran's loss had shocked them all. But for his grandmother it was a blow from which Asim feared she'd never recover. Unless she had something else to focus on.

With a sigh, he sank onto the arm of her chair and covered her age-knotted hands. He knew he'd regret this.

'You really want Jacqueline Fletcher here?'

Her hands stilled. 'I promised Imran.'

In their family a promise was an unbreakable bond.

Imran and Jacqueline Fletcher. Just how close had they been? The question had taunted him through the long night.

Asim closed his eyes, thrusting aside the futile wish that his grandmother's peace of mind could be achieved through other means. The only way forward was to take control of the situation, however unpalatable, and mould it into what you wanted.

'And if she proves unworthy of your trust?'

'I may be getting on in years, Asim, but I'm not in my dotage.' The indignation in her tone was a relief. 'I'm still a good judge of character. And talent.' She gestured to the papers on the table. 'Read those and tell me she's not gifted. She's got a journalist's instinct for a story, but it's tempered with humanity and respect.'

'Respect?' It wasn't a word he associated with the press.

'Read them and see.'

To please his grandmother, he scooped the papers up. The last thing his crowded schedule permitted was leisure for reading.

'You'll let her stay?'

Reluctantly he inclined his head. 'Since you wish it.'

'You won't regret it, Asim.'

'I hope you're right.' He would permit no one to hurt either his sister or his emotionally fragile grandmother. If Jacqueline Fletcher crossed that line she'd answer to *him*.

Jacqui paced the antechamber. Sitting still wasn't an option. Her response to a problem was to resolve it quickly. Except the Sultan had been unavailable all day. One didn't simply interrupt a busy head of state, no matter how infuriating and highhanded his attitude.

'His Highness will see you now.'

Jacqui spun round to see a young man gesturing her towards an open door.

Her empty stomach clenched. This was it. Lady Rania had assured her this morning that she'd persuade her grandson. But, remembering his severe expression and the glint of honed steel in his eyes, Jackie wondered if anything would shift him when he'd made up his mind.

Once she'd have been sure she could persuade him, but her self-assurance had shattered, leaving her questioning her judgement in coming here.

Yet if Jacqui didn't have this project, what did she have? Her insides heaved as she fought panic.

'Thank you.' She straightened her jacket with clammy hands and entered.

Though she was prepared, the sight of the man standing near the vast desk made her breath catch. He was taller than she remembered and memory hadn't exaggerated the breadth of those shoulders. Or the keenness of that stare.

Briefly she wondered if she should curtsey but knew she couldn't carry it off. Besides—heat seared her—after he'd had an eyeful of her nude body last night it was a little late for such niceties.

'Good afternoon, Your Highness.' Her gaze took in his finery: a long grey tunic embroidered at the high collar and hem, worn over pale, loose trousers that tucked into boots. No dagger at his side this time, but he wore a neat white turban threaded with silver. He looked imposing, his spare features harsh.

'Ms Fletcher. Please sit.'

And let him tower over her?

'Thank you but I prefer to stand.'

'Fine. What I have to say won't take long.'

Jacqui's insides tumbled in a sickening corkscrew. She planted her feet in her low-heeled shoes and braced herself. She should have argued her case last night but she'd been swaying with exhaustion after twenty-four hours of travel and then the trauma of the nightmare.

He paced closer and she had to make a conscious effort not to retreat. His gaze pinioned her like a hunter marking his prey.

Atavistic fear quivered through her as he came close and she read something in his stare that wasn't simply disapproval or dismissal. Something made her remember the brush of the silk coverlet against her bare skin and the strange jittery sensation deep in her core. She swallowed hard.

'You're lucky to have such an advocate, Ms Fletcher.' He was so close his breath warmed her and his hot spicy scent teased her nose. 'My grandmother is very taken with you. So I've decided you can stay.'

It took Jacqui whole seconds to take it in. She goggled.

'I can?' A smile trembled on her lips but they were too stiff to curve properly. Relief was a swoop of sensation through her chest so strong it hurt. She'd been so sure he'd banish her from the palace, perhaps the country.

'You may.' There was no lightening in his expression. If anything, it sharpened. He leaned closer, looming so her pulse jumped. 'But I have conditions.'

Jacqui nodded, feeling the force of his disapproval. 'Yes?' Her voice was a scratch of sound.

'One, absolutely no photos without permission.'

'Of course. I—'

'Two, no attempt to report on my family's personal lives. A social history is one thing, digging for gossip is another. I won't hesitate to sue if necessary.'

Outrage stirred. 'That's not what I'm here for!'

Astonishingly his hand reached out to cup her chin, tilting it up till his face filled her vision. Tension snapped between them and an unfamiliar sensation shot through her as his fingers splayed over her throat, reinforcing her vulnerability to his superior strength.

No man had ever held her like that. Jacqui was torn between wide-eyed anxiety and a sudden, startling jab of excitement. She hated men who threw their weight around, who encroached on women. But as she arched back in his hold part of her thrilled at his masculine power.

She blinked. She must be going mad.

'My family is precious to me and I won't have them harmed.' He paused, his jaw tight. 'I've seen what damage the press can do.'

Slowly she nodded, surprised and a little daunted by this glimpse of the man behind the royal title. The man she was sure would bring retribution on anyone who hurt those for whom he cared. Curiosity stirred.

'Three.' He paused, his gaze flicking to her parted lips then to her eyes. To her dismay her mouth tingled from that look. 'You will sign a contract agreeing to these terms and I will meet with you regularly for updates on your progress. I intend to take a very personal interest in this book of yours.'

Jacqui swallowed. 'Of course.' She made to jerk her head away but his grip firmed. He didn't hurt her but the sensation of being at his mercy sent anxiety scudding through her, as it was meant to. Her jaw clenched. 'There's no need to assault me to make your point.'

'Assault?' His brows rose. 'I'm simply reminding you that while you're in my home, and in my country, my will is law. If you attempt to take advantage of my family you'll pay dearly. Understood?'

'I understand.' For a moment longer Jacqui stood unmoving. Then abruptly she slumped from the knees, her body weight dragging his arm down, pulling him off-balance. A twist, a jerk and she was free; another quick movement as he reached to support what he presumably thought was her fainting body and now it was she who gripped him, her thumb hard on the pressure point in his hand. His skin was firm and warm under hers.

Her chest pounded as adrenalin shot through her blood. She stifled a grin at the surprise in his coal-dark eyes. Suddenly, for the first time in months, she felt strong and confident. It was a heady relief after so long doubting herself.

'And I hope *you* understand, *Your Highness*, that I won't be intimidated.' Beneath her touch his pulse throbbed an infuriatingly even rhythm. 'If ever I want a man to touch me, I'll invite him.'

Slowly his mouth curved in a smile as lethal as a scimitar. 'I'll be sure to remember that, Ms Fletcher.'

Strangely, his words didn't reassure.

CHAPTER FOUR

'Is SHE ON your list of potential brides?' Asim's grandmother whispered as they stood side by side, farewelling guests from the formal reception.

He stiffened. He hadn't sought the old lady's help to find a wife but that didn't mean she wouldn't try to sway him.

'I'm keeping my options open,' he said as he watched the young woman in question leave with her parents. They'd loitered till the very end of the evening and he wondered if they'd hoped for some signal of preferment. If so they'd waited in vain. The girl was nice enough, but...

'She's very pretty,' his grandmother murmured. 'Very well brought-up.'

So well brought-up she'd barely spoken till Asim had asked her questions she had to give more than a 'yes' or 'no' answer to. Even then she'd kept her eyes downcast.

His gaze shifted to a knot of people so engrossed in conversation they hadn't realised the reception was breaking up. At its centre was a familiar tawny chestnut head. Jacqueline Fletcher, nodding at something one of the country's most renowned lawyers said. Even from here he saw the flash of her bright eyes. Asim couldn't imagine her standing meek and silent before a man her parents wanted her to marry.

His lips twisted in a grim smile as he remembered how she'd been anything but meek. She was too opinionated, too outspoken for comfort.

'And she's obviously eager to start a family.'

Startled, Asim turned to stare at his grandmother, only then realising she referred to the woman who'd just left.

'That's a definite plus,' the old lady murmured, 'Since you want heirs. Did you know she volunteers at the children's hospital? She adores children.'

'I'd noticed.' She'd only become animated when talking about children at the hospital and, blushing, about her hopes for a large family.

Asim liked children. He wanted his own. But he'd felt uncomfortable with a woman who seemed to have no interests beyond that.

'Her mother tells me she's an excellent cook. I suspect she'll be a wonderful home-maker.'

Asim arched an eyebrow and stared down at his grandmother. 'Why the hard sell? It's not as if I'm likely to starve for want of a good cook.' A wide gesture took in the remnants of the superb buffet supper prepared by the royal chefs.

'I'm just pointing out her good qualities. Why are you so touchy?'

He shrugged, frowning. Why *did* he feel dissatisfied? Tonight had been arranged so he could vet a potential bride in a setting which wouldn't make his interest obvious. Yet the result was strangely disappointing. 'I'm sorry. I thought I knew what I wanted and now I'm having second thoughts.'

She nodded. 'A man like you needs more than a sweet mouse, Asim, even if she is a domestic goddess. You need a real woman.'

He discovered his eyes were fixed again on Jacqueline Fletcher. He blinked as his grandmother's words sank in. A real woman.

But not one like his unwanted guest. So she could hold her own in conversation and had an enquiring mind. That was all. She didn't even dress to make the most of her assets. That dark suit would have been acceptable at a business meeting, but not tonight, where the women wore full-length gowns of impeccable quality.

Did she aim to draw attention to herself in some perverse way? Or did she think to hide herself behind the boxy cut of that jacket? Perhaps she'd worn it because of him. Did she really believe the unflattering style would make him forget her svelte, alluring body now he'd seen it laid out before him?

'Asim, dear. You're scowling.'

His jaw firmed and he stiffened as he realised his grandmother was right. He'd been Sultan for ten years, had been attending formal events since childhood. Concealing his thoughts in public was second nature. Until now.

'Allow me to escort you to your suite.' The deep voice was as rich and tempting as the thick Arabic coffee sweetened with wild honey that was a local specialty. It slid right through her insides, scorching as it went.

Jacqui swung round to find the Sultan beside her. Her pulse throbbed faster and an unsettling frisson pulled her skin taut. She'd been so busy saying goodnight to her new acquaintants she hadn't heard him approach.

All evening she'd kept her distance, though he drew her gaze constantly. A head taller than most of the glamorous crowd, he looked magnificent in pale trousers and a high-necked tunic of coppery gold that complemented the saturnine darkness and chiselled authority of his features. This time his turban was black.

Beside him she felt like a drab sparrow. For a fleeting moment she wished her travel wardrobe included something sexy and feminine, until reality punctured the illusion. She didn't own anything like that. Besides, she'd look ridiculous, a scarecrow pretending to be a fairy princess.

'Your Highness, thank you for the invitation to tonight's reception. You have such interesting guests.'

His dark gaze was impenetrable. She should be used to it. She saw it every day in his office when he subjected her to twenty minutes of questions and answers more gruelling than any editorial inquisition. Twenty minutes in which he assessed her with the intensity of a scientist viewing a lower life form.

And never once had she discovered the man behind the formal interrogation. She sensed a sharp intellect and decisive mind but there'd been few glimpses of the man she'd met that first night, the one whose quick distrust, kindness and latent sexuality had fascinated her.

Just as well. She didn't need that distraction.

'Had, Ms Fletcher. The evening is over.'

She looked around and realised he was right. The last scattered guests had left.

'Then I'll say goodnight too, Your Highness. Thank you again.'

'I'm glad you enjoyed yourself.' He fell into step beside her and she was inordinately conscious of his height and the swing of his arm close to hers as they exited the opulent room. He turned with her into the wide corridor away from the marble and gilt public rooms.

'Really, there's no need to see me to my door.'

'It's not out of my way.' He gestured for her to precede him under a stone archway decorated with carved calligraphy and semi-precious stones.

Reluctantly she stepped through. Those short daily interviews were unsettling enough. Walking empty corridors with him reminded her too strongly of that first night when he'd found her naked and screaming. He made her feel vulnerable, as if her defences had been scraped away like a layer of skin by the hot desert wind.

Or maybe it's because you're so aware of him as a man. A hot, sexy man.

His hand shot out and grabbed her elbow when she stumbled.

'I'm fine.' Jacqui made to tug out of his hold but found she couldn't.

His eyes weren't blank any more. What she saw there made

her breath quicken and sent a charge jolting to the apex of her thighs. Heat seared to the tips of her ears as she identified her body's reaction.

Arousal.

Jacqui swallowed over a throat lined with sandpaper.

For days she'd assured herself she'd imagined the throb of desire that first night. She'd focused on her work, interviewing Lady Rania and poring over documents. She'd kept her reports to her royal host businesslike. But in the dark of her solitary room each night she'd felt a rush of heat that made a liar of her.

Her breath quickened as he tilted his head, watching.

Then abruptly she was free, his strong fingers sliding away.

'Forgive me, Ms Fletcher. I realise you didn't invite that.' His lips curved in a wry smile that set her heart battering her ribs.

It took a moment to realise he referred to her defiant announcement that if she wanted his touch she'd invite it.

Suddenly Jacqui remembered the warmth of his skin on hers that first night. How his dangerous smile had undone something vital inside her. How, even when annoyed at his superior attitude, she was always *aware* of him.

'I should go. I have a busy day tomorrow.'

She turned into another corridor and infuriatingly he fell into step. He was so close she heard the faint swish of silks and linen as he strode beside her.

'So I understand. My grandmother is excited by the prospect of you meeting her old friends. I gather they're spending the afternoon with you, discussing harem life.'

'You know about that?' Jacqui hadn't told him in advance, suspecting he'd object to her spending time with women who were intimately acquainted with his family. He'd made it clear his family was off-limits. The discreet presence of a guard who trailed at a distance whenever she left her suite to meet Lady Rania or investigate the deserted harem constantly reminded her that she was here under sufferance.

If she hadn't been so engrossed by her research, or so

desperate to make a success of it, she'd have bridled at the surveillance. It made her smile grimly that, after the dangers of her old job, now she was relegated to pure desk work Sultan Asim felt he had to take precautions against *her*.

'My grandmother has spoken of little but this gathering.' He paused. 'Whatever comes of this project, I must thank you for bringing pleasure to her at a very difficult time.'

Jacqui's pace faltered. It was the last thing she'd expected to hear.

'I'm pleased you think so. But it's she who's helping me. Without her involvement this project wouldn't be possible. When Imran...' She cleared her throat. 'When your cousin mentioned the possibility of interviewing her I hardly dared hope she'd agree.'

'It's that important to you?'

She nodded. More than he could know. What had begun as an interesting idea for the future had become her lifeline, her only option. And one final homage to her friend.

'Please.' He gestured and Jacqui stared, discovering they'd reached the spacious courtyard outside her suite. 'Take a seat.' He led the way to a pair of comfortable looking chairs in the garden.

Jacqui hesitated. 'I really should—'

'I'd like to talk to you.' He stood, a commanding figure bathed in moonlight. It gleamed on the fine fabric of his clothes and turned his eyes to a dark glitter.

Instinct warned against a tête à tête in the darkness. But he was her host. She was indebted to him. She couldn't walk away.

Reluctantly she stepped from the lit passageway and took a seat, struggling to sit upright when the cushions invited her to lounge. He sat turned half towards her, half towards the long pool that shimmered invitingly.

Silence surrounded them.

'I'm curious,' he said at last. 'Why would a woman like you embark on this particular project?'

'A woman like me?' She strove to keep the indignation from her voice. What was he accusing her of now?

His reluctance to have her here, his hawk-like scrutiny of her research and her daily guard proved he didn't trust the press. But she'd hoped she'd allayed his concerns and he'd begun to trust her a little.

'I've read your profile, Ms Fletcher. You're one of Australia's youngest foreign news reporters and well regarded. You received an award for media excellence, though you were in hospital and missed the ceremony.' Jacqui tried and failed not to stiffen at the casual mention of the time when shock and guilt, as much as her injuries, had incapacitated her. 'You rarely take leave and when you do it's to follow another story. You have a reputation for doggedness and for grasping the bigger picture.'

'You've checked me out.' It shouldn't surprise her yet Jacqui sat straighter, nerves jangling.

'Of course. Don't pretend you haven't done the same.' Jacqui felt the challenge in his stare though his eyes were shadowed.

Finally she nodded. 'You inherited the crown at twenty-five. You were educated in France and England, including at the Royal Military Academy Sandhurst. You've got a Master's degree in business administration.' She paused, reflecting on those old reports of extreme sports and hard partying.

'Despite your early reputation for…adventure, since taking the throne you've gained a name as a broker in diplomatic and trade negotiations and as a leader of vision. You've built on your nation's loyalty to your family and are well respected.'

'*Touché*, Ms Fletcher.' Laughter threaded his voice, making it far too appealing.

Her fingers tightened on the arms of her chair. Sitting in the darkness with this man whose presence sent her senses into hyper-awareness was a supremely bad idea. Her nostrils twitched. She wished he'd doused himself in some expensive aftershave any man might buy. Instead, she guessed that far too appealing spice and man mix was innate to him.

'And so?'

'And so, after checking your credentials, I'm intrigued. Why step away from your career to write about a lifestyle that no longer exists?'

'I hope plenty of people will be interested in reading about life in a harem.'

'Because sex sells?'

He leaned towards her and she shifted back. 'The book won't be about sex.' She waved a hand. 'Or only in part.'

'But that's what readers will expect.'

Jacqui shrugged. 'I want to paint a portrait of a vanished way of life.'

'The question remains. Why give up a challenging, successful job for which you're receiving accolades to write this book?'

Her breathing hitched and when she swallowed it felt like she'd gulped a block of ice. It froze her from the inside. She tried to prise her fingers from their claw-like grip on the arms of the chair but couldn't.

He leaned closer. 'I'm surprised your network has given you time off for this. Surely they want you doing what you do best?'

Jacqui bit down a sour laugh. *What she did best.*

What she *used* to do best.

'I didn't take leave,' she admitted in a rush, the blood pounding in her ears. 'I resigned.'

Even now the admission dealt her a sickening blow. After years building her career it still stunned her that she'd actually walked away from the only thing that had given her purpose and identity—her work.

As long as she could remember she'd wanted to be a journalist. Now that part of her life was over and it was no more than she deserved. Because of her Imran had lost his life. The price she paid was small by comparison. Her shoulders inched high as tension radiated up from her clawed hands.

In the other chair her inquisitor sat comfortably, fingers steepled together.

'I see.' Something about his inflection suggested that, even if he didn't see the whole picture, he guessed most. The idea of him silently dissecting what she'd said pushed her into speech.

'I'm sure your grandmother has told you about the essays I've written.' She snatched a breath and hurried on. 'They were well received and I'd always thought one day I'd try my hand at a book.' Like when she retired.

'It's good sometimes to work on something longer term, without the quick demands of current affairs reporting.'

Except she'd thrived on pressure and deadlines. Being without them now created a new sort of pressure, increasing her fear that she wasn't cut out for this longer project. Was this all a huge mistake?

'And yet it's a remarkable decision for a woman with such a promising career,' he mused. 'To cut herself off from work which, from what my cousin used to say, was a vocation, not a job.'

Jacqui's breath hissed between her teeth. This man was too insightful.

'I assure you I'm devoting all my energies to this. I'm not playing at it.'

He waved his hand dismissively. 'But you must understand my doubts about this unlikely career choice. Especially when it coincides with heightened media interest in my sister's whereabouts.'

'You think I'm here to get a scoop on your sister?' Jacqui frowned. 'If that were so, surely I'd be staking out the private Caribbean island where she's staying?' That was where the pundits reckoned she was hiding, licking her wounds after a disastrous love affair.

Jacqui shook her head. Tunnel visioned as she'd been, she hadn't considered Princess Samira relevant. 'There was I thinking you doubted my qualifications. Or that I intended to write some titillating fiction about sex slaves rather than a well-researched history.'

'Both crossed my mind.' The admission was a slap in the face, making her skin tingle and igniting a spark of professional pride. 'But what I've gleaned from our daily interviews and my investigations has reassured me somewhat.'

'Somewhat!' Annoyance spiked. How disappointed he must have been when she'd reported on her research. So far she'd focused on marriage celebrations and the training of young girls in domestic skills like preparing the spectacular sweets for which the royal court was famous. Nothing at all salacious.

He shrugged casually, the movement drawing attention to those wide, straight shoulders. 'Your arrival just as Samira is being hounded by the press is too coincidental.' He paused. 'I've allowed you to remain for my grandmother's sake, but I can't be completely easy with your explanation.'

'You don't have much time for the press, do you?'

'My caution comes from experience.' His voice was steely.

Jacqui remembered the reports about his lovers and his jet-setting lifestyle before he'd inherited the throne. Even now he captured headlines wherever he went. The combination of stunning looks and extreme wealth guaranteed it. Then there were older reports she'd skimmed about his parents' volatile relationship. They'd provided perfect fodder for sensationalist media outlets with gossip about break-ups, lovers and jealous rages.

'I'm a journalist, not a paparazza!'

'So you tell me.'

Jacqui pursed her lips, thinking. He'd given her support… so far. But he could change his mind at any stage. Only one thing would convince him—the truth.

A shudder ripped through her and she hunched forward, her arms automatically crossing, holding tight, as if that could keep the pain at bay.

She could keep her secrets and hope he didn't change his mind about letting her stay. Or tell him what he wanted to know. Tell him what she'd not told a soul.

His patient silence, the sense of a listening presence in the anonymous darkness, won out. Or maybe she was just tired of hugging the truth to herself.

'Everything I told you is true.'

'But there's more.'

Yes, damn him. There was more. She sucked in a sustaining breath.

'I can't do that job any more. I've tried and...' She shook her head. 'I just can't.' Jacqui heard the wobble in her voice and bit her lip. 'I tried being in the field again and I just...shut down. I couldn't function. Even being in the newsroom, working at that end, with the bustle and the people and the pressure, it was too much.' She blinked and lifted her head to stare up at the clear, bright moon. She remembered staring at a moon like that from her lonely hospital bed that first night, when she still couldn't believe the horror she'd witnessed.

'Ever since the bombing, since Imran died, I haven't been able to work.'

'Post-traumatic stress?'

She lifted her shoulders in a tight movement. 'Trouble sleeping, trouble handling more than one task at a time.' It almost killed her to admit that. She'd been so proud of her professional skills. 'Trouble with loud noises and too many people.' On bad nights she couldn't even face darkness, fearing sleep and the nightmares it might bring. And beyond all that was guilt that she'd led Imran to his death. *She'd* been responsible.

'Tonight was the first night I've been able to stand being in a crowd of people without searching for suspicious packages or jumping at shadows.'

She told herself that was progress, but in some ways tonight had only made it all worse. For she'd spent the evening in conversation with such fascinating people, people she'd normally pursue for an interview. She'd had an idea for a report on current regional trade negotiations, but the thought of following it through had made her queasy. She'd been second-guessing herself, wondering if the idea was as good as she believed or if her judgement was flawed.

Forcing herself to face him, she laid herself bare, ignoring the shrieks of her ragged pride.

'I *need* this project. Once I realised I couldn't go back I had nothing. No job, no hope for the future. Until your grandmother and I corresponded again after...Imran.' Jacqui swallowed over the obstruction in her throat and forced herself to continue. 'She was so enthusiastic, I realised the project was too big for the article I'd planned. It needed a book. So here I am.'

Jacqui didn't add that her work defined her. Relationships had never succeeded for her. She'd never belonged anywhere as she had in journalism. Burying herself in reporting, building a life around her professional goals was all she had.

Moonlight silvered the strong lines of his face as he surveyed her.

Did he believe her or still think this was a conspiracy to uncover dirt on his sister? Had she bared her secret shame for nothing? Was he going to kick her out?

'Thank you for sharing the truth.' His voice was rich and slightly rough, like crushed velvet rubbing on bare skin. 'I suspect you haven't shared that with many.'

None. But she refused to tell him that.

Jacqui was an intensely private person, having learned to rely only on herself from the day her parents had split. It had been difficult, discovering at ten that neither of your parents loved you enough to want you full time. That you came a poor second to their new families. That you didn't belong except as an unpaid babysitter. But it had made her strong. She gave thanks now for that strength.

'I realise it was difficult for you.'

She nodded, her throat still closed.

'I'll continue to monitor your progress' He paused and she felt his scrutiny like a touch. 'But you've put my mind at rest for now.'

For now? What hoops did she have to jump through to win this man's approval?

Jacqui felt wrung out. She wasn't sure she had the stamina to go another round with the Sultan, no matter how desperate she was.

Abruptly he stood. 'Come, it's late. I've kept you from your bed.'

In the gloom he extended his arm and for an insane moment Jacqui thought he meant to accompany her to bed. A jagged slash of heat scorched her, resolving into an eddying pool of liquid warmth deep in her abdomen.

'In my country a handshake is a sign of trust.'

Reluctant despite the unlooked-for compliment, Jacqui reached out and took his hand. It was just as she remembered, firm, warm and strong.

Instead of the expected handshake he pulled her to her feet till they stood toe-to-toe, close enough for her to feel his breath on her forehead. The heat in her belly flared and sparked and a new kind of tension stirred.

There it was again, that searing stare that spoke of things far more intimate than news stories or remembered anguish. Breathlessly Jacqui told herself it was a trick of the moonlight that made his eyes glitter.

Yet instinct made her pull free of his hold. Not because of what she thought she saw there but because of the answering hunger growing inside, banishing the last glacial chill of memory.

She'd never known such an overwhelming response to a man. It made her want to run and hide.

'Good night.' She kept her head up, resisting the impulse to rub away the imprint of his touch. It was too unsettling but she knew better than to reveal that.

'Come, I'll see you to your door.'

'There's no need to go out of your way.' Her voice sounded scratchy and breathless and she cursed this sudden rush of hormones.

'It's not out of my way at all. Haven't you realised yet that you're staying in my private wing?'

Even in the darkness his slow smile packed a punch that made her reel.

'So if you need me in the night I'm not far away.'

CHAPTER FIVE

Asim stared across his desk at the woman before him, her head bent over her laptop.

Afternoon sun caught amber and russet tints in the hair she'd scraped back from her face. Idly he imagined it loose like it had been that first night, catching the light in a nimbus of gold and autumn hues.

He frowned. Blonde or brunette, or even tawny chestnut, no woman distracted him from his purpose.

His purpose was to protect Samira, no matter how tempted he was to believe Jacqueline Fletcher's tale of desperation. Yet hearing her voice catch as she'd told him why she'd begun this work, watching the moonlight silver a face pinched with pain, he'd wanted to comfort her.

Instinct told him her pain was real. But years of experience warned him never to trust a reporter. For too long they'd fed like jackals on his family. If he made a mistake trusting her when he shouldn't it would be Samira who'd suffer. The thought tightened every sinew.

Besides, Jacqueline Fletcher wasn't what she seemed. Her clothes were so drab and unfeminine it was suspicious, as if she aimed to deflect his attention but took the camouflage too far.

He'd seen her pearly skin, the flash of vivid amber eyes, the russet of pubic hair and the rose pink of her full-body blush. And he wasn't forgetting any time soon.

Heat doused him as she looked up. He felt wrong-footed,

as if caught ogling an innocent. An innocent whom his cousin had trusted.

'Here's the reference I wanted.' Her head tilted to one side as if she tried to read his expression and Asim stiffened as guilt eddied.

Instantly the shimmer of brightness in her eyes dulled and doubt jabbed him. Could she be such a good actress?

'Go on.'

She paused but didn't look away. Asim felt admiration stir. So often he merely had to hint at disapproval to find others giving way. Clearly his frown had no such impact on Ms Fletcher.

'It's a reference to diaries kept by...' she looked down to check her facts '...your great-great-aunt Zeinab.'

'And you found this where?' It was the first Asim had heard of royal diaries.

'There was a paper in the royal collection your grandmother thought would interest me. She arranged for your chief archivist to show me and it mentioned the diaries.'

'Tell me more.' This research project expanded before his eyes. First interviews with his grandmother, then visits to abandoned parts of the palace accompanied by various building experts, then meetings with an ever-expanding group of his grandmother's old friends. Now the royal archives. When would it stop?

So much for his hope he'd soon see the back of Jacqueline Fletcher.

'It mentioned arrangements to teach the ladies in the harem geometry, astronomy and poetry.'

Asim nodded. 'All are traditionally important to my people. Astronomy and geometry aid navigation in the desert and poetry is prized among all the arts.'

Again that tilt of her head. 'Yet the women of the palace weren't likely to navigate alone across the dunes.'

Asim shrugged. 'You think one should learn only the immediately practical? What about broadening the mind?'

'I agree.' Her gaze dipped. 'It just surprised me that your ancestors felt the same way, especially when it came to educating women.'

He repressed anger. Wasn't this the sort of too easy assumption many outsiders made? 'Despite the stories you've heard, many of my predecessors were enlightened. They sought beautiful, clever women as their consorts, women whose company they could enjoy. Educated women who could share their lives as well as their beds.'

'Which is why I'd like to access Zeinab's diaries. They will be invaluable—'

'No.' A journalist prying into intimate family details? Even after generations the diaries could reveal material better kept private.

'But if I could—'

'It seems to me you have plenty of sources already.'

He supressed a smile as her eyes flashed. No longer drab despite her dowdy clothes, Jacqueline Fletcher looked vibrantly alive with her flushed cheeks and pouting lips.

'The diaries will give a new perspective to the project, adding depth and texture.'

'I take your point, Ms Fletcher, but I prefer to keep such private material private.'

She met his gaze, her brow pleated.

Enough. Asim glanced at his watch. It was time for his next meeting. He pushed back his chair.

She stood, planting her palm on the desk and leaning forward. As if he were an equal, not an absolute ruler who'd already granted her great favour.

'Your Highness.' The way she said his title was anything but obsequious. 'Don't you see? This could be a chance to provide an insight into a woman who was both educated and well regarded. The diaries could provide material to refute the sort of assumption I just made.'

Asim paused. She had a point, damn it. If this book was to be written, better it be done properly.

'I'll consider the matter and discuss it with the head archivist.'

She shook her head, leaning in till the faint sweetness of her skin reached his nostrils. 'I talked to him and he...' she paused '...didn't see it as a priority.'

'Didn't he?' Asim could imagine it. The head of that department was a dry old stick who wouldn't have taken kindly to Jacqueline Fletcher's enthusiasm.

'No. But if you were to take a personal interest...'

Asim huffed out a laugh at her persistence, her sheer front. She didn't take no for an answer, no matter how demure she pretended to be. Sooner or later something would catch her interest and she'd light up in enthusiasm or outrage.

She was never dull.

'Very well.' He made a quick decision. 'I'll look at these diaries and, if appropriate, you will be allowed access under supervision.' His raised hand silenced her thanks. 'I understand that while you speak our language you can't read it fluently, so a staff member will translate any relevant sections.' A carefully picked curator who would protect the royal interests.

The radiance of her smile sent a trickle of heat through him and his mouth firmed.

Jacqueline Fletcher was convincing as an honest, dedicated writer rather than a conniving, duplicitous opportunist. But Asim wasn't completely sure yet.

The only thing he could be sure of was that his attraction to her was a complication he could do without.

If you need me in the night I'm not far away.

It had been days since the Sultan had said that but the words taunted Jacqui as she slid through the water.

Surely he hadn't intended it to sound so...intimate. As if he expected her to invite him into her bed. Yet the sizzle of electricity between them was real. Even she could recognise desire.

Unless the sizzle was only *her* body's response to a potently masculine and charismatic man, not his response to her. Her mind and her body had let her down these past months. Had she imagined the sultry interest in his hooded eyes, projecting her own breathless awareness onto him?

Had he *really* brought her to his apartments in case she suffered night terrors? She spluttered, swallowing water.

She'd been so busy branding Sultan Asim high-handed, she'd disregarded the soft spot he'd shown for his grandmother and his protectiveness to his sister. He wasn't just an arrogant potentate. He knew how to care.

Could that caring extend to her? It seemed unlikely. Yet the alternative, that he desired her, was impossible.

Jacqui had no illusions about her sex appeal. She'd been a gawky tomboy, always playing sport with the boys. Puberty came late and no one noticed since her body had steadfastly refused to grow curves like other girls'. She'd simply stayed one of the boys. Not the sort of woman to attract a man like Sultan Asim with his renowned eye for beauty.

She remembered her few attempts in her teens to discover the secret of looking feminine. Her mum had pretended she was still a little girl and her stepmother, when forced to, had bought the same T-shirts and jeans for Jacqui as for her sons. She'd viewed Jacqui's occasional efforts to dress up as selfish attention seeking.

So Jacqui had taught herself with the help of hand-me-down magazines. The results had been spectacularly awful. There'd been no one to warn her that the pink frilly dress she'd spent all her savings on and the vibrant hot-pink lipstick made her look like a clown. Or a transvestite, as one of the little cats in her class had exclaimed.

By the time she was working Jacqui had learned the best she could achieve was neat professionalism and to avoid bright colours and clingy fabrics. Better to blend in than draw attention to her shortcomings.

A slamming door made her turn, treading water.

Late afternoon light slanted across the courtyard as a tall figure strode to the pool. Jacqui's eyes bulged and she almost forgot how to stay afloat until instinct shook her lax limbs into movement.

She'd thought him imposing fully dressed. But the Sultan of Jazeer had a body that looked even better without clothes. Almost without clothes. White swim shorts rode low on his hips, revealing acres of burnished skin.

Hot needles of excitement pricked Jacqui's flesh as she watched his easy, athletic lope. Those shoulders were even wider than she'd imagined, his body lean but well built. The dusting of dark hair across his chest emphasised the bunch of muscles as he moved.

She exhaled, trying to slow her racing pulse as she tracked the line of dark hair that arrowed down, plunging beneath his shorts.

Belatedly her brain engaged as she realised where she was staring. And that he watched her.

Jacqui struck out for the far edge of the pool, splashing in her haste.

She had sex on the brain, and it was the fault of Lady Rania and her friends. What had begun a few days ago as a small reference group of old ladies had grown with daughters, granddaughters and friends who saw their afternoon gatherings as an excuse for socialising. When Jacqui had asked about preparation for marriage in the harem, soon they'd been swapping stories that made her blush.

The art of pleasing a man sexually had been an essential part of a harem education. The trouble was now Jacqui's head was full of images of her trying those techniques on the Sultan's taut, powerful body!

Obviously she'd been cooped up here too long. She was having some weird harem fantasy.

At last she neared the edge and reached out, only to find him standing there, hands on hips, watching. Shock made her suck in a breath that turned out to be water and sent her under.

Spluttering, she grabbed for the rim of the pool. Instead of hard tiles she felt warm flesh. An instant later the water rushed by as he hauled her straight up and out of the pool. Jacqui found herself planted on her feet, his hands spanning her waist as she bent, coughing.

Was his touch hot or was that searing sensation her nerve endings going into overload?

Finally Jacqui blinked and straightened, hyper-aware of his hands encircling her middle. His long fingers made her waist seem tiny.

Her vision was filled with a broad chest that just asked to be touched and a squared-off jaw that proclaimed male power. She curled her hands into fists, fearing she might do something unforgiveable like reach out.

Yet when she made to shift away his hold firmed.

Shakily Jacqui pushed her sodden hair back and raised her face. Dark eyes surveyed her from under half-lowered lids.

That flagrantly carnal look seared her into silence. Her breath caught as his gaze dropped to her mouth. To Jacqui's horror she felt her nipples pebble as erotic energy zapped through her.

Why was he looking at *her* like that?

'Thank you, Your Highness. But I can stand without help.'

'Asim.'

'Sorry?' She stared at his mouth, not trusting her ears.

'I reserve the right to use first names with women I save from drowning, Jacqueline.'

The sound of her name in that deep, rich voice sent a quiver of excitement through her.

She was in deep trouble.

'I don't think that's necessary, Your Highness. Besides, I wasn't drowning.'

'Asim.' His fingers curled in, securing her, and she fought not to wriggle with pleasure. 'Say it.'

He looked every inch the arrogant prince with his austerely aristocratic features. His nostrils flared, his eyes narrowing to glittering obsidian shards.

Heaven help her, he was more powerfully attractive than any man she'd ever seen.

'Really, there's no need.'

His eyebrows rose loftily and there was steel beneath the velvet of his voice. 'You reject my offer of friendship?'

Asim looked at the woman in his hold and felt hunger rise, sharp and raw. She couldn't be trusted. She was a journalist, one of the breed that had feasted on the carcass of his parents' marriage and now preyed on his vulnerable sister. He'd be a fool to let her close.

Yet when he looked at her he saw simply a woman.

An infuriating, challenging, surprising woman who didn't know when to shut up or when simply to obey.

A woman who in her sleek, rust-brown one-piece swimsuit looked like a naiad. Water sluiced over her lithe frame, accentuating each streamlined curve and hollow. Her limbs glowed in the late-afternoon light, giving her a luminous quality that made her seem otherworldly.

Except the woman beneath his hands was real, so fine-boned his fingers almost spanned her waist.

But it wasn't her waist that drew his attention. His gaze fixed on her lips, pink and inviting.

'Asim,' she said finally in a throaty murmur that sounded more like invitation than capitulation and made his blood rush hot and hard.

'That's better.' His voice was a low growl and he heard her gasp.

He wanted to hear her gasp like that while she lay beneath him and he took them both to paradise.

Jacqueline Fletcher invaded his peace. Every day she visited his office to report progress. She was businesslike and brisk but those stunning slanted eyes would flare amber fire when something fascinated her. Then she'd forget her formality and her whole being would come alive with an enthusiasm Asim wanted to capture and taste.

Each day it grew harder to concentrate on her words or remember the need to be suspicious. He wanted to strip away her shapeless trousers and loose shirts and touch the pearly skin he remembered. His body tightened as he imagined her writhing in pleasure against him.

Except he was in the process of selecting a bride. He had no time for sexual diversions. Besides, honour dictated he shouldn't seek a mistress and a wife at the same time.

His brain said that. His body refused to listen. It told him a few hours' diversion was exactly what he needed.

Her teeth snagged on her bottom lip and he lifted one hand, pressing his thumb there, feeling her swift intake of breath.

'Don't. You'll draw blood.'

'Then let me go. I don't want this.'

Liar.

Asim was tempted to demonstrate how much she wanted precisely this. It would be easy to kiss her till she surrendered. He'd carry her to a bed and relieve them both of the pressure that had built inexorably since the night he'd found her naked in the harem.

'Please, Asim.'

Whether it was the fact she pleaded, this prickly, opinionated woman, or the way she said his name, in a voice barely concealing distress, Asim felt a fist lodge in his chest. Reluctantly he opened his hands and stepped back.

She looked up, those feline eyes gleaming with a slumbrous heat that made a mockery of her protest and his caution. Then he read the tension in her mouth. She'd paled, the tiny smattering of freckles across her creamy skin standing out like blood on parchment.

'I'm sorry I intruded.' She ducked her head and spun away. 'I should have realised you might want the pool.'

The fist in his chest twisted.

'Don't!'

Alarmed, she stared back over her shoulder.

'Don't apologise.' He breathed deep, filling the void in his lungs. 'I don't like it when you're…meek.' The words surprised him as much as her. He felt the shock of that admission reverberate through him, even as he saw it ripple across her face.

He didn't approve of the way she argued with him, refusing to be silenced after he'd made a decision. It happened daily when she tried to wheedle access to records or palace staff or ancient pavilions that had been locked up as unsafe generations ago. Yet seeing her hesitant and downcast was like watching a bright light dim.

For long seconds their eyes locked. Long enough for him to notice that in the syrupy late-afternoon light her eyes flashed with shards of gold.

Slowly her mouth eased into a crooked smile.

'In that case, Asim…' She paused over his name as if savouring it. 'I promise not to be meek with you again.'

She scooped up her towel and wrapped it around herself, hurrying towards her room. But her chin was up and her shoulders back and, despite his body's howl of protest at her departure, Asim found himself smiling.

CHAPTER SIX

'It's gorgeous, but I can't accept it.' Regretfully Jacqui tore her gaze from the liquid fall of pewter silk in her hand and turned to Lady Rania.

'Of course you can. You'll look marvellous.'

'It's kind of you but unnecessary. I'll wear my skirt and jacket to the dinner.' Seeing the other woman's raised brows, she hurried on. 'I'm here for business, not pleasure.'

Lady Rania shook her head. 'You have a lot to learn, Ms Fletcher. There is no reason why business cannot be spiced with pleasure, or why a lovely young woman cannot make the most of herself. After all,' she continued with a glance at Jacqui's long-sleeved top, 'The dress is modest.'

Jacqui didn't know how to respond. She couldn't admit she'd never worn a formal evening gown and had no wish to start. This slinky dress would highlight the deficiencies of her lanky frame. There'd be nowhere to hide in it.

Yet the slide of silk through her hand was seductive.

Jacqui wondered how it would feel, wearing this designer original against bare skin, and shivered. Maybe because her riotous imagination pictured strong, bronzed hands stripping it off her—Asim's hands.

Carefully she laid the dress over the exquisitely upholstered sofa. Everything in the dowager's apartments was delicate and feminine, everything Jacqui wasn't.

'It's just…' She wiped her palms down her trousers.

'Yes?' The old lady gestured for her to sit. 'You know it would give me immense pleasure to do this for you, Ms Fletcher. I don't think you realise how much your project has meant to me.' She smiled wistfully, a small hand gesture conveying a hint of frailness Jacqui had never noticed before. 'Everyone these days is interested in moving forward but never in looking back. It does an old woman good to be useful again. My friends and I have been useful, haven't we?'

'Absolutely.' Jacqui leaned forward. 'You've been a mine of information. My research would never have got off the ground without you.' She paused, wondering if the dress was meant as a farewell gift. Was this a signal her stay was about to end? 'I had hoped to continue working with you a little longer...'

Lady Rania smiled gently. 'I look forward to that. In the meantime, allow me to do this. Tonight will be a formal dinner and it would please me if you wore my gift.'

Put like that, Jacqui had no choice. 'Thank you.' She eyed the spectacular fabric and gulped. She could do this. She couldn't offend or disappoint the woman who'd been so good to her. 'I'm honoured by your gift.'

'Excellent.' Lady Rania sat straighter, that hint of frailty abruptly extinguished by her radiant smile.

Three hours later Jacqui took a deep breath and looked in the mirror.

She blinked and looked again.

That was *her*?

The woman in the mirror looked subtly elegant. Not ungainly or scrawny. A few weeks of eating the delicious palace food must have helped her put back on the weight she'd lost. She wasn't much of a cook at the best of times and in the months following Imran's death preparing meals had been too much bother.

Jacqui stroked her palms down the fragile silk covering her hips and thighs and felt a ripple of excitement glissade across her skin. She knew nothing about couture but even she recognised this had been styled by an expert. From the delicate drape of the cowl neck that made the most of her less than impressive bust, to the belt of silver metal links that cinched her waist and the full-length sweep of skirt, the dress was fabulous.

She twisted, frowning as she surveyed the narrow slit at the back of the bodice. It was just wide enough to prevent her wearing a bra. But what was the point of it when she was covered from neck to toe?

Swivelling back, she stared again. With her shoulder-length hair up in a deceptively casual knot that had required the expertise of Madame's personal attendant, and subtle make-up that enhanced her eyes and glossed her lips, she didn't look like boring old Jacqui Fletcher.

She recalled the way Asim called her Jacqueline in that slow, lilting way, as if he rolled the sound around his mouth. Did she look like a Jacqueline now?

She'd always thought it ironic her parents had chosen such a feminine name for a tomboy like her. Jack suited her better. But tonight… She cocked her head and a slow smile spread across her face. Trepidation gave way to excitement.

Tonight perhaps she had it in her to be Jacqueline for a few hours.

Asim dragged his attention back to the pretty brunette beside him. Her hands fluttered like tiny birds as she talked. Delicate colour flushed her cheeks and her eyes sparkled. The acid green of her halter-neck dress showed off her smooth olive skin to perfection and her glossy curls danced.

She laughed and without pause launched into another line of conversation. Asim's smile grew fixed.

No one could accuse her of being meek. She was talkative and friendly. Her trill of laughter turned heads and made their neighbours at the long dining table smile. Nor had she mentioned children. Instead of being fixated on babies her conversation ranged from the economy to her work in television and the latest reality television show, about which Asim now knew more than he wanted.

After two hours in her company he longed for silence.

Fortunately as Sultan there were many demands on his time. He and his wife need not live in each other's pockets. If he wished, he could avoid her easily.

After all, he didn't seek a love match. A shudder skipped down his spine at the thought. With his parents' example before him he knew any such relationship would turn destructive. That was the nature of love, at least in his family. He had no doubt he carried the same defective taint as his parents. Children of dysfunctional families usually did.

No, he didn't do love. He wanted a mother for his children and a helpmeet. She'd take her place at his side and share the burden of official entertaining.

Yet why saddle himself with a chatterbox, no matter how bright and cheerful? Asim wanted a woman who could hold her own in conversation but also knew when to hold her tongue.

Unbidden his gaze slid down the table to the svelte vision in silver that had robbed him of speech when she'd entered the room.

He stiffened, horrified at the way his attention kept straying there.

Jacqueline Fletcher wasn't the woman he sought. She didn't chatter, but she was more likely to question his decisions than support them. Right now she fielded the attention of two diplomats, a businessman and a cabinet minister who, rumour had it, was on the lookout for a new bride after a recent divorce.

Heat rippled under Asim's skin. She'd played him for a fool. All those weeks she'd covered herself up, he'd almost believed she was uncomfortable showing off her body.

Now she flaunted herself. With that clinging dress moulding her ripe breasts like a lover's caress, she might as well have worn a sign saying 'open to all offers'. And this after she'd pushed him away that day at the pool!

If she wanted to hook a man to enliven her stay, his royal dinner wasn't the place.

With a scowl he turned back to his companion.

'Where do you think you're going?'

Jacqui slammed to a halt, her hand going to her throat as that familiar, deep voice sounded behind her. To her horror, awareness unfurled in the pit of her stomach. If only she could conquer this response to him. But it grew worse, not better. She'd spent half the night snatching glances at him entertaining VIPs, among them a number of beautiful women.

Snagging a shallow breath, she turned and there he was, resplendent even in the low light of the quiet corridor, wearing a tunic of scarlet silk shot with silver, dark-grey trousers and a matching turban. All the other men tonight, even the handsome young diplomat who'd been so attentive, had faded into the background near Asim.

He stalked towards her, every inch the autocrat, his mouth a straight line, his look brooding.

'I repeat, where are you slinking off to, Ms Fletcher?'

'Slinking?' She stiffened. And *Ms Fletcher* when she'd finally got accustomed to Jacqueline? 'I'm not *slinking* anywhere.'

He halted less than an arm's length away, well inside her personal space. Jacqui frowned. Since that day at the pool he'd been scrupulous about maintaining his distance.

'No? Then why carry your shoes if not to be quiet?'

'They're new and they rubbed.' She'd felt like Cinderella leaving the ball, knowing the night's magic was over when she'd had to remove the sandals.

'But you've missed the way to your suite.' If anything his expression grew sterner. What was his problem?

'I wasn't going there.' She hadn't wanted the evening to end. Attending a royal banquet was an affair to remember. The company had been fascinating and she'd basked in the pleasure of knowing she looked almost pretty. She was too wired to sleep.

'You have an assignation?' Asim moved closer, his brow lowering. His expression made her shuffle back, disquiet rippling across her nerves. Suddenly the isolation of this rarely used corridor struck her.

'Assignation? No.' She stared squarely back at those dark eyes, indignation swelling. Was this about her supposedly digging up dirt on his sister? She'd thought they'd moved on from that.

'But this is the way to the rear gate of the palace.'

'It is?' She shrugged. 'It's also the way to the harem. I thought I'd sit in one of the garden courtyards for a while.' She'd avoided the one near her rooms ever since Asim had hauled her out of the pool and her body had gone into meltdown.

'Is there a problem, *Your Highness*?' She was sick of the way he stood there, glowering. She hadn't done anything wrong. She could have eaten her dinner with her fingers rather than the exquisite antique gold cutlery and he wouldn't have noticed; he'd been too busy gawping at the vivacious beauty at his side. 'If not, I'll go.' She moved past him, her happiness stupidly dashed by his hostility.

A hand snaked out, shackling her wrist and pulling her to a halt mid-step. Jacqui gasped. Even through the long, fitted sleeves his touch singed.

'What did you think you were doing, wearing *that* to the banquet?' His gaze scorched a trail from her neck to her breasts and lower, to where the silk flared over her hips before swirling to the floor.

The tone of his voice mixed anger with disapproval and for a moment hurt assailed her. Then she recalled Lady Rania's delight when she'd seen Jacqui in the dress, and the interest in her dinner companion's eyes.

'Dressing for dinner.' She bristled. It was on the tip of her tongue to tell him to take his bad mood and shove it, but he had the power to eject her from the palace. She drew a slow breath and pretended not to notice the way his gaze flickered on the movement. 'Your grandmother—'

'No!' He raised his free hand. 'Don't bring her into this. This is about why you chose to wear that—' he gestured disparagingly to her beautiful dress '—to an important royal occasion. You must have known the effect it would have.'

Jacqui stared up at him, seeing a flash of fury, and felt her eyes widen. He was serious. And he was mightily offended.

To her horror something crumbled a little inside. Could she have got it so wrong? Had Lady Rania been too polite to tell her she'd been mistaken about the gown suiting her? Had the diplomat's assiduous attention been too over-done? Could he have felt sorry for her, trying to masquerade as glamorous when she wasn't?

Jacqui swallowed and it felt like razor wire lodged in her throat. She'd never been a good judge of fashion. Had she been blinded by the beauty of the dress into thinking it could transform her with a mere slither of its silk?

A horrible churning sensation filled her insides. Normally she didn't worry too much about how she looked. But tonight she'd thought...

'It won't happen again, Your Highness.' Her voice was wooden but she refused to look away and let him see how much the truth hurt. 'Next time, if there *is* a next time, I'll wear my suit.'

He nodded stiffly. 'That would be preferable to making an exhibition of yourself.'

Jacqui tore her hand from his, anger and hurt spiralling uncontrollably. It was one thing to know her limitations after having her stepmother harp on them so often, but it was horrible to hear *him* spell them out.

'Damn you!' She snarled the syllables between gritted teeth. 'That's a horrible thing to say.' Her breath sawed in her throat as she strove for breath. 'We can't all be glamorous and sexy like you but that doesn't give you the right to belittle others for the way they look.'

Jacqui marched away, only to catch herself up on her long skirt. Cursing under her breath, she scrabbled at the slippery silk, lifting it enough to walk, and strode off.

She'd gone two steps when he grabbed her elbow and swung her round to face him.

CHAPTER SEVEN

'You're not serious.'

But those amber eyes spat fire at him. This was no joke. And there was hurt in the twist of her mouth.

His stomach dived.

'Never more so.' Her jaw angled so she could look down her nose at him, despite the fact he was so much taller. This woman had sass.

She also had sex appeal in spades. Only iron willpower kept his hand on her elbow instead of skimming up that shimmering fabric and cupping her firm, high breasts. His gaze dipped inevitably and he saw her nipples tighten as if responding to the hunger inside him.

'Oh!' She stamped her foot on his but she was barefoot and it had no impact. 'Let me go. Now!' She thrashed in his hold, trying to get free.

'Be still, Jacqueline. You'll—'

'Don't you *dare* "Jacqueline" me. It's Jacqui. Or Jack.' Her mouth trembled and pain smacked him in the chest.

'You've got it wrong.'

'Oh, I have, have I? So you didn't come stomping after me to tell me I shouldn't have worn this?'

'No. Yes.' Asim gritted his teeth, infuriated with himself as much as her. Even now he couldn't believe his behaviour. He'd insulted her, grabbed her, hurt her. *Spent the whole evening lusting after her.* 'You don't understand.' Hell, *he* didn't understand! Where was his calm? His easy charm? Where was his dislike of reporters?

Her eyebrows arched. 'It's late, Your Highness, and we've both said enough. If you'd refrain from manhandling me, I'll be on my way.'

'Manhandling you?' Frustration ignited, fanned into a roaring inferno by guilt and raw need. '*This* is manhandling.'

He grabbed her other arm and swung her round, pushing her backwards. He heard a soft 'Ooh,' of surprise as her back hit the wall. Those mysterious eyes opened wide as if for the first time she sensed what it was to be at a man's mercy.

Not that he'd harm her. He just wanted her to shut up and listen.

Her tongue darted out to slick her lower lip and heat drilled into his belly. It was a habit she had when nervous. The first few times she'd come to his office, only that had given away the fact she knew how precarious her position was, that he'd look for any excuse to get rid of her.

Now, as then, the unconscious movement tore at his self-control. That mouth of hers...

Consciously he relaxed his grip, but not enough for her to slip away. To be sure he stepped in close so they stood toe-to-toe, their breaths mingling.

'I shouldn't have spoken like that.' His words sounded stilted, emerging from stiff lips. He wasn't used to apologising. He wasn't used to letting emotions get out of hand or blurting words before he considered them. He was renowned for diplomacy!

'No, you shouldn't.' Her eyes narrowed like laser-sharp sunbeams, scoring his skin. 'But you've made your point and I want you to let me go. I'm very tired.'

Liar. The energy running through her slender frame all but gave off sparks. His hands tingled just holding her through the silken sleeves.

Asim slammed a door on his thoughts before he could contemplate holding her bare flesh.

'I didn't mean what you think.'

'Of course you didn't. I must have imagined it all.' Sarcasm dripped from each syllable, but it didn't quite mask her hurt, and again Asim felt pain stab him in the gut.

He'd known she was affected by recent trauma but how could he have guessed she also had a warped self-image? It seemed impossible that a woman so intelligent and feisty should so underestimate herself.

'You think you don't look glamorous and sexy?' He couldn't quite keep the disbelief from his voice.

She stood ramrod-stiff. 'Don't! You've said enough on the subject.'

Asim shook his head, his gaze locked on hers. That fiery stare sent blasts of heat running through his blood.

'I didn't say it right. My complaint wasn't that you looked...' He searched for a word then remembered her usual camouflaging clothes. 'Drab.' He heard her swift intake of breath. 'It was because you sashayed into the dining salon looking like sex in heels. You turned every male head and sent the ambient temperature soaring.'

'Why are you doing this?' Her voice was ragged, her mouth tight as she skewered him with wide, hurt eyes.

'Because you don't believe me.'

'Of course I don't believe you! It's nonsense. The place was littered with beautiful women. You were surrounded by them. What would it matter if I...?'

Her words petered out and abruptly she turned her head away. Instantly, like a switch flicking off, the current of electricity arcing between them died.

'If you distracted every man in the room?' Asim didn't want to think about that but it was too late. He already knew the answer.

Because he wanted her for himself.

He'd felt sick to his stomach when her companion had spent the evening leering at her. Asim knew every man there had imagined tearing that dress away and having her for themselves.

Inexplicably Asim had felt betrayed. *He'd* been the only one to know her secret—that beneath those unflattering clothes lurked a delicious body ripe for the plucking. Now the secret was out.

'Because,' he ground out, 'I didn't want every other man there wanting you too.'

Her face swung back, eyes locking with his, and the shock of urgent hunger slammed into him again.

She just had to look at him...

'I don't know what game you think you're playing but it's not funny.' Her voice was brittle. 'I've had enough.'

Asim told himself to release her, to talk to her again in the sterile safety of his office, not in the dim seclusion of the old palace where they were totally, tantalisingly alone.

The trouble was he hadn't had enough. He hadn't even started. He felt his control snap and didn't give a damn.

'Did you even look in the mirror before dinner?' Anger roughened his voice. Anger at her for tempting him beyond endurance. Anger at himself.

'Stop it.' Her voice wobbled and this time the jab to his chest was a knife carving right through his ribs.

He let go one of her wrists and lifted his hand to her cheek. It was pale as cream and soft against his knuckles. His hand drifted to the neat whorl of her ear, to the ornate, dangling earring that emphasised the bareness of her throat.

'With your hair up your throat looks so slender, so fragile. And these...' he flicked the silvery earring so it tinkled '...draw attention to the sexy curve just here.'

He bent and pressed his lips to the tender spot where shoulder and neck met. She started and her pulse jumped beneath his lips. The scent of her was rich in his nostrils and he licked the spot, drawing in her taste. Apricots, that was it. Sweet with a hint of tartness. And skin like pale cream.

Slowly he drew back, the air heavy in his lungs as he dragged in a breath.

'Please, Asim—'

He stopped her words with a finger to her lips and felt their lush promise. His belly tightened.

'And this.' His hand skimmed the folds of fabric that fell in a curve from her shoulders. 'It's there to draw attention to your breasts.'

'But I'm completely covered.' Her voice had that husky weight that never failed to please him. 'I couldn't be more covered up.'

Asim nodded. 'Exactly. Whoever designed this knew what they were doing. All that lusciousness covered but on display.'

His gaze dropped to her breasts, high and proud and temptingly close. 'Are you even wearing anything under there?'

She tugged in his hold as if to break free and he slammed her arm up against the wall, the weight of his own holding her in place. To be sure, he planted his free hand on the other side of her head, caging her.

'I couldn't wear a bra,' she murmured defensively, and his body hardened. 'There's a slit in the back of the bodice.'

'Ah, the slit.' He surveyed her face, watching colour rise. 'It's masterful. That tiny sliver of pale skin when you move or turn. You have no idea how tantalising it is, do you?' Even now he read uncertainty in her eyes. She looked dazed but she held her mouth tight as if fearing to believe him.

'Sometimes a glimpse of the forbidden is more arousing than a blatant display of flesh.'

Her eyes rounded.

'Even these...' deliberately he stroked his index finger down one tight sleeve from shoulder to wrist '...simply make a man want to see what they conceal.' He breathed deep, relishing her sweet scent.

Asim dropped his hand to the shimmering folds of her skirt. 'This too.' He couldn't resist laying his palm flat as he dragged his hand up her thigh. Silken material over warm flesh, the combination was pure seduction.

He felt her tremble. Somehow the movement transferred

to his hand and it grew unsteady as he moulded her hip and tugged her close. His fingers spread, shaping her taut buttock.

'Tell me you're wearing something under this,' he growled, then shook his head. 'No. Don't. I don't want to know.'

He was rigid with arousal. He pulled her close so her heat cushioned his erection and his eyes sank shut, her gasp loud in his ears.

'Believe me now?' Asim's lips twisted in self-mockery but it was beyond him to pull back. For weeks he'd imagined slipping off her concealing clothes and losing himself in her firm, lithe body. Especially when in her enthusiasm she forgot protocol and argued with him, her face vibrant, her whole body animated. That was when he was in danger of forgetting himself. Too often he'd wanted to capture that quicksilver energy and naiad's body for himself.

'You're hard. For me?'

Her free hand fluttered at his hip. She wanted to touch him? The thought sent control spiralling.

Opening his eyes, he fell into amber fire. 'There's no one else here, Jacqueline.' She didn't object to him using her name this time.

'Every time you move in that dress the light shimmers on each curve and hollow. Did you know that?' He slid his palm over the tight curve of her bottom then back up to the gentle swell of her hip. 'Every delectable feminine inch is on show.'

He reached the belt of silver links and insinuated his fingers beneath it. 'And, as for this, it makes your waist look tinier than ever.' Plus it subtly gave a man ideas that would probably shock the woman before him. About chaining her to his bed.

Desire dragged at his belly and he had to force himself into stillness.

'I don't know what to say.' Her voice shook as she blinked up at him. 'Really?'

How could she doubt with his erection pressing into her belly? He was on fire.

'I forbid you to wear that dress in public. It's too distracting.'

Her lips curved in the tiny, delighted smile. He drank in the sight. It was the first real smile he'd had from her, not a polite social expression but a gift from the heart.

'I'm sure you could manage.' She looked down, the fringe of her eyelashes screening her gaze.

'Oh, I'd manage.' He snatched in a laboured breath. 'I'd scoop you up and take you straight back to your room.'

'Like a naughty child?' She pouted and heat zeroed straight to his groin.

'Not at all like a child.' Asim gave up the struggle with the remnants of his conscience and let his hand slide up to cup her breast. 'Like the desirable woman you are.'

'Oh!' She leaned into his hand, filling it with her bounty.

'Exactly,' he whispered from his suddenly parched throat. He'd wanted to touch her all night and the reality didn't disappoint. She arched, pressing closer, and satisfaction welled. At least he wasn't the only one drowning in this tide of hunger.

She looked up at him through her lashes, the picture of provocation. 'Then what would you do?'

His laughter was a harsh bark of self-derision. He was the sensualist, and she the woman who had to be convinced of her sex appeal, yet he was the one teetering on the brink.

'I'd make love to you till your bones melted and you couldn't walk.' He breathed deep, rapidly losing himself in the image he'd created. 'Then I'd do it all again.' His desire for her was stronger than anything he remembered. Outstripping his need for any recent lover. Far beyond anything he'd felt for the bridal hopefuls paraded for him.

'I wish you would,' she murmured, lifting her head so he read answering desire in her bright eyes.

Instantly energy crackled through him and delay was impossible.

Seconds later she was high in his arms, held against his chest as he strode through the night. Her hands clasped his neck and even that innocent touch sent rivers of fire rushing through him.

'Where are we going?' Her throaty voice was eager, not shocked, and Asim smiled. Only minutes ago she'd doubted her sex appeal. Jacqueline Fletcher was anything but predictable.

He darted a look at her face. That wide-eyed stare made her look almost innocent. To a man used to seasoned lovers, it was refreshing.

'To a bed.'

Despite the rigid tension screaming through his aroused frame, he almost smiled at her expression: doubt, trepidation and excitement.

'So far?' Her brow knitted as she pouted.

Asim stumbled to a halt. She was going to kill him. He wanted to find a flat surface and get her under him. Failing that... His gaze traversed the carved pillars lining the corridor. No. Taking her hard and fast against a wall wouldn't come close to satisfying his hunger.

'Unless you're carrying protection concealed somewhere.' His gaze dipped to her breasts, wobbling delectably as he strode faster, proud nipples erect beneath the fragile fabric.

His breath was a harsh scrape of sound as he finally turned into the corridor to his private wing.

'I can walk. You don't have to carry me.'

And let her go? Not likely. He wasn't releasing her till they'd finished what they'd begun. Besides, he enjoyed the feel of her in his arms.

'There's no need.' Ah, there was the door, just ahead.

'I'm too heavy.'

'Hardly.' Asim shouldered the door open and let it swing shut behind them.

'But I'm so tall.'

He frowned at the discordant note in her words and paused mid-stride. Something was going on in that convoluted, surprising mind of hers that he didn't understand.

Heavy...

Tall...

'You're tall for a woman,' he said slowly, watching her expression freeze, 'But that's good.' Her brows twitched in surprise. 'It means we'll be well-matched in bed.' His erection throbbed in eager agreement. 'I've been fantasising about those long legs of yours. I want to feel them wrapped around my waist when I'm moving inside you.'

Her mouth popped open in an O of astonishment as if he'd shocked her to the core. Yet she hadn't been shocked when he'd described his need for her, only eager.

'As for heavy.' He shook his head as he crossed the foyer. 'You're a lightweight. Even now with a little flesh on your bones you don't weigh much.'

'You noticed I'd gained weight?'

Of course he'd noticed. He'd been fixated on her body since that first tantalising revelation.

'This isn't my room.' Her head swivelled.

'No, it's mine.' There was protection in the bedside table and it was beyond him to last out any longer. Already his hands shook, not from carrying her, but from the effort of not ravishing her on the way.

Gently he laid her on the bed, his heart pounding with anticipation. Her dress flared like liquid silver, draping and cupping her delicious body. Already part of his brain was analysing the best way to rid her of it, even as he took a moment to relish the seductive picture she made.

Without turning, he yanked open a drawer and fumbled for condoms, planting a handful on top of the bedside table. Those amazing eyes fixed on the movement and she swallowed.

Dredging up the last grains of self-restraint, he dropped his arms.

'I want you, Jacqueline.' So much his chest felt like it was bound by steel bands. 'Tell me now if you don't want this.' He prayed he had the strength to let her go.

She shook her head and he nearly died. Then she stretched out one slender arm and his pulse revved into life again. 'I want you too. You have no idea how much.'

No game playing, no flirting, just honest need. Her directness was more arousing than any erotic foreplay.

'Oh, I think I do.' Asim snatched her hand and planted a kiss on her palm, then pressed it to his chest where his heart thundered.

In one swift movement he was on the bed, reaching around her for the dress's concealed zip. She stiffened.

What now? His patience was worn paper-thin from holding himself in check. Was this after all some coy game? Yet a look at her face disabused him of that.

'Jacqueline?'

'You first.' Her eyes didn't meet his. Instead she fixed her gaze on his high collar as she fumbled to find how it opened. 'Please.'

No woman had ever asked him to strip for her. Usually it was him watching his latest lover with anticipation.

'Very well.' He stood, quickly shucking his shoes, his hands making short work of the fastenings on his jacket. Moments later it dropped to the floor and he hauled his collarless shirt up over his head, flinging it away. His eyes met hers and the current of sexual energy between them almost blew the back off his skull. Her gaze raked his torso as if he'd spread a banquet before her and she didn't know where to start.

He knew where he wanted her to start. He was hard as the stone quarried to build this palace. His hand dipped to his waistband, his temperature skyrocketing as her gaze followed the movement. Then he thought better of it. Once he was naked this would be over in minutes.

Instead he untucked the end of his silk turban. His hand moved deftly in the familiar task but the intensity of her stare invested it with a sensual significance that turned his blood heavy, making each pulse a ponderous thud that reverberated low and deep.

Eyes holding his, she wriggled off the bed and reached for the fabric in his hand. It arced as she tossed it, a ribbon of bright silk disappearing beyond the bed.

Still she didn't touch him, though her breath wafting across his collarbone was pure sensual torment. His hands clenched.

Grave eyes held his then she spun around, bending her head, giving him unfettered access. Her nape was dewy perfection, drawing his lips as he unfastened the couple of buttons at her neck then tugged the zip till the curve of her spine was revealed, a sinuous invitation. He heard the click of metal as she undid her belt and it dropped.

'Yes!' With one swift movement he wrenched her sleeves down from the wrists so the dress slid off her shoulders to slither with a delicate hiss to the floor.

Creamy perfection filled his vision. He followed the sweep of her back and grinned. No wonder there'd been no line to mar the perfection of her silhouette. His uncertain seductress only wore a thong of champagne lace. It accentuated the perfect ripeness of her derriere and the tantalising swell of her streamlined hips.

'You're so beautiful, Jacqueline.'

There was no holding back. One step brought him flush against her, his erection snug in the groove between her buttocks as he bent his knees. Asim kissed her nape, his hands unerringly finding the soft bounty of her small, high breasts.

His groan was drowned by her hiss of pleasure as he rolled her taut nipples between his fingertips and gently bit her shoulder. A judder rippled through her and she stiffened, her breath hoarse. Then her hands covered his, pressing him closer as she arched, her backside pushing against his arousal, obliterating anything like a plan for seduction.

Had he ever had a woman so responsive? He bent further, raking his tongue up her vertebrae, tasting apricots and cream and the hot tang that was Jacqueline.

She shifted against him and Asim feared he'd come before he'd had a chance to feel her flesh against him. This woman's power to seduce astonished him. Her hands on his were desperate, the swivel of her hips not a practised, sultry invitation but a jerky thrust of unadulterated need and all the more provocative for it.

Slipping one hand from her grip, he arrowed it to the lace between her thighs. He needed to be there *now*, to impale himself in that delicious softness, but he couldn't bear the time it would take to shuck his trousers and strip her thong away. Instead his questing fingers slid straight to her sweet spot and instantly she bucked, making stars whirl as the friction between them morphed from arousing to incendiary.

Her hand slid down his arm just as he pushed two fingers inside her tight heat. Asim felt the quiver begin deep within her and ripple out till it became a quake that made her shudder and rock against him.

CHAPTER EIGHT

WHEN THE WORLD stopped spinning, Jacqui was flat on her back looking up into jet-dark eyes. They glittered, fiery, as Asim raked her body with a scorching look.

Gasping for breath, her limbs liquid, Jacqui didn't have the strength to cover herself when he zeroed in on her breasts.

Heaven knew what magic had happened tonight to make a man like Asim want her but she was past caring. She intended to revel in every single second of it. No doubts. No regrets.

A callused palm brushed her nipple and she jolted as a current of fire raced straight to her womb. She frowned. How could that be, after the climax he'd given her?

His hand stroked back and she reached for him, fingers curling around those wide, straight shoulders, revelling in the silky, hot feel of taut skin over bone and muscle.

She tugged him close. 'I need you.' The aching emptiness inside cried out for Asim.

He shifted, propping himself over her, and she felt the hard, hot length of his body, unfamiliar and utterly breath-taking. She'd been so dazed she hadn't noticed him strip his trousers. Heavy muscle and the tickle of masculine hair created a friction that was unbearably wonderful.

'Please, Asim.' But he ignored her urgency. Slowly he lowered his head and licked her breast and she gasped, her legs flopping open to cradle him.

'So lovely,' he murmured as his gaze collided with hers. 'I

haven't been able to get them out of my mind since that first night. So pert and ripe.' He lowered his head again and tugged gently at her breast, sucking her nipple till Jacqui's head thrust back and her body bowed up into his.

'And so sensitive.' His deep voice was smug. Through slitted eyes she saw dark satisfaction on his taut features.

She swallowed hard, a knot in her throat as she realised she'd never felt so close to beautiful in her whole life as she did now.

He cupped one breast and her breath hissed in ecstasy. 'They're beautiful. Like ripe, fresh fruit. I love that you don't need to wear a bra.' He paused, his brows bunching. 'Except in front of other men. But when you're with me you can go braless.'

There it was again, that domineering tone of a man used to giving orders and getting exactly what he wanted. But Jacqui was too stunned to care.

Since puberty she'd been conscious of her lack of curves. She'd never had to fight men off, like some female colleagues, yet here was Asim...

He dipped his head to suckle her breast and fire zapped her. She arched almost off the bed at the feel of his mouth on her. Was it like this every time? She tunnelled her hands in his thick hair, holding him close, and felt something under her ribs melt.

When you're with me. He made it sound like they'd be together a lot.

He's being kind, whispered a familiar voice. The cutting voice of her stepmother and the girls at school. But how could she heed it as she watched Asim and felt the magic he wrought? The glory of it drowned everything else. Heat drenched her.

'Asim.' She didn't recognise that rusty voice. 'I want you.' She'd never wanted anything so much in her life.

She dragged his head up, making him growl low in his throat as he released her nipple. Their gazes clashed and the febrile shimmer in his might have scared her if she hadn't already left caution far behind. 'I need you.'

His fierce expression didn't ease and Jacqui feared he intended to keep teasing her.

On a surge of desperation she shoved his shoulders, pushing him onto his back, rolling with him till she straddled his hips. The strength beneath her reminded her that she only managed it because he let her, a quizzical gleam in his eyes.

'You like to be on top?' His voice rasped gravel across each sensitive spot. She gasped as her over-stimulated senses threatened to explode just at the sight and sound of him and the furnace of heat that was his erection, hard and amazing between her legs.

She gulped as need and trepidation vied for supremacy. She couldn't bear it if he pulled back now. 'I just can't wait.'

Jacqui reached down to find him already sheathed and her pulse raced even harder. He was heavy and thick in her unsteady hand. She fumbled and almost sobbed in desperation, hating her inexperience.

Asim brushed her fingers away. Seconds later firm hands cradled her hips, guiding her as he thrust up in a long, slow surge of power that halted when she gasped. Jacqui couldn't help it—the feeling of impossible fullness stole her breath.

'Jacqui?' Asim's voice was husky with disbelief. 'Is this your first time?'

She clutched his shoulders, panic rising. She'd come this far, further than she'd ever been with any man, and she wanted it all, with Asim. All these years wondering and now...

'Sorry to disappoint.' She snagged another breath, feeling the tension in her body begin to ease. 'It's just been a while.' If she told him she was a virgin he might stop and she couldn't bear that.

Still he scrutinised her, his brow pleating, and she sensed his doubt. She licked her dry lips, her whole body trembling, waiting for rejection.

After what seemed an eternity he pulled her gently down, filling her inch by slow inch. She had to fight not to let her eyes bulge at the amazing sensations.

He watched her face like a hawk. His jaw was set, his nostrils flared, but it was the look in Asim's eyes that made her heart clutch. He held her captive with those eyes and she never wanted to be free.

Tentatively she rocked her hips, feeling the friction and the heavy throb of pleasure. When she did it again strong hands clasped her, helping her find the elusive rhythm.

He urged her high as he withdrew and bucked up, reaching, she was sure, right to the core of her. Lightning shimmered across her vision. Once, twice and she started to shake. A third time and her legs liquefied.

A tumble of movement and she was on her back, pressed deep into the bed, her vision filled by Asim. His eyes holding hers, his lips drawn in a grimace of pained pleasure, he thrust one more time and the world shattered in colour and light and sensation, overwhelming her.

Shuddering at the delicious shockwaves, Jacqui clutched him close as he powered on and, with a roar of triumph, reached his own pulsating climax.

The awesome force of his orgasm deep within and the juddering intensity of his steaming hot body surrounding hers smashed open some unseen barrier. Jacqui felt tenderness and an unprecedented tug of protectiveness.

She cradled Asim tight with the last of her strength. With trembling fingers she stroked his thick hair while he shuddered in her arms, his breath hot in the valley between her neck and shoulder.

Later they lay entwined, her head on his shoulder, his arm draped around her waist, his other hand spread on her thigh, holding her to him.

'Jacqueline, are you sure you're all right?'

Jacqui smiled drowsily, a delicious shiver rippling through her at the way he said her name. He made it sound mysterious and feminine, and for the first time in her life somehow…right.

'All right? I've never been better in my life.' She threaded her fingers through his. 'Thank you, Asim.'

* * *

Jacqui hurried down the wide corridor, grateful for her flat shoes. If she'd tried to run in the heels she'd worn last night...

She put a brake on her thoughts. Last night was over.

Asim had made that clear when he'd discreetly left her to wake in his bed alone. And she'd been grateful. She had no experience of mornings after and she'd needed time to process everything.

Heat swirled in her belly. Last night had been extraordinary. Magical. She'd felt desired and desirable, sexy and treasured. She'd woken to a sense of well-being that eclipsed grief and doubt. She was grateful to Asim for that gift.

Her gift to him would be proving she had no unrealistic expectations. He needn't fear she'd read too much into kindness and passing attraction.

For him, that was. For her... Well, it hadn't passed. The night together had only made her eager for more, despite the slight ache between her legs. She stifled a smile, remembering in glorious detail her unaccustomed exercise.

Jacqui buttoned her jacket and strode faster. She was late. Her visit to the old harem baths had been fascinating and the female historian informative. But, when the woman had learnt Jacqui had never experienced a traditional Jazeeri bath and massage, she'd insisted that be righted immediately. She'd said Jacqui couldn't write about the process unless she experienced it.

So for the last several hours Jacqui had been bathed, exfoliated, rinsed, covered in herbal concoctions, massaged and scented till she glowed. Every pore felt alive and she was preternaturally aware even of the scrape of cloth over her tingling body.

Or was that the effects of a night of hot sex?

She'd discovered she was a woman with needs, and she'd never been as aware of herself as a sexual being before. She'd never felt so happy in her life.

The shade of Imran rose in her mind and she waited for guilt to slice into her. It was a sign of the change in her that instead it was Imran's grin she recalled, his laughter. The way he'd always urged her to take chances.

Jacqui shook her head. Whatever her needs, she had to sublimate them. A woman had her pride. Sighing over Asim wasn't an option. Yet her pulse tripped as she entered the royal offices.

'Sorry I'm late,' she said to Asim's secretary. 'I got caught up.' Her hand rose to the unfamiliar silky camisole peeping above the deep V of her jacket.

She might have been on time but, opening the wardrobe to grab her trusty suit, she discovered a skimpy camisole instead of her serviceable grey top on the next hanger. There'd been a note pinned to it, an apology from Lady Rania, saying an accident in the laundry had damaged her top beyond repair and offering this replacement. As if Jacqui's ancient cotton top and this fragile garment—spun, she suspected, from gilded spiders' webs—bore any similarity. Even the shade of it, between old gold and amber, was luscious. And disconcerting to a woman not used to wearing anything that drew attention to herself, like bold colours.

Yet what could she do but accept it and hurry to her appointment?

Now, though, as Asim's secretary entered the Sultan's office, Jacqui wondered if she'd done the right thing. Her fingers fluttered over the delicate fabric. Against her skin it felt like a whisper, not clothing. A whisper that teased like the memory of Asim's breath on her bare skin.

Horrified at the sultry heat unfurling within her, Jacqui turned towards the water cooler, stopping as Asim's secretary returned.

'His Highness will see you now.' He smiled and held the door open and Jacqui had no choice but to enter.

Her mouth turned as arid as the great Jazeeri desert when the door closed and she confronted Asim. He stood by the windows, the glare turning him into a formidably large silhouette, his face in shadow.

Jacqui's heart hammered a tattoo against her ribs and she sucked in a breath, grateful he was too far away for her to register the spicy scent of his skin. It had lingered in her nostrils all day, a tantalising reminder.

What to say?

She swallowed and tugged her jacket.

Casual. She needed to be casual and calm. As if last night hadn't blown her self-possession to smithereens then put her back together a different woman.

Jacqui opened her mouth.

'Take it off.' Had his voice been so deep last night? It burred through her, stirring the blood in her veins.

She blinked. 'Sorry?'

'The jacket. It's an offence to my eyes. Take it off.'

At that tone of command her hand jerked up automatically to the button of her jacket before she realised what she was doing.

'I beg your pardon?' She tried to inject her voice with hauteur, but what emerged was a breathless gasp. She'd been prepared for embarrassment and the need to assure Asim she wasn't some lovesick fool. She hadn't expected this.

'So you should. It's appalling.' He crossed his arms. 'Wear it near other men. Never with me.'

Jacqui sucked in air. Again that hint that they'd be alone again and, from the gravelly undercurrent in Asim's voice, intimate.

She shook her head. She was imagining things. 'No thank you.' Best to treat his words as an invitation to be comfortable during their meeting. 'I prefer to keep it on.'

'And I prefer never to see it again.' He paused and when he spoke again his voice was a sultry ribbon of invitation. 'Take it off for me, Jacqueline. Or should I come across and do it for you?'

His words terrified her. It was one thing to tell herself she could pretend to be aloof and quite another to do it if he came near.

She fumbled the button open then peeled the jacket off,

covering the wash of heat across her bare arms and shoulders by taking her time putting it on a chair.

When she turned back she heard a sharp intake of breath.

'Lovely,' he murmured in a voice that turned her blood to sweet, heavy syrup. 'As lovely as I recalled. And you remembered not to wear a bra for me.' His words scraped to the core of her where her insides seemed to be melting. 'I approve of the colour too. You should wear it more often.'

Jacqui licked her lips, about to tell him the camisole was a gift from his grandmother, when her brain slipped into gear. He thought she'd gone braless for him? That she'd wanted to please him in the hope that they'd...?

She gulped, shocked. Wasn't that exactly what she'd done? She'd told herself she was running so late and it wouldn't matter if she was braless as no one else would know. But *she'd* known and with every step, as her tight nipples grazed cobweb-soft silk, she'd thought of Asim.

'Now your hair. Take it down.'

'No! Anyone could come in.'

'No one disturbs the Sultan unless invited.' He spoke with such certainty it hit her anew that he was a man used to having every order obeyed. 'Now, take it down.' Dimly she registered surprise as excitement rather than anger rippled through her.

Part of her wanted to comply. The part that had come alive under his touch and the velvet caress of those dark eyes, not to mention that potently deep voice. But this was broad daylight. They were in his office. They couldn't...

The molten heat between her legs told her they could. That she wanted to.

'Last night I stripped when you asked me, Jacqui.'

Is that what he wanted? A striptease? Her heart hammered so heavily against her chest she wondered if she'd feel bruised later. A shot of adrenalin, heady as neat alcohol, pulsed into her blood.

Her? Strip for him? Horror merged with excitement to skate

down her backbone then burrow through her belly, transforming into butterflies the size of buzzards.

She hated baring her body.

Yet last night he'd made her believe he looked at her skinny frame and saw a different woman to the one she knew.

Fear sliced through her and embarrassment. That pulled her up short.

Did she really want to go back to being the woman she'd been before last night? The woman who hid herself in nondescript work clothes? Even if all she'd experienced with Asim was an illusion, it was an illusion she craved.

Did she dare? Anxiety cramped her stomach.

Her hands went to her ponytail. A few practised flicks and her hair fell in waves around her cheeks and shoulders.

'Now the trousers.' His voice was gruff. She couldn't read his face. Yet even after a single night she recognised the edge in his voice. No matter how he tried to hide it, Asim was as desperate as she. At least she hoped he was.

Praying he was right and no one would dare enter, she snapped open the button on her waistband, lowered the zip and wriggled till the fabric pooled at her feet. She felt shockingly vulnerable yet daring.

Her skin was so sensitised the air on her legs felt heavy. She breathed deep and told herself she wouldn't regret this. She wouldn't allow herself to.

'Now come here.'

Gingerly she stepped out of her trousers, leaving her shoes behind, and padded across the carpet. With each step tension coiled higher, till she stopped before him. Now she read his expression and was glad she hadn't been able to earlier. He looked so fierce that heat licked inside. His eyes glittered as she imagined those of his warlike ancestors might have when they'd spied a trade caravan loaded with riches entering their realm.

She shivered and rubbed her hands up her arms.

'You're cold?' Still he didn't touch her. She shook her head and he nodded, a tiny, knowing smile lifting the corner of his mouth. 'You won't be for long, Jacqueline. Sit on my desk.'

She followed his glance to the antique desk, bare except for a sleek computer and a single tray of papers.

Arousal shuddered through her as she pictured making love on that gleaming surface. It would be hard, fast and satisfying. She wanted him so badly she almost obeyed without a word of protest. She, who'd never been intimate with a man before last night!

'You're sure no one will come in?' Excitement and dread warred.

'Be assured, Jacqueline. We won't be disturbed. My secretary has left and locked the outer office on the way out.'

Her eyes widened. 'You told him to? But he'll know we're...' She shook her head as words failed her.

A small voice inside jeered that, standing almost naked, she'd left it late to have second thoughts.

'Fahid is utterly discreet. You have nothing to worry about.' Asim stepped closer and at once the vast study shrank. She felt crowded, excited and aroused, yet at the same time annoyed.

This was utterly unfamiliar territory. Last night had turned her inside out, made her question long-held certainties and put her trust in a man she barely knew. Even so it had felt right.

Now, abruptly, standing half-dressed while he calmly gave orders, unease spiked. If only Asim had come to her, embraced her, done something other than bark instructions. Tension crawled along her shoulders. Indignation rose. She might be desperate but she had some self-respect.

'Do you make a habit of seducing women on your desk?' The words shot out and she raised her chin, battling to hide churning distress.

She didn't expect declarations of undying devotion but she wasn't some convenience, available to satisfy a passing itch.

Nevertheless, she had to fight her needy body that swayed towards him as if seeking a caress from its master.

He strode forward till they almost touched. His brilliant

gaze raked her; the subtle scent of his skin filled her nostrils, weakening her knees. He radiated heat that hazed her skin.

'I have never seduced a woman here.' He paused and Jacqui was surprised to see him swallow. 'My desk has been used for nothing but paperwork.' His eyes narrowed to glittering darts that scraped her skin. His voice was steely. 'I spend my days and many of my nights here working, not dallying with women. As for Fahid guessing...' Asim's shoulders rose in a shrug. 'It seemed preferable to have privacy rather than run the risk of interruption.'

'Because you were so sure I'd give you what you want.' And he'd been right. Jacqui had bared herself to camisole and panties, desperate for his touch. Were her doubts just delaying tactics so she didn't have to acknowledge she was putty in his hands? Her stomach cramped.

'What we *both* want. Don't deny it, Jacqueline. I see the flush of arousal on your perfect skin. Your pulse races and your beautiful breasts are rising fast because your breathing is too shallow.'

He was right. Her body betrayed her. She wanted him.

Yet she needed more, proof this meant something to him too. That they were equals in this.

Doubt lingered. Why had Asim made love to her? Had he been motivated by pity and mere convenience? Last night she hadn't thought so but today he seemed so cold and uninvolved. It was hard to shake a lifetime of self-doubt.

'Then why haven't you touched me?' Despite her intentions it sounded like a plea.

He shook his head, his face grim. 'Once I touch you, Jacqueline, there'll be no holding back, no time for finesse. I've spent the whole day waiting for you, and I'm not a patient man.'

Startled, Jacqui gazed up at that strongly sculpted face and felt heat squiggle through her. Now she saw more than his piercing gaze. A pulse throbbed at his temple. His squared jaw was set and the tendons visible in his neck spoke of tension. Tension *she'd* put there? Heady relief and pleasure filled her.

His big hands flexed as if resisting the urge to reach for her. The movement drew attention to the bulge in his trousers she hadn't noticed earlier.

Remembering the heavy, delicious weight of him, the softness of satin over forged steel, her inner muscles contracted. His body fascinated her but last night, though they'd shared more intimacies than she'd ever experienced, he'd been the one exploring her body. She'd had no chance to satisfy her curiosity.

'Sit on the desk, Jacqueline.' His voice was harsh but she caught an edge of desperation. 'I promise you'll enjoy it.'

'No.'

'No?' Asim's head reared back, his eyes rounding. He'd been so sure of her. And not used to anyone denying him what he wanted. 'What do you mean, *no*?' It was a roar of outrage.

Jacqui licked dry lips as excitement and trepidation warred. She made herself meet his eyes.

We're equals, she told herself. He might be lord of all he surveys but she wasn't his subject. Besides, something had changed after last night—the way he'd confronted her hang-ups and shown her they meant nothing to him. Her body hummed with arousal and a woman's curiosity.

'No, I don't want you to take me on your desk. Not yet.' For now she said it aloud she was shocked at how appealing it sounded.

'Then what do you want?' His brow furrowed in a scowl.

For a moment longer she hesitated, but her body, primed by a day of physical pampering and now by proximity to Asim, had no doubts.

She dropped to her knees and heard his hiss of indrawn breath. Reaching out, she flicked open the button at the top of this trousers and tugged the zip.

'This,' she said, reaching for him.

CHAPTER NINE

SHE WAS KILLING HIM.

Hour by hour she drove him quietly insane.

Asim frowned as strode from the stables. His ride hadn't cleared his head. It was filled with Jacqueline. Her sighs as she snuggled up to him in bed; the look of exhilaration when he told her how beautiful she was.

The spark of devilment in her eyes when she occasionally convinced him to let her take the lead in sex. He tightened as heat flashed through him. Remembering her hands on him, her mouth—hot and sultry and a little clumsy—brought him to fever pitch all over again.

He'd wondered that first night if she was a virgin, but she'd been adamant and he'd let himself be persuaded. Now he was convinced he'd been right. Jacqueline was passionate and eager but definitely inexperienced.

Or she had been.

Asim's jaw clenched. At least that had relieved his earlier discomfort that he might be poaching on his cousin's territory. Imran really had been just a friend. But now there was guilt that he'd seduced a virgin. A decent man would have pulled back straight away, respecting her innocence. But with Jacqueline Asim feared he had no control.

She was a *houri*, an enchantress.

She was disrupting his well-ordered life.

Was he mad, having an affair with a journalist? Logic should say yes but instinctively he trusted her.

He grimaced and entered the palace, nodding to a guard.

Sleep he could do without. He preferred to spend the midnight hours exploring Jacqueline's insatiable appetite for passion. She interfered with his work too. Those daily briefings on her research became long interludes that left him smiling and sated yet still hungry for her.

Worse, she interrupted his thoughts. Yesterday during another round of trade negotiations he'd found himself recalling her pithy assessment of one foreign diplomat. On impulse he'd changed his carefully laid approach to test what she'd suggested was a weakness in the foreign position. And the hunch had paid off! She'd been correct.

He should thank her; she'd saved him time and effort. Yet that crossover from lover to advisor niggled.

Asim kept his women separate from his public life.

That would change a little when he had a wife, of course. His wife would be intelligent and experienced enough to deal with diplomats, royalty and all manner of VIPs. But in the meantime it disturbed him that he found himself thinking about Jacqueline so often.

That was another thing. She stymied his search for a bride. How could he devote himself to that important task when the passion between them flared so hot? Obviously it would dim with time, passion always did, but in the meantime he owed it to himself, and his country to choose an appropriate wife. Yet lately the few he'd seen hadn't come close to arousing interest.

One had been superficially suitable: engaging, intelligent and well-bred. But he'd felt no spark of attraction. How could he spend his life with a woman if he wasn't interested enough to bed her?

Another candidate he'd mentally dismissed as too short. Too short! Just because he relished the fact that when he kissed Jacqueline he didn't have to fold himself in half to reach her lips.

Plus the feel of her long, slim legs locked around his waist was currently one of his greatest pleasures.

Asim grunted in self-disgust. At thirty-five he needed to find a suitable wife and start a family, securing the throne for the future. He couldn't afford to fixate on a woman as his father had done with his mother. Their passion had been unhealthily intense, turning into a sick relationship that had damaged all the family.

Starting today, Asim would do what he should have been doing: focus on his search for the perfect queen.

'I'm so glad my grandmother finally brought you to visit.'

Jacqui watched her companion twirl her long sable hair. It was a nervous gesture Princess Samira had repeated several times since Jacqui had arrived.

The princess was a beauty. The harsh, extravagantly male cast of Asim's aristocratic features were, in his younger sister, softened. They had the same hooded eyes, though in his sister's case they were a rich sherry colour. Her mouth was lush, not thin, and her jaw, though determined, wasn't uncompromisingly hard.

Yet despite her beauty there were shadows under her eyes and she had a lustreless quality as if weighed down by unimaginable woes.

'I'm honoured you invited me.' And intrigued that Lady Rania had left them alone after half an hour.

Jacqui's chest squeezed in sympathy as the princess fumbled the traditional coffee pot she'd been tending, her hand unsteady. She looked tired and fragile but her minuscule frown as she concentrated on pouring the honeyed coffee into tiny cups reminded Jacqui of Asim.

But everything reminded her of Asim. He was in her thoughts constantly. She spent the night flush against his big, naked body, and even when she dreamed it was of him, not the horror that had haunted her for months.

'Thank you, Your Highness.' Jacqui accepted a steaming, fragrant cup.

'Please, call me Samira.' The other woman smiled and Jacqui caught her breath at the impact a little animation had on her face. More than beautiful, she was stunning. No wonder the press was avaricious for photos. That face would sell millions of magazines.

It took a moment to realise the other woman's smile had faded.

'I'd be honoured.' Jacqui was surprised at the unlooked for offer. 'Thank you, Samira. And I'm Jacqui.'

'Not Jacqueline, as my brother calls you?'

Jacqui froze, the cup halfway to her lips. 'He talks about me?' Intimate as they were, she hadn't expected him to discuss her with his sister.

A mischievous smile tugged Samira's mouth. 'More than I suspect he realises. But my grandmother and I don't tell him.' She lifted her cup to her lips. 'Now I've begun to know you a little, I understand why.'

Jacqui wondered what sort of back-handed compliment that was. Except the princess struck her as genuine and friendly. And they had something in common: Asim.

Why did everything come back to him?

It was because he'd taken over her world, turning it from dark grey to glowing brightness.

He'd made her happier than she'd dared hope.

And he made her feel special. So special it scared her, made her worry this couldn't be real. She'd never felt such closeness, even with her family. Was she imagining he cared for her because she wanted it to be true? Was she extra needy because of the stress she'd gone through?

'Tell me more about your project, Jacqui. I was too…unwell to attend the sessions with my grandmother and her friends. But I'd like to hear more.'

An hour later they were on their second coffees and the conversation had veered through traditional Jazeeri dresses to the silvery grey designer original Jacqui had worn at the formal dinner.

'You mean you designed it?' She leaned forward, admiring the portfolio Samira had produced. There were sketches, fabric swatches and photos of finished dresses. All were stunning, ultra-feminine in an unfussy, eye-catching style that instantly appealed.

'Grandmother wanted to give you a gift.' Samira smiled. 'She is so excited about your book and the sensitive way you're approaching it. She wasn't sure you had something suitable for Asim's formal dinner.'

'I don't. Didn't.' Jacqui shook her head. 'I still can't believe you designed that amazing dress. And these. They're gorgeous.'

Samira shrugged. 'It's a very trivial talent, nothing compared with the work you do—'

'Nonsense!' The word shot out and belatedly Jacqui wondered if she'd been too forthright when Samira stiffened.

Jacqui had enjoyed their conversation so much she'd almost forgotten her companion's royal status, and that they'd just met. It felt as if they'd known each other for ages. 'I'm sorry. I didn't mean to be rude.' Even now Samira didn't smile and the shadows were back in her eyes. Jacqui wondered if it was just her break-up with her actor boyfriend that had wounded her, or something deeper.

'What I meant was that we each have talents and should be grateful for them. I could never design anything as beautiful as this.' She gestured to a photo of a blonde model whose evening gown of midnight blue swirled around her like a dream.

'You're gifted in a way that brings beauty into the world. Much of my job dealt with an uglier reality. It was necessary, because people have to know the truth about the world around them, but they need beauty too.'

Perhaps that was why her book was giving her a new sense of optimism. Despite the negatives to harem life, there was great beauty and grace too, personified by the remarkable old women she'd been privileged to meet.

'You should be proud of your talent, Samira. These are amazing. But you've only designed for friends? Why aren't you doing this professionally?'

'A good question, but not one for today.' Asim's deep voice came from behind her and instantly her flesh prickled in awareness. She drew in a breath, willing her pulse not to racket so fast, afraid her response to him would be too obvious. Since they'd become lovers it grew harder to pretend in public.

'Asim!' Samira smiled. 'I didn't expect to see you again today. I thought you were working.'

Jacqui turned. Asim filled the doorway, resplendent in a turban and embroidered tunic of dark blue. His stern features gave nothing away but suddenly she recalled his furious accusation when she'd first arrived, that she'd come to ferret out a story about his sister.

Is that what he thought? His hooded eyes were impenetrable but the line of his shoulders was stiff.

'I was stood up for my meeting.'

'Stood up?' Samira frowned. 'Someone cancelled a meeting with *you*?'

His gaze switched to Jacqui. Her blood sizzled and the breath stuck in her throat.

Suddenly Samira laughed. It sounded breathless, as if she was out of practice. 'Your meeting was with Jacqui?'

Jacqui blinked and looked at her watch. Samira was right. Jacqui should have been in Asim's office ten minutes ago. She'd lost track of time.

'Who else would dare be late for an appointment with you?' Despite the teasing lilt in Samira's voice, Jacqui couldn't find an answering smile. Not when Asim's scrutiny skewered her where she sat.

An apology rose to her lips but she knew it wasn't her tardiness he took issue with. It was that she was with his sister after he'd forbidden such contact. She stared back. 'I'm sorry, Asim.' To her chagrin she stumbled over his name. 'I'll come now.'

Still he said nothing and Jacqui was appalled at how that wounded her. Did he trust her so little after what they'd shared?

'Or you could stay too,' Samira offered.

Asim prowled across and put a hand on his sister's shoulder. His expression softened. 'I'd like that. But Jacqueline and I need to discuss a few things. I'll return later.'

I, not we.

'Thank you for your hospitality, Samira.' Jacqui got up and pasted on what she hoped was a convincing smile. 'I enjoyed our time together.' Far from being a pampered princess with no thoughts outside her social calendar, Samira was someone Jacqui wanted to know better.

'I'll look forward to your next visit.'

Jacqui smiled but said nothing, guessing Asim would ban any such visit, if he didn't simply banish Jacqui from the palace. Her stomach dived. He wouldn't keep her here if he thought it compromised his sister's well-being.

Lovers they might be, but theirs was a physical relationship, despite the late-night chats they shared about everything under the sun. An hour ago she'd have said they'd begun to know each other, sharing their tastes in books and politics and their mutual love of chess. But, looking into his dark eyes, Jacqui saw no warmth. She felt hollow.

Repressing a shudder, she followed him.

Asim remained silent as they traversed the palace. Instead of going to his office, they went to his suite.

So he could oversee her packing? Jacqui's stomach twisted in mixed fury and hurt as she bit down instinctive protests. She would wait till they had privacy.

As soon as they entered his private wing she spun to face him. 'I suppose you're going to accuse me of engineering a meeting with Samira so I could sell a story to the gutter press.'

'Are you?' He leaned against the door jamb, crossing his arms. He looked smugly superior, and devastatingly sexy despite that harsh expression.

Pain smacked her in the chest as she realised how much his

trust had meant. For he *had* trusted her these last weeks. The guard shadowing her as she roved the palace had disappeared the night of the banquet and lately Asim had even discussed some of his work, describing at least in broad terms various projects and negotiations. She'd loved the sense that they shared more than sex, stupendous as that was.

'Of course I'm not. You know why I'm here.' When he didn't respond she stepped into his personal space, so close her breasts almost brushed his crossed arms.

'Except you don't believe me, do you? One of your palace spies came tattling that I was with Samira and you raced to save her from my evil clutches.'

Pain scored deep. She'd thought he believed in her.

'Palace spies?' His brows lifted, accelerating the fire in her blood.

'You know. The guards who used to watch me.'

Slowly he shook his head and for a moment she'd have sworn amusement flickered in his eyes. 'Actually, it was my grandmother who told me.'

'She did?' Jacqui took a step backwards, only to find she wasn't going anywhere. Asim's hands were firm on her elbows.

'Not so fast, my little firebrand.'

'Hardly little!' She didn't need his condescension.

His mouth curled at one corner in an almost-smile that did ridiculous things to her insides and made her despair of her own good sense. How could she be attracted to a man who patently didn't trust her?

'Compared with me, you are. Deliciously so.' He pulled her in, his arms wrapping round her. 'Tall enough to fit me but slender and fine-boned and, oh, so sexy.'

She shoved his chest but made no headway. He held her and her insides melted like chocolate in the Jazeeri sun. Her weakness appalled her.

'What a shame then that you don't believe a word I say.'

'Who said I don't, *habibti*?'

'But you…' Her words petered out as she watched that smile take hold and turn into a grin. 'You let me believe…'

'I merely preferred to have our discussion in private rather than where we might be overheard. I never said I didn't believe you.'

'Then why didn't you *say* something?' She shook her head, the wind taken out of her sails.

One large hand tugged her hair loose of its ponytail.

'Far better,' he murmured. 'I like your hair loose. You look like one of our Jazeeri lionesses with that spark in your amber eyes and your tawny hair rippling around your shoulders.' His voice dropped to a seductive caress. 'I love it when you argue, Jaqueline. You have such fire. Such passion. And I want it all.'

He pulled her closer and she was stunned to feel his arousal against her belly. Instantly the fierce roil of emotions within transformed to familiar hunger as instinctively she moulded herself to him. Asim threaded his fingers through her hair, pulling her face to his.

'Yes,' he murmured against her ear, 'Like that.'

'No!' She tried to insert space between them, levering herself back from his chest, even though the movement pushed her lower body against his and the friction there felt so good she almost groaned.

'Wait,' she gasped. 'You mean you deliberately picked a fight to watch me lose my temper?' Disbelief warred with something unbelievably close to delight.

'I did nothing, *habibti*, but say I wished to speak with you. You did the rest and I'm man enough to enjoy the fireworks.' His hand slipped down to her breast and she saw stars as he gently kneaded the sensitive mound.

'You, you arrogant, conniving—' Her head lolled as he nipped her earlobe and insinuated his hand beneath her shirt, tweaking her nipple. Fire arced, drawing her tight against his body.

'And you don't mind at all, do you, my sweet?' he murmured as he kissed his way down her throat and delight rippled through her. 'Because you're not intimidated and making up is so very, very satisfying.'

Jacqui opened her mouth but all that emerged was a feathery sigh as she succumbed to his expert touch.

With a tight smile Asim swung her round so her back was to the wall. Then he proceeded to show her exactly how satisfying making up could be.

CHAPTER TEN

ASIM LEANED INTO HER, chest heaving, trembling in the aftermath of a climax that had blown him apart. Stars faded behind his closed lids.

He nuzzled the tender skin at the base of her neck, inhaling the scent of summer-ripened apricots. She shuddered and clenched around him one last time and impossibly he felt a flicker of renewed response.

Virile he might be but Jacqueline Fletcher pushed him to limits he'd never thought possible.

Was that why he'd sought her out in Samira's rooms rather than whittle down the list of bridal candidates? He'd returned from his ride determined to give that task his full attention and instead he'd given in to temptation again. He hadn't been able to settle as the clock had passed the hour for their usual appointment.

It disturbed him, how his usual control deserted him around her.

'Asim?' He loved hearing her voice like this, low and breathy. 'You should put me down.'

For answer he widened his stance, wedging her tighter against the wall, her legs still around his waist. He didn't want to let her go. He wanted her right where she was.

How long would it take to convince her she wasn't too tall or her perfect breasts too small? That she was beautiful? It didn't matter. He enjoyed demonstrating how wrong she was.

Except one day he'd have to put her aside when he took a wife. The realisation exploded his sense of well-being.

Some internal organ he couldn't identify clenched hard in denial.

He distracted himself by kissing her bare shoulder. 'You have the most perfect skin,' he murmured. 'Like cream. How did you grow up in Australia and not get covered in freckles?'

'I have freckles!'

'A smattering on your nose and a couple on your hands, no more.'

'My mother insisted I cover up in the sun and I kept the habit of wearing long sleeves. It wasn't difficult. Summers in Tasmania are short.'

She wriggled and reluctantly Asim decided it was time to move. The condom needed disposal, then they should talk.

Minutes later, after a slow kiss that left Jacqueline satisfyingly silent and starry-eyed, Asim headed for the bathroom.

His jaw set as he saw his reflection in the mirror. The dishevelled clothes didn't bother him, but the unfamiliar expression in his eyes did. It was more than sexual satisfaction. More than smugness at having silenced the most argumentative, feisty woman he knew.

There was something disturbing about that look. He wished he knew what it was. Just as he wished he understood his feelings for Jacqueline.

They were lovers—simple.

Yet he'd never let any woman so close. Physical intimacy was one thing, but she'd inveigled her way into other parts of his life, his work, his thoughts, even his decision making.

He'd come after her to warn her about Samira. Not to warn her off—and that was another disturbing factor. With Jacqueline he'd slid too easily past distrust into acceptance that she was a woman of honour who wouldn't harm his sister.

Asim breathed sharply, bewildered by his faith in her. Such trust went against every instinct. Asim had spent a lifetime standing alone, forced to rely on no one but himself.

His little sister had needed protecting as a child in the hothouse atmosphere of his parents' unstable passion. They'd been so caught up in their roller-coaster relationship they'd used her as a pawn in their battles one day and neglected her the next. Samira still needed protection.

His grandmother... He trusted her and cared for her, but she hadn't been there when he was young and now it was his role to look after her.

Yet with Jacqueline, who wasn't even family, he found himself wanting to share parts of himself he never had before.

Asim shook his head. He was not becoming fixated on her. He was *not* repeating the mistakes of his father. He was in control.

Jacqui sat back in a chair beneath a courtyard tree and closed her eyes, drawing in a shaky breath. As if that could calm her racing pulse.

She and Asim had just had frantic, raunchy, scream-out-loud sex against a wall and all she could think of was doing it again.

This was getting out of hand. She'd never thought of herself as highly sexed. If anything she'd wondered at her lack of libido. Was she becoming a sex addict?

Or, worse, addicted to Asim?

He'd tricked her into anger just to watch her temper catch fire! He'd been unrepentant and smug and she hadn't been able to resist him. She hadn't much put up even token resistance when he'd stripped her clothes away and taken her hard and fast and, oh, so satisfyingly. If anything, the remnants of her fury had added extra sizzle to the scorching experience.

The warm breeze stirred her clothes, reminding her of his breath on her skin. She sighed.

'Pleasant thoughts?' A finger trailed down her cheek, her throat, to swirl around her peaked nipple and she sat up with a jerk, eyes snapping open. Eyes as dark as midnight met hers and longing throbbed through her. To touch him, but more, so much more.

Shock hit her. She told herself it was the aftermath of the best sex of her life.

Pity she didn't believe it.

Asim sank into a chair turned towards hers. He looked cool and collected, as if she'd imagined the last half hour. Jacqui felt again as if she played catch-up.

'I want to talk to you about Samira.'

Jacqui blinked. 'I'm not going to do a media piece about her.' Surely he knew that?

Asim raised his hand. 'I know you didn't come here to investigate her. I know it was my grandmother's idea to bring the two of you together.'

'But?'

'You need to know my sister is fragile at the moment.'

Slowly Jacqui nodded. 'I'd picked that up.' It wasn't just the rings under Samira's eyes but her mention of having been unwell and her patent lack of strength. 'Being hounded by the paparazzi on top of that very public break-up must have been incredibly stressful.'

Since Samira and her boyfriend had once been dubbed the world's most beautiful couple, the media had gone into frenzy at their spectacular bust-up. Lurid details of his affair and the disruption to the blockbuster film he'd been shooting only added fuel to the flames.

'The press won't leave her alone. They want the inside story on her heartbreak.' Asim spoke through gritted teeth and Jacqui reached to cover his hand. Instantly he turned his, meshing their fingers and holding tight.

Funny how that small gesture stopped Jacqui's breath.

He was a remarkable man, the Sultan of Jazeer. His modern country still adhered to many ancient traditions. She imagined a lot of men in his situation washing their hands of an unmarried sister whose love life was so public, or who even *had* a love life.

As if reading her mind, he spoke. 'She's an adult and she makes her own choices. Living overseas seemed to suit her.

She was so excited about her textile and design course. She excelled at it too.'

He paused, watching a pair of tiny birds flutter in the trees.

'Then she fell in love.' His voice rang hollow on the word. Clearly he despised the man Samira had fallen for. How could he not? 'To say it wasn't a good match is an understatement, but despite her gentleness my sister is stubborn.'

'Possibly it runs in the family.' His head swung around, eyebrows lifting, and Jacqui shrugged. 'Both you and your grandmother have decided views, even if your grandmother isn't quite so...'

'Domineering?'

She saw the gleam in Asim's eyes and smiled. 'There are times when that can be quite invigorating.' Jacqui's gaze slid towards the entry foyer where he'd just taken her so thoroughly.

He laughed and the sound shivered through her, a rare treat.

'But not all the time?' His expression sobered. 'Suffice to say she fancied herself in *love* with the louse.'

There it was again, that condemnation on the word 'love'.

'When he betrayed her it came out of the blue and her world crumbled.' Asim scowled, his expression rough hewn. His fingers tightened on hers, almost to the point of pain, and she sensed suppressed violence.

Samira's ex-lover was incredibly lucky Asim hadn't exacted revenge. It would be in character, unless Samira had pleaded with him for mercy. Even the few minutes she'd seen brother and sister together had revealed Asim's strong feelings for Samira. If she'd begged him to stay his hand he would have done it.

'What you don't know is that there's more to the story than a love affair gone wrong.'

Late sunlight sneaked through the branches and gilded Asim's jaw. It might have been cast in bronze for all the softness she could see. A pulse beat rapidly at his temple. Once more she was reminded of an ancient warrior, eager for combat.

He drew a slow breath and eased his grip. When he turned she saw heat in his eyes, but regret too.

'Samira is recuperating from more than the shock of his betrayal.' He paused and for the first time ever Jacqui sensed him hesitate. 'I can't betray her confidence by saying more, but I want you to know and be prepared. Samira isn't strong, either physically or emotionally. More perhaps than is obvious.'

Concern etched Asim's features. She respected him all the more for not sharing his sister's private affairs without permission.

Her mind whirled. What could have made such an appalling situation worse? But it was none of her business.

'You need to know, to take that into consideration as you get to know her.'

Startled, Jacqui stared up at him. 'You seem very sure that's going to happen.'

Amusement lightened his stern features. 'I know you, my little firebrand, and I know my sister. Now you've met, there's no chance of keeping you apart.' He pulled her hand onto his thigh and clamped his palm over it so she felt the flex and bunch of hot muscle through his trousers. 'It would be counterproductive trying to keep you apart.'

Jacqui tilted her head. 'Because it's not worth the argument?'

He shook his head. 'Because you're good for her. She's been in hiding too long. I heard you telling her she was talented and should pursue her work. You talked about her gift of creating beauty and she *listened*. I saw it in her face.' His voice roughened.

'You have no idea how hard it's been to break through to her. Or perhaps it's that you're an unbiased outsider, so your words count more. Whatever the reason, I want to thank you for what you did today.'

Warmth filled Jacqui. When he looked at her that way the world brightened.

'You brought a breath of fresh air with you. I saw it as soon as I walked in on you two. It's the first time in ages I've seen roses in her cheeks.'

'When she smiles your sister is breathtakingly lovely.'

Asim didn't smile in agreement. To Jacqui's surprise, his mouth tightened. 'It's a burden she's carried all her life. Just like our mother.'

'A burden?' To Jacqui it seemed a benefit.

'Beauty like that doesn't guarantee happiness. It attracts trouble. Stunning women become invested in their looks and how people view them. As they age it undermines their sense of themselves. They panic and become demanding, needing more attention, more proof of their beauty.' He shook his head. 'It would need to be a very secure and confident man to marry a gorgeous woman. Otherwise he'd spend his life fretting over whether she's unfaithful.'

Jacqui opened her mouth to ask how he knew so much about it. But of course he did. His mother had been one of the beauties of her age. Jacqui had seen the press photos. Plus she'd skimmed reports linking his mother to one eligible bachelor after another, stories hinting all wasn't well in the Jazeeri royal marriage.

'Hopefully one day your sister will fall in love with a man who values her for herself, not just the way she looks.'

Asim snorted. *'Love?'*

'You disagree?'

'I don't believe in it.' Jacqui felt him tense beneath her touch. 'At best it's a fool's dream, something the weak hang onto.'

Jacqui frowned, disturbed more than she could say by his dismissive attitude. 'Your grandmother doesn't strike me as weak or foolish yet she believes in love.'

'My grandparents lived in a different time.' He lifted his shoulders. 'Maybe love was possible then.' He shot her a dark stare. 'Why? Do you believe romantic love can solve all your woes?' His look was sharp, almost accusing. She felt it cut, despite the comfort of his hand on hers.

'I don't know. I hadn't thought about it.' She'd never

dreamed of Mr Right sweeping her off her feet. She'd never allowed herself to dream, except about achieving her next professional goal.

Suddenly it struck Jacqui how wonderful it would be to have more than her career to look back on when she was old. How wonderful to share your life with one special person.

'What is it?' He leaned close, as if he could read the lightning-bolt flash that momentarily blinded her.

What would it be like to share her life with Asim? The trembling shock of the idea couldn't douse effervescent delight. A lifetime spent getting to know Asim, discovering his secrets as he uncovered hers. A lifetime feeling more special, more alive, than she'd ever been before. The idea was so heady she felt dizzy.

'Jacqueline?'

She met his probing gaze and found herself wondering if his children would have the same dark eyes, like black velvet.

She tried to tug her hand free. Asim simply tightened his grip, leaning towards her. Panic filled her and she went on the attack.

'Just because your parents weren't in love doesn't mean it's not possible.'

'Oh, but they were. In love.' His lips twisted in a parody of a smile. 'At least that's what they called it. I thought it was a battle for supremacy, one playing off the other. They covered it all—sickly sweet romantic gestures and times when no one existed but the pair of them, not even their children. But more often it was jealousy, sulks, rages and ultimatums, then break-ups and reconciliations. They tried to use Samira and me in their one-upmanship but they lost interest in us as soon as they reconciled.'

'It sounds awful.' Surely that sort of volatile, chaotic childhood would leave its scars? He'd hinted it had affected Samira. How had it affected him? Jacqui wondered if this explained why Asim liked being in control and having his commands obeyed. He thrived on order and logic.

'And as a result you don't believe in love?' She needed, desperately, to understand him.

'Perhaps there are some lucky couples who've found it, but I suspect most of them put a good face on it. The best you can hope for is an amicable marriage with someone you respect.'

'That sounds very businesslike.' Perhaps at last she'd discovered a cultural chasm between them. Until now there'd been little, apart from Asim's tendency to expect instant obedience to his wishes, to reinforce the different worlds they came from. As she refused to be obsequious, and they usually negotiated an agreed position when she wanted something for her research, she'd pushed that to the back of her mind.

'Why not? Marriage is the most important venture in a person's life. It deserves careful consideration rather than some impetuous decision influenced by a hormonal rush.'

Jacqui smiled wistfully. 'I can't imagine you doing that.'

'I should hope not!'

She looked into his severely sculpted features and tried to imagine him doing anything as impulsive as falling in love. He was so contained.

Yet Asim could act on impulse. Like when he audaciously made love to her at unexpected times and places. Sometimes he shocked her, novice that she was to this game of passion. He also made occasional impulsive decisions, though he'd label them instinctive, when he pursued an unexpected tack in his diplomatic work. Those flashes of intuition added to his reputation for brilliance.

'How about you, Jacqueline?' His fingers stroked the back of her hand. 'Have you ever fancied yourself in love?'

'Never.'

'Really?'

He looked so intent she had to ask. 'Why so surprised?'

His gaze shuttered and he looked away. 'I thought females were susceptible to romantic fantasy.'

'Not this one. I suppose I spent too much time with boys to see them as anything to fantasise about.'

'Lots of brothers?'

'In a way.' She paused, hesitating. Asim knew her weaknesses, her dreams and fears. What would happen if she shared her past too? She was used to protecting her privacy. Would opening up make her even more vulnerable to him?

He sat, waiting as if he had all the time in the world. The comfort of his presence, his touch, in this beautiful, peaceful garden worked its magic and she felt her shoulders relax and drop.

'Half-brothers and step-brothers.'

'Your parents were busy.'

'You could say that.' She huffed out a breath of laughter. 'They split when I was ten. But there were no fights or shouting. Just...coolness. One day we were together and the next they were moving on to their new families.'

His fingers tightened. 'They already had new families?'

Jacqui nodded. 'My father was seeing a woman who already had three boys. The eldest was just a year younger than me. My mother moved away and by the time she remarried she was pregnant with the first of two sons.'

'So you stayed with your father?'

Even after all this time Jacqui felt that familiar stab of hurt at being unwanted. Not once in her life had she felt truly loved.

Was that why Asim's attention made her so happy?

Her mouth flattened. 'No. They decided it was best to share responsibility so I went back and forth between the households.'

Asim shifted, closing the distance between them. 'It doesn't sound like you were happy.'

She lifted her shoulders. 'The boys weren't bad, though sometimes they really enjoyed getting their babysitter into trouble.'

'You had a babysitter as well as your parents?'

'No. I was the babysitter. My mother...' Stupid to let it get to her after all this time. 'My mother was more interested in her new family. I was a bit of an embarrassment to her and my stepmother made it clear I was only accepted in her house if I made myself useful.'

'And your father?' Asim's voice was terse.

She shook her head at the sight of the militant spark in his eyes. 'My parents aren't bad people. They never maltreated me. They were just more focused on their new families.'

'Leaving you adrift.' There it was again, that trace of angry protectiveness. Like when he'd accused her of having a distorted body image. Secretly she adored arousing his protective instincts. Even for a capable, modern woman there was something thrilling about a take-charge man wanting to make things right for you.

'I wasn't adrift. I made my own way. I dreamed of becoming a journalist and learning independence early helped.' He didn't look convinced. 'Besides, given the number of men in current affairs reporting, knowing how the male mind works is a distinct advantage. All those years coping with testosterone-filled teens was great grounding.'

Asim gave a bark of laughter. 'That would explain why you've never been intimidated by me.'

Jacqui kept her mouth shut rather than correct him. There'd been times, especially in the beginning, when she'd felt completely out of her depth and more than a little daunted. That was before she'd realised that behind his tough exterior and ruthless decision-making lurked a man of compassion and surprising tenderness.

'We're well matched, Jacqueline. Both of us are pragmatists. Neither of us is foolish enough to fall for the fantasy of romantic love.'

She looked into those gleaming eyes, saw his satisfied smile and felt some of her bright, glowing pleasure grow dull and brittle.

CHAPTER ELEVEN

ASIM WALKED WITH his entourage through the throng, exchanging greetings. They'd assembled in the plain where festivities were traditionally held. Once, tribes had travelled days by horse or camel to get here. Tonight, on the tenth anniversary of his accession to the throne, most had driven and some had flown around the globe.

There was laughter and feasting after a day of entertainment: displays of horsemanship, archery and shooting as well as athletics, dancing and horse racing.

Satisfaction buzzed. Jazeer had prospered and developed in ways that made him proud. He wasn't solely responsible, but his government had achieved much, far more than under his father's unstable rule.

He neared the gateway to the royal enclosure, on high ground abutting the citadel. The crimson and gold Jazeeri royal banner flared and snapped in the breeze.

Movement beneath it caught his eye and he paused, his breath locking.

How did she do it?

He should be immune to Jacqueline Fletcher or at least accustomed to her presence. She spent every night in his bed and they shared more hours awake than he had shared with any previous lover. Yet still she made his heart hammer.

His gaze roved over the slim figure in amber. She was stunning, a beacon glowing in the early evening light. Her dress shimmered, the long skirt moulding her neat hips and giving a tantalising hint of gorgeous long legs.

Immediately desire throbbed, as if his body had been trained to respond to the mere sight of her. He registered vague disquiet. This fascination should be ebbing. Instead it had escalated.

He wanted to be with her, stripping off that dress that flowed over her slender curves like apricot syrup. This on the night when he should be rejoicing in his achievements and the accolades of his people!

She made him want to forget his duty. He wanted to lose himself in her. Or at least be with her, seeing her delight in the spectacle and listening to her refreshingly honest assessment of everything, from the pageantry to the behind-the-scenes lobbying by guests. He sensed danger in the way she distracted him, making him lose focus. It was his duty, his responsibility, to keep control and protect those, like Samira, who relied on him.

Asim made himself turn. It was a test of willpower that he stay away.

His grandmother and her cronies would take Jacqueline under their wing. He'd remain here, doing his duty till it was time for the fireworks.

As the light faded and he finally made his way back to the enclosure a ruffled press secretary raced over to report a breach of security. Amongst the invited media, a cameraman and reporter from a major magazine were on the premises. A magazine that had pursued Samira relentlessly. Its staff had been banned from all royal premises. Yet they were in the royal enclosure, large as life.

Asim marched up the hill, barking questions to his stumbling retainers.

How had they entered? He couldn't believe his efficient security team had slipped up so badly.

But there was a conundrum. For it appeared the pair had press passes that had been checked and double checked and proven genuine.

Only years of self-discipline prevented Asim taking the steps three at a time. The Sultan of Jazeer never publicly showed haste or fury. He topped the rise and his heart pumped an aggressive rhythm.

It was worse than he'd thought.

A sweeping look took in the cluster of photographers held back by security staff. Their lenses were trained on the platform overlooking the plain below. On it posed women dressed in flamboyant rainbow colours. Among them he saw Jacqueline in full-length amber looking luscious as toffee and, in a gown of deepest violet, Samira.

Asim halted, pulse hammering, barely able to believe his eyes. Samira hadn't planned to attend. When he'd tried to persuade her weeks ago she'd claimed she needed time before facing crowds again. What was she doing here?

A barrage of sound hit and the sky exploded in fireworks.

Asim was stalking forward, his jaw clamped, when a hand touched his arm. About to shake it off, he looked down into his grandmother's concerned face.

'Don't worry. I'll get rid of them.' He started forward but her hand tightened.

'No. That's exactly what you won't do.'

'Sorry?' He couldn't believe his ears. The old lady had supported his strategy to protect Samira.

'They're here now. If you cause a scene it will fuel the flames. Look—they're not talking to Samira, just taking photographs.'

Asim followed her gesture, confirming that, while Samira was in full view of the press, his staff kept them from questioning her. The women came together in a neatly choreographed move and posed for the cameras, a burst of multi-coloured light adding to the spectacle.

'It's deliberate,' he murmured, taking in the scene properly for the first time. The beautiful women, the glamorous dresses, the backdrop of ancient fortifications and stunning pyrotechnics. The scene would enthral millions of avid viewers.

'Of course,' his grandmother responded. 'Don't inflame the situation.'

Grimly Asim nodded, forcing himself to stand and watch those vultures snap photo after photo.

Yet he felt betrayed. Someone in his palace had arranged this press intrusion and put Samira at risk. A few weeks ago she'd barely had the energy to stir herself and here she was, posing like some catwalk model for the paparazzi.

When he got his hands on the person who planned this, they'd wish they'd never been born.

Jacqui wondered if the smile she'd pasted on looked convincing or was a grimace of stress. These days she didn't like crowds and being on show, a reluctant model for Samira's gorgeous creation, shredded her nerves. But Samira had insisted, latching onto this opportunity with a feverish determination that convinced Jacqui she had to do her bit to make it a success.

Even though it meant keeping it secret from Asim.

No doubt he'd get on his high horse when he discovered what they'd done, but when he saw how well it worked he'd accept it was a masterstroke.

Of course he would.

But no one had mentioned fireworks.

Each crack of sound plunged her back into that day of chaos, blood and death.

The acrid scent of gunpowder turned her stomach. The whole display was torture, testing her resolve to the limit, cracking it till she feared any minute she'd fling herself to the ground, curling in a foetal position as the world shattered around her.

Another explosion splintered the air and she flinched. The hairs on her nape and arms prickled and she fought to keep the contents of her stomach down as terror iced her blood.

'That one was close.'

Mouth dry, she nodded at the reporter, trying to feel grateful for the mundane observation.

'And it seems to have been the finale of the show. Now we can talk.'

'Of course.' She'd been unable to think or speak during the barrage. Now she frantically drew on her reserves of strength, hoping years of experience in front of the camera would come to her aid.

She wasn't used to being interviewed. She'd shunned even her network's request for an interview after the bombing. But surely she could do this for Samira. Jacqui gripped her hands tight together.

Tentatively she began, confidence building as she followed the script she and Samira had developed. The interviewer tried to probe about Samira's private life but it was easy enough to turn the conversation back to what they'd agreed: Samira's dresses and her design style; the celebration; the magnificent citadel as a backdrop for what promised to be a blossoming design career. He even asked about her presence here and Jacqui relaxed a little more, describing her research and the generosity of the royal family.

'So tell me, Jacqui. What's happening between the princess and her ex? Our readers are desperate for more. You're an insider now.' The reporter leaned close, his smile gloating as he returned to his favourite subject. 'Just a hint will do and we can develop the story further.'

Jacqui forced her features into a smile, though she gritted her teeth. She'd known he wouldn't want to accept her 'no comment', but he'd have to.

'I—'

'You have all you need for your story.' A deep voice sliced through the night air, making her jump. 'The interview is over.' Long fingers gripped her elbow, turning her inexorably to face the tall man looming out of the night. Dark eyes flashed.

'Your Royal Highness.' The reporter half-bowed but managed to thrust a microphone forward.

Asim ignored it, ignored him, towing Jacqui away past security staff and VIPs. They didn't hurry but moved purposefully, though Asim paused occasionally to exchange pleasantries with guests.

Only Jacqui, with his hand anchoring her like a manacle of iron, guessed the tension riding him. It vibrated, a palpable force that sent shivers of apprehension through her.

'Should you be seen holding my arm?' she hissed between clenched teeth as the photographers turned their lenses towards them. 'Surely it's not a good idea to—'

'Don't presume to give me advice on appropriate behaviour.' His whisper cut like a blade. His grip tightened almost to the point of pain and Jacqui sucked in a shocked gasp.

Instantly Asim's hold relaxed but the angle of his jaw spoke of trouble, of fury barely contained.

'I need to see Samira.' Jacqui turned her head. 'She did so well but she needs—'

If his voice had been dangerous before, it was lethal now. '*Never* presume to tell me what my sister needs.'

A glacial chill crackled down Jacqui's backbone.

He paused and drew in a mighty breath that lifted his impressive chest, reminding Jacqui of the latent power in his big form. A power he carefully leashed when they were together. She sensed he was on a knife-edge of control and anxiety feathered through her.

Asim wasn't a violent man. But she'd never seen him like this. Even his controlled pace spoke of barely contained ire.

They left the royal enclosure, passed the guards and entered the passageway that led into the palace then wound confusingly. Still he didn't speak and with each tap of her heels Jacqui's tension screwed to breaking point. She should say something, explain, but her tongue stuck to the roof of her mouth.

They emerged in a garden surrounded by a pillared arcade. No lights shone but the moonlight revealed the old harem courtyard. A breeze whispered through the leaves of a climbing vine, making a desolate sound.

There to the left was the chamber where she'd woken from her nightmare to discover Asim standing over her.

It seemed a lifetime ago.

Asim swung her to face him. In the silvery light he looked as grim and forbidding as an ancient idol awaiting a blood sacrifice.

Jacqui swallowed and met his eyes. She'd known this would be tough. Keeping tonight's plan a secret had weighed on her conscience, but Samira had been insistent she needed to do this her way, not Asim's. In the end Jacqui had banked on the fact Asim would be so happy seeing his sister emerge from seclusion that his anger would be short-lived.

How wrong she'd been.

'I was warned against you, you know.' The words were a sliver of sound on the night air, slashing through her neat justifications.

'Warned?' Jacqui frowned, thrown by the change of subject. Wasn't this all about Samira?

He didn't let her go, just stood toe-to-toe, staring down at her as if he wished he'd never laid eyes on her.

She felt bruised by that look, her heart thundering in distress.

'You don't think your presence in the palace or my bed is a complete secret, do you? From the first I've had advisors warning me against you. Not least my press secretary. He said you'd cause trouble.'

'Now hang on there.' She stiffened. Asim's press secretary had been part of Samira's problem. 'I haven't caused any—'

'Really?' His head reared back, lips curling disdainfully. 'I should have known better. So what's your excuse? Are you saying you didn't inveigle your way in here by playing on the sympathies and grief of an old lady?'

Jacqui's breath hissed in. 'No!'

'That you had no compunction using any tactic you could to get close to us? To me and my sister, particularly my sister?'

Abruptly he released her and stepped back, his expression sharp and accusing.

Something cracked open inside her and she knew pain would

follow as soon as the shock wore off. Jacqui had expected concern over their tactics but not *this*!

'Did you think my staff wouldn't discover it was you who persuaded Samira to approve the press passes for those vultures?' His face thrust forward into her space, his demeanour intimidating. 'You think no one heard you promising him an *exclusive* interview?' Asim shook his head and Jacqui could have sworn she read regret on his grim features, not simply anger.

He lifted one hand and swiped it down his face, as if rubbing away an unpleasant sight.

The sight of her?

Hurt warred with indignation as Jacqui stared, disbelievingly, at her lover. The man she'd grown closer to than anyone else in her life. Something crumpled inside.

How could he speak to her like this after what they'd shared?

What, sneered a tiny voice, *sex? You think that makes you special to him? How many women do you think he's had? You're just a novelty.*

Correction: *were* just a novelty.

She gasped as pain sliced deep. Her chest heaved and her head spun from lack of oxygen.

'Samira and Rania *trusted* you.' Asim's voice had lost that pulse of terrible anger. Instead it sounded hollow, like the aching void that opened up inside Jacqui's chest. 'And I let them. I *encouraged* them.'

He shook his head. 'So tell me, Jacqueline, what's your excuse? Money? They'd pay a pretty sum for a scoop. Or was it a chance to get back into reporting? Have you had enough of your self-imposed exile from the media?'

Jacqui opened her mouth but no words emerged. It felt like something had broken inside. It took all her strength to stand there, facing him.

She firmed her lips. What was the point, explaining herself when he'd already judged her?

With anyone else she would have tried, but with Asim…

He of all people should know her well enough to give her the benefit of the doubt. She'd *trusted* him, reached out to him as she never had to anyone.

Piercing regret filled her and she knew that soon it would be replaced by anguish. Oh, she could give him the explanation he said he wanted, but should she have to? What was the point? She felt battered in places she couldn't even name. Places deep within.

Finally she shook her head.

'Nothing to say? You surprise me.'

Yet still he lingered, hovering like some great, dark cloud about to swoop down and engulf her. As if he actually *wanted* her to persuade him.

When she remained silent, her gaze fixed on a point over his shoulder, he finally moved.

'Later,' he warned in a low growl. Then he marched away into the night.

Asim returned to the celebrations, accepting compliments and congratulations. Yet he acted on autopilot, his mind on the woman he'd left in the harem.

He'd waited for her to convince him there was some error, that her blatant betrayal of trust was a mistake. He'd *wanted* her to persuade him.

Even with the evidence of his eyes and the reports of his staff he hadn't wanted to believe she'd betrayed them.

He'd wanted to believe in her.

A flash of light filled the air, a thunderous explosion that turned heads and made bystanders jump. Asim whipped his head around, relaxing when he realised it was one final sally from the pyrotechnics.

But with the realisation came something else. Something disquieting.

Only now with a cooler head did he recall a detail he hadn't registered before. When he'd approached Jacqueline and the reporter, he'd been intent on their words, on what secrets she might give away. Now memory conjured up her tight, defensive stance, the way she'd flinched at the fireworks.

She had a fear of sudden loud noises. She'd admitted it herself, and he'd seen it the day they'd turned a corner in one of the palace gardens and frightened some birds that had shot up into the air with a loud clap of wings. The sound had been like a muffled gunshot and Jacqueline had dived for cover, only his grip on her arm stopping her.

She still suffered from the trauma of that explosion. Hadn't he soothed her more than once when she'd cried out in her sleep, her skin hazed with heat and her limbs twitching in terror?

Would she have submitted herself to the trial of a fireworks display for a cash payoff from some magazine?

His ingrained distrust told him, yes, people did remarkable things for money.

Instinct told him the scenario was wrong. Jacqueline wouldn't corrupt herself like that. She appreciated beautiful things, but her idea of beauty was more likely to be a faded, romantic mural than riches. The usher who'd shown her the crown jewels had reported she'd been as fascinated by the intricately embroidered silks worked by the harem women as by the fortune in gems they'd worn.

Asim frowned. If she'd wanted to sell her story, why do it here?

His gaze moved to where his sister sat with her friends and grandmother. To a casual eye Samira looked bright and cheerful. But Asim had known her all her life. He'd seen her pull on that smiling mask too often. This evening taxed her to the limit.

Doubt shivered through him.

No. Not doubt. *Certainty*.

He recalled the times he'd seen Jacqueline and Samira, heads together, chattering like long-lost friends. The way Samira, with her usual impulsiveness, had opened her arms to this stranger. And Jacqueline's rare, glowing smile when the pair were together.

She'd done this for Samira.

She'd braved the crowd and the barrage for her new friend.

How often had she said Samira needed to stop running and face the world? And he, so used to protecting his kid sister, had known it was too soon.

Whatever the rights of the matter, he had his answer. Loyalty, not personal gain, had motivated her.

What else would have got Jacqueline up on the dais in front of cameramen, dressed in one of Samira's sexy creations? This was the woman who still couldn't quite believe in her own physical allure.

Asim scrubbed a hand over his face as the enormity of what he'd said to her sank in. Her glassy stare and the stark whiteness of her features in the moonlight as she'd refused to explain told their own story.

'Asim?' He turned.

A lifetime's practice at hiding emotion came to the rescue. 'Had enough, Samira? It's been a big night.'

'It has. But a success, don't you think?'

'A huge success. And it was an unexpected pleasure having you present. Thank you, little one. I'm proud of you. It took a lot to face everyone and you did it in style.'

If only he'd thought sooner about what the effort had cost Jacqueline.

Samira shrugged. 'It was time I stopped hiding. After all, I haven't done anything wrong.'

'On the contrary!' His sister had been a victim, first of her scumbag of a boyfriend and then of the paparazzi.

'That's what Jacqui said. She said I should hold my head up and look the world in the eye.'

'Did she?'

Samira nodded. 'That's what she does when things don't work out. She said sometimes pretending to be confident, even when you felt horrible inside, is enough to get you through the tough times.'

Asim's chest squeezed.

That was what Jacqueline had been doing, parading herself in that slithery silk dress in front of the media, surely her worst nightmare come to life. And then to do it under a cannonade of fireworks! What guts that had taken.

Had her proud defiance as she faced his blistering accusations been her pretending to be confident when she felt *horrible inside*?

'Asim? Are you all right?' Samira clutched his arm, her expression concerned.

'Of course.'

He almost laughed aloud that he could lie so smoothly. Far from being all right, he was ashamed of himself. How could he have got it so wrong?

CHAPTER TWELVE

JACQUI WAS SITTING by the campfire when she heard the four-wheel drive.

She hadn't tried sleeping. How could she when her mind churned over Asim's accusations? Instead she huddled into her jacket as if that could counteract the chill that spread from her bones rather than from the pre-dawn desert air.

She'd thought to get away somewhere isolated and quiet. Solitude had always helped when things were tough. But now all she felt was alone.

Had Asim taken that from her? The last of her resilience?

The idea scared her almost as much as the slashing pain that tore through her when he'd looked at her with distaste and accused her of treachery.

The hum of sound became a roar as a vehicle crested the dune, headlights flooding her campsite. She clambered to her feet, one hand up to protect her eyes, her movements as slow and stiff as an old woman's.

The headlights dipped as the vehicle rolled towards her and for the first time Jacqui felt a sliver of doubt about coming here alone. Isolation didn't guarantee safety. If Imran had been alive he'd have scolded her for taking such a chance, haring off in the middle of the night into one of Jazeer's national parks. What if she bogged the vehicle in sand or got lost? What if she found herself at the mercy of men who had no respect for a lone woman?

Jazeer was generally a safe country but there were always exceptions.

Jacqui spun around towards her four-wheel drive as the other vehicle pulled to a halt. The door opened and the hairs at her nape rose. She sprinted for her vehicle and had her door open, ready to leap into the driver's seat, when a voice stopped her.

'Jacqueline!' Not just any voice. *His* voice.

How could that be?

Why wasn't Asim partying? It was his night. Her too-vivid imagination had conjured images of him celebrating with one of the sophisticated beauties who'd hung on his every word.

Their liaison was over. There was nothing to stop him taking a new lover. An unseen blade sank between her ribs at the thought of Asim with another woman.

She'd give anything not to face him now.

Slowly she turned. He stood silhouetted by the lights. Broad-shouldered and bare-headed, legs planted wide and hands on hips. In what looked like jeans and a shirt, he was rangy and hard as a cowboy.

But he wasn't anything so simple. He was the hereditary Sultan of Jazeer. His word was law. People raced to anticipate his wishes. He was feted and revered. And what he wanted he always got.

Jacqui peered into the darkness but saw no other vehicles.

'Where are your henchmen, Asim?' Her voice was harsh. 'No security staff to take me into custody? No officials to deport me as an undesirable alien?'

He paced forward, his tall frame looming larger than ever. 'Are you all right?'

The question threw her off balance.

'Jacqueline?' A sharp undercurrent bit through his words.

'Oh, I'm just dandy,' she jeered, planting her hands on her hips. How dared he ask if she was all right? 'How kind of you to enquire.' She breathed deep, shocked at how the sight of him affected her. She was torn between wanting to escape into the desert and the desire to fling herself into his arms. 'Or did you come to accuse me of stealing a vehicle? Is there a manhunt for me?' After tonight nothing would surprise her.

'I came alone.'

The timbre of his voice made her shiver.

'How did you find me?' She'd got permission days ago to borrow a vehicle for a research trip to the Asada oasis, but when she'd arrived at the garage after midnight it was deserted. She'd simply flung her bag in, grabbed the keys and scrawled her name on the register.

'Satellite tracking on the four-wheel drive. Desert conditions make it a necessary safety precaution.'

'I see.' But she didn't. Why follow her into the wilderness?

Jacqui sagged against the vehicle, exhaustion stealing over her. She didn't want to face Asim. Not until she'd shored up her defences.

'Why don't you come back here?' He gestured to the place by the fire where she'd huddled.

Jacqui stiffened. 'For a cosy fireside chat?' She shook her head, hair flicking around her face, reminding her that the evening's sophisticated hairstyle had disintegrated into a haphazard mess. She hadn't taken time to tie her hair back, or even remove the make-up Samira had painted on her. 'You've already said everything.'

'Not everything, Jacqueline.' She wished she could see his expression rather than just his silhouette against the headlights.

She stood mute. Instinct told her to run, get as far from Asim as she could. She couldn't take more of this slashing pain. Logic told her he'd simply follow. He knew the desert and she had no hope of escaping.

Pride locked her knees. She refused to retreat again.

'Please?' He sounded as uncomfortable as she felt.

Finally, with a ragged shrug, she stepped forward. What choice did she have?

Stiffly she took her seat by the fire, aware of Asim standing to one side. She'd been right. Worn denim clung to his muscled thighs and he wore a black sweater and serviceable boots. She almost wished he wore his regal finery. He looked too potently masculine, too approachable and real in casual clothes.

Real enough to rip shreds off her, she reminded herself, wrapping her arms tight around herself.

Finally he sank cross-legged to the ground on the other side of the fire. The easy movement reminded her of the fluid strength in his hard-packed body. A strength that had always attracted, even awed, her.

Jacqui hunched her shoulders, dragging her gaze away.

'If you're not here to arrest or deport me, why *are* you here?'

'To apologise.'

The prompt response stunned her and she found herself staring across the embers into a face of forged bronze and shadows. Something quick and hungry sparked between them as Jacqui met Asim's eyes. She blinked, telling herself it was a trick of the light or her own stupid, yearning heart.

That same heart catalogued his taut features and she could almost pretend to find regret and shame there. Shame? Not likely. Not from a man like Asim.

'You don't say anything.'

Jacqui shook her head, not trusting her voice. Asim apologising? Was anything so unlikely? Even if he'd learned the truth, since when did an absolute monarch feel the need to apologise?

'You don't believe me?'

She swallowed, her throat arid as the desert around them. 'I don't pretend to understand you, Asim.' She'd thought she knew him, that he knew her too, but she'd deluded herself. Tonight's outburst confirmed that.

Slowly he nodded, his eyes never leaving hers. 'It's not easy, what's between us.'

'There's nothing between us!' Not after what he'd said. He'd lacerated that fragile, delicate thing between them.

'If that were true I'd be in the palace, sleeping the sleep of the just.' His lips twisted. 'Or entertaining a new lover in my bed.'

Jacqui couldn't prevent her gasp as ice pierced her breast and ripped through her insides.

'Exactly.' His eyes bored into hers as if he delved deep into her secrets, to the woman she'd never shared with anyone. 'There's still this connection and even my suspicions and disappointment couldn't sever it.'

'You're wrong, Asim. You *have* severed it. I feel nothing for you. I don't even know why you're here.'

His stare unnerved her. It took all her willpower not to fidget, to pretend she felt whole instead of raw and bleeding.

'Do you have any idea how I felt when I went to your room and couldn't find you?'

'Relieved? Triumphant?'

Slowly he turned his head from side to side. 'Gutted. As if someone had taken a dagger to my belly.'

Jacqui stared, her mouth gaping. Had he really felt it too? That slash of pain? Asim was many things: autocratic, suspicious, tender, thoughtful, assertive and generous, but never vulnerable.

'You're lying,' she croaked. But as she said it she knew that was one thing she'd never accuse him of—dishonesty.

Yet to believe him meant he cared about her, which he'd already proved impossible. Jacqui frowned, her thoughts tumbling over themselves.

'Why would I lie?' He leaned closer. 'You think I *enjoy* admitting this?' He paused and Jacqui felt his hesitation like a weight.

'I couldn't find you in my suite, or yours. I couldn't find your clothes, except those two evening dresses, and I felt…' He shook his head, his mouth a grim, flat line.

'Do you understand the dangers you face out here?'

The abrupt change of subject disorientated Jacqui and she shook her head.

'The dunes are treacherous. What if you'd rolled the vehicle?' His eyes flashed. 'What if you'd hurt yourself with no one knowing where you are?'

'But I didn't.' Her brow puckered. He hadn't chased after her in case she ran into car trouble.

'And you're alone.'

'I'm an adult. I'm used to being alone.' Independence had been bred into her early. Conveniently she ignored the fact that usually when she'd travelled in risky locations she'd been with Imran or another colleague.

'A woman alone can be vulnerable to unscrupulous men.' He paused, letting that sink in. 'And you know about our lions?'

Jacqui stiffened, her eyes frantically scanning the darkness beyond the firelight. 'No one mentioned lions.'

'Jazeer was famous for them and there's a tradition that, while lions live in the Jazeeri wilderness, our people will remain safe from external threat. Over the years their numbers dwindled to near extinction but in the last decade there's been a programme to re-establish them in this national park.'

'Not here?' She shivered, remembering a pride of lions she'd seen in Africa devouring some poor antelope.

'In an enclosure not too far away. Rangers have stopped poachers trying to kill them for so-called sport.' He paused, his expression grim. 'It's dangerous for you here alone. Such men flout the law. I doubt they'd respect an unprotected woman.'

'You came here to make sure I was safe?' Jacqui's jaw tilted. She wasn't some chattel to be protected.

'Partly that.' He lifted one hand and raked it through his dark hair, leaving it rumpled. Jacqui remembered the feel of it through her fingers, like a soft, thick pelt inviting her touch. A twinge of heat flickered.

'I had to know you were safe. And we have to talk.'

'You've already said more than enough.' She didn't have the stomach for more. She wasn't sure how much longer she could stop her hurt showing. Pride only stretched so far. 'It's late, Asim. I'm tired and fed up. You've seen for yourself that I'm fine. Why don't you go back to your palace and leave me be?'

His arm dropped. 'Because I was wrong.'

'Pardon?' Jacqui felt her eyes bulge.

'I made a mistake.' His eyes locked on hers, sending a sizzle through her blood. 'I jumped to conclusions when I should have known better. I accused you of dishonesty, of manipulating my sister for your own ends, and I was wrong. Totally wrong.'

Silence engulfed them, but for the soft crackle of the low fire and a faint whisper across the sand. Jacqui held herself taut, disorientated and almost scared of what he might say next.

'I behaved badly, Jacqueline, and I ask your forgiveness. I realise you were doing what you thought best for Samira.'

Jacqui leaned back, as if to sever the force field that drew her towards him. It was harder than it should have been, resisting the temptation to believe him.

'How do you know? What did Samira tell you?' Sourness filled her mouth. How easy for him to believe her now his sister had revealed the truth. Yet when Jacqui had needed his trust it hadn't been forthcoming.

Asim shook his head. 'It wasn't Samira. I knew as soon as I returned to the celebrations and more fireworks exploded. Finally my brain kicked into gear. If you'd wanted to sell a scoop, you wouldn't have picked anywhere so public. If you'd betrayed us you'd have done it quietly, not surrounded by my people and loud detonations. The whole scenario was wrong.'

He leaned forward and Jacqui thought she saw tenderness in his eyes. 'I realised too late how strong you'd been, supporting Samira when she most needed it. How much you gave of yourself to help her. I should have been thanking you, not attacking you. An apology isn't sufficient but, believe me, I'm sorry for what I said, what I believed.'

Jacqui read sincerity in his expression and heard the warmth in his voice, yet something held her back. He'd destroyed something inside her with his mistrust. She wasn't ready to let him close again.

She'd never let anyone as close as Asim, not even Imran, and tonight's devastating events proved how dangerous that was. She'd opened herself to a world of hurt. She should have known better. Her family had taught her she didn't have what it took to inspire love but she'd thought at least Asim respected her. His rejection after slowly winning her trust and her regard had shattered her.

But, oh, it was tempting to accept his change of heart. Her weaker side wanted to forget his earlier contempt and pretend tonight hadn't happened.

'If only Samira had confided in me this wouldn't have happened.'

But it had, Jacqui thought miserably. Nothing could erase it.

Was she being precious, too wary to accept his apology? But nothing had prepared her for the devastation his distrust had wrought.

'Samira thought you wouldn't agree if you heard our plans. Your press office has been adamant she remain out of the public eye. She was sure you'd take their advice again.'

Asim frowned. 'That's only ever been for her protection. When she first came back she was in no state to face anyone.'

'But she's better now. She's stronger than you think.'

'You believe I'm over-protective?'

Jacqui shrugged, surprised at how easy it was to talk about Samira instead of what lay between them. 'Isn't that what older brothers do?' She'd been almost wistful, hearing Samira talk about how Asim tried to shelter her.

Jacqui had never known that sort of protectiveness. You learned resilience early when you were unwanted. 'And your media advisor was all for keeping Samira isolated.'

'Samira said you disagreed.'

Jacqui shrugged. 'He could have reassessed the situation when Samira felt better.'

'So you came up with tonight's scenario.'

'Samira and I did together. As I said, she's stronger than you think.'

He nodded. 'She is. Between you, you've turned the secret of her isolation on its head. The press think she's spent her time working on what will be a stunning formal fashion collection. They're slavering for more. That sort of interest could be a springboard to a successful career.'

Jacqui smiled, relieved that he could see the positives in what they'd done. 'She's talented enough to do it too.'

'I can't thank you enough, Jacqueline.' His voice dipped to a low note that never failed to do funny things to her insides. 'You've been a true friend to Samira and my grandmother. You've given them both something they needed at a very difficult time in their lives.'

His intensity made her skin prickle and she rubbed her hands up and down her arms.

'It was only—'

Asim raised his hand. 'It wasn't *only* anything. When you arrived here I expected trouble and instead you've done my family considerable service. A service that deserved far more than my distrust.' He drew a slow breath. 'If there's anything I can do to make amends, you must tell me. We owe you so much. *I* owe you.'

Words trembled on her tongue. Hungry, eager words that would reveal how much she wanted from him.

Jacqui firmed her lips rather than blurt them out. She hugged her knees. She'd experienced so much with Asim, more than she'd ever expected, and still she wanted more. The depth of her neediness scared her. Was there no end to it?

Better to keep her distance. After all, though he'd apologised, he'd made no move to close the gap between them. Wasn't it safer that way?

Yet she couldn't staunch the slow bleed of hope and happiness. She wanted to be held and caressed and treasured.

The realisation almost stopped the air in her lungs. She'd begun to want too much.

'There's nothing I need,' she said briskly. 'Except to finish my research.' Turning from his searching gaze, she looked towards the rising sun, a glimmer on the horizon. 'I plan to visit the Asada oasis before I leave Jazeer. It used to be a favourite with the royal harem ladies and I want to take photos.'

The idea of leaving was like a physical blow. Her time in the palace had passed too quickly. She'd lived from day to day, not daring to think ahead, throwing herself into her project and immersing herself in the wonder that was her affair with Asim. Each day had been a revelation to a woman who'd thought never to smile again.

But her time was up. Regret shivered down her backbone.

Even if Asim's distrust hadn't shattered her illusory peace, the realisation of her vulnerability to him would have.

'We can do better than that. I'll take you to the oasis and you can stay in the royal pavilion there. It's rarely used, but I guarantee you'll love the old rooms.' His tender smile made Jacqui's stomach dip. She almost cried out at the sense of loss engulfing her.

It was one thing to know their affair was over. It was another to find the courage to move on. She couldn't seem to switch off her feelings.

'Thank you, but I couldn't impose.'

'Don't treat me like a stranger, Jacqueline.' His smile died, his voice turning harsh.

Why she fidgeted under his gaze, she didn't know. He was the one who'd been at fault, not her.

But he was trying to make amends, wasn't he?

The trouble was she wanted more than access to royal buildings from Asim. Much more.

She wanted his arms around her in the night when she woke from a nightmare. She wanted that gleam in his eyes as they made small talk at some official reception, promising delicious intimacies to come. She even wanted to debate politics with him! Spending a tranquil hour chatting with Asim at the end of the day had become one of her greatest pleasures.

Now she felt bereft.

It struck her how rootless she was. For years she'd had no real home. Visits to family were short and infrequent and her flat was a spartan place she didn't miss. She'd felt more at home in Asim's palace than she could remember feeling any time in the last eighteen years.

What did that say about her life?

Asim tossed a piece of wood onto the fire, watched the sparks flash and heard the greedy hiss as flames took hold. In the flare of light Jacqueline's face was pensive, almost sad.

His gut twisted. He needed her smile, her gurgle of throaty laughter, the flash of animation in her sultry, amber eyes.

He needed *her*.

The realisation was stark and undeniable.

He needed her as he'd needed no other woman.

That made a mockery of his attempts to negotiate a compromise.

He didn't want compromise! He wanted Jacqueline.

It was only now he'd lost her that he understood how important she was.

Asim frowned. He couldn't recall another lover having had such an impact. He chose his women for their beauty and good humour, for intelligence and sophistication. For their ability to please.

Jacqueline Fletcher was just a little too sharp and questioning, a little too unpolished. Yet she charmed his family, his courtiers and guests, and she charmed him. Her passion was instinctive rather than subtle, honest rather than practised. He liked her mind, her inquisitiveness, even her damned independence.

Even after tonight's fiasco the link between them was strong. The sizzle of passion hadn't faded, though inevitably it must. He'd known enough women to understand that. Besides, nothing that burnt so bright could last indefinitely.

Yet Asim acknowledged with a flash of disturbing insight that he'd never be content to part from Jacqueline till this ardour faded.

He didn't want other women. He'd even let his bridal search stall, distracted by her.

Giving her up wasn't an option. Not yet.

He had to win back her trust.

Asim drew in a slow breath and faced the unpalatable fact he'd been avoiding. Jacqueline wouldn't be won over by platitudes and a trite apology. She needed to know the whole truth.

She deserved to know it.

CHAPTER THIRTEEN

'You believe me to be overprotective.'

Beyond the flames Asim saw Jacqueline shrug but she said nothing.

He unknotted his hands and flexed his fingers. When that reporter had pumped Jacqueline about Samira, Asim had come within an inch of decking him. Hot fury surged and the need for violence had twanged every taut sinew. As if the man he'd spent a lifetime moulding himself into—honourable, thoughtful and judicious—was a sham.

As if he'd reverted to the unbridled, unthinking emotion that had been his parents' hallmark.

His sudden lust for blood, his desire to wrap his fingers around the reporter's throat, had made a mockery of everything he'd striven to be. Distaste filled his mouth.

'You know my parents had a troubled marriage.'

Jacqueline lifted her head as if startled at the direction of the conversation. Slowly she nodded.

'My earliest memory is the sound of fighting. Not physically,' he added quickly when he read her expression, 'Though there were lots of breakages. Ornaments and mirrors didn't last long in the royal apartments.'

Asim paused, remembering. 'I used to lie in bed, listening to the rhythm of the arguments. I became expert at reading the progress of a fight. I'd tell myself it would be over soon, when my parents kissed and made up, or temporarily separated.'

He shook his head. Amazing how some memories stayed fresh. His parents had soured his view of marriage and taught him that so-called love was a curse to be avoided at all costs. Was it any wonder he'd been in no hurry to find a bride? Shackling himself to a life partner, even in a carefully arranged transaction devoid of romance, was a step he'd put off for years.

'I protected Samira as much as I could.'

'They hurt her?' Horror edged Jacqueline's voice.

'Not intentionally. But she suffered. One minute she was petted and fussed over, and the next they were too busy screaming at each other to notice her. The poor kid never knew what to expect from day to day.'

'Nor did you.'

He blinked. Was Jacqueline taking his part?

'I was older. I'd learned to cope. But for a long time Samira thought she was to blame for their unhappiness, or when one of them stalked out and wasn't seen for weeks. She had nightmares for years, night terrors, they called them. I used to sit with her and try to keep her safe.'

'Surely you had a nanny or someone to look after you?'

Asim smiled humourlessly. 'We had plenty, but they never lasted. Either my mother sacked them because she believed they were seducing our father, or he sacked them because he believed they were spying for her.'

Asim rolled his shoulders.

'The details don't matter. I just wanted you to understand that Samira has always been vulnerable. She was caught in the middle of our parents' wrangling and she was distressed by it.

'They were never happy for long and when they were apart they spent their energy trying to best the other. Eventually my mother decided to use Samira to help her cause.' Asim breathed deep, ploughing his hand through his hair. He hated thinking of his parents.

'I found her being quizzed by a "friend" of our mother. The woman was a journalist and she put words into Samira's mouth, twisting innocent statements into appalling accusations about our father. Samira was thirteen and distraught, trying to set the record straight and horrified at the way everything she said was distorted.'

'That's awful! No wonder you don't like reporters.'

Asim permitted himself a tiny smile. 'Some more than others. I've learnt they're not all tarred with the same brush.'

Jacqueline's eyes met his and heat punched low in his belly. 'What happened?'

'Our father stopped the story, but years later rumours circulated. It was too late to worry about them. Our parents died suddenly in an accident and I had more urgent things to worry about than sourcing lies in gossip columns.' Accession to the sultanate at twenty-five, in a country damaged by his father's ineffectual rule, had been no picnic.

'The point is Samira blamed herself.'

'She was just a child! No decent journalist—'

Asim lifted his hand. 'I know. But ever since then she's had a horror of dealing with the press.'

'That was why she was adamant about me being interviewed tonight instead of her.' Jacqueline nodded slowly. 'She said she usually managed with a smile and a "no comment".'

'That worked until Jackson Brent.' Asim watched his hands clench into fists. This time he felt no remorse at the tide of loathing that filled him. If he didn't know it would make things worse for his little sister, he'd enjoy taking the actor apart with his bare hands.

'A smile and no comment is probably the best thing she could have done,' Jacqueline said. 'It lifted her above the rest of the players in that little drama. It showed she has class and integrity. She won a lot of sympathy.'

'She shouldn't have to win public sympathy!' The words slid out between gritted teeth.

'I know, Asim. I understand.'

He met Jacqueline's eyes over the fire and there it was again, that arc of energy, that link between them, as real as if she'd touched him. He read her regret and somehow it calmed him.

'What you don't know is the full story. I spoke to Samira before I came here and she agreed to me telling you.' He'd hated even asking.

'I know enough.' Jacqueline frowned. 'Her boyfriend, her lover…' she paused on the word and Asim wondered what she was thinking '…had an affair with his married co-star. Her husband caught them and is dragging his wife through an acrimonious divorce. Now the press are dragging up every detail of both their marriage and the relationship between Samira and Jackson Brent.' She spread her hands. 'Since Samira is gorgeous and talented, plus she's a princess with wealth and an exotic background, it's not surprising the press want her story.'

Asim inhaled slowly, a familiar weight crushing his chest. 'But what they don't know, what they must never know, is that Samira was pregnant at the time.'

'Oh, Asim!' Jacqueline's eyes bulged, her face a mask of horror. 'She didn't…?'

He nodded, his gut clenching as he remembered his sister, parchment-white and dazed, her face marred by the salt tracks of tears, lying beneath a starched sheet, a nurse hovering. 'She miscarried just after she arrived here. Whether from the stress or whether it was going to happen anyway, no one could say.'

Asim had never felt so helpless, so utterly useless, in his whole life.

'I'd always done my best to look out for her. It went against every instinct to do nothing when she hooked up with Brent. But I told myself she had to grow up some time. She had to make her way in the world.' He dropped his head, torn between shame that he hadn't done better by Samira and frustration that she'd made him promise not to exact revenge on Brent.

'I wasn't much of a protector. All I could do was look after her till she recuperated and give her privacy.' The feeling that the world had spun out of his control, that there was nothing he could do for someone he cared for, wasn't one he ever wanted to experience again.

'You did the best you could. You did all anyone could.'

Supple fingers closed around his fist and a jolt of power sizzled through him. Jacqueline had moved to sit beside him, he realised. Her arm was across his, her slim frame warming his side.

Asim clamped his other hand over hers, unwilling to let her slip away again. He didn't try to understand how her touch, her sympathy, could ease his turmoil. He simply accepted that they did.

He breathed deep, drawing in the scents of sand and warm, sweet woman, and felt that terrible roiling in his stomach quieten down.

'You were right, Asim. You had to let her go. She's not a child.'

He stared at their joined hands. They looked so *right*.

'Samira was so fragile, so distraught, we feared she might have a complete breakdown. The one thing I knew was she had to be kept safe from the press.'

'And then I turned up, bearding the dragon in his den. No wonder you hated the idea of me staying in the palace.' She squeezed his hand and, despite everything, Asim's mouth turned up at the corners.

'I've been called many things but never a dragon.'

'Really?' He caught a lighter note in her voice. 'But it's so apt. You're very fierce and proud, and handsome, in a dangerous sort of way.'

Asim huffed humourlessly. 'Don't forget fire-breathing.' His hold on her tightened. 'Jacqueline, I'm ashamed of how I reacted tonight. I saw you with that reporter and I lost it. I should have known better.'

Jacqui felt the ripple of tension through Asim's broad shoulder and arm. Regret laced his voice as he squeezed her hand and she felt the last of her fury fade.

She'd been hurt, unbelievably hurt, but now she understood what had driven Asim and why he'd overreacted.

'I'm not surprised you lost it,' she murmured eventually. 'Tonight pressed every one of your hot buttons: your fears for

Samira, your need to protect her, your distrust of the press. Even down to the idea of a female journalist taking advantage of her.' It all made a skewed sort of logic.

'But you didn't deserve that tirade. You put yourself out for my sister.'

Jacqui shrugged. 'She's a good friend.' Amazingly, after just weeks, it was the truth. They had clicked in a way Jacqui never had with another woman. In the past she'd kept to herself, focusing on work, the part of her life where she felt competent, where she *fitted*. Her friendships had been limited to colleagues and her job meant she was often moving on. Only Imran had been a constant, keeping in touch even when they weren't working together.

'So I understand now.' He paused. When he spoke again his voice was gruff. 'What you did for her—not just managing the press, but posing with her model friends to show off her designs for the cameras—that took real guts.'

Asim was right. Being photographed with a bevy of beauties had tested her. It was one thing to bask in Asim's assurances, quite another to parade for the press. Only knowing how much it meant to her friend had kept her there. Samira's need was greater than hers.

'Then there were the fireworks.' Asim shifted and she looked up to see his eyes fixed on her. 'How did you manage? You hate loud noises.'

Jacqui lifted her shoulders, arrested by the gleam of warmth in that look. Heat trickled through her where just a short time ago there'd been an arctic chill.

'I don't know. The first bang nearly had me on the ground, till I realised everyone was looking up and smiling. After that it was easier.' No point admitting every eruption of sound had jarred through her like the crack of doom.

'You're a remarkable woman, Jacqueline Fletcher.'

Her eyebrows rose. 'All I did was help Samira choose how to face the public. She just needed a positive angle.'

Asim shook his head. 'Don't downplay it. I know your

demons.' His thumb stroked her wrist. 'I've seen the nightmares and I've watched you break into a cold sweat at a sudden loud noise.'

Jacqui squirmed, trying to move away, but he wouldn't release his grip.

'I'm fine.'

'But you never talk about it.'

Her breath snatched in as tension clamped her ribs. 'There's nothing to talk about.'

Asim said nothing. Reluctantly she looked up to find him regarding her through narrowed eyes.

'What? You think everything would suddenly be better if I relived it all?' Sharp anger rose. He knew nothing about it! She'd been through it all multiple times in counselling.

'It seems to me you're reliving it anyway. How often do you dream of Imran?'

Like air rushing from a punctured balloon, Jacqui's ire bled away. No matter how she tried to escape, the memories crowded back. Memories of that day, the doom-laden sense of guilt and regret, rather than recollections of her friend alive and happy.

She shook her head, hunching her shoulder.

'Jacqueline!'

'What?' She met his stare, striving for defiance and finding only pain. She pulled air into her tight lungs. He refused to back down.

'Have you seen a dead body, Asim?'

He nodded.

'Have you ever seen someone blown apart by a bomb?' She snatched another breath, the movement jagging pain through her chest. 'What about a street full of debris, where it's hard to make out what used to be people? Living, breathing people who just seconds before were—' Her next breath was a sob and she stopped, sinking her teeth into her lip, trying to fight the trembling that radiated from somewhere deep inside.

'I've seen that too,' he said quietly. 'It's unspeakable.'

Jacqui's gaze lifted to his and held. She saw old pain and anger, and something that made her feel suddenly not so alone.

'But you weren't responsible,' she murmured. Asim was a protector, a statesman, a man who worked for peace in his region.

'Nor were you.'

Jacqui's eyes blurred. 'I led him into it. It was my fault. I had the scoop. I should have checked it out before dragging him in.'

'Why? So it could have been you lying there in a bomb crater and not Imran? How would that be better?'

Jacqui yanked at his hold but Asim's grip was implacable.

'Imran has people who grieve for him. Your grandmother, you. People who—'

'And you think no one would miss you?'

She lifted her shoulders, trying to imagine the reaction of her parents and half-siblings if she'd died. They'd have been shocked but would they really have missed her?

'You're wrong, *habibti*.' A strong hand cupped her face, lifting it till she stared into stormy eyes. '*We'd* miss you—Samira and my grandmother and me. And so would your family.'

Ridiculously Jacqui felt her lower lip tremble. She didn't cry except in her sleep when the nightmares devoured her. Yet Asim's tenderness unplugged the dam of grief she'd held at bay so long.

'He had all his life ahead of him,' she mumbled. 'And it was snuffed out because of me. I should have taken precautions—'

'Listen to me.' Asim leaned closer, his breath warm on her face. 'It wouldn't matter what precautions you'd taken. Imran was his own man. He'd have been there with you if there was a chance of a scoop. He lived for his job.'

His thumb grazed her bottom lip and she swallowed at the tenderness of the gesture.

'You think I don't know that? He was my friend.'

'But you didn't know him intimately.'

Jacqui peered up at Asim, trying to read his expression. 'If you're asking whether we were lovers, the answer is no.'

He shook his head. 'I wondered that when you first arrived, but as soon as we made love I realised that wasn't the case. You were a virgin, weren't you?'

Jacqui frowned. 'Did it matter?' She'd lied so he wouldn't stop. Because she'd wanted more than anything to be one with him. Her mouth flattened. If only sex was all she wanted from Asim. If only life were so simple.

'It mattered that you shared something precious with me, Jacqueline. Something to be treasured.'

The gleam in his eyes unnerved her.

'You were talking about your cousin,' she said briskly.

For long seconds she thought he wouldn't accept the change of subject. Finally he spoke. 'I meant merely that you didn't know Imran as intimately as someone who'd grown up with him.'

Asim's mouth curved reminiscently. 'Let me tell you about my cousin. He could climb before he could walk and he never walked when he could run. His nickname in the family was "Trouble" because he was always in strife. Luckily he had nine lives, like a cat, because he was regularly falling off roofs or down wells or under horses. He took risks others wouldn't.'

'Even you?' Jacqui couldn't imagine Asim being left behind by his cousin.

'I never seemed to collect the injuries Imran did.'

So, they'd been as bad as each other.

'When he got older he found a passion in rally driving.'

'I've seen the photos.' Jacqui smiled wistfully. Imran had looked in his element, dusty, dishevelled and elated, leaning against a car that looked as if it had barely survived the rigorous course.

'It wasn't till he went to college and discovered a love of cameras and film that he became focused. He found his purpose. Some of those stories he got…' Asim shook his head. 'He didn't get them waiting on the sidelines to be assured it was safe.'

Reluctantly Jacqui nodded. Imran had been up to any challenge when it came to getting a story. That had drawn them together in the beginning. She'd put it down to his commitment to his job, but had there been an element of thrill-seeking too?

Of course there had been. But Imran had also been professional, taking appropriate precautions in risky situations, at least when she was around.

'At first I wanted to blame you for his death. I was looking for a scapegoat.' Her breath snared as he voiced the guilt she'd carried so long. 'But I couldn't do it. It just didn't fit.' He paused, his eyes capturing hers. 'You can't tell me my cousin would have waited for you to reconnoitre the situation alone.'

Jacqui blinked. When Asim put it like that... But the fact remained it had been her tip-off, her responsibility. 'I led him into danger.' She swallowed.

'No.' Asim shook his head. 'You told him what you'd learned. If he'd wanted, he could have turned back. Couldn't he?' His eyes held hers. 'Jacqueline?'

'I suppose.'

'Is it likely he'd have waited for you to go off alone and track down the story?'

Under that unblinking ebony stare Jacqui found herself confronting the harsh truth.

'No.' The word burst out. 'No, he wouldn't have waited. But that doesn't mean I feel any less guilty.'

'Because you survived and he didn't.' Asim's arm curved around her shoulders, drawing her into his warmth. 'He didn't die because of you, Jacqueline, but because someone cared more for their own ends than the lives of innocents.'

'I—' She shook her head, her mouth working.

'It's okay to grieve for him, *habibti*, so long as you understand you're not to blame.'

Jacqui huddled into Asim's big frame, drawing comfort. What he said wasn't new, the counsellor had said something similar, but for some reason it seemed to make more sense. Because Asim had known Imran? Because they were here in the desert Imran had loved? Or because Jacqui was finally ready to move on?

She buried her face in Asim's sweater, breathing in the spicy scent of his skin. Tears leaked beneath her eyelids and she wrapped her arms around him, holding tight as he gathered her in and rocked her.

Jacqui drew a shuddering breath.

She'd come out here because Asim had broken her heart. Now it felt like he'd put it back together again.

CHAPTER FOURTEEN

'IT'S UTTERLY GORGEOUS.'

Asim watched Jacqui's eyes widen as she stepped into one of the rooms at the old royal pavilion. She turned slowly, taking in the delicately coloured wall murals and the shallow pool in the centre of the floor, now dry, that glittered with a mosaic of semi-precious stones.

She walked to the wide seats running the length of the walls, dragging her fingertips over the silk cushions, exclaiming over the fine fabric and delicate embroidery.

She was so tactile, so sensual. Asim remembered the way she stroked his flesh or tangled her fingers in his hair whenever they lay together. How, even when physically spent, he enjoyed those soothing caresses.

Regret pierced him. He wasn't ready to give her up.

If anything, understanding her better and admitting his faults to her as they sat by the fire in the early hours had made her more rather than less appealing. His body craved her with undimmed urgency.

How long before this attraction waned? Weeks? Months? He'd never had a relationship like this. It was new territory.

Asim folded his arms as she pushed open a window and leaned out to take in the oasis view. She wore jeans and a rumpled shirt, her hair loose around her shoulders, and he couldn't take his eyes off her.

No wonder his scheme to find a bride had come to naught! He was bewitched by Jacqueline Fletcher.

It had been a mistake, trying to vet well-bred beauties when he was enthralled by this tawny-haired lioness.

She fascinated him. He'd never known a more contradictory woman—brave when standing up for others or for her work, yet vulnerable and unsure of herself. Responsive and generous, yet abrasive when she thought she was being dismissed.

'It's like an Arabian Sleeping Beauty's palace. There are even roses climbing up the wall. You can smell them.' She turned. 'I wonder if they're the ones the women used to make perfume? Did I tell you about that in Zeinab's diaries?'

'You told me. But I suspect they gathered petals from the palace gardens. There used to be acres set aside for roses.'

'Were there?' She frowned. 'I didn't know. There's so much I haven't had time to finish researching. But I'll make do. If it's okay, I'll call your staff sometimes to check details.'

'Why not check them yourself here?'

Her gaze caught his, a flare of amber that scorched before sliding away. 'It's best if I leave. After last night you don't want...'

'What don't I want?' He paced towards her, watching the tension creep up her shoulders and neck.

'You made it clear we—'

'I made it clear I'd been a fool and that I regret it.' He stopped close enough to note the quick rise of her chest.

Her eyes darted to his, surprise clear in their depths. Asim's mouth quirked mirthlessly. 'Fool' wasn't a word he used of himself but last night it had been true.

And he'd be a fool to let her leave when there was still such pleasure to be gained from their affair. Asim was a man whose life was ruled by duty but he wasn't into unnecessary self-denial. What they had was too good to throw away.

'Stay in Jazeer and finish your work, Jacqueline. Write your book.' He brushed the hair from her face, sliding his fingers over her satiny cheek to cup her face. He felt her tiny tremor and saw her eyelids flicker and knew she wanted this too. 'Stay with me.'

Jacqui looked into that harsh, beloved face and felt torn in two. She wanted to snuggle close and agree to whatever Asim wanted. But last night had revealed with devastating clarity the dangers of their relationship. When he'd turned on her, it had cut her to the core.

She'd never had a lover before. Maybe that was why she felt so…connected? She'd never been so drawn to a man, never trusted one as she'd trusted him.

Surely it was dangerous to give so much? Life had taught her to expect rejection. That she wasn't the sort to inspire love or long-term relationships.

'You're thinking too much.' His fingers rubbed her brow. 'Stop analysing, *habibti*. Can't we agree to make the most of what we have?' He leaned in and kissed the corner of her mouth, teasing her with the promise of more. Inevitably, longing awoke.

Jacqui leaned back, bracing her hands on his upper arms, only to find that gave him access to her throat. Ruthless as he was, Asim didn't hesitate to kiss her there, nuzzling each sensitive spot till her knees wobbled and her nipples peaked.

'Don't! I need to think.'

Dark eyes held her. 'Then think about how good we are together. About the pleasure we give each other.'

His voice was mesmerising. She felt it reverberate deep in her belly, felt her caution splinter.

'Do you want to give that up?'

She shook her head before realising. His smile, pure satisfaction, warned her she'd given away too much.

'But I think some distance would be sensible.'

Asim scowled. He really was used to getting what he wanted.

'What's to be gained by separating? We're good together.'

'There are more important things in life than sex.' Asim

overwhelmed her; he had from the first, with his earthy sexuality and potent charm.

'Don't we share those too?' His eyes narrowed to gleaming slits. 'Don't we swim together and play chess; debate politics, current affairs and literature?' He paused. 'I've never spent half the night just talking with a woman. I've never shared so much of my life.'

Asim's face was grim and Jacqui knew he remembered those revelations about his family.

Suddenly it struck her how out of character that had been. He'd been brought up to be Sultan, raised for the solitary role of ruler, shouldering vast responsibilities and keeping his own counsel. Being dictatorial came naturally. Yet with her he'd stopped to listen, even changed his mind on some things, like giving her access to those diaries. He'd trusted her with information she guessed he'd shared with no one else, like those childhood memories and his fears for Samira.

How could she not be moved by that?

Maybe he cared more than she realised. Was that why he wanted her to stay?

Jacqui tried to squash an urgent buzz of excitement that maybe Asim felt as she did.

She waited but he said no more. Should she walk away, preserve her heart and find sanctuary elsewhere?

Or was it too late?

Had she already gone too far?

Fear spiked, pinioning her where she stood.

'Jacqueline?' His hands tightened on her arms.

It should have made no difference but she couldn't help thinking how much she'd miss the sound of him saying her name in that deep, honeyed-coffee voice if she left.

'I'll think about it.' She bit her lip, knowing she prevaricated.

Asim frowned. Clearly he wanted more.

So did she. Badly.

Finally he released her. Instantly she felt bereft. How could she want his touch even as she feared it was wrong to stay?

'Think about it here. We'll stay a few days and I'll show you the desert.'

Jacqui goggled. 'A few days? You can't do that. What about your meetings? Your schedule?' Any idea she might have harboured about his royal role being a sinecure had been shattered by the sight of his daily schedule. Often he didn't stop work till late evening.

Which meant the time he'd devoted to her really *had been* precious.

Perhaps she was being naïve, expecting more when she already had so much.

'I'd planned some down time after last night's celebration. There will be some appointments to move and arrangements to make if we're to stay here.' Already he was pulling out his phone. 'Leave it to me.'

The sun was setting, its peach and cinnamon blaze gilding the oasis as they rode back from the desert.

Jacqui's blood tingled under her skin from excitement and exertion. Her mare snorted and she laughed in sheer delight.

'I knew you'd make a good horsewoman.'

'Sweet talker!' She turned to Asim, so at ease in the saddle beside her. He looked relaxed, his smile making something flutter high and hard in her chest.

How precious this day had been. She didn't want it to end. 'I suspect your teaching, and the fact you chose such a well-mannered horse, had something to do with it.' She leaned forward, whispering to the mare. 'You wouldn't let me fall, would you?'

'You underestimate yourself. With more practice, you'll be a very good rider.'

Jacqui smiled. 'The only thing that will surprise me is if I can walk when I dismount. I suspect I'm going to be stiff and sore from my first ride.'

'Don't worry. A warm bath and a slow massage will do the

trick. I'll take care of it personally.' Asim's eyes glowed with promise and Jacqui didn't have it in her to argue. Under that look she melted, her very bones liquefying.

All day he'd kept his distance and all day she'd chafed at his restraint.

So much for caution.

They'd spent the day exploring the faded finery of the royal pavilion—a sprawling building designed for short retreats. They'd swum in oasis pools and explored caves in a nearby hill where archaeologists had found evidence of an ancient settlement. They'd picnicked lavishly by the oasis, courtesy of staff who'd driven from the city to make the old place comfortable. Then Asim had given her a riding lesson on the most beautiful Arab mare.

'It's been a magical day, Asim. Thank you!'

'I'm glad you've enjoyed yourself.' The warmth in his expression made the air catch in her throat.

Her resolve to keep her distance had shattered as they'd shared their day. Somehow that proved more intimate than love-making, especially after their campfire revelations. The last twenty-four hours, even Asim's accusations and apology, had drawn them closer.

Jacqui couldn't stop wondering if for Asim, too, this was more than a fling, more than convenient sex.

Had it ever been that for her? She'd tried to tell herself so, but from the first this had been about far more than simple need. It was all about Asim and the wondrous way he made her feel.

They stopped by the stables and Asim swung down, passing his reins to a servant.

'Let me help you.' Moments later she was in his arms, pressed to the steady beat of his heart. His eyes met hers and Jacqui knew it was useless to pretend. She'd crossed the point of no return weeks ago, possibly the night Asim had first made love to her, all the while lavishing her with praise and whispered endearments.

Or perhaps it had been earlier, when she'd seen him with Lady Rania, proud yet patient and protective, revealing an emotional bond that told her he was a man capable of caring deeply.

Or even when they'd argued about her being in the palace—having access to things that had never been shared with an outsider. There was something about sparring with Asim that made her feel vibrantly alive.

She curved her hands around his neck and leant close as he nodded to the stable hand and strode towards the main building. She'd never grow tired of how precious she felt, scooped up in his arms. As if she was some delicate treasure.

It was too late to walk away. The die was cast. She'd give him what he wanted, what they both wanted.

There was only so much a woman could take.

Asim's mobile phone rang as their bath water cooled. His gaze shifted to the bedroom and he frowned.

'Answer it,' she urged, forcing herself to lift her head from his solid shoulder. 'It must be important.'

Lolling in the massive sunken bath, her body lax and deliciously replete, Jacqui couldn't begrudge him his call. In the time she'd known him, this was the longest Asim had gone without a meeting. After the first flurry of calls this morning to arrange his time away from the capital, his private line had been silent as he'd devoted his time exclusively to her.

'Possibly.' But he leaned in to kiss her full on the mouth in a lush caress that liquefied her already weak limbs. Then gently he put her aside to stand, water sluicing down the strong planes of his body.

Jacqui's eyelids dropped to half-mast as she took in the display of masculine perfection before her. Too soon, though, he'd grabbed a towel and, grinning at her reaction, strode from the room.

'I'll wait for you in the bedroom.'

She sighed and wondered if it were possible for this day to

get any better. It had started abysmally but now she felt like she floated on cloud nine.

Finally she made herself move, getting out and wrapping a fluffy bath sheet around her. She was towelling the ends of her hair, walking towards the open bedroom door, when she heard Asim.

'No, cancel the princess's visit.' He paused. 'I know it's short notice but I've had second thoughts. It can't go ahead.' A longer pause. 'No, not her either. I'll explain when I'm back, but for now put the whole schedule on hold. No more eligible women.'

Jacqui paused and looked over her shoulder to where Asim spoke on the phone. He stood, magnificently bare-chested, wearing only a stark white towel around his hips.

His eyes caught hers and something about his expression made her still. She couldn't put her finger on it. Tension? Worry? Determination?

Misgiving feathered cool fingers across her nape. Something wasn't right.

She turned away and reached for a comb, tidying her damp hair while he finished the call. Even then she waited a few extra moments before entering the bedroom, unable to shake a sense of foreboding.

'All finished?'

'Yes.' Asim turned away and took his time putting the phone on the bedside table. She couldn't read his face. For some reason that only added to her nebulous anxiety.

'That sounded intriguing. No more eligible women?' Jacqui put a smile she didn't feel in her voice.

Asim turned, faint colour washing his craggy cheekbones. 'No.'

Warning became a nagging bite of worry. It wasn't like Asim to be monosyllabic. When he said no more, Jacqui turned towards the wardrobe. She wouldn't push.

'I should tell you.' He paused. 'Even though it's ended now.'

Jacqui spun around. 'What's ended?'

Asim palmed the back of his neck as if massaging tight

muscles. The action drew attention to the formidable strength in his biceps and shoulder, and the musculature of his torso.

They'd been lovers for weeks and still Jacqui was distracted by the sight of him.

'You might want to sit.' He gestured to the wide bed. Instead Jacqui sank onto a nearby sofa. Instinct urged against lolling on a mattress when Asim had news for which she needed to sit. Unease rippled again.

'I'm thirty-five,' he said, pacing, then turning to face her. 'The last male of my family.'

She nodded. The Sultanate of Jazeer had been in the hands of the same family for hundreds of years. She'd been fascinated by the way a modern state was melded to such ancient tradition, like the right of one man to rule.

He walked towards her, stopping less than a metre away, so she had to tilt her head up.

'I've been looking for a wife.'

Jacqui felt the air rush into her lungs in a gasp. Her eyes bulged. Finally she forced herself to exhale, ignoring the way her head spun.

Was it really so surprising?

Yet shock sank claws of steel into her defenceless body.

'You want an heir.' Of course he did. He needed to secure the succession. Wasn't that what they called it?

Yet for some reason the air seemed suspended in her lungs and tightness banded her ribs. It might be logical but that didn't lessen the impact of his bombshell.

'And a spouse. A family.' He paused. 'I've been putting off the day for years, far too busy enjoying myself when I was younger, and more recently dealing with the business of government.'

Jacqui sat back, letting the couch support her wilting frame. Asim and…a wife? She worked to swallow a knot in her throat.

What did this have to do with her?

At the back of her mind a tiny flicker of an idea ignited, but ruthlessly she blanked it out, refusing to let herself go there.

This wasn't some fairy tale, not with Asim looking so sombre. She knotted her hands in the thick, plush towelling on her lap.

'No questions?' he probed.

Hundreds of them. She settled for the most obvious. 'Why tell me now?'

Again that tiny flare of excitement she couldn't quite extinguish. But, reading his body language, Jacqui sensed there was nothing for her to be excited about. Anxiety drew every tendon and muscle tight.

Asim slowly exhaled and, despite everything, she had to work to keep her eyes on his face.

She was lost and she knew it. Too late now to think of drawing back to protect herself.

'For weeks I've been checking out prospective brides. Almost from the night you arrived.'

Jacqui couldn't stop the abrasive laugh that burst out. 'But obviously not because of my arrival.'

The steely gleam in his eyes confirmed it and that tiny, optimistic spark burnt itself to a lifeless cinder. She knotted her hands, willing her lip not to tremble.

'No, I was in a temper that night because someone had let the cat out of the bag. I'd been faced with some very obvious match-making in a very public situation.'

'And you didn't like the prospective bride.'

His nostrils flared. 'I wouldn't touch her with a barge pole.'

It was stupid to experience an easing of the pain cramping her chest at his words. But Jacqui didn't want him attracted to anyone but her.

Then the import of his words sank in.

'You've been *checking out* women all the time we were...?' She swallowed convulsively, tasting rising bile.

Quickly he took the seat beside her, turning towards her. But he didn't touch her. How telling was that?

Jacqui blinked, her mind reeling. Half an hour ago he hadn't been able to keep his hands off her. And she'd been just as greedy. After believing they'd lost each other last night, their loving had been urgent and phenomenally satisfying. The way he'd held her afterwards, collapsed against his chest in the cooling water, she'd felt the epicentre of his attention. She'd even got a fillip of delight at the idea this retreat to the desert was as romantic as a honeymoon!

'Don't look like that!'

'Like what? Like a woman you played for a fool?'

Asim clasped her hands before she could pull away.

'It wasn't like that.'

From somewhere Jacqui dredged up hauteur, anything to conceal the splintering pain.

'No? What *was* it like, Asim?'

'It was long planned.' He lifted one shoulder. 'I decided what I wanted in a bride and my advisors came up with a list.'

'How very methodical.'

This time both shoulders rose and fell. 'How else could I do it? It wasn't as if I was going to fall madly in love.' His mouth kicked up at one side in a bitter smile that twisted her heart. 'Besides, it wasn't just about choosing a wife but a queen. I'd be stupid not to think carefully and make the right decision.'

Jacqui pressed a hand to her chest, trying to sort her tangled emotions. Hurt pride and savage disappointment were easy. Harder to deal with was the sensation deep in her soul that she'd sustained a critical injury from which she wouldn't recover. There was even part of her that understood Asim's logic.

'So all those royal dinners and receptions...' She stopped, remembering the parade of beauties at his side. She'd spoken to some of them, articulate, sophisticated women who came from a completely different world from hers.

Just as Asim did.

The realisation was a punch to the belly that made her gasp.

'Jacqui?' He raised his hand to her face and she reared back.

'Don't!' She drew a sharp breath, then another. 'So I wasn't supposed to care that you were sleeping with me while you *courted* other women?' It was an old-fashioned word but it implied an intrinsic respect that had obviously been lacking in their affair.

'I never courted any other woman.' His voice grated. 'I never got further than meeting them. I wasn't interested in any of them.'

Jacqui laughed, the sound a broken rasp. 'I'm sure your advisors have plenty more candidates. Let me guess. All from fine, Middle Eastern families, with excellent breeding and the best possible education, all—'

'What would you have had me do?' Asim burst out, his hold on her tightening. 'Look in the soukhs and back alleys for a bride? Of course I searched for someone who'd be personally compatible as well as someone who could handle official royal duties.'

The devil of it was he was right. Wasn't that what royals did, arrange dynastic marriages?

She drew a shuddering breath and looked towards the window framing the view of the oasis. The sky was indigo now. Her day of magic was over.

'I never meant to hurt you, Jacqui. You must know that.' This time when he palmed her cheek she didn't have the strength to pull away. She shut her eyes and told herself soon she'd gather the will to move.

'What's between us…it wasn't planned. You felt it too, that spark that drew us from the first. It kept getting stronger and stronger. I hadn't planned to take a lover, now of all times, but resisting became impossible. You know it.' He tilted her chin.

She opened her eyes and lost herself in the velvet depths of his gaze. Her heart felt bruised and battered and so full she thought it might burst.

'I've never lied to you.'

'Except by omission.'

Gravely he regarded her. 'You're right. It was dishonourable of me. I tried to pull back but I couldn't resist you. You were always *there*, in my consciousness, and no matter how I tried I couldn't keep fighting temptation.' He shook his head.

'I sound like a kid making excuses! The truth was, after that first night, the night I seduced you, I hadn't a hope of putting you aside. You're in my blood.'

His hands moved to her shoulders, as if to prevent her moving.

If he only knew. Nothing on this earth would make her shift now.

For all the hours they'd spent talking, Asim had never spoken so frankly about his feelings. It was as if he shied from admitting softer emotions.

How did he see their relationship? Lust? Friendship with benefits? Or something more?

'And now?' Her voice was stilted by tight vocal cords. 'What happens now, Asim?'

His hands curled around her shoulders in a rhythmic caress. He leaned in.

'I've told my staff to cancel all arrangements to meet...' He stopped, as if choosing his words carefully. 'Anyone else. It was a foolish idea.'

Jacqui's heart soared as she read the warmth in Asim's eyes.

'It's impossible to consider potential brides when you and I have this.' One hand slid across her bare shoulder to stroke the sensitive skin of her neck.

'Really?'

'What do you expect?' His mouth edged up in a smile. 'You're a lover who'd distract any man, Jacqueline. It's nonsense even to think of such things while we're together.'

Jacqui stiffened, her brain chugging into gear despite the distraction of Asim's caresses.

While we're together. Was she imagining it or did that imply an end date?

'So you want to keep me as your lover?'

His brow knotted. 'Of course! What we have is rare. I've never had this with any woman.'

'For how long?' Her lips felt stiff.

'However long the passion lasts.' His smile was taut as he

stroked her neck. He plunged his fingers into her hair, massaging her scalp in a sensual caress that turned her to jelly. 'What we have is too good to give up yet.'

Yet.

Despite the desire to loll back against his touch and let him seduce her into ecstasy, it wasn't going to happen. Not this time.

She hadn't slept with Asim expecting him to declare undying devotion. Like him, she'd been overwhelmed by the force and physicality of their passion. But always there'd been another element for her. Something more profound. Something she'd done her best to ignore.

Something that was all about emotion.

She could ignore it no longer. Not when it sliced her in two, knowing Asim relegated her to the role of sexual partner. Or was the word 'mistress' when the man you slept with ruled a country?

With strength she hadn't known she possessed, Jacqui ripped herself from his hold and surged to her feet, stumbling out of his reach. She pressed a hand to her roiling stomach where her lunch threatened to rise.

'Thank you for explaining where I stand.' Her words were sharp as broken glass. 'It's good to have it spelled out.' It wasn't good; it was a raw, bleeding wound that made her want to curl up in a ball and die.

'Jacqueline?' Asim looked astonished. Was he really so sure she would be content with his scenario? Of course he was. She'd fallen into his arms like a ripe plum.

'So I'm good enough for an affair but not for anything more lasting. Just a bit of sex on the side.' Fury warred with hurt.

He catapulted to his feet. His dumbfounded look would have made her laugh if her throat hadn't seized up.

'It's not like that!'

'Isn't it?' Her hands found her hips through the towel swathed around her. Out of the depths of her anguish came a strength she hadn't known she possessed. It ran like fire through her veins, urging her on to blast him with the truth.

'If it's not like that, then let me suggest an alternative arrangement. Instead of testing all those aristocratic beauties, why not marry *me*?'

Her pulse thudded so loud she could barely hear herself speak but she refused to back down.

'I can offer something they can't. I'm in love with you.'

CHAPTER FIFTEEN

IN LOVE?

Asim formed the words but no sound escaped.

His eyes bulged and something slammed into his chest. Dazed, he looked down but there was nothing, no projectile, no wound. Yet it felt like he'd been shot. He felt the impact spreading through his torso, a shockwave that would have floored him if he'd been standing.

In love.

The words conjured every nightmare memory. They were his worst fear made real.

Jacqueline was speaking. He watched her lips move, heard a harsh rip of sound, but couldn't make out the words.

He stared into her flushed face and read the fierce intensity of her amber gaze. Anguish and defiance glittered in equal measure, flaying him where he sat.

What had he done?

An instant later he was on his feet, stalking to the door, then the window, then back.

She was silent now, looking at him with huge, shadowed eyes.

'You don't mean it.' She couldn't.

But Jacqueline didn't play games. From the first she'd been open, not coy. What you saw was what you got. No feminine wiles.

She stood watching him, her eyes too big in her face, her

damp hair tousled round her shoulders and a bulky towel wrapped around her slim body. Yet she looked more regal than any of the aristocratic women his advisors had selected.

She looked at him as if he was something unsavoury she'd inadvertently stepped in.

'I don't say what I don't mean.' That throaty voice played havoc with him.

Asim shook his head, trying to clear it, telling himself there'd been a mistake.

There'd been a mistake all right!

He'd been so caught up in his need for her, giving in to the fever of attraction, he hadn't been able to keep his hands off her. Even when he'd realised how little sexual experience she had.

Instead of pulling back or taking time to make the ground rules clear, he'd thrown himself into their affair with a single-mindedness he couldn't remember experiencing.

But Jacqueline wasn't like his usual lovers— experienced, sophisticated, ready to move on when the time came, even if some of them had been a little wistful.

Jacqueline was from a different mould.

They said women confused sex and love. Was that what had happened? Perhaps she'd imprinted some fanciful, romantic dream on him because he'd been the one to open her eyes to sensual pleasure.

Asim swiped his hand over his jaw, the rasp of stubble loud in the aching silence.

Why hadn't he taken better precautions? This was the sort of emotional minefield he'd sought to avoid all his life.

Perhaps because he hadn't wanted to know what she felt, in case it meant leaving her before he was ready?

Guilt thwacked him across the chest. But there was indignation too. He'd never once intimated their affair might turn into something permanent. He hadn't encouraged such notions.

But nor had he taken the precautions he should have.

'I'm sorry, Jacqueline.'

The colour bled from her face, making her smattering of

freckles stand out. She didn't look regal now. She looked like a kid who'd been bullied. Or a woman dealt a fatal blow.

Instinctively he started towards her, his gut burning with guilt, but she shoved out a hand, palm towards him.

'No!' She gulped. 'Don't.'

Asim watched her breasts jump with each jagged breath. Each scrape of her breath scored his conscience.

He'd been intent on pleasure and she'd been...

Hell!

He spun away to pace the room.

'I never meant this to happen.'

'So you don't love me.' Her voice was surprisingly strong. He turned to find her backed up against the window, as if trying to get as far as possible from him. His belly cramped on the thought.

But he couldn't lie. 'I already told you. Love isn't for me. I've seen too much of the damage it does.'

'So you couldn't...' she paused then breathed deep '...come to love me?'

How proud she looked. Even now, laying herself on the line like this.

Slowly Asim shook his head. Regret and guilt ran through him like a knife through ripe fruit. He'd never believed it could happen, but he almost wished he *could* love her. He hated what he had to say. And that he had to say it to *her*.

'I care for you more than I've ever cared for any woman, Jacqueline. I admire you. I like you. You're one of the most remarkable people I've ever met.' His voice vibrated with regret. 'But don't look to me for love. You'll never find it. I was inoculated against it at an early age. My parents did that. Growing up watching love tear them apart and almost destroy Samira and me...' He shook his head. 'It's impossible. I'm sorry.'

'And what if you're wrong? What if it wasn't love that destroyed them?'

She stepped forward, eyes blazing. 'Just because your parents were self-absorbed and caught in a destructive relationship doesn't mean love is like that.' Her fisted hands jammed onto her hips, pulling the towelling fabric tight against her slim figure.

Her passion called to him as it always had. He wanted to snatch at it, hold her close and burn in the fire that inevitably flared between them.

Except he knew it for lust, and she believed it to be something altogether more dangerous.

Asim ran his palm around the back of his neck where tendons pulled so tight pain pounded the back of his skull.

'Whatever you call it, I don't want it. I never will.'

Did she sway or was it a trick of the light? Asim braced ready to catch her.

But Jacqueline was made of sterner stuff. She wrapped her arms around her torso in a way that spoke of pain but she stood firm.

'You believe you'll never fall in love?'

It hadn't happened yet. Asim opened his mouth to say so then thought better of the words. He'd hurt her enough. 'It's not possible.'

She bit her lip. To hold back words, or a cry of distress? Asim might be incapable of love but he was no ogre. He cared for this woman, respected her. The sight of her pain was impossible to bear.

'Jacqueline...'

'So you can't offer your wife love.'

He frowned, his outstretched hand dropping to his side.

'No. Not that.' There would be respect and liking, and sex of course, but his bride, when he chose one, wouldn't expect hearts and flowers in a dynastic marriage.

'I see.' She turned and leaned against the window, her neat profile clear against the night sky. Asim's gaze lingered on the smooth curve of her shoulder and the supple turn of her calves beneath the voluminous towel. She was like a creature of moonlight, endlessly enthralling.

He turned away. He had to end this now.

'I have a proposal.'

'Yes?' He swung back.

She laughed briefly and the mirthless sound made the hair on the back of his neck shiver. 'A real proposal.' She turned from the window to face him, her hands straight at her sides like a guard on duty. 'Save yourself the time and bother of interviewing all those women and marry me anyway.'

Asim stared. He couldn't be hearing this.

'I'm not a princess or an aristocrat but there are more important things.' Her slender throat worked as she swallowed. 'I'm intelligent and well-read. I speak your language and I'm getting more fluent every day. I'm loyal and honest and I can be discreet. You know that. I'm even-tempered.' She shrugged and the ghost of a smile skated across her lips. 'Most of the time I'm even-tempered.'

She paused, her eyes searching his, and he wanted to tell her to stop, not do this to herself, to him. But before he found the words she continued.

'I'm a quick learner and with help I'll pick up what I need to know about royal etiquette and protocol. Your grandmother likes me and Samira too. I'm sure they'd help.' This time her smile was real if faint. 'Samira would help me learn to dress the part. And I'm good with people; you know that. I can hold my own at your fancy receptions and with more time I'll learn not to flinch at the sound of fireworks or a twenty-one-gun salute.'

'Jacqueline—'

'I'll make a good wife,' she said in a rush. She clasped her hands tight and he couldn't dispel the uneasy sense that she pleaded with him.

Asim didn't want that. It made him feel wrong inside. His gut, his chest, cramped. His vocal cords froze.

She stepped closer, her tone earnest.

'I'll give you the children you want and you'll always know I'll have your best interests at heart. None of those other women care for you like I do. That must count for something.'

He shook his head, for the first time in his life words failing him.

'Asim—'

'Don't, Jacqueline. Please just...don't.'

Spots of colour appeared on her cheekbones. She stood stock-still, watching him.

'You don't think I'm good enough?' Her voice was ragged and something within Asim nosedived at the pain he heard there.

'It's not that. Never that. How could you think it?' But he remembered her self-doubts and the way trauma had dented her confidence.

He wanted to lie and say it would be okay, that they could marry and she'd be happy. But he respected her too much.

'This isn't about you.' He paced so close he read the tension in her lips and the pain in those over-bright amber eyes. What he saw there almost undid him. He wanted to protect her from hurt. He, who hadn't been able to protect his sister!

'Any man would be proud to have you as his wife.'

'But not you.' Her voice was hollow.

Asim shook his head. 'I'd be proud but I couldn't do it to you. What sort of marriage would it be where you loved and I didn't?' He reached for her then caught himself and pulled his arm back.

'You believe in love, Jacqueline. You *can* love. You deserve the same from the man you marry. You deserve a man who can love you too.' The notion of her with some other man tore a hole through Asim's belly and he almost staggered.

'If we married...' he paused and swallowed, moistening his arid mouth '...it would be unfair and unequal. I'd feel guilty for not giving you what you wanted, not living up to your dreams, and you'd grow out of love eventually. You'd resent me and wish you'd never taken me on.'

'Is that what happened with your parents, Asim?'

'This isn't about them!'

Couldn't she see? Didn't she know she was offering herself

as a sacrifice to a marriage that would destroy her? He couldn't do that to her, despite the selfish part of him that wanted to grab her before she changed her mind.

He breathed deep then regretted it as he caught the scent of apricots. Would that always remind him of her?

'I'm honoured by your offer, Jacqueline. But I can't take advantage of you like that.'

She stepped forward, crowding him. 'I want you to.'

Asim stared into her face, taut with fear and hope, and felt panic that he might weaken. He might not be in love, but he cared for Jacqueline, and he didn't want to leave her.

But he knew his duty to her even if she didn't.

'The woman I marry will not love me, nor I her. It's better that way. Anything else would be unfair on her.' He paused. 'I care for you too much to do that.'

Silence hung between them. Asim couldn't tear his gaze from hers. He wanted to find words to cushion the blow he'd dealt but there were none. He could only protect her by telling her the truth.

Finally she moved, turning her head from side to side like a boxer who'd taken one too many punches.

'In that case, Asim, I'd be grateful if you'd arrange a vehicle.' She looked him in the eye and he felt hurt slam through his chest. 'It's time I left.'

CHAPTER SIXTEEN

THE SUN SHONE BRIGHTLY, turning the park's avenue of old trees into a bower of dappled green light, a welcome respite from Melbourne's summer heat.

But, instead of the neat path and regimented trees, Jacqui pictured the Asada oasis, its crystalline pools and delicious havens of green. When she inhaled she almost smelled the desert sand and spices.

A shout of laughter jerked her head up and she watched a family cross the grass, like so many others heading for the Grand Slam tennis tournament along the Yarra River.

Her eyes lingered on the tall, dark-haired man in the group as he swung a tot onto his shoulders, the other children clamouring for a ride. Then she ripped her gaze away, ignoring the way her chest clamped.

Swerving to avoid them, she set off for the edge of the park. Her hotel was there, across the road, and her hour was up. Each day she forced herself out of the hotel for a walk, to exercise and try to lose herself in the crowds.

Not that it was possible to lose herself. Nothing, not work or the familiarity of her own country, had managed to make her forget, or offer respite from pain. She'd even opted for an anonymous hotel rather than her tiny flat while she finished her book, hoping the novelty might take her mind off the cold weight in her chest.

Jacqui hesitated, wondering if she should try harder. Maybe

order something at the café in the centre of the park and watch the people. Except it was near the Fairies Tree, a mecca for parents with young children.

Jacqui lengthened her stride, heading for the road. When had she become such a grouch that the laughter of children unsettled her?

Since she'd discovered Asim was planning his own family with some other woman.

Jacqui would never bear his child, or hold him close, or have him look at her in that way that made her heart flutter.

She grimaced. That look had merely signified lust. She'd just been too naïve to recognise it.

Had he found his bride? Jacqui had avoided the news, not wanting to hear of a royal betrothal. Pain tore at her throat and roughened her breathing.

With a quick look at the traffic, she stepped onto the road, crossing to her hotel.

That was when she heard the hubbub and saw the security cordon. Jacqui frowned. It was a pleasant hotel with a view over the Treasury Gardens but it wasn't one of the luxury premises visited by VIPs. Yet she saw a news camera beside the entry and a phalanx of staff at the top of the stairs.

Distracted, Jacqui hesitated, then had to scurry to the pavement as a limousine drew to the kerb.

The crowd surged, held back by men in dark suits. The hotel manager hastened from the head of the stairs as the limo door opened.

Curiosity stirring, Jacqui watched a tall figure emerge from the back seat. A figure with wide shoulders and a jacket of steel-grey shot with midnight blue. The slanting morning light caught the rich, matching fabric of his neat turban and accentuated an arrogant slash of a nose that perfectly matched his proud, honed features.

A tingling began in her fingers and toes as numbness swamped her. Even her breath suspended as she took in that oh-so-familiar visage.

Then, in a rush, the blood pounded in her ears and her breath sawed on a gasp that seared her lungs.

She stumbled as she swung around, lurching against a bystander and almost falling as she willed her feet to keep moving. Anywhere. So long as it was away from here.

Asim, here! What did it mean?

It couldn't be coincidence. For one thing, he'd never mentioned planning a visit to Australia. For another, this wasn't the sort of palatial hotel to house heads of state. For another...

Jacqui couldn't think of another but instinct shouted he was here for her. Why, she didn't know, but she wasn't staying to find out. She wasn't up to treating Asim as a casual acquaintance.

A shout came from behind her. Was that her name?

Jacqui didn't turn but walked faster, clutching her lightweight cardigan around her.

Lights at a crossing flashed green and she hurried across, joining the jostle of pedestrians.

Her heart was hammering, her breath was uneven and her teeth had an alarming tendency to chatter. Swept by the crowd, she scurried along one block then another, until she reached a pavement café. Shock took its toll. Knees rubbery, she dropped into a chair at a table by itself, half-hidden by a planter box.

Jacqui grabbed the menu then laid it down. It shook so badly she couldn't read it. No matter; she'd ask for something sweet and full of chocolate. Something to counteract the shock of seeing Asim.

Had she imagined him? He couldn't really be here.

'Jacqueline.' That deep voice ran like treacle through her body. Instead of stiffening in surprise, Jacqui found herself slumping, exhausted by the inevitable. Had she really thought to escape?

What Asim wanted he always got and for some reason he wanted to see her.

Anger sparked. Couldn't he leave her alone? Couldn't he see she was trying to get on with her life?

Slowly she raised her eyes and flinched as her heart gave an almighty thump of recognition and longing. He towered over her, broad and imposing and impossibly sexy, despite the stark concern etched into his spare features and the grim line of his mouth.

'You shouldn't be here, Asim.'

'I know. I'm supposed to be on a state visit to France.'

'And interviewing brides.' The words jerked out.

Without asking, he took the seat opposite, propping his arms on the table as he leaned close, scrutinising her.

For the first time that day Jacqui gave a thought to her appearance. Hair in a high ponytail, already coming down around her ears, bare of make-up and dressed in lightweight trousers, T-shirt and cardigan, she was hardly prepared for an interview with royalty.

She'd hoped if she saw him again—and she *had* hoped— that she'd look serene, aloof and even beautiful.

Jacqui bit her lip, her eyes lowering.

Asim was the only one who'd called her beautiful.

'Don't.' His hand snaked out and captured hers, clamping it to the table. She gasped as fire sizzled through her veins. The fire she'd told herself she'd imagined. But memory hadn't exaggerated.

One touch from Asim was all it took.

Dimly she was aware of a bustle on the pavement. She turned. Heavy-set security men were trying to block a couple of cameramen from filming. But she noticed a number of mobile phones raised in their direction.

She supposed she should be concerned that he'd made her the subject of gossip just by following her down the street, but that was the least of her concerns.

'You're creating a scene. You should go.'

'I don't give a damn.'

Her eyebrows arched. 'Those are TV cameras. You're making a spectacle of yourself, a target for the sort of stories you hate.'

To her amazement, Asim smiled. The impact rocked her back in her chair and made her forget about trying to wrest her hand free.

'Recent events have put my dislike of the press in perspective.'

'Recent events?' Her stomach plunged and she sat straighter. 'Has something happened to Samira?'

'No, she's thriving, though missing you.' He leaned close and she almost lost herself in the dark velvet of his eyes. 'But there are far worse things than providing fodder for the press.'

Jacqui doubted that. Asim's prejudice was strong. 'Like what?'

'Like losing the one woman in the world who can make me happy.'

His fingers tightened on hers as she recoiled, her spine hitting the back of her seat. The sound of traffic and people blurred to white noise.

'Don't!' It was almost a shout. 'Don't,' she whispered. 'Whatever you're up to, I don't want to be part of it. I walked away, remember? I'm getting on with my life.' No matter that she had yet to discover a spark of interest in anything.

'Oh, I remember, Jacqueline.' His mouth curved in a baring of teeth she could only call ferocious. 'To my everlasting shame, I remember. That's why I'm here. To tell you I'm sorry for what I did, pushing you away.'

Jacqui stared at his harsh expression but hadn't a hope of guessing what he thought.

'It's a long way to come for an apology.'

'You don't think you deserve it?'

She leaned close enough that his spicy scent tickled her nose. Involuntarily she breathed deep, savouring it. Her automatic reaction fuelled an anger she'd hoped had passed. 'What's wrong between us can't be fixed by an apology, Asim.'

To her amazement he paled, the gleam in his eyes extinguished like a flame snuffed out.

'Don't say that.' His hand tightened almost to the point of pain.

'It's true. You want a blue-blooded princess for a cold-hearted marriage. An apology won't change that.' As abruptly as it had flared, her indignation died, replaced by sorrow. 'You can't help what you feel and nor can I. At least you were honest with me at the end.'

His other hand joined the first, engulfing hers on the table.

'That's where you're wrong.'

'Sorry?' Jacqui gaped. Distressed as she was, she knew Asim was a man of his word. Even that last evening, her heart shredding to bleeding tatters, she'd seen his regret. He hadn't wanted to hurt her.

His jaw looked as solid as the stone of the Jazeeri citadel. Only the double-time flick of a pulse at his throat betrayed him.

'Asim?' She was used to him in control, managing every situation, even the business of despatching his unwanted lover.

He didn't look in control now.

'I wasn't honest with you.' The words were a bare rumble of sound, drawing her closer till their heads almost met. 'I told myself I was. I was even proud of myself, in a perverse way, for making us face the brutal truth that we couldn't be together. For bringing everything into the open.'

His nostrils flared on a deep breath and his eyes flickered shut. When they opened again she read something in his expression she'd never seen. It held her trapped as surely as his hands.

Something in her chest seemed to roll over. Her heart?

'I was afraid, Jacqueline. Afraid to face a truth I wasn't ready for.' He swallowed hard. She watched the muscles of his throat work and tried to understand what made him so vulnerable.

One bronzed hand rose to stroke her cheek and it was her turn to swallow as the slow caress evoked sensations she'd thought never to know again. Hot tears glazed her eyes and she fought to stop her mouth crumpling.

'My darling.' His voice was for her ears alone. 'Can you forgive me? I'd spent a lifetime convinced there was no such thing as love, at least for me. I was a coward, terrified to face the emotions you made me feel. I didn't see I'd already fallen for you.'

Jacqui sucked in a stunned breath. 'You love me?' Her heart stuttered then sped to a gallop. She tried to sit back, to digest this, but his hand slid to the back of her neck, warm and compelling, keeping her close.

'I don't deserve you, not after the pain I caused us.' He breathed deep, his chest expanding mightily. 'But I love you, Jacqueline Fletcher. It took me less than a day after you'd left to realise my fatal mistake. I drove you away, not because I didn't care but because I cared too much. I was too cowardly to face that.'

Jacqui blinked. She could read his expression now. It was open and clear. The light she saw there shone like a beacon in the grey that had shrouded her since she'd left him.

'I admire you, *habibti*. I'm fascinated by you, more attracted than I've been to any woman—and I admit there have been a few in my past.' A slashing gesture summarily dismissed them all.

'I care about you. Your happiness is more important than my own. I've never felt that with any woman, but I want only good things for you. I want to spend my life cherishing you and building our lives together. If I hadn't been a coward at Asada I'd have recognised it then.' He shook his head. 'I'd been too busy believing I could control my feelings, never guessing I'd loved you for weeks.'

'You had?' Jacqui was dazed, drinking in his words.

'At least from the night you wore the silver dress.' His eyes glittered with a heat that scorched her from her cheeks to her toes. 'I told myself I was seducing you but all along it was you with your innocence and honesty and courage, seducing me.' He smiled. 'Or maybe it was even earlier. You were in my thoughts all the time.'

Jacqui told herself dreams couldn't come true this easily.

'But I'm not like the women on your list. I'm not aristocratic or—'

'You're the woman I want, Jacqueline. No list would do you justice.'

'What about your parents? You said...'

Asim shook his head. 'I said a lot of things. Most of it rubbish. How could I fear what we have together? We're not my parents. You're strong, courageous and loyal and I...' He shrugged those broad shoulders. 'I rely on you to teach me about love.'

Jacqui slipped one hand free and covered his, her heart swelling. 'You're already an expert, Asim. Your love for Samira and your grandmother is there for all to see.'

'Does that mean you'll have me? You forgive me?' His voice, a gravel whisper, dragged like a rough caress across her skin.

'Asim! Are you asking what I think you're asking? Here on a Melbourne street corner?' A bubble of hysterical laughter threatened, fed by shock.

'Why not? Unless you'd prefer I got down on one knee. Is that how it's done here?'

His chair scraped back on the pavement and Jacqui lunged forward, grabbing both his forearms.

'You can't be serious!' She glanced around to see a crowd had gathered, barely held back by his bodyguards. Even the traffic seemed to have slowed and, sure enough, at least one cameraman had his lens trained on them.

'I've never been more serious about anything in my life. I want you as my lover, my wife, my queen.'

'But...' Words failed her. Her heart was so full she felt like laughing and crying at the same time. And hugging Asim and never letting him go. 'But you can't propose here. Look at me: I'm wearing an old *cardigan*!'

Asim's face broke into a smile that stole her breath all over again. 'You'll start a trend, my darling. All the fashionistas will want one in just that shade of brown.'

He stood, pulling her to her feet, his body sheltering her from the crowd.

'Very well, I'll take you somewhere more suitable and ask you to be my bride.' His face sobered, his hold tightening. 'On condition you promise to say yes.'

Jacqui stared up at the one man in the world she'd ever love and understood for the first time that phrase about your heart singing. Hers was doing it right now.

'Jacqueline?' Was that fear in Asim's voice?

She lifted her palm to his face and sighed at the dear familiarity of him.

'That can be arranged, Your Highness. On condition you take me somewhere very, very private. After this…' she gestured to the thronged footpath '…I want you all to myself.'

Asim's eyes glittered with a promise she'd never been able to resist and his mouth curved in a smile of pure satisfaction. Jacqui didn't bother to protest when he scooped her into his arms and strode to the limousine waiting at the kerb.

'I knew this would be a marriage of like minds,' he murmured in her ear. 'Those are my thoughts exactly.'

* * * * *

MILLS & BOON®

Classic romances from your favourite authors!

40% OFF!

Whether you love tycoon billionaires, rugged ranchers or dashing doctors, this collection has something to suit everyone this New Year. Plus, we're giving you a huge 40% off the RRP!

Hurry, order yours today at
www.millsandboon.co.uk/NYCollection

MILLS & BOON®

Two superb collections!

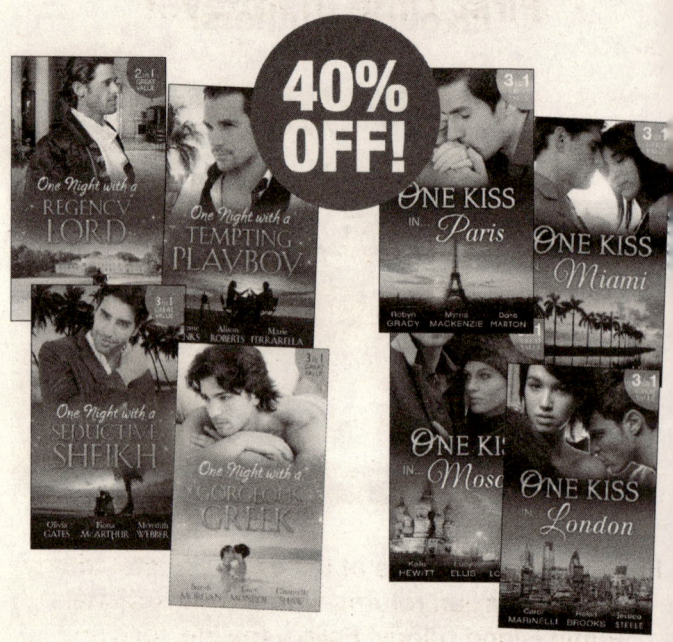

40% OFF!

Would you rather spend the night with a seductive sheikh or be whisked away to a tropical Hawaiian island? Well, now you don't have to choose! Get your hands on both collections today and get 40% off the RRP!

Hurry, order yours today at
www.millsandboon.co.uk/TheOneCollection

MILLS & BOON®

First Time in Forever

Following the success of the Snow Crystal trilogy, Sarah Morgan returns with the sensational Puffin Island trilogy. Follow the life, loss and love of Emily Armstrong in the first instalment, as she looks for love on Puffin Island.

Pick up your copy today!

Visit
www.millsandboon.co.uk/Firsttime

MILLS & BOON®

Why not subscribe?
Never miss a title and save money too!

Here's what's available to you if you join the exclusive **Mills & Boon Book Club** today:

- *Titles up to a month ahead of the shops*
- *Amazing discounts*
- *Free P&P*
- *Earn Bonus Book points that can be redeemed against other titles and gifts*
- *Choose from monthly or pre-paid plans*

Still want more?
Well, if you join today we'll even give you
50% OFF your first parcel!

So visit **www.millsandboon.co.uk/subs**
or call Customer Relations on **020 8288 2888**
to be a part of this exclusive Book Club!

MILLS & BOON®
MODERN™

POWER, PASSION AND IRRESISTIBLE TEMPTATION

A sneak peek at next month's titles…

In stores from 20th February 2015:

- **The Taming of Xander Sterne** – Carole Mortimer
- **At the Count's Bidding** – Caitlin Crews
- **The Real Romero** – Cathy Williams
- **Prince Nadir's Secret Heir** – Michelle Conder

In stores from 6th March 2015:

- **In the Brazilian's Debt** – Susan Stephens
- **The Sheikh's Sinful Seduction** – Dani Collins
- **His Defiant Desert Queen** – Jane Porter
- **The Tycoon's Stowaway** – Stefanie London

Available at WHSmith, Tesco, Asda, Eason, Amazon and Apple

Just can't wait?
Buy our books online a month before they hit the shops!
visit www.millsandboon.co.uk

These books are also available in eBook format!